Tom Hawkins... As she looked at him through
the steam from her coffee, Jane
thought how strange that a face so
forbidding and irregular could become,
in so short a time, so pleasing to her eyes.

...Man From Interpol. How alien that sounded,
without reality, like the title of a book or a
movie. And how impossible now to think of
him that way. He was just...a man, a flesh-and-
blood man, in need of a shave, a shower and a
good night's sleep, a man who had covered her
with his jacket and watched over her while she
slept, a man whose hands had touched her in
intimate places, a man whose tongue she'd
tasted.

A man who played games in which the stakes
were human lives.

How could this have happened? Jane thought.
To me?

Dear Reader,

April's offerings from Silhouette Sensation® are irresistible! We know the holidays are upon you, but that's even more reason to take time to indulge yourselves a little. Come and meet Kathleen Creighton's HEARTBREAKER, embittered Interpol agent Tom Hawkins; he's all man.

Next, we have *A Man To Die For* from Suzanne Brockmann. Carrie Brooks ends up on the run with this gorgeous but dangerous guy who *says* he's a cop, but the last time they met he was kidnapping her!

We're finishing Beverly Bird's WOUNDED WARRIORS mini-series this month with *A Man Without a Wife*, the story of a mother who wants to see the son she had to give up—she's heard that his adoptive mother has died; little does she know that he has such an attractive and intimidating dad! Look out for more books from Beverly as her new trilogy begins in June.

Finally, the ever popular Maura Seger brings us *Heaven in His Arms*, about how one of the worst days of Lisa Preston's life became one of the best. And it all started with a car crash!

Have fun!

The Editors

Never Trust a Lady

KATHLEEN CREIGHTON

*Silhouette, Silhouette Sensation and Colophon are
registered trademarks of Harlequin Books S.A., used under licence.*

*First published in Great Britain 1998
Silhouette Books, Eton House, 18-24 Paradise Road,
Richmond, Surrey TW9 1SR*

© Kathleen Modrovich 1997

ISBN 0 373 07800 5

18-9804

*Printed and bound in Great Britain
by Mackays of Chatham PLC, Chatham*

KATHLEEN CREIGHTON

has roots deep in the California soil, but has relocated to South Carolina. As a child, she enjoyed listening to old-timers' tales, and her fascination with the past only deepened as she grew older. Today she says she is interested in everything—art, music, gardening, zoology, anthropology and history, but people are at the top of her list. She also has a lifelong passion for writing, and now combines her two loves in romance novels.

Other novels by Kathleen Creighton

Silhouette Sensation®

Demon Lover
Double Dealings
Gypsy Dancer
In Defence of Love
Rogue's Valley
Tiger Dawn
Love and Other Surprises
Wolf and the Angel
*A Wanted Man
Eyewitness
*One Good Man
*Man of Steel

Silhouette Desire®

The Heart Mender
In From the Cold

Silhouette® Christmas Stories 1992
'The Mysterious Gift'

*Into the Heartland

Prologue

Tom Hawkins hit the steering wheel with the heel of his hand as a silver Peugeot zipped around him on the right with barely inches to spare. *"Idiot!"* he snapped, adding his favorite filthy epithet in French.

The traffic on the Corniche President John F. Kennedy had come to a halt once more, to the symphonic accompaniment of blaring horns and shouted insults. Hawk glanced at his watch and swore again, softly and this time in English. No way around it, he was going to be late for his meeting with Loizeau.

He settled back with a resigned sigh and reached for his cigarettes, deliberately avoiding even a glance at the spectacular Mediterranean view on his left, where windsurfers' sails swooped and darted like butterflies over molten copper breakers. It was just such scenes of almost searing beauty that made him hate this city so much. Marseilles reminded Hawk of New Orleans. It seemed to him that there was something false about both places...something sinister and treacherous lurking just beyond the raucous gaiety. The face of evil behind a Mardi Gras mask.

Death riding on a carousel, smiling and waving to the children as she goes round and round, biding her time...

Hawk's cigarette broke in two as he stubbed it out in the car's ashtray. He'd blocked the image almost before it had formed in his mind, but the lapse, however brief, left him shaken.

It was full dusk when he pulled up in front of Loizeau's antique and curio shop, inconveniently located in the labyrinthine quarter of old Marseilles known as *Le Panier.* The streets in The Basket were largely deserted at this hour, most of its residents locked up safe and snug in their upstairs apartments, and all sensible tourists apparently heeding their guidebooks' warnings against being caught in the area after dark.

It was very quiet; he could barely hear the clanking of the masts in the harbor below. What sounds there were carried through the narrow, sloping streets on dancing tendrils of the mistral, along with the smells of fish, fuel and cooking. Somewhere a baby cried, a radio screeled Middle Eastern dissonances; rival cats sang threats to each other in a nearby alley. A lone car engine gunned, shifting gears, then growled away into silence.

As he stepped out of the car and turned the key in the door lock, Hawk found himself discreetly, and out of old habit, checking to make sure his weapon, a nice Walther 9-millimeter pistol, was where it should be, nestled in its holster against the small of his back.

He paused, fingers still curled around the car keys, to study the building in front of him. Gray stone and stucco, pocked with patches of decay like open sores, but fresh white paint, he noticed, on the wooden door and on the louvered shutters that flanked both second-story and street-level windows. A bedraggled red geranium bloomed in a warped wooden box right below a hand-lettered sign in the downstairs shop window that said, *FERMÉ.* The other ground-floor windows along the gently curving street were dark and tightly shuttered, while the second- and third-floor shutters stood open to the warm spring wind, spilling yellow light and looping ropes of softly swaying laundry across the darkening canyon below.

Loizeau's shop was dark, too, but the shutters were still folded back, open and welcoming, and above Hawk's head the living quarters' windows were closed up tightly, with not the faintest gleam of light leaking through the slats.

Noting—even enjoying a little—the small frisson of unease

that stirred across the back of his neck, Hawk stepped to the door of the shop and raised a hand to knock. For a moment more he hesitated, then tapped lightly on the thick, age-roughened wood. He listened, then, calling out, "Loizeau? *Ouvrez, s'il vous plaît,*" tapped once more.

He drew a breath, held it and closed his fingers around the doorknob. It turned easily. He froze, but only for an instant. His gun was already warm and heavy in the palm of his hand as he eased the door open and slipped silently through it.

He knew at once. He could smell it. Death had been here, recently and almost certainly with violence.

Every sense—including a well-developed sixth—on full alert, Hawk crouched low and waited. He listened with every nerve, every cell in his body, listened for the sounds of fear and menace, stifled breathing, adrenaline-driven heartbeats, the brush of fabric over gooseflesh, the trickle of sweat, the stirring of hackles. *Nothing.* But his instincts had already told him the room was empty. Whoever had brought Death into it was gone.

But not *long* gone. If he needed more evidence of that fact, it came when his free hand, braced on the floor for balance, encountered a sticky warmth. He noted it automatically and without revulsion, while another part of his mind was on instant replay, reviewing every detail of every impression it had recorded from the moment he'd driven into that street. *Crying baby, radio, fighting cats...a car shifting gears, driving away...*

Five minutes, he thought. *If I'd been five minutes sooner...*

He stood, his movements brisk and efficient now, hitting the light switch with his elbow as he tucked his gun back into its holster. The shopkeeper, Loizeau, lay on his back near the door and stared sightlessly at the ceiling. He appeared to do so with three eyes; the one in the center of his forehead oozed a dark, congealing trickle. Other than that, oddly enough, his face was untouched. It was the back of his head and most of its contents that had splattered over the glass case immediately behind him. A glass case filled with lovely things gathered from the far corners of the world, trinkets made in cloisonné, beautiful objects of ivory, jade and gold.

Hawk didn't bother to feel for a pulse. An easy death, he thought, gazing dispassionately at the iron-gray moustache that framed a mouth frozen in an O of eternal surprise. The man probably hadn't even seen it coming. So the killer was a real pro—a thought that didn't cheer Hawk. It meant that, in all likelihood, he wasn't going to find what he'd come for.

Still, he had to be sure. Regretfully aware of what he was doing to someone else's crime scene, he began a careful search of the body and its vicinity. After giving the same attention to the cluttered desk, with as much success, he paused, fingers drumming restlessly on the blotter. Hawk didn't suffer defeat well. His mind was once again on rewind, zapping back to this afternoon's telephone conversation with Loizeau...

"*Oui, monsieur,* I can have the information for you, but you understand, the time difference in the United States—"

"I understand. You are absolutely certain the item I am interested in was shipped—"

"Oh, yes, yes, quite certain. I remember that consignment very well. The seller insisted it was to go to Rathskeller's and to no one else. But there will be no problem, *monsieur,* no problem at all. I have here the shipping receipt, I am certain they will have no problem tracing it. Perhaps you wish to make a telephone bid—"

"I might just do that. I'm interested in the one painting, as I believe I mentioned. My wife—you understand, she has her heart set on it. I'd like to surprise her. If you can get me the lot number—"

"Yes, yes, of course, *monsieur.* I understand very well. If you would care to call again after *sieste*...shall we say, four o'clock? I will have the information for you by that time."

"I'd rather come by the shop, if that's okay. How late are you open?"

"Until six, *monsieur. Bon...bon...*I look forward to being of service..."

Hawk stared down at his restlessly drumming fingers and at the thick paper blotter beneath them, willing his mind to methodical processes.

"*I have here the shipping receipt.*" Okay, if the shopkeeper had had it, where was it now? Gone, of course, having almost certainly left with whoever had left the man's blood and brain tissue congealing on the glass display case. Why? Because the information the killer—and Hawk—needed was written on it.

Hawk's fingers stopped drumming and began instead to stroke

the surface of the blotter, slowly, delicately, like a lover's caress. He could see Loizeau, picture him sitting here in this very spot, pulling the phone closer as he checked the telephone number on the shipping receipt. Picking up a pen, poising it over that same receipt while he waited for the overseas connection. Smiling, nodding as he jotted down the lot number. That piece of paper, the shipping receipt, was gone. But the blotter...

It took him longer than he would have liked. He kept having to remind himself to go slowly. Be careful. Take it easy, Hawkins...don't blow this. He even felt a little silly doing it, painstakingly rubbing graphite over a small piece of white paper, like making leaf rubbings in kindergarten.

Silly? There was a dead body cooling at his feet. And maybe a lot more lives—uncounted thousands of lives—at stake.

So he kept at it, while darkness crawled like a villain through the streets outside the shop and tension cramped his hand and coiled around the back of his neck, and in the end his hunch and his patience paid off. It was there, all right, imprinted in the blotter where Loizeau's hand would have rested as he sat at his desk with the telephone cradled between his ear and shoulder, busily making notes. Hawk's rubbing produced a perfect negative in the shopkeeper's neat, if somewhat prissy, hand: Rathskeller's—Lot #187, 3/22, Arlington, Virginia.

He sat for a moment, looking down at the piece of paper in his hand. Then, releasing his breath with a soft hissing sound, he folded it once and tucked it away in his shirt pocket. Like it or not, it looked as though he was going home.

Chapter 1

The evening air was soft and smelled of lilacs. It flirted with the draperies at the long, open windows, played around the edges of the ballroom like a maiden too shy to join in the dance. Out on the glittering dance floor, laughing couples dipped and whirled to the strains of a waltz, in breezes of their own making.

"Jane? Dear, are you coming?"

With regret, Jane Carlysle allowed herself to be pulled out of the eighteenth-century Viennese ballroom and back to the foyer of the West Arlington Community Center, where her friend Connie Vincent was waiting for her with, it appeared, some impatience.

"Sorry," she murmured, drawing her fingertips once more across the silky surface of the ornately carved baby grand piano she'd been leaning against. "I was just...coming."

"Do you think this is for sale at this auction?" she asked Connie, who was peering at her over the tops of the half glasses she wore perched on the very tip of her nose—glasses that were kept from jeopardy only by virtue of the chain that was attached to the earpieces and looped around her neck.

"The piano? I should imagine so. It has a tag and a lot number, hasn't it? Here, dear, why don't you queue up for registration while I go and grab us a couple of catalogs.''

"How much do you think it'll go for?" Jane persisted with faint hope, although she was sure she knew the answer.

Connie shot her an amused look as she confirmed it. "Oodles."

Shuddering, Jane muttered, "I thought so. I have fatally expensive tastes. As you know."

Jane knew Connie had good reason to be familiar with her tastes, since Connie's shop was directly across from the bank where Jane worked, and right next door to Kelly's Tearoom and Bookshop where she usually ate lunch. She and the antique shop's new owner had hit it off right away, although Jane wasn't quite sure why. The truth was, they had very little in common. Connie was originally from London, unabashedly middle-aged, unmarried and childless, though Jane had an idea there had been a Mr. Vincent somewhere in a rather murky past. Now, though, Connie's life seemed to be her business—antiques, a subject upon which she seemed to be something of an expert—and travel.

When Connie wasn't out of town on one of her buying trips she and Jane had lunch together several times a week at Kelly's Tearoom. What someone as well traveled and sophisticated as Connie found in the relationship, Jane couldn't imagine. She, on the other hand, thought the English antiques dealer was the most interesting person she'd ever met. She particularly enjoyed hearing about all the exotic places Connie had traveled to. Vicarious adventures, after all, were probably the only kind she would ever experience. With the exception of the couple of years encompassing her divorce, Jane's life had been notably uneventful, and she saw very little likelihood that things were going to change much in the future.

While Connie went in search of catalogs, Jane joined a small knot of people loosely bunched in front of the registration desk. While she waited her turn—and for Connie to return—Jane studied the crowd that had gathered in the community center's carpeted foyer, awaiting the opening of the auditorium doors. People-watching was an occupation she'd always enjoyed, and this gathering of veteran auction-goers seemed an interesting and varied bunch. Male and female in almost equal number, rather quirky in their dress, most of them. Quirky, but prosperous—antiques were expensive. Mostly middle-aged, or older.

Jane suddenly had to hide a smile. She was remembering what her daughter Tracy had said to her on the phone when she'd mentioned she was going to an auction with Connie.

"Mom, *antiques?* You're never going to meet any decent men at an antique auction. Trust me—they're all these wimpy old gray guys with glasses on the ends of their noses. Mom, listen, the best place to meet cool guys is at a car auction— better yet, trucks. What you do is, you act really helpless, like you don't know which one to bid on..."

Honestly. Sometimes she just had to laugh at Lynn and Tracy's efforts to set her up with male companionship—like worried mamas with a spinster daughter on their hands. But the truth was, she'd accepted long ago that she would likely spend the rest of her life without a partner. She'd accepted it when she'd made the decision, at nearly forty, to end her marriage of twenty-one years. The idea seemed to distress the girls when she pointed it out to them, but Jane knew that the odds were against her finding anyone, given her age and a lifestyle that included mostly other women, retirees and college students. And especially given that she had no intention whatsoever of going out and *looking.*

Not that she hadn't *thought* about it...having a man in her life again. Not that she didn't miss some aspects of male companionship. She missed sex, of course. She really did. It made her very sad, sometimes, to think that she was never going to feel that particular tingle again, never going to feel a man's hands touching her in intimate places, never feel the weight of a man's body, the smell of him...the warmth... Oh, dear. Okay, she missed it a *lot.*

But the rest—the companionship and the sharing, reaching out to take someone's hand walking down a rainy street, reading aloud from the paper over breakfast coffee, laughing over some silly private joke, finding each other's eyes across a crowded room—those were things she'd never known, even when she was married. She couldn't very well miss something she'd never had.

Could she? And if not, what was this misty, achy feeling all of a sudden? *Bother.*

She was normally a positive, optimistic and upbeat person. She wasn't sure what had made her thoughts take off in such unexpected directions, unless it had something to do with Lynn going off to Europe in a couple of months and Tracy choosing a college clear out in California.

She was glad when Connie returned with her arms full of catalogs and a combative gleam in her eyes. The last person ahead of Jane in the registration line was just moving aside. Thrusting the stapled pages of auction listings at Jane, Connie snatched two information cards and moved quickly to an adjoining table.

"Here, dear, fill out one of these and get your number so we can go inside. They're opening the doors—do hurry, I'm eager to see what's on today." Her voice was breathy with excitement; it was a side to the usually genteel antiques dealer that Jane had never seen before.

"Do I really need this?" Jane asked a few moments later as she struggled through the crowd in Connie's wake, juggling her purse, catalog and a stiff white card with a large black number 133 on it. She was frowning at the latter. "I hadn't planned on buying anything."

Connie shot her an exasperated look. "Not buy anything? Then why on earth did you come along?"

"Because I've never been to an auction before," said Jane with a shrug. "I wanted to see what it was like. Oh my goodness..." The crowd that had been carrying her along like a bit of flotsam had suddenly surged through a pair of double doors and into a vast room, where it spread out and dissipated among the treasures displayed there like a flash flood on a desert floor. Jane was left behind in a quiet eddy near the doors, stunned and gawking.

Connie gave her another look, this one both knowing and amused. "Yes, as you can see, there is something for everyone. Best keep the card, dear, in case you find yourself caught up in the excitement of it all. If you did find something you wanted to bid on, then where would you be?"

But Jane was already wandering ahead through a marvelous maze of inlaid sideboards and clawfooted settees, porcelain jars and Tiffany lamps, hideous brasses and glowing Oriental rugs. It was the kind of thing she could do quite happily for hours, just looking, letting her imagination fly unfettered to times long past and places she would never see. Ancient China...the London of Dickens and Victoria...Paris in *any* age...a tall ship under full sail... And memories. Images from her own past, her grandmother's house, her childhood...

Her cry of delighted recognition drew Connie to her side. "Find something, dear?"

"Look—an honest-to-goodness Roy Rogers cap pistol!" She held it out, draped across her palms like a ceremonial sword. "I don't believe it—it has the holster, and everything. My brother had one just like this when we were kids. I wonder— oh, Connie, it does—it even still has a box of caps! That smell..." She ducked her head, sniffed and was instantly awash in a memory. *Sitting on the back steps at Gramma's on a hot summer day, hitting caps with a hammer...*

She gazed down at the toy pistol, suddenly aching with that same blend of joy and sadness that had assailed her earlier, in the foyer. "You know, I used to envy my brother. He had the real six-shooter, and all I could do was point my finger and yell, 'Pow-pow!'"

About then it occurred to her that her companion was looking at her with something akin to alarm. She laughed and hastened to explain, though she had an idea it wasn't something someone as sophisticated as Connie could ever understand. "You know, the game, Cowboys and Indians? Well, actually, my parents were liberals—we weren't allowed to shoot at Indians, even imaginary ones. I think the game was more like Good Guys and Bad Guys."

"Let me guess," said Connie, looking amused. "You were the good guy."

"Well, no, my brother was, actually. He had the Roy Rogers pistol. But since I was the bad guy, at least I always got to die. That was fun." But she sighed as she stared down at the small silver-colored pistol in its decorated leather holster. "I always wanted one of these things. I asked, every Christmas and every birthday, but no one ever paid any attention to me."

"Strange request for a young gel," Connie remarked, then cocked her head and added, "Though it does seem a bit unfair, your brother having one, and not you."

"Oh, but you see, in those days girls were expected to be

girls, and boys, well, you know." Jane shrugged. "Hey—I wanted a catcher's mitt, and nobody paid any attention to that request, either."

And suddenly she found herself wondering whether things might have been different if just once someone had bothered to listen, or pay any heed at all to what she'd wanted.

But as quickly as it came to her, she shrugged away the thought. She was happy. She had a good, full life. A home of her own, no money worries, an okay job, two terrific kids, good friends. Her life had no room in it for regrets.

But...her hands lingered as she was replacing the toy gun on the display table. She asked Connie very casually, "How much do you think this would go for?"

Connie peered at the pistol without enthusiasm. "Oh, I don't know, dear, it's so difficult to say with these nostalgia collectibles. It rather depends on who's here, if you know what I mean. If there happens to be someone else in the crowd who's terribly keen on a Roy Rogers cap pistol, the price could go quite high. Or, you might be lucky and get a bargain. Why don't you note it down in your catalog, if you're interested? Give it a whirl."

"Maybe I will." Jane was surprised to discover that her heart was suddenly beating faster. "I could give it to my brother." *Liar, liar, pants on fire,* a voice inside her whispered. Jane knew that voice. It was the voice of a nine-year-old tomboy who'd once dearly coveted her brother's Roy Rogers cap pistol. "For Christmas," she added, breathless with suppressed desire. "Where do I—how do I find it in here?"

"This little sticker right here, do you see? It has the lot number." Connie showed her how to find the listing in the catalog, loaned her a little jeweled pen and waited patiently while she circled the number, then took her by the arm, saying firmly, "Now then, Jane, do come have a look at these oil paintings. I know you are fond of the Impressionist style—these aren't terribly good ones, I'm afraid. But one or two are actually quite... There now—what do you think?"

Connie had halted before a temporary wall of pegboard on which an assortment of paintings, prints and mirrors had been hung for display. More paintings occupied a Victorian settee nearby. Still others sat on the bare floor, propped against ar-

moires and table legs. Jane scanned them quickly—some con-
temporary limited-edition signed prints that she knew from experience would be out of her price range, a few Victorians,
either gloomy and dim or hopelessly sentimental, the usual flor-
als—before pausing at the one Connie was purposefully tapping
with the frames of her glasses. She tilted her head and regarded
the painting doubtfully. "I don't know...the colors...it's kind of
murky, don't you think?"

And then suddenly her gaze shifted. She felt herself begin to
smile. "Oh," she murmured. "Now *this* I like."

It was an oil, not large, more or less in the style of Renoir, a
pair of dancers against the backdrop of a crowded ballroom
floor. To Jane, it was as if the artist had looked into her mind
and painted her daydream. She could almost feel the graceful
movements of the dancers, hear the lilting strains of the Viennese waltz, feel the softness of the spring evening, even catch
the sweet scent of lilacs drifting through the open windows. The
faces of the dancers had only been suggested, but somehow Jane
knew that they were not just casual partners, but lovers.

Oh, yes, she thought. This was for her. Like the magnificently
carved baby grand, the little painting touched chords in her
imagination—only this, perhaps, she could actually afford.

"It would be perfect above my old piano," she announced.
"How much do you think it will go for?"

Connie considered, head tilted, lips pursed. "Oh, I shouldn't
think it would be too much—as art, it hasn't any particular value
at all. It's really a matter of whether it suits one's taste and
purpose, isn't it? Jot it down, dear. You might get it for a song."

Jane squinted at the tiny tag affixed to one corner of the
frame, found the corresponding lot number in her catalog listings and made a bold check mark beside it. She was beginning
to get the hang of this. She turned to Connie, flushed with ac-
complishment, as though the painting were already hers.
"There—that's done. Now I think I'd better quit before I...oh,
what's that you have there? Did you find something else? Let
me see."

Connie chuckled. "It is addictive, isn't it?" She gave the
painting she was holding a disparaging glance. "Oh, no, dear,
not for you. Another one of those gloomy Victorians—quite
dreadful, really." Jane could see what appeared to be a sailing

ship foundering in a garishly green-tinted, storm-tossed sea. Connie was right. It was dreadful.

"The frame isn't at all bad, though." The dealer turned the painting, assessing it through her half glasses. "I might just pick up one or two of these for the shop, if I can get them at a nice enough price. If you're quite sure there's nothing else you want to have a look at, you might just go and find us some seats. I suspect they'll be getting under way very shortly."

Jane was glad to take the suggestion, though her excitement was somewhat dampened by worry as she made her way through the crowd that was slowly beginning to drift toward rows of folding chairs that had been set up in the center of the huge room facing a low, temporary stage. Her mind was on her checkbook, doing some depressing mental math as she tried to decide how much of her modest balance she could afford to spend on either the Roy Rogers six-shooter or the painting of the dancers. Not very much, she feared.

She found two unclaimed chairs about two-thirds of the way back, just a few seats in from the aisle, deposited her catalog and purse on one to save it for Connie and settled into the other. A group of men were gathered on the stage in a purposeful-looking cluster. One, a short, dapper man in a suit and tie, plump and glossy as a ripe plum, from the toes of his polished black shoes to his shiny black slicked-down hair, separated himself from the rest and took up his post behind a wooden podium. As he lifted the microphone from its stand, a woman seated at a card table next to the podium handed him a sheet of paper. He glanced down at it, then beamed upon the crowd like a kindergarten teacher on the first day of school.

"Ladies and gentlemen, good morning, and welcome to another fantastic Rathskeller's auction...."

Jane sat with her hands clasped in her lap like a well-behaved child on the first day of school while the auctioneer read the policies and conditions of Rathskeller's Auction House. He was finishing up when Connie slipped into the seat beside her.

"Just in time," Jane whispered. "I think they're about to start. Are these seats okay?"

Connie gave a quick look around, then said, "This will do fine, dear." She sounded a little out-of-breath. And looking quite pleased with herself, Jane thought. Her eyes had that feisty gleam that always made Jane think of a little white hen who's just spotted a particularly juicy grasshopper.

Up on the stage, the auctioneer hitched the mike cord around with a flourish and said, "All right, now, ladies and gentlemen, let's get the bidding under way with a few of these items you see here..." One of several young men wearing white shirts and red baseball caps with Rathskeller's printed on them held up a small metal object so everyone in the crowd could see it. "Okay, lot number one in your catalog is a World War II infantry compass. And, here we go, ladies and ge'men, whatumahbid for this fascinating WWII compass...okay, who'llgimmetwenny, umbidtwennytwenny..."

The words tumbled out of the auctioneer's mouth like marbles out of a bag, while here and there among the crowd a white card flashed, then over there another. There was a certain rhythm to it. Each time a card appeared, one of the white-shirted men would instantly point it out to the auctioneer, arms waving and pointing like semaphores, until there were no more cards to be seen—save one.

And then..."Sold!" *Down* came the gavel onto the podium, and the crowd subsided with anticipatory rustlings and murmurings while the lady at the table noted the buyer's number and the selling price. And then, while the white-shirted men carried the item to a holding area to await its new owner, the rhythm began all over again. Jane thought it was terribly exciting.

"I just don't see how you do it so calmly," she said as the gavel fell and Connie made a triumphant notation in her catalog. "Maybe you could bid for me?"

"Nonsense, dear." Connie looked very much like a cat with a mouthful of feathers. "Nothing to it. Tell you what—why don't you have a go at it a time or two. Bid on something you don't particularly care for, just for the practice. You do have to keep your wits about you, of course. Jump in early, and get out when the bidding gets serious. That way you'll get the hang of it and you won't be so nervous when it really matters. Like this, dear—watch."

It looked so easy when Connie did it.

The first time Jane poked her number 133 tentatively into the view of the eagle-eyed men in the white shirts, she thought she might actually faint. When one of them pointed at her, it might as well have been with a loaded pistol; she subsided hastily, shaking like a leaf.

But it got easier each time she tried it. Soon she began to feel like an old hand, especially when she noticed that the men in the white shirts were beginning to look in her direction, now, in anticipation. By the time the Roy Rogers cap pistol came up for bid, she was ready. She felt calm. While the auctioneer was describing "this prize piece of Americana," Jane closed her eyes and repeated her absolutely top bid over and over in a whisper, like a mantra, or a prayer. Then she lifted her card.

Her confidence lasted exactly as long as it took the bidding to soar beyond her "absolutely top" bid. How high could a toy cap pistol go? What, after all, was another ten dollars? Twenty? Her heart was pounding like thunder; she could hardly hear the auctioneer. Lips pressed tightly together in determination, she kept her card in the air, even though it was now shaking like a reed in a windstorm.

"Well done!" said Connie when at last the auctioneer had intoned, "Sold...number 133!" She added gently, "You can put your card down now, dear." Her voice seemed to come from the bottom of a well.

"I did it! I can't believe it—I just bought a Roy Rogers cap pistol!" Jane's whisper was a high, ecstatic squeak. "I think I'm gonna faint." Actually, what she thought she might do was fly, right up out of her chair and on through the roof and into the clouds. "Whew, I think I need to get something to drink. How about you? Can I get you a cup of coffee or something?"

"Later, perhaps..." Connie was frowning, turning the pages of her catalog, following down the list with her little jeweled pen. Jane had gathered up her purse and was halfway to her feet, when the other woman suddenly clutched her arm and pulled her back. "Quick, Jane—have a look. Isn't that your painting coming up there?"

Jane shook her head. "It's a long way off yet. I should have plenty of time—"

"No, no, I'm certain that's the one you were so fond of. There, you see? It's the next one up, I think."

Jane fumbled through her catalog. Yes, there it was, the lot number she'd circled, still at least twenty items off. But there

was no doubt about it, the painting of the ballroom dancers—
her painting—was at that very moment up on the stage, sitting
on an easel at the auctioneer's elbow. "What number is it?"
she hissed at Connie. "What does it say?"

"Number 187, I believe. It just says, 'Oil Painting, Framed.'
A bit of a mix-up, apparently. Oh, well, never mind, these things
happen. There you are—it's started. *Good luck.*"

And just that quickly, the bidding was under way. Jane sat
perched on the edge of her chair, lips pressed and heart pounding, and presented her card to the gleeful spotter like a swords-
man leaping into battle. At first, to her dismay, the bidding was
brisk, but when two or three bargain hunters dropped out early,
she felt a surge of triumph. *Yes! It's mine.*

But no—oh no! Now she could see that every time the spotter
pointed to her, with his other hand he immediately jabbed the
air above her head. Someone was bidding against her! And
seemed every bit as determined as she was.

Outraged, she turned around to see if she could identify the
villain who was trying to take *her* painting away from her.
Yes—there he was. He was easy enough to spot, standing behind the last row of chairs. A man, and one who was not the
slightest bit gray or wimpy, and certainly not old. In fact, he
looked almost indecently young and handsome and fit, in spite
of the banker's gray suit, white shirt and conservative tie he was
wearing. He was very dark, swarthy, almost, with an arrogant
nose and eyes that should have been beautiful. Jane thought he
looked like some sort of Arab prince, or...*no*—a terrorist, that
was it. The kind of person who hijacked airplanes and bombed
school buses.

"Connie," she whispered in dismay. "What am I going to
do? I already spent too much on the cap pistol. I can't afford
to go much higher on this piece."

But Connie's seat was empty. Jane hadn't even noticed that
her friend had left. Where in the world could she have gone?
And at the worst possible time! What should she do? She
couldn't keep bidding like this, she couldn't!

What if she won? Her stomach clenched at the thought of
what this was going to do to her bank balance. She knew she
had to be responsible and give up the painting. *She had to stop
now.*

And then suddenly it was over. *Whack!* went the gavel, the auctioneer bellowed, "That's gone...number 133!"

Stunned by the unexpected victory, almost unable to believe it, Jane turned to look at the man she'd bested. Incredibly, he seemed to have vanished.

She was frowning perplexedly at the place where he'd been standing only a moment ago, where now a small knot of people were engaged in a peculiar flurry of activity, when Connie settled into her chair. She gave her gray curls a pat and her tweed skirt a tug, then turned to Jane, eyes bright and birdlike with expectancy. "So sorry, dear—nature's call, you know. Do tell me, how did it go? Did you get your little painting?"

"I got it," said Jane absently. She still felt dazed.

"Oh, bravo, dear!" Connie was beaming at her like a proud mama at a ballet recital. "Well done."

Jane shook her head, frowning still. "Yeah, well, I don't know how I got it. This man was bidding against me, and he was really determined, too. Then all of a sudden, he just...quit. Connie, what's going on back there, do you know? Seems to be some kind of fuss."

"I suppose it is a bit of a fuss," murmured Connie, planting her half glasses firmly on the tip of her nose and turning to her catalog once more. "Nothing to be concerned about, dear. These things do happen."

"Happen? *What* happened?"

Just for an instant, Connie's eyes met hers over the tops of her glasses, bright with what was unmistakably amusement. And something else that couldn't possibly have been triumph. "I'm afraid it appears some poor chap has fainted."

Chapter 2

Hawk couldn't figure out how she'd managed it. He could see that the guy on the floor was already stirring, so whatever she'd used, it hadn't been lethal, which in his estimation made the operation that much more admirable. He could think of several ways it could have been done, both electrical and chemical; it was the timing that had him stumped.

She was good, no doubt about that. She'd fooled him, and there weren't many, living or dead, who could say that.

The Middle Eastern guy, now, the fainter—Hawk had spotted him for a player right off the bat. It hadn't been hard; the guy looked about as much like an antiques lover as a fox looks like a chicken.

Those two women, though—he'd never have figured them for a game like this. Two nice suburban ladies looking for bargains, that's how he'd had them pegged. Although the tall brunette was a fox, all right, and the older one—come to think of it, that one did sort of resemble a chicken, a plump little gray hen. But what in the hell was she to the other one? Mother, friend or aunt, maybe—surely not an accomplice. In any event, Hawk figured she was probably just along for window dressing, part of the camouflage. Effective, too; he hadn't given them a second glance.

Though, to be honest, there'd been a time when the younger woman might have turned his head and quickened his pulse, those first few years, the bad years when the glimpse of any tall, slender woman with short dark curls and a certain way of walking, a way of holding her head, her chin just *so,* could spin him around, trembling, like an electric shock straight to the heart. He'd gotten over that, thank God. Just as he'd gotten over waking up in the night thinking he'd heard a child crying.

He straightened, suddenly alert. The dark-haired woman was on the move, squeezing past people's knees with polite, apologetic "Excuse me's," making her way to the center aisle. He watched as she came toward him, his whole body tense with concentration, little electrical currents of excitement coursing through him. He could feel his skin ripple with it, feel his hair rise. If he'd been a cat, his tail would have twitched. He was the hunter, watching the unsuspecting prey—dangerous prey, to be sure, but at the moment the advantage was all his.

But she was edgy; he could tell by the way she licked her lips as her eyes darted toward the crowd of Good Samaritans gathered around the man on the floor, by the way her hands clutched the straps of her shoulder bag, as if she expected someone to try to snatch it from her. Sensing his presence, perhaps, like a leopard sensing the lion.

From his hiding place behind a rack of Oriental rugs he studied her, paying attention to things that couldn't be easily altered by a disguise. For instance, it was the particular shape of her eyes and the way they were set—not too deeply, but not prominent, either—that interested him, rather than the fact that they were the greenish-gray of deep sea waters, dark-lashed, with a little fan of smile lines at the corners.

Those lines and another set, like parentheses, around her mouth told him she was probably somewhat older than he'd thought—late thirties, maybe even forty. Which made it unlikely her hair color was entirely natural. That rich dark mahogany had been a good choice, though, maybe it even had been her natural color once upon a time. And the style suited her—short, but softly curling on the back of her neck and feathering around her

face in a way that set off her cheekbones. He'd remember those
cheekbones.

Nice body, for forty or any age. She wore her clothes well,
with a certain style and natural elegance that was as much a
product of health, vitality and good posture as it was proportions. Her clothes seemed of good quality but not designer, expensive but not ridiculously so—brown wool slacks and rust-
colored turtleneck, tan tweed blazer with leather trim on the
lapels and pockets. Nice shoes—some kind of short boot with
a bit of a heel, comfortable-looking but elegant, too—and
matching leather bag. No rings on the fingers that were still
wrapped in a death grip around the strap of the shoulder bag,
which didn't surprise him; she had the self-indulged look of the
well-off recently divorced.

Overall, the effect was simple, tasteful, and... What she had,
Hawk realized suddenly, was that indefinable something called
class.

He still couldn't quite make the woman as Loizeau's killer,
though of course he couldn't rule out that possibility, either.
Whoever she was, she wouldn't catch *him* off guard again.

He waited until the double doors that led to the foyer had
closed behind her before he left his cover among the Oriental
rugs and followed. The crowd of compassionate busybodies
around the fainter was dispersing as he passed. The gentleman
himself had moved to a chair, where he sat slumped and sullen,
engaged in a conversation with one of the Rathskeller people
that appeared to consist, on the unfortunate man's part, mostly
of monosyllables and head shakes. He appeared both dazed and
furious; his skin still had the waxy, old-ivory look of someone
in imminent danger of losing his lunch.

Hawk almost ran his quarry down in the foyer—literally.
He'd assumed it was the ladies' room she was heading for so
purposefully, so he wasn't expecting it when he pushed full tilt
through the double doors and found her standing only a few feet
on the other side. She had her purse open and was frowning at
something in her hand—her checkbook, it appeared.

He pulled up just shy of plowing into her. As startled as he
was, she looked up, straight at him, and murmured a breathy
apology. He managed a curt nod, maintaining just enough poise

to reach for his cigarettes as something of a distraction while he moved a safe distance away from her.

His thoughts were in turmoil. Dammit, she'd done it again. Caught him by surprise.

That didn't make him happy, but it wasn't nearly as unsettling as the impression he'd gotten from that one brief look into the woman's eyes. A sudden widening...brightening...an impression of breath caught and held, like a child tearing paper off a birthday present. Young eyes. *Innocent eyes.*

A soft, throat-clearing sound penetrated the tumult of his thoughts. He turned toward its source, a cigarette poised halfway between the pack and his lips. The woman was gazing at him, the parentheses of lines around her mouth and the fan at the corners of her eyes both deepening as she shifted her gaze meaningfully toward a prominently displayed No Smoking sign.

Ah, hell. With a nod that was just barely polite, Hawk turned his back on the lady and strolled down the foyer toward the front entrance. One look through the glass doors assured him that the icy drizzle that had snarled traffic on the beltway that morning and caused him to miss the auction preview was still falling. That fact made his desire for a cigarette that much more compelling, and did nothing to improve his temper.

He considered his options while he gazed out at glistening gray walkways bordered by bowing daffodils and beds of drenched pansies, tapping the cigarette restlessly against the pack. He could feel the woman's presence there in the foyer behind him. Feel her watching him. Studying him, as a moment ago he'd studied her. It wasn't a feeling he liked.

Deciding that no nicotine craving was worth letting the woman out of his sight, and getting wet and chilled to the bone in the bargain, Hawk dropped the unlit cigarette into a trash container near the doors. He was tucking the pack into his pocket, when the woman's voice startled him once again, wafting from the far end of the foyer like a puff of a breeze on a still spring afternoon, unexpectedly warming, amused and sympathetic.

"It is a bother, isn't it?"

"I beg your pardon?" His own voice was hard-edged, partly with suspicion, partly in self-defense.

She gestured with her left hand, with the checkbook she still held. "Smoking. They do make it as difficult as possible for you these days, don't they?"

Hawk gave an all-purpose shrug and moved toward her, his mind spinning with possibilities. He paused when there was still some distance between them and said warily, "You're not a smoker."

The lines around her mouth appeared briefly, a rueful little smile that didn't touch her eyes. "Not me. Married to one for twenty-one years, though."

"Ah." He nodded and turned a shoulder toward her—not impolitely, just a firm but gentle closing.

Which she ignored. Her voice came again, same friendliness, same sympathy tinged with amusement. "I take it you're here with someone." He turned his head, looked at her along one shoulder, eyebrows lifted. Her smile asked pardon for the liberty. "Somehow you just don't look like the antiques type. Are you here with your wife?"

Hawk shook his head, again unprepared for the apparent openness, the casual friendliness of the woman. Then he muttered, improvising like mad, "I'm meeting someone. A...friend." He made a quick movement with his head toward the outer doors, conveying, he hoped, a touch of annoyance. "Apparently she's late."

The woman nodded in a commiserating sort of way. "Probably stuck in traffic. It's really nasty out."

"Yeah," said Hawk. "That's probably it."

And then, for a change, she was silent. It was a curious, almost expectant little silence. She seemed to be studying him again, but he didn't want to risk making eye contact with her to find out for sure. There wasn't much he could be certain of where this woman was concerned, but all his instincts were telling him he didn't want her gazing into the windows of his soul.

She took a step toward him. He tensed. Then, "Hi—I'm Jane Carlysle," she said, and held out her hand.

It would have been impossible not to take it. It was a strange sensation, Hawk discovered, shaking hands with someone who might be a cold-blooded and accomplished assassin. Wouldn't be the first time he'd done it, of course; he wasn't sure why this time was different. But he could feel those currents of excitement racing around under his skin. Feel his perceptions sharpen and his chest tingle, as if he'd just sucked in a lungful of crystal-clear, bone-cold air.

"Tom—Tom Hawkins," he said, and watched her smile lines deepen once again.

He doesn't smile, thought Jane. A shame, too; she had a feeling he might be quite nice-looking if he did. Not that he was unattractive as he was—quite the contrary. It was just that there was something rather off-putting about his rugged, slightly asymmetrical features...a certain hardness to his mouth, a coldness in the eyes. She thought that if he would only smile it would make all the difference in the world. She thought she would very much like to make him smile.

Before she could wonder why that should be so, before she could even begin to wonder how to go about it, she saw the man's eyes shift and darken, foreshadowing the touch she felt an instant later on her elbow.

"Excuse me, miss, uh, ma'am?"

Turning, Jane recognized the very same individual who, only a short time ago, had been bidding furiously against her for her precious painting. The man she'd last seen stretched out on the auditorium floor surrounded by curious auction-goers and concerned employees of Rathskeller's. The "Arab terrorist"—though at the moment he didn't look capable of terrorizing anyone. His hair was mussed, his tie askew and his olive-toned complexion had a decidedly greenish tinge, all of which played strongly to her compassionate nature and mother-hen instincts.

Reflexively, she put out a hand to touch his arm and, in a voice husky with concern, said, "My goodness, are you all right?"

The man waved that aside with an impatient grimace. He glanced around, then took Jane's elbow and maneuvered her a couple of steps closer to the auditorium doors and away from the third party present. That accomplished, he lowered his head and said in a low voice, "Can I talk to you a minute? About that picture..."

Jane's heartbeat quickened. Chilly little currents of unease stirred across the back of her neck and shivered her skin with goose bumps. For some reason, she found herself looking over her shoulder, searching for the unsmiling stranger named Tom Hawkins, as if he represented some sort of haven, or rescuer.

She was relieved to find him over near the windows, only a polite distance away, scowling at his watch.

She turned back to the "terrorist," mentally fortifying herself the way she did when she was forced to be firm with one of her daughters. "Sir, I'm sorry about what happened to you, but—"

"I'd like to buy it from you." Keeping his hold on Jane's elbow, the man reached inside his jacket and pulled out a wallet. The fingers on her arm were tense as wire. "I'll pay you cash. What was the final bid? I'll top it by a hundred."

Jane's breath caught; jolts of alarm shot through all her nerves and muscles. Instinctively, she took a step backward, jerking her arm free. "I don't want to sell it. I just bought it."

"Please." The man held up both hands, palms out, almost, it seemed to her, in supplication. "I know you probably think I'm nuts. Maybe I am nuts." He made an unconvincing attempt to smile. "The thing is, well, darn it, I really wanted that particular painting. See—it's my fiancée—she just fell in love with it. I was going to get it for her as a surprise. That's why money's no object, okay? I was willing to go as high as it took." Another of those stiff, almost painful-looking smiles. "If I hadn't passed out like that—I don't know what happened. I mean, I've never had anything like that happen to me before."

"Maybe it was the excitement," Jane suggested, her natural compassion now struggling with an inexplicable sense of guilt. It made her feel awkward, almost embarrassed. "You know, if you're not used to auctions…"

The man's smile was wry, and much more believable than his previous attempts. He snorted and said, "Maybe," in such a tone of gloom and disappointment that Jane began to feel sorry for him.

But dammit, *she* loved that painting, too. It was hers—she'd won it fair and square. "I wish I could help you," she said with a helpless shrug. "I really do. But I just—"

"Ah, come on," the man pleaded, opening his wallet. "I told you, money's no object. Try me—name your price."

Jane gave an incredulous laugh. This whole thing was just so *bizarre.* Again she glanced over her shoulder, searching for the tall, angular form of the man called Tom Hawkins. Yes, he was still there, over by the windows, standing with his back to her, looking out at the rain, restlessly jingling things in his pockets. And yet, she had the strangest feeling he was listening to every word, missing nothing.

"I'm sorry, Mr...."

"Campbell—Aaron Campbell," he offered eagerly, as if he hoped the name might head off the inevitable.

Campbell? "I'm truly sorry," she said, making her refusal as kind and as firm as she knew how, girding herself against her own generous instincts. "I wish I could be unselfish about it, but it happens that I've fallen in love with that particular painting myself. I know how much you must want it, but I also know that if I did give in and sell it to you, I'd very much regret it. I'm sorry..." She was backing away from him now, a hand upraised as if to physically ward him off. "I'm sorry."

Still he persisted, following her beseechingly, holding something out to her—a business card. "If you should change your mind—"

"I won't. Really. Please...I'm sorry," Jane gasped. Discovering that the auditorium doors were there at her back, she groped for the handle and pushed through them, throwing out one more anguished, *"I'm sorry."* The last thing she saw as the doors swished shut was a look of black and impotent fury.

Inside the auditorium, the auctioneer's voice droned on.

"There you are," said Connie, appearing at her elbow. "I wondered where you'd got to. Everything all right, dear? You look a bit whacked."

"Oh, I'm fine." Jane was already finding it hard to recall what it was, exactly, that had been so unsettling about the confrontation with the persistent Mr. Campbell. His eyes, perhaps. Something about his eyes...

"You won't believe it," she said to Connie with a short, incredulous laugh. "That man—the one who was bidding against me for the painting? He just offered to buy it from me. He told me to name my price. Can you imagine?"

Connie's glasses tumbled from their customary perch on the end of her nose, coming to rest before reaching the limits of their tether on her ample, sweatered bosom. Her eyebrows shot up. "You didn't sell it to him, did you? Oh, my dear, after all that!"

"No, of course I didn't," Jane assured her with a huff of

indignation. "Are you kidding? I love that painting. I'd never sell it. So—how are *you* doing? Buying lots of good stuff?"

She straightened as she spoke and pushed away from the doors, but the nerves on the back of her neck and between her shoulder blades still prickled with a strange *awareness*—she'd never felt anything like it before and couldn't think what else to call it—awareness of the two enigmatic and vaguely upsetting men she'd left on the other side of them.

Hawk turned away discreetly as the gentleman he'd just heard identify himself as Aaron Campbell plunged past him, through the glass doors and out into the rain. Under different circumstances, he might have allowed himself a smile; to say Mr. Campbell was pissed was like saying a hurricane might be a little windy. Hawk half expected to see steam rising from under the coat collar the man had hastily turned up against the drizzle.

He considered following Campbell. But it was the Carlysle woman who had the painting, and judging from the fire in his eyes, Campbell didn't seem like the type to give up the game so easily. A sudden vivid image of the shopkeeper Loizeau staring up at the ceiling with his three vacant eyes wafted through Hawk's memory. An image of the tall brunette in those same circumstances wanted to follow, but he blocked it with a reflexive rejection that surprised him. For some reason, the thought of those sea-gray eyes clouded and empty of all light and life made him feel queasy, like a bubble of indigestion lodged at the back of his throat. He told himself it was only because he couldn't see her as Loizeau's killer, and if she wasn't, then she didn't deserve to die. No matter who she was, or where she fit into the picture.

And that was the next thing he had to find out. *Who in the hell was this Jane Carlysle?* Watching the slick way she'd neutralized Campbell during the bidding, he'd figured her to be a player for sure. After seeing her up close, talking to her, he'd thought, okay, not one of the bad guys—CIA, maybe. Even, God forbid, the FBI. He'd been thinking maybe it was time for a little team effort, a limited pooling of resources. As long as the good guys won, right?

Now, though, after seeing her with Campbell, he was beginning to consider a whole new possibility. One that made the bad taste at the back of his throat even more bitter. What if Jane Carlysle was exactly who and what she appeared to be—an innocent antiques lover who just happened to have fallen in love with that particular painting? What if—jeez, stranger things had happened—Campbell really had fainted? Sure wouldn't be the first time an innocent had gotten caught in the crossfire of someone else's war....

Enough. The grimace with which he banished that thought was more of annoyance than pain. God, he wanted a cigarette.

The young woman at the reception desk looked up as he approached, elegant eyebrows arched in welcome. "Yes, sir, may I help you?"

Hawk glanced at his watch and made his smile as charming as he knew how. "Sorry to bother you, but I wonder if you can tell me—I think this is where I'm supposed to meet my wife. She called me this morning—major crisis—apparently she'd gone off without her credit cards."

The woman laughed in mock dismay. "Ooh, a real disaster."

Hawk did his lopsided smile again, accompanying it with a chuckle. "For me it's more of a disaster when she has 'em. Anyway, I don't seem to be able to locate her."

"Have you taken a look inside? Perhaps she's gone back to the auction."

Hawk nodded. "I checked a while ago. Didn't see her, but it's a pretty big crowd. I wonder, would you mind checking her registration card for me? Just to make sure she's checked in."

"Certainly. Name?"

"Carlysle—Jane."

"Carlysle...let's see...how is that spelled?"

Hawk's heart lurched. *Shoot.* Well, hell, he had a fifty-fifty chance. He had his mouth open to take a stab at it when the woman said, "Oh, yes, here it is. Jane Carlysle—from Cooper's Mill?"

Hawk exhaled and put the smile back on. "That's the one."

The receptionist plucked the card from the file and placed it on the desk in front of her. Hawk tried not to crane too obviously. "Well, according to this, your wife plans to pay for any purchases by check."

"*My* wife? Can't be! Let me see that...." And as he'd been

certain she would, the receptionist obligingly turned the card
around. He leaned over and gazed at it long enough to commit
Jane Carlysle's—with a Y—North Carolina driver's license to
memory, then straightened with a sigh. "That's her, all right.
Well. I guess I'd better find her and see what she wants to do.
Maybe she's already paid up and gone. Is that possible?"

"For that, you'd have to check with the office—that's through
the auditorium, door to the, um, right of the stage. She'd need
to pay for her purchases there, then pick them up in holding.
That's in the backstage delivery area—there's a loading dock
there, for large items. I suppose your wife might have gone out
that way, if you—"

Hawk muttered, "Thanks, I'll check," as he turned away. He
pushed through the auditorium doors on a surge of adrenaline,
nerves already kicking in to full battle readiness. He was pretty
sure he knew now where Campbell had been going in such a
hurry.

"Look, there he is again," Jane said in a loud whisper, tight-
ening her grip on the shopping bag containing her precious Roy
Rogers cap pistol as if she expected an imminent mugging.
"The man I told you about, the one who was bidding against
me, the one who tried to—to bribe me."

Connie's slightly protuberant blue eyes glittered dangerously.
She shifted, moving closer to Jane, her stocky body lending
unspoken support. "Yes, yes, I see him. Never mind, dear, stand
fast, don't let him intimidate you. You won the battle, fair and
square."

"Right," said Jane, breathing through her nose. She watched,
hovering anxiously, while a Rathskeller's employee carefully
wrapped the painting of the ballroom dancers in layers and layers of brown paper. It was the last of the lot, thank God. Connie's purchases—and there had been a good many of them—
had already been loaded into her van, which was conveniently
parked near the foot of the loading ramp.

It was there that Jane had spotted the ubiquitous Mr. Campbell, leaning against the fender of an anonymous black sedan,
arms folded and ankles crossed, seemingly oblivious to the cold
and wet. Watching. Waiting.

Jane shivered and turned her back to him. "I wish he'd just give it up," she said crossly to Connie as she accepted her wrapped parcel from the young employee. "I've already made it perfectly clear to him that I've no intention whatsoever of selling this painting. I *love* this painting. You know, people like that seem to think they can have anything they want if they just pay enough money. He gives me the creeps—oh!" Turning with the painting in her hands, she'd clumsily barged right into someone. "Oh—I'm so sorry. Please excuse me, I..." And then she stopped, bemused, completely forgetting what it was she'd meant to say.

"We meet again," Tom Hawkins said with a smile.

Well, okay, so it wasn't much of a smile—a lopsided quirk of the lips that didn't soften the forbidding terrain of the rest of his face one iota. She found it oddly endearing. "Mr. Hawkins," she breathed, her own smile blossoming without reservation. "Tell me, did you ever find your friend?"

He gave his head a rueful waggle. "The girl at the front desk suggested I try back here, but..." His shrug had the same elusive charm as his smile. "I don't see her anywhere, so I guess I must have missed her. Oh, well..."

"I'm sorry," said Jane, which was a bald-faced lie.

"Me, too." He gave another little *c'est la vie* shrug, then, as if suddenly remembering his manners, stepped forward to take the paper-wrapped parcel from her. "Here, let me give you a hand with that. Where are you ladies parked?"

"That won't be necessary," said Connie in her iciest and most dismissive upper-crust British.

It was a tone designed to give frostbite to a penguin, but its effect on Tom Hawkins seemed to be quite the reverse. By no stretch could the smile he turned on Connie be considered rueful or lopsided. And it did affect the terrain of his face—all of it. It touched his features like the sun coming up on an Arctic landscape, squinting his eyes and lighting his skin with color and warmth. Jane didn't know about Connie, but her own re-action to that smile was about the same as if she'd taken a slug of Canadian whiskey, neat.

"Thanks," she gasped over the beginnings of Connie's pro-test. "That's very kind of you." She edged around her friend with a whispered, "It's okay," and fell into step with the man, who was already starting down the ramp with her burden.

"That's us right there, the dark blue van." She waited while he wedged the painting into the back of the van. She surrendered the bag containing her Roy Rogers cap pistol when he turned to ask for it. When he had tucked that away, as well, she heard herself witlessly babbling profuse thanks, saw herself poking out her hand with a lamentable lack of grace, realized that she was as out of breath as if she'd been the one doing all the toting and lifting.

"My pleasure—glad I could help." Without the smile, his face was once more grave and careworn, though not so forbidding, perhaps, as she'd first considered it. And his handshake was firm, and very warm.

"Anything else to go in here? No?" He slammed the van's doors, tested them to make certain they were closed properly, then nodded politely to Connie, who was protectively hovering. "There you go, you're all set. You ladies drive carefully now." With a brief nod to Jane, he turned and started back up the loading ramp. Halfway up, she saw him pause to light a cigarette, hunching over his cupped hands to shelter against the drizzle.

"Who was that?" Connie demanded as she turned the key in the van's ignition, her tone sharp and battle-ready.

Jane chuckled, and realized at once how artificial it sounded. How exhilarated she felt—but that was just from the cold, wasn't it? And so breathless—which was easily explained, especially at her age, by the ordinary bustle and fuss of settling in and buckling up. Oh, but she *had* found that man attractive—and what was wrong with that? It had been a long time since she'd felt that particular buzz, and she'd damn well enjoyed it.

"A man I ran into in the lobby," she said in a bright and casual tone that was as fake as her smile. "He was waiting for a girlfriend, I rather imagine. It doesn't look as though he's made connections yet." With patent insincerity, she added, "Poor guy."

"Well, one can't be too careful," Connie said as she edged the van out of the line of parked cars. "These days, you never know."

Chapter 3

Hawk tucked his lighter away and continued up the ramp without looking back. He didn't need to look to know that the blue van was pulling away from the curb, or that the man named Campbell was already behind the wheel of his black rental sedan, set to follow. He'd be doing the same, of course, when the time was right, and in the meantime, he wasn't concerned about losing sight of the van. The small electronic device he'd planted on the top edge of the back door would make the vehicle easy enough to locate.

In the shelter of the loading bay's overhang he lingered a while to smoke his cigarette, to any interested observer just a poor nicotine addict enjoying his fix. But while he waited for the calming effects of the drug to take the edge off his adrenaline high, his eyes were busy scanning the parking lot and nearby streets and alleyways. When he was satisfied that no one else besides Campbell was taking any particular interest in the two middle-aged ladies in the dark blue van, he drew on his cigarette one last time and dropped it to the concrete, squinting against a lingering tail of smoke as he ground the stub beneath the toe of his shoe.

He dusted his hands together, then shoved them into the pockets of his charcoal-gray overcoat and moved to the steps, moving quickly now and with purpose, taking the short way to the parking lot. God, he could still feel the tingle. Feel it in the palms of his hands, feel it crawling all the way up his arms and across his shoulders, along the back of his neck and into his scalp. As he'd felt it a few days ago outside Loizeau's shop in Marseilles, and again just moments ago, holding that damn painting in his own two hands. The tingle of excitement. *The thrill of the game.*

As he zigzagged his way through the busy parking lot, in a midafternoon gloom that was only partly mitigated by the premature illumination of mercury vapor lamps, it occurred to him that he might be in danger of becoming addicted to the tingle.

And why not? Why not, when it was one of the few real pleasures he allowed himself these days. No risk of emotional involvement attached, a helluva lot safer than sex and probably only marginally more hazardous to his health than cigarettes or booze.

Besides, holding that painting, knowing what was hidden inside it—hell, it would give any man a thrill to realize that right there in his hands was the key to the future of civilization as we know it, the beginnings of the next holocaust, the fate of millions of innocent lives. Wouldn't it?

But Tom Hawkins acknowledged and accepted the truth about the man he'd become, which was that the wildfire racing along all his nerves hadn't been ignited by any of those things. No...he knew that what he'd felt, standing in the rain with that painting in his hands, was more like what a fighter feels with the throat of a vanquished foe pulsing in his grasp. The elation of a poker player who's just been dealt a pat hand. The emotion that had surged through him then was the same one that fills the breast of the chess champion just before he utters the words, "Checkmate."

No...for a man to think about the fate of children and nations at such a time, he would first have to care about those things. But Hawk had learned the hard way that caring bears a terrible price. And that it was one he no longer cared to pay.

He spotted his rental car in the next row over, went straight to the trunk, unlocked it and took out his briefcase. He tucked it under his arm while he relocked the trunk and let himself into the car, then placed it carefully on the seat beside him until he'd gotten himself settled in behind the wheel and relocked the doors.

After a quick but thorough check of all neighboring vehicles, he punched in a number combination and opened the briefcase. Inside was a smaller case that resembled a laptop computer. This Hawk turned toward him, flipped up the screen and began to touch keys. When he had the monitor screen green and glowing, he selected a disk from a small assortment in his briefcase and inserted it in the laptop. A moment later a map of eastern Virginia appeared on the screen. A few minor manipulations gave him Arlington and its environs. Close enough, for now. He marked his own waypoint, then sat back and lit a cigarette while he studied the screen through narrowed eyes.

Generally speaking, Hawk disliked high-tech toys, especially anything that relied too heavily on computers. It was his firm belief that they couldn't be trusted. Also that they were short on flexibility and utterly lacking in imagination and loyalty. He wouldn't like to have to count on one in a crisis. The Global Positioning System was an exception, probably because he'd had one on his boat for a good many years now and had gotten used to it. These days, he considered a GPS unit an indispensable modern convenience, rather like a microwave oven.

But he still knew how to boil water the old-fashioned way, if it came to that.

The rapidly changing numbers on the LCD screen told him that the van was still moving, albeit slowly. He glanced at his watch. Rush hour—small wonder. No need to follow just yet.

He turned on the car's engine, adjusted the heater and ran the windows down a crack to let out his smoke, then took the cellular phone from its box in the center console and punched in a number he knew by heart. While he waited for the connection, he parked his cigarette between his lips and reached inside his coat, searching for the small piece of paper he'd tucked away in his shirt pocket.

He was squinting at it when a familiar, French-accented voice snarled in his ear. "Interpol—Devore."

"Hawk, here. I'm on the cellular. Better scramble."

There was a short pause before the U.S. bureau chief spoke

again, with tension crackling in every syllable. "Go ahead. Have you got it?"

Hawk chuckled, though no one hearing it would have mistaken the sound for humor. "Not yet. Working on it. Listen, I need for you to call in a favor from our friends at Quantico." He paused, smiling darkly to himself, for Devore's rumble of discontent; there was nothing one law enforcement agency hated more than having to ask another one for help—especially when one or the other was the FBI. "Don't worry, it's just a little one. I need anything you can turn up for me on a Jane Carlysle—that's Carlysle with a 'y' and an 's'—address, Cooper's Mill, North Carolina."

He read off the driver's-license number he'd scrawled on the back of one of his bank deposit slips, waited until Devore gave it back to him, then rolled the paper into a slender tube and held it to the glowing end of his cigarette. He watched it sprout flame while he listened to Devore's inevitable questions—questions he didn't have any answers for. Yet.

"Hold on a sec," he said, interrupting Devore in midsentence, and dropped the burning paper into the car's ashtray. "Time to go. I'll get back to you." He'd just observed that the coordinates on the GPS monitor screen had remained unchanged for a significant length of time, which meant, in all probability, that the blue van had reached its destination. He broke the connection on Devore's tinny protest, stashed the phone in its box more abruptly than was probably good for a delicate piece of electronic equipment and reached across it to tap keys on the laptop.

When he had the van's location pinpointed on his street map, he sat back with an audible "Huh!" of surprise. He didn't need to look up the address in his directory; it was one he knew well. He'd stayed in that hotel himself, a time or two. Had a nice view of the river, the tidal basin and the Washington Monument. In a few weeks, when the cherry trees were in full bloom, it would be downright spectacular.

And what the hell, he wondered, were those two women doing back in the middle of town? It didn't make sense. If *he'd* just gotten his hands on one of the most devastating and sought-after pieces of information since the A-bomb blueprints, he'd be hightailing it out of town with the goods as fast as he could.

The more he thought about it, the more he had to wonder about the Carlysle woman's role in all this. In fact, he couldn't get the woman out of his mind. As he backed out of the parking space and circled the lot to the exit, nosed into traffic and set a course toward the Potomac, her name played in his memory like a phrase from a song, a bit of melody sung in her own gentle voice: *"Hi, I'm Jane Carlysle."* He saw her face floating above his head like a loopy white cartoon balloon.

The weirdest thing was, he could still recall the way she *smelled.* It wasn't even anything he could put a name to—not a particular scent, or a certain brand of perfume, but rather an elusive combination of things, like soap and bath powder, deodorant and hand lotion and shampoo, a smell that was uniquely her own, and at the same time achingly familiar to him. It had come wafting out of his past, from the depths of forbidden memory, calling to mind not just a particular woman, but a particular *kind* of woman.

He spent some time thinking about it before he came up with the word *ordinary,* but he wasn't happy with it. The way that word was used, it usually meant nothing special, and that wasn't what he meant at all. What he meant by the word *ordinary,* as applied to a woman, was, well, *nice.* The nice, everyday kind of woman, the moms, the sisters and sweethearts. The kind of woman a man gets married to, the one he wants nursing his babies, humming in his kitchen. The kind that puts a smile on his face every day of his life when he sings out, "Hi, honey, I'm home."

That's what Jane Carlysle smelled like. A nice...ordinary woman. So how come that nice, ordinary woman had just walked off with a package people were killing one another for?

He was beginning to have a bad feeling about this. A very bad feeling.

"Are you sure you don't mind my staying?" Jane asked, turning reluctantly from a breathtaking view of the Washington Monument.

Connie closed the lid of her small overnighter with a snap and glanced at her in surprise. "Heavens, no—are you sure you don't mind my going? I feel as though I'm abandoning you."

"You're not," Jane protested. "Please don't think that for a minute. I'll just catch a shuttle to Raleigh-Durham, and one of the girls can pick me up there. I did say I might like to stay over, spend a day or two in Washington—I've only been once, and it was such a long time ago."

Connie sighed. "I know, and it's a lovely idea. I'd stay on with you, dear, but to tell you the truth, I'm about all tripped out. I'd barely unpacked after my last jaunt, you know, and it was hi-ho, off to the auction." She chuckled, pausing on her way to the bathroom to give Jane's arm a comforting pat. "Believe it or not, even an old globe-trotter like me develops a longing for her own bed and cozy slippers from time to time."

"That's right," Jane said with just a touch of wistfulness, "I'd forgotten you'd just come back from a trip. You were in Europe again, weren't you?"

Connie's eyes rolled expressively. "Oh my, yes, and not a very successful trip, either, I'm afraid. The weather was positively dreadful."

Jane had no reply to that, since she couldn't imagine any weather terrible enough to take the thrill out of Europe. She murmured inanely, "Well, I guess spring is late everywhere this year," and turning, gazed again at the shimmering city beyond the window. The Washington Monument's floodlit column had been rendered somewhat fuzzy by all the mist in the air, so that it seemed to glow in the lavender dusk like a ghostly candle.

Disneyland for adults—that's what David had called Washington. He'd promised to take her there, someday, but as with most things where Jane was concerned, it hadn't been very high on his priority list, and he'd never quite gotten around to it. So, of course, one of the first things she'd done after the divorce— right after covering up the gray in her hair and having her crooked front teeth capped—was take the girls to see the Capitol. Three days, that was all the time she'd felt she could afford to take off work, those first uncertain, terrifying months on her own. The girls, too young to fully appreciate the experience, had complained about the heat and sore feet. Jane had gotten blisters on her feet, too, but she hadn't minded.

She'd promised herself then she'd go back when she had more time and see everything she'd missed. Why hadn't she?

After all, there'd been nothing—and no one—to keep her from it. Time just seemed to go by so quickly.

"That's it, I believe," Connie announced, giving her hands a brisk dusting as she emerged from the bathroom. She hoisted the strap of her overnighter to her shoulder and turned to survey the room once more. "Don't believe I've forgotten anything. Now, dear, did you bring up everything you wanted from the van? Anything to go down? Are you sure you don't want me to carry your painting home with me? I should think it might be rather a nuisance, especially on one of those dreadful little shuttle planes."

"The painting isn't really all that big," Jane said. "I think it'll fit in a shopping bag. Anyway, if not, I'll wrap it and ship it home. I'm going to take your suggestion, though, I think, and have it appraised while I'm here. That man, Campbell, being so interested in it—and I didn't buy his story about his fiancée being wildly in love with it, not for a minute, did you?—it just makes me wonder." She hitched a shoulder and added defensively, "Well, stranger things have happened. You read about them all the time—priceless manuscripts turning up in an attic, some old master bought at a yard sale for pennies."

Connie had the grace not to smile, but merely said solemnly, "Quite so, dear. As I said before, if you're at all uneasy about it, it can't hurt to be sure, can it? Let's see, now, did I jot down the address of that art dealer friend of mine in Georgetown for you?" Muttering to herself over Jane's grateful demurrals, she planted her half glasses on the end of her nose, produced her little jeweled pen and scrawled a name on a piece of hotel stationery. "There you are, dear. I'm sure there are any number of good dealers in the area, but this reference might save you some time. And let's see...where's your little popgun?"

"Oh, damn," said Jane. "I guess it's still in the van." With all the fuss over the painting, she'd all but forgotten the Roy Rogers cap pistol she'd fought so hard for. "I'll walk down with you and get it. I need to buy some things downstairs, anyway...oh, wait, that reminds me—your toothpaste."

She detoured into the bathroom to get the tube she'd been sharing with Connie since the evening before. Such a ridiculous thing to forget, toothpaste! But then, she'd be the first to admit she wasn't very experienced at this traveling business.

Connie waved away the tube of toothpaste with a breezy, "Oh, heavens, dear, keep it. I have plenty at home. Well, that's it, then—I'm off."

"Wait, just let me get my purse." She planned to stop in the gift shop and pick up a map of Washington with a Metro schedule, and maybe a paperback to read. She'd already planned to order a light supper from room service and spend the evening planning the next day's sight-seeing.

Having retrieved her purse, Jane followed the other woman through the door and pulled it firmly shut, pausing for a moment to make sure it had locked securely behind them.

Hawk lit his third cigarette and told himself it was to ward off the carbon monoxide fumes in the parking garage. God, he hated stakeouts. Too much dead time. Too easy, in those long, lonely hours, for the mind to slip its leash and run untethered into shadowed corners, sniff out forbidden tidbits and drag them triumphantly into the light. He was forced, at times like that, to be doubly vigilant, his concentration divided between making sure he missed nothing that was going on around him, while at the same time making himself deaf and blind to the images that flickered unbidden across the blank screen of his mind.

Mentally reciting poems or lyrics helped, as long as he was careful not to pick the wrong song. He was trying to remember the third verse of "The Battle Hymn of the Republic," when he heard the ding of the elevator bell, and then voices and footsteps coming down the row.

He sat very still in the shadows, making no sudden moves that might draw their eyes his way, and watched the two women approach the back of the blue van. The shorter, gray-haired one had a piece of carry-on luggage slung over one shoulder and a set of keys ready in her hand. The Carlysle woman carried only a handbag and wasn't wearing a coat.

Hawk waited until the older woman had the back door to the van unlocked and both women had turned away from him, then sat up straight and adjusted the earpiece he'd already inserted in his left ear. He propped the directional microphone on the dash, aimed it like a pistol and thumbed it on, wincing at the swish, crackle and resonating *thump* the shoulder bag made as it settled onto the floor of the van next to a pile of paper-wrapped parcels.

He thought, as he adjusted the volume, that of all his electronic toys he probably disliked listening devices most. Necessary as they might be, to him there was something sleazy, something nasty and voyeuristic about eavesdropping on people's private conversations. And sometimes the worst moments were when there wasn't any conversation at all.

"Drive carefully now." That was Carlysle. The two women were hugging each other.

"Of course, dear."

"I just wish you weren't getting such a late start."

"Oh, never mind that. Actually, I rather like driving at night. And if I do start to nod off, well, then I'll just pull off somewhere and take a room for the duration. Do stop worrying, Jane. I'm an old hand at this, you know."

"I know." The Carlysle woman was laughing. The effect was unexpectedly intimate, so close in his ear. "I suppose you're the one who should be worrying about *me*."

"Oh, you'll be fine, dear." The back doors of the van slammed shut, making Hawk wince again. "Just keep your door locked, and a good firm grip on your handbag at all times."

The woman was climbing into the driver's seat now, getting ready to leave. Carlysle was obviously staying. But where was the damn painting? He hadn't seen it in the van, but he hadn't gotten a very good look, and he couldn't be certain...

"Oh, and do give that art dealer friend of mine a ring. I'll be most interested to hear what he has to say after he's had a look at your little picture. As you say, one never knows..."

Okay, that answered *that*.

"I will—first thing tomorrow. I'll call...." The van was backing out, Carlysle standing back, waving goodbye. She watched a moment while the blue van rumbled off toward the exit, then turned and walked purposefully back the way she'd come, toward the elevators. He could see that she was carrying something in a small plastic bag, the kind supermarkets give you to carry your groceries home in. Whatever was in it, Hawk noted with amusement that she was making sure to keep a good firm grip on it, as well as her handbag.

While Mrs. Carlysle was waiting for the elevator to arrive,

Hawk did another visual check of the parking garage. Still no sign of Campbell. So either the two women had managed to lose him, or the man was pro enough to stay out of sight. Hawk was betting on the latter.

The ding of the elevator bell finally came while he was in the middle of stashing the GPS and other toys into his briefcase. He had to slam it shut, quickly spin the lock and drop it into the back seat, then almost dive out of the car and sprint for the closing elevator doors. When he got close enough to see the "L" on the indicator panel light up and stay lit, he changed direction and made for the stairs instead.

By taking them two at a time, he managed to get to the lobby just in time to catch a glimpse of Mrs. Carlysle crossing from the elevators, heading toward the row of shops near the main entrance. She had her back to him, still walking with that purposeful stride, still keeping a death grip on her parcel and purse.

Hawk watched her for a moment longer than he probably should have, just liking the way she looked from that angle. She had a sexy walk, he decided, mainly because she so obviously had no intention whatsoever of being sexy. Unbidden, the thought came: *A nice lady...*

After a moment, he hitched his shoulders, stuck his hands into his overcoat pockets, focused his gaze somewhere off her starboard bow and followed.

He had a bad moment when she paused to window-shop at the ladies' boutique, and he had to take evasive action by popping into the nearest handy open doorway. It happened to be the florist's shop, which he later decided must have been Providence, or perhaps just pure dumb luck.

He could feel his hunter's senses coming alive as he browsed among the silk-flower arrangements in the front window, all the while keeping a close eye on Mrs. Carlysle as she made her slow, oblivious way down the row of glitzy little hotel shops. This was the part of the game he liked best, the stalking game, the cat-and-mouse maneuvering...no toys required, just skill, finesse, a cool head, steady nerves and quick wits. He was good at it, maybe because to him it *was* a game. A dangerous game, to be sure, and sometimes the stakes were life and death. But then, Hawk didn't place a whole lot of value on the one, and wasn't afraid of the other, so he didn't worry overly much about the odds.

When he saw his quarry go into the gift shop, he decided it was probably now or never. He opened the refrigerated display case in the florist's shop and plucked out the first thing at hand, an arrangement of spring flowers in a vase, some tulips and daffodils, a few pink roses and some lilacs. He could have done without the lilacs—too many memories associated with lilacs— but there wasn't time to be fussy. He paid for the bouquet with cash.

After a quick detour to check on the Carlysle woman—she was browsing the paperback-book racks now, and if she was anything like most of the women he knew, that meant she was going to be there a while—he marched up to the front desk, presented his flower arrangement and growled in a weary it's-past-my-dinnertime-and-I-wanna-go-home tone of voice, "Flower delivery for Jane Carlysle?"

The snappily dressed and frighteningly perky young woman behind the counter tapped computer keys, jotted a note to herself, then gave him a radiant smile and chirped, "Thank you, sir, we'll have the flowers sent right up."

Damn. Hawk muttered, "Right...thanks," and turned away. What else could he do? Hotel security these days was a pain in the butt.

He dawdled toward the main entrance, thinking hard and pretending to browse through the rack of brochures near the concierge's station while he kept an eye on the front desk and his expensive and futile bouquet.

It must have been a slow night, because it was only a few minutes before he saw a bellman approach the desk. The perky clerk handed him the handwritten note, after which the bellman picked up the flowers and headed for the elevators at a brisk clip. Hawk made a show of looking at his wristwatch as if he'd suddenly changed his mind about an appointment, and followed.

The bellman was lucky; an elevator opened right up for him. He stepped on and the doors whooshed shut just as Hawk, timing it perfectly, arrived to punch the Up button. While he waited for the next elevator, Hawk watched the floor indicators above the one the bellman had taken light up in slow and steady sequence...two, three, four, five, six...seven. Seven it was, then, unless—but no, the numbers were lighting up in reverse now. A few moments later, there was a ding, and those same doors opened invitingly for him.

Hawk rode to the seventh floor in a tense, anticipatory calm, cocooned in a cottony silence. Everything seemed to be moving much too slowly, though he knew mere seconds had ticked by before the elevator doors whisked open at last on an elegantly furnished foyer, lit by wall sconces and decorated with fresh flowers.

He spotted his flowers sitting on the floor in front of a door about halfway down the long, softly lit corridor to his right. There was no sign of the bellman, or anyone else.

Hawk glanced at his watch. Incredible as it seemed, no more than ten minutes had passed since he'd left Mrs. Carlysle perusing the racks of romance novels in the hotel gift shop. How many more minutes did he have? He didn't need many—with the small device he carried in his pocket, he'd have the security lock open in a matter of seconds. Seconds more to nip inside, grab the painting and get back out again, then pray she didn't catch him hightailing it down the hall toward the stairs. Piece of cake.

Please, God, he thought, just let her give me two more minutes.

Under the circumstances, he didn't think it unreasonable to assume that in this case, at least, God might be on his side.

At first it seemed his assumption might be correct; his nifty little electronic decoder worked exactly the way it was supposed to, unlocking the door without a hitch. Soundlessly, he eased it open, slipped inside and pulled it shut after him.

He barely had time to register the fact that the room was in total darkness, and that it was odd, because in his experience, women almost always left a light on when they exited a hotel room they expected to return to alone. That insight only took a split second. But by then he already knew the reason for it.

He wasn't the only person in the room.

His sixth sense told him first, before the faint stirrings in the air currents, before the furtive but unmistakable rustlings of a body diving into cover. Grateful now for the total darkness, Hawk felt for the opening that would be the bathroom doorway, found it on his right, as he'd guessed, slipped into it and crouched low, listening with held breath for the whisper of other respirations. Silently cursing his own thundering pulse as he tried to tune his radar to another heartbeat.

The sound he heard instead was deafening by contrast: the swish and *click* of a plastic key card going into, then out of the lock.

He hardly had time to swing the bathroom door to and flatten himself behind it before the outer door opened. He heard a soft gasp, then a thud and a rustle.

What now? No choice—he had to risk a look through the crack he'd left in the bathroom door. What he saw nearly stopped his heart; he had to bite down on his lip to keep from groaning. There was Mrs. Carlysle, dead center in the damn doorway, bathed in light from the corridor, a perfect target. And in her two outstretched hands, what was astoundingly and unmistakably a handgun.

Two thoughts flashed into Hawk's mind, following each other with the speed and clarity of electronic pulses. The first, with a surge of gladness he didn't wonder about until much later, was, *Thank God! She has to be an innocent—no professional would be so stupid.*

The second thought was, if the other person in that hotel room was the same one who'd put a bullet between Loizeau's eyes, Jane Carlysle was a dead woman.

Chapter 4

Jane told herself it was because she'd been distracted by the flowers. She'd been so busy asking herself, "Who on earth would send me flowers? And *why?*"

But even so, the instant the door opened, she knew that something was not as it should be. Something was different. Something was missing.

For a moment—just a moment—she even thought she must be in the wrong room. At least that would have explained the flowers.

But she couldn't possibly be in the wrong room. This was *her* room, number 722, the very same one she'd left not half an hour ago to go down to the garage with Connie.

And...well, of course! *Now* she knew exactly what was missing. It was the Washington Monument. She'd been looking at it before, and it was the last thing she'd seen as she'd pulled the door closed behind her. But now the curtains were drawn, the room in darkness. And she'd left the desk light on...

All that realizing took place in the space of time it took her to utter one small exclamation of surprise and alarm. What she did next required even less time and no thought at all, and she couldn't for the life of her account for the impulse.

She let go of her purse, reached into the plastic bag that held her Roy Rogers six-shooter and pulled it out. It slid smoothly from its holster, nestled nicely in the palm of her hand. And the next thing she knew, she was holding it the way she'd seen policemen do in the movies, with both hands and at arm's length, and was aiming the toy pistol at the dark wall of draperies right where the Washington Monument was supposed to be.

And what then? Up until that moment, her mind had been operating on autopilot, or like a computer purring smoothly through its set-up program. Now it waited with a blank screen, cursor patiently blinking, for further instructions. And she had none whatsoever to give it! She thought...*nothing*. No review of the course of action chosen, no consideration of better alternatives, no what-ifs or should-haves. Stranger still, she *felt* nothing, not even fear.

Perhaps there just wasn't time. Because that curious blankness could have lasted no more than the span of a heartbeat or two, and just as she was beginning to get a glimmer of an idea that maybe, just maybe, it was a very stupid thing she'd done, the blankness exploded into violence and total confusion.

Something struck her—from the side, she believed, although for some reason she fell forward, suddenly and hard, so that the wind was knocked out of her. As she lay gasping and retching on the scratchy hotel carpet, she felt a tremendous weight come down between her shoulder blades, as if someone had knelt there, on one knee.

She knew a second or two of absolute terror as hands touched her...fingers searched along the side of her neck... There was a ghastly pressure. Panic-stricken, unable to struggle or even draw a single breath, she wanted to scream, to cry out. But no sound came from her mouth. And then darkness drifted down around her, almost gently, as if someone had thrown a blanket over her head...

And then, just as gently lifted it. She found that she could breathe again, and hear all sorts of confusing noises—thumps and scuffles, muffled shouts and running footsteps. She could see, although her range of vision consisted mostly of the underside of a hotel bed. And for some reason, she felt so weak that the notion of lifting her head, even to improve the view, was utterly beyond her.

She would have been content to stay where she was for a while longer, but it seemed only a moment before she felt the vibrations of footsteps scuffing and jarring the carpet nearby. The bed that loomed alongside her jiggled violently, and then urgent hands were gripping her hips, her waist, her shoulders. She felt those hands pulling her back, turning her over.

She heard a man's voice, raspy with alarm. "Ma'am—are you all right?"

She muttered automatically, "I think so."

But as the hands pulled and hoisted her to a sitting position, her head began to pound and the darkness to descend once more. Quite by accident, she found that if she hastened the darkness by closing her eyes and then wrapped herself inside it like a nice, safe cocoon, she could concentrate all her willpower on fighting the nausea. She felt quite clever to have made that discovery, and would have preferred to stay indefinitely in that safe, lovely darkness.

"Here, put your head down," the voice commanded, coming now from a great distance, somewhere on the other side of the darkness. "Don't get sick on me now."

The idea of passing out or throwing up on her shoes in the presence of a total stranger was all the inspiration Jane needed. Cautiously opening her eyes, she found that her view now consisted of the hotel-room carpet and her own feet. From that fact, her sluggish powers of deduction reasoned that she must be sitting on the edge of the bed with her head tucked between her knees. Besides being hideously uncomfortable, she found it a mortifying position to be in, especially since a stranger was sitting beside her and holding her firmly by the shoulders.

At some point, he'd also apparently closed the door, but turned on only the entry light. She didn't know whether to be sorry there wasn't more light, or glad.

"Are you all right?" the man asked for the second time, in a gravelly, dispassionate voice that Jane suddenly realized was familiar to her. "Want me to call someone?"

She gasped. "Oh, God, no!" The idea appalled her. "No, I'm okay. *Really.*" She tried a somewhat gingerly stretch.

Her Good Samaritan instantly let go of her shoulders but

stayed where he was, close beside her, his body touching hers, as if he thought she needed bolstering.

And she did—oh, she did! All the willpower she'd employed moments ago to keep her wits and her lunch, she called upon now to keep from throwing herself into those strong masculine arms. To keep herself from thinking about how lovely it would be to have those arms around her while she blubbered and snuffled into the man's nice broad chest.

Instead, she let her eyes drift shut again, drew a long breath and rotated her head carefully. "Oh, my," she murmured. "What on earth happened?"

"I was hoping you could tell me," the now *very* familiar voice said dryly.

Recognition came like a clap of thunder. Jane's eyes flew open upon a facial landscape so forbidding and at such close range, she pulled back from it with a soft, reflexive gasp. "Mr. Hawkins—it *is* you. What on earth are you doing here? I'm Jane—Jane Carlysle—from the auction, remember?"

He seemed to be regarding her with puzzling intensity. "Oh, I remember you," he said, and something about the way he said it made her heart stumble.

While she pondered that phenomenon, he got up and turned on the lamp on the dresser. On the way back, he stooped to pick something up from the floor. "I guess this must belong to you," he said, and held it out to her on the palm of one hand.

"Oh, God." Instead of taking the offering, she put a hand over her mouth to stifle a giggle. Then, to her dismay, she began to shake, but not with laughter.

Tom Hawkins looked at her for a moment, then shifted his grip on the toy pistol he held in his hand, hefted its weight, sighted along the barrel, pulled back the hammer. He squeezed the trigger and listened almost thoughtfully to the crisp metallic *click*.

"Quite a weapon," he drawled with more than a hint of sarcasm. "What were you gonna do, throw it?" It was only when he transferred a steely blue gaze back to her that she realized he was angry.

To Jane, seeing anger in the eyes of a stranger was so unexpected—it seemed so very *personal*, somehow—it was as if she'd been doused with cold water, or slapped smartly across

the face. Her head cleared. Her shaking subsided. She sat very
straight and still, immersed in a strange calm that was almost
like being suspended in weightlessness.

"I don't know what I meant to do with it," she said in a
hollow voice. "I don't think...the fact is, I *didn't* think. It was
stupid, of course. Right now I can think of at least six things I
should have done instead. I don't know what got into me."

Hawk found it impossible, suddenly, to be so close to her.
He went to sit on the other bed, shoulders hunched and hands
clasped between his knees, and studied the woman who had just
become his biggest problem. Her face was very pale, and there
were dark smudges under her eyes. She should have looked
older, he thought, with her makeup gone and her hair all mussed
and curling with the humidity in a way that could only be natural, but for some reason she didn't. She looked incredibly
young. And frightened. He hadn't expected that.

"You were damn lucky," he said harshly. "You know that,
don't you? If I hadn't come along when I did—"

"I know." She caught in a breath hungrily, as if she hadn't
had one in a while, then repeated, "I know. I haven't even
thanked you." She looked sideways at him. Amazing, he
thought, how expressive those sea-gray eyes of hers could be—
and a reminder to him to keep his own shielded. "I'm very
grateful you happened along. How did you—I mean, it's such
a coincidence, isn't it?"

There was a nuance in her words that didn't escape Hawk.
He laughed, hoping to head off her suspicions with a certain
gruff charm. "No kidding. You're the last person I expected to
see here. Hey, I was on my way to the elevators—going down
to get a bite to eat, as a matter of fact. And I hear this yelp and
a thump, and the next thing I know, this guy comes tearing out
of here with this package in his hands—"

"Package—oh my God, my painting!" She shot to her feet.
He could have told her it was a bad move. He put out a hand
to steady her when she swayed.

"Hey, it's okay—it's right there, on the bed." He put his
hands on her shoulders and eased her down, narrowing his eyes
when he looked at her, trying hard not to see how pale and
vulnerable she was. "I...more or less persuaded the bast—uh,
guy—to leave it behind." His lips tightened and stretched in a

smile while his jaw clenched with the unpleasant taste of lies. Necessary lies, he assured himself. "Unfortunately, I couldn't persuade him to stick around and explain why he was making off with it. Hey," he added, all innocence, "isn't that the one you just bought, today at the auction?"

She nodded, then winced.

"Headache?" he asked gently.

She nodded again, closing her eyes this time. "He...did something to my neck—right here." She cupped the place with her hand, rubbed briefly, then let the hand drop. Her eyes opened, fixed unnervingly on his face as she said in a soft, puzzled voice, "I think...I must have passed out. It's so strange...I really think he was going to kill me."

Hawk didn't say anything. He watched his hands as he placed one on either side of her neck, watched his fingers search for the spot he knew very well, trying to block out the way her skin felt, the way it had felt such a short time before, when he'd stopped for just a second or two, the life force pulsing beneath it. Soft and warm. Vibrant and strong. *Alive.*

He tried to block out awareness of those eyes of hers, so near he could see the tiny lines that gave away her age. Tried to deny the strange, tense silence that had fallen between them.

He couldn't look at her eyes, so he shifted his gaze to her mouth. And that was a mistake. He hadn't expected it to be so full and soft...or so near. His heartbeat grew strong and heavy; his mouth went dry and his vision blurred. He could feel the moist warmth of her breath on his lips, like a summer promise.

Shaken to the very soles of his feet, he pulled his hands away from her and growled, "Lady, if he'd wanted you dead, we wouldn't be having this conversation."

But even with the safer distance between them, for several moments longer they sat in that curious state of silent tension, in a kind of *connectedness* God knows he didn't want, but didn't know how to end. Her eyes seemed to be asking something of him. He felt as if he ought to apologize to her.

But exactly what would he be apologizing for? The fact that it was he who'd knocked her down and put her out of commission, when by doing so he'd probably saved her life? The fact that he wanted to kiss her—very nearly *had* kissed her—or the fact that kissing her was the one thing he wasn't about to let himself do?

And then suddenly, like a rubber band stretched too far, the suspense broke. Hawk shifted even farther away from her and they both spoke at once.

"Did you see who—"

"—Must be some painting."

He rebounded first, answering her question with a shake of his head. "He was wearing a ski mask."

For some reason, that information seemed to unnerve her as nothing else had. She muttered, "I don't believe this," then added with a touch of asperity, "What *is* it with that painting, anyway? First that man Campbell tries to buy it, then he wanted to bribe me, and now someone—" She broke off midsentence, her eyes darting to Hawk's with the unspoken question.

He answered it with a shrug of apology. "Sorry. No way to tell if it was the same guy. I told you—he had on a ski mask." At least *that* much was true.

"Must be some painting," he remarked once more, keeping his tone light, with only a touch of irony. Picking up the flat, paper-wrapped package he'd placed so carefully on the bed next to him, he held it up tentatively in front of Jane, who was chewing her lip and frowning thoughtfully at nothing. "Okay if I take a look at it?"

"What? Oh, okay, sure..." She obliged him by holding it while he tore the tape that crisscrossed the back and peeled aside the layers of brown packing paper. A moment later, he had it in his hands. *The prize. Game, set...match.*

"It's nice," he said, surprised to discover that he meant it. Funny, he wouldn't have expected that little weasel Jarek Singh to have such good taste in art. Not that it mattered; it could be Elvis on black velvet, for all he cared. What he wanted was hidden somewhere in, on or behind this damn painting, and all he had to do now was get it out of the woman's clutches long enough to find it.

An idea came to him, based on something he'd overheard earlier, in the parking garage. Keeping his voice carefully neutral, he said, "I take it it's not supposed to be valuable?"

"No." She rose, gingerly at first, then with more confidence,

and moved over beside him so she could look at the painting
with him.

He found himself bracing automatically for her nearness. Apparently not at all affected by his, she was silent for a while,
gazing down at the painting as if she'd never seen it before.
Then she caught a quick breath and said in a puzzled tone, "I
was told it isn't. I just bought it because I like it. The style
reminds me of Renoir—I've always liked Renoir." She gave a
short laugh. "Of course, this *isn't*. I'm certain of that. But it's
more than that. It just..." Her voice trailed off, but she went on
staring at the dancers in the painting. There was something about
the tilt of her head that made her seem...wistful.

"Maybe," Hawk said, releasing the painting into her keeping
with a casual shrug, "somebody knows something you don't."

Her eyes flew to his, not guiltily, but with a little lift of surprise and gladness, in the way of one human being discovering
another of like mind. "That's just what I thought! You don't
think it's silly, do you? Things like that do happen." Again she
gave that ripple of laughter he was beginning to recognize as a
signature of hers. "Not to *me,* of course. But suppose..."

"If you'd asked me this morning, I'd have said not a
chance," said Hawk dryly. "But after what just happened, I'd
have to wonder. *Somebody* obviously wants that painting pretty
badly." He paused a beat before adding, "Maybe you should
have it appraised."

She nodded, her face thoughtful. "Oh, I plan to. I'd already
planned to, after that man Campbell offered me so much money
for it. And after this..."

"I might be able to help you there." He said it with just
enough diffidence, not too eager. "I have a friend at the Smithsonian—he could probably recommend somebody. I'll give him
a call, if you want. You could take the painting in tomorrow
morning."

That ought to give Devore plenty of time to get somebody in
place, he thought.

She laughed and said faintly, "My goodness, the Smithsonian."

But Hawk knew he was losing her. He was an experienced
enough hunter to know when his quarry had sensed the trap.

Her smile was strained, now, her body tense, and her eyes slid sideways, reluctant to meet his.

Or maybe, he told himself, it was just that she was feeling better now, more her usual self, and her natural self-preservation instinct was kicking in. He was well aware that an animal suffering from trauma will tolerate invasions of its comfort zone that a hale and healthy one never would. Human beings were no different.

Or, it could be that Jane Carlysle was simply experiencing the normal edginess of a woman—a *nice* woman—becoming aware that she was alone in a hotel room with a strange man. Small wonder if she was feeling leery, after that near slip of his. He'd have to be a lot more careful about that in the future. And he would be. It had just snuck up on him, that's all. It had been a long time since he'd felt that kind of attraction to a woman. A long, long time.

But, either way, his moment had come and gone. Time to drop back and punt, he thought. Let her get her confidence back, and wait for another chance.

"Just an idea," he said with a shrug.

"I appreciate the offer." She leaned forward to prop the painting against the pillows at the head of the bed, and shot him a quick smile over her shoulder before she straightened—not seductively, more like a peace offering, he thought, but felt the sudden lurch in his belly anyway, like a plane hitting an air pocket. "I really do—it's very kind of you. But I already have the name of an appraiser—I believe he has a gallery in Georgetown. I'm going in to Washington first thing in the morning anyway. I'll just take the painting with me then."

"Oh—okay, well, that's good." Nothing more to be done now, he told himself. Time to go. And yet he felt a curious reluctance. He told himself it was the painting he hated to leave behind. "That's good...sounds like you've got it covered." He edged toward the door. "I guess if you're sure you're okay..."

"I am—really." She followed him, moving in that fidgety way people do when they don't know quite what to do with their hands. "And thank you. For saving my—" She broke off, gave that little embarrassed laugh of hers and amended it to, "My painting. I don't know what I'd have done if you hadn't..."

"My pleasure," Hawk said, and reminded himself to smile. "Glad I happened to be in the right place at the right time." He stopped suddenly, as if the thought had just come to him, and made one last try. "Listen, maybe you should get somebody to go with you when you take that painting in tomorrow. You know, if somebody's crazy enough to try this..."

"Oh, no, that's okay, I'll be fine." She said it hurriedly, automatically, the usual polite demurral. Then, as she thought about it, he saw her smile slip a little. "Anyway," she added staunchly, "I'm prepared now. Forewarned is forearmed, right?"

His thought exactly. This time he didn't give her the smile she wanted. Instead, frowning, he said, "Are you sure? I have a couple of appointments, but I can probably—"

"Oh, no—no, really." It was firm, final. He heard it in her voice, saw it in the set of her mouth.

"Well, okay then. Be careful." His hand was on the doorknob. He turned it and pulled. "Lock your door."

Instead of a reply, he heard a soft, stifled sound, and turning, found that she'd crisscrossed her body with her arms and covered her mouth with one hand. Above it, the eyes that clung to his were suddenly troubled, frightened, confused. He'd never seen such tattletale eyes.

"Oh, I will." Her words came muffled through her fingers. "And I *did*. That's just it. I know I locked my door when I went out. How on earth did he get in here?" She shivered.

Hawk tapped the small sign that was mounted on the door near the security bar. "Ma'am, I could tell you about six different ways. That's why they tell you to put the bar on when you're in here, and not to keep valuables in your room."

"But what I don't understand," she persisted, her voice low and still shaken, "is how he knew this was *my* room. It's not even registered in my name, and anyway, the hotel wouldn't give out that information. How did he know?" It was hitting her now, he could see that—the sense of violation that every victim of violence experiences. It would probably take some time before she felt safe again.

The door was open now. Hawk held it while they both stood in silence, looking down at the arrangement of spring flowers on the floor.

"Looks like somebody's sent you a present," he said in a neutral voice.

She bent slowly and picked up the flowers. "It's a mistake— it has to be," she said in a frightened voice. "I don't know anybody who'd send me flowers. The only ones who even know I'm here are my kids, and I can't think why—" She broke off as he reached over and turned the little white card on its plastic stake so she could see "Jane Carlysle" plainly written there. Just the name, and nothing else. She whispered, "I don't understand."

"Don't you?" Hawk's mouth twisted as he touched a sprig of lilac with one finger. "This...is probably how he knew. It's one of the tricks—call and order something to be delivered to a particular person, then watch and see which room it goes to." He let the hand drop to his side.

She whispered, "My God."

He felt grimy, uncomfortable in his own skin. Ashamed. Her stricken eyes clung to his, framed in daffodils and tulips. The smell of lilacs hung in the air between them, making his nose burn and his eyes ache. He hadn't been prepared for this. Desperately, he hardened himself against the memories, the guilt, and her.

He said thickly, "Well, now you know," and turned.

He'd taken only a few steps when she called to him. "Mr. Hawkins..."

She'd never know what it cost him to pause and look back, when he knew she'd be standing where he'd left her, with her arms full of those damn flowers.

"Mr. Hawkins," she asked, her voice steady, her face pale but resolute, "are you with the police?"

For some reason, the question didn't surprise him. Nor did the fact that she'd said police, not cops. *A nice woman...* He wondered later if that was why he didn't simply lie to her.

Instead, he muttered, "Not in this jurisdiction," and walked away, this time without looking back.

After Tom Hawkins had gone, Jane closed and locked her door and barricaded it with the security bar. Then, for a time, she just stood with the flowers in her arms, struggling to think, to make decisions, to regain some measure of control. Control of herself, her life and her circumstances.

Recent events had shaken her more than she wanted to admit to herself, and certainly more than she'd ever admit to a stranger, especially one as attractive as that enigmatic Mr. Hawkins. After all, she was a full-grown woman—a middle-aged woman, if she was completely honest with herself—and ought to be accustomed by now to dealing with life's unpleasant little surprises.

Okay, so she'd never been the victim of a violent crime before. These things happened all over the world, to millions of people, every single day.

Grow up, Jane. Join the club. And pull yourself together. You're always complaining that nothing exciting ever happens to you.

A perfect example, she thought, of "Be careful what you wish for!"

So, okay, first of all, what to do with the flowers? It wasn't in her nature to blame them for the fact that they'd been used for evil intent. And they were so beautiful—some of her favorites, in fact. She'd always particularly loved lilacs.

Closing her eyes, she dipped her face into the center of the bouquet and inhaled that sweet, familiar scent; she felt the cool touch on her cheeks and eyelids, light as a kitten's kisses, and felt the tremors of emotions she couldn't name. Which was something that had been happening to her quite a lot today, for some reason.

But those longings that had come over her at the auction had been vague and restless, a strange, sweet ache for something she'd never known and probably never would know. This was much more specific, and if she didn't know what it was she was feeling, at least she knew *why*. Because standing there with her eyes closed and the smell of spring in the air, all she could see was the tall form of Tom Hawkins, walking away from her down that long hallway without looking back. Walking away...and out of her life forever.

Oh, but she couldn't give in to emotions of any kind right now. And she would not. She even had a formula—how did it go? Oh, yes, she remembered it well. Swallow hard a few times...concentrate on breathing deeply until the weakness passes... Then, *do* something. Find a job, a purpose.

So, as if it were the most important job in the world, she carried the flowers into the bathroom and gave them a drink of water, then dried the florist's vase carefully so it wouldn't leave a ring on the furniture and placed it on the dresser, arranging it nicely in front of the mirror. The fragrance of the lilacs seemed to fill the room.

I should eat something, she thought. From experience, she knew she'd feel better if she did. But, oh dear, how could she leave her room unguarded? What if *he* was out there somewhere, watching, waiting for her to do just that?

This time the wave of emotion was easier to identify. What it was, was pure panic. Suddenly she could feel it all over again—the sensation of falling, of utter helplessness, the weight on her back squeezing the breath out of her lungs. She felt warm fingers on her neck, the awful, terrifying pressure, the pounding, the gentle darkness...

Trembling, she sank onto the bed, groped for the phone and clumsily punched the Operator button. For a moment, hearing the unexpected words, "Front desk," her mind went blank. Then her own voice responded calmly, "Room service, please." The very normalcy of her request helped to quiet her panic, although it continued to roll and churn through her insides.

After the girl at the front desk had cheerfully connected her with room service, she ordered the only thing she could think of at that moment, even though she wasn't particularly fond of hamburgers, and absolutely *never* ate French fries.

Music, she thought desperately as she cradled the phone, reaching for the TV remote. That's what I need. Please, God, let there be something on PBS.

But PBS was showing a nature film, and the idea of watching Serengeti lions tear into a zebra wasn't at all appealing to her right then. Neither were the talk shows, police dramas, old movies, sitcoms and infomercials offered by the other channels. The best she could find was the cable channel directory, which was playing classical music as background—Vivaldi, she thought. Or maybe it was Mozart. She turned up the volume as far as she dared, then sat restlessly fiddling with the remote control as her eyes darted around the room in search of further distraction.

She thought about the paperback romance novel she'd bought to read that evening, the map of Washington she'd meant to study, the sight-seeing plans she'd intended to make. But she didn't feel like reading, or planning. She couldn't think. Her mind was a jumble of fragmented thoughts and impressions. She felt exhausted and wired at the same time.

What she wanted was simply to talk to someone.

She thought about calling the girls. She knew she should— they'd be expecting to hear from her, since she always checked in with them when she had to be away overnight. But of course she didn't dare tell them about *this*. It would only alarm and upset them. And besides, she was the mom, she was supposed to be the strong one, the steadfast, sensible one; her children were supposed to come to *her* for comfort and strength, not the other way around. And if she called them and tried to act as though nothing was wrong, they'd know. They'd hear it in her voice; she'd never been any good at hiding her feelings.

She supposed she should report the incident to hotel security or the police. Doing so would certainly give her an opportunity to talk, but she had an idea it would, in the long run, bring her more headaches than solace.

What she really needed, she thought, was a friend. Just a friend, with a sympathetic ear and a strong shoulder. Like Connie, who was more than likely halfway home to Cooper's Mill by now, or blissfully asleep in some roadside motel. She thought of David, who had never listened or given her much support or solace, even when they were married. She thought of a stranger named Hawkins who had sat beside her, almost but not quite touching, just in case she needed him.

For the first time since the terrifying days leading to and then following her decision to divorce David, loneliness seemed overwhelming. It came suddenly, like a bad cramp. Doubled over with the pain of it, arms across her belly, she rocked herself back and forth, entombed in the darkness of her own desolation. She kept saying to herself, Dammit, dammit, I thought I was done with this. I thought I was stronger. *I thought I'd taught myself not to need.*

And so she had, until tonight, when a stranger's touch had awakened her to her own reality, like a bright light turned on in a room where she'd grown accustomed to darkness. Once before such a thing had happened to her, and her life had been forever changed.

A knock on the door and a muffled, "Room service," jolted her badly. Trembling, she went to eye the hotel waiter's starched white coat through the peephole. She instructed him to leave the tray outside the door, and only after he'd gone and she'd verified that the hallway was completely deserted did she unlatch the safety bar and open the door long enough to snatch the tray and carry it inside.

She wolfed down the hamburger without tasting it, left the French fries untouched, then prepared for bed, taking meticulous care to floss and brush and cleanse as she always did; she'd always found routine reassuring. After that, she put on the peach-colored silk pajamas she only wore on those rare occasions when she slept away from home and crawled between the starched and tucked hotel sheets. With the pillows from both beds stacked high behind her shoulders and the light burning brightly over the nightstand, she channel-surfed until her eyes burned and her head ached. Then, at least, she could welcome the darkness with relief rather than dread. But she didn't find solace in it, nor sleep, either.

Sometime in the dead of night, it came to her and she threw back the covers and sat up, clutching the edge of the bed. Clammy. Trembling. And one thought in her mind: *wet wool.*

That was what was wrong. She'd smelled it. She'd felt it. His coat had been wet. And yet he'd told her he'd been on his way *out.* Hadn't he? Yes, she was sure he'd said so. On his way out to get something to eat, that was it. Tom Hawkins had lied to her. *Why?*

His story about "happening along" at just the right moment—had that been a lie, too? And if he hadn't just "happened" to be there, it followed that he must have been there for a purpose. Was the purpose something to do with *her,* or her attacker?

It has to be something to do with the painting, she thought. It has to be.

Slowly, she turned to look at it, propped against the head of the other bed, the graceful figures only faint pale shapes in the almost darkness. *He* was there at the auction, she thought, forcing her plodding thoughts along dim and scary paths. He'd seemed so nice, so helpful. And tonight, he'd just happened to be *here*, out of all the hotels in the city, in time to save her painting, if not actually her life. Such an amazing coincidence.

She got up, padded barefoot around the foot of her bed and made her way to the other one, where she shoved the discarded wrappings aside and sat facing the painting with one leg drawn up on the unrumpled spread.

She thought about the man Campbell—he'd wanted the painting badly. So did the man in her room tonight.

And what about Tom Hawkins? He'd been there at the auction, where Campbell was. And he'd been here tonight, where Campbell—or whoever—was. Was it Campbell he wanted, or the painting? Was he a cop, or wasn't he?

Not in this jurisdiction. What an odd answer that was, now that she thought about it. What kind of law enforcement officer would be tracking a man—or a painting—out of his jurisdiction? If the damn thing was stolen, why didn't he just say so? And most of all, why would he lie about so simple a thing as whether he'd been coming or going?

She knew there wasn't any use going back to bed, not then. She sat in the armchair, curled up and wrapped in the bedspread, gazing out the window at the floodlit Washington Monument until her eyes ached and the vision blurred.

Tomorrow, she vowed. Tomorrow I'm going to find out about that painting, once and for all.

She had a feeling she hadn't seen the last of Tom Hawkins, either. Whoever he was.

Chapter 5

"Emma? Sorry to call so late..."

"Tom? Oh, my goodness. Tom, is it really you?"

With the phone pressed painfully against his ear, Hawk listened to the compassionate, gentle voice he hadn't heard in so long and remembered so well. *Jen's voice.* "It's me, Emma. I hope I didn't wake you." The voice hadn't sounded at all sleepy, but then that was Emma.

"Oh, Tom, what a lovely surprise! No—no, as a matter of fact, I was waiting up for Frank. He's grading papers—spring break starts next week. He should be home any time. Oh, he'll just hate that he missed you. Where are you? Are you in town?"

"I'm in town, but—"

"Oh, how wonderful. Can you come for a visit? We'd both love to see you."

"I wish I could, but it's business, and I'm pretty tied up. I just called..." He paused to take a breath, both because the ache in his chest needed easing, and because the fact was, he didn't know why he'd called. "...to say hello."

"We've missed you, Tom." The voice had grown softer. The sadness in it leaked from the receiver and into his soul. "It's been so long. Seven years..."

"It was yesterday!" He regretted, but was unable to blunt, the harshness in his tone.

There was a pause, and then, "I wish you'd come home, Tom. I think...perhaps you need to."

"Emma..." His voice cracked. "I can't."

"Jennifer wouldn't have wanted this for you. You know she wouldn't. It's time, Tom." There was a pause and then a whispered, "Time to say goodbye." And he knew she was crying.

"Soon," he growled, his voice guttural with pain. "I'll come for a visit. I promise. Listen, say hello to Frank for me, will you?"

"Of course I will. Oh, Tom, I'm so glad you called. I just wish—"

"Good night, Emma."

"Tom? Be good to yourself..."

He gave her the chuckle she wanted and hung up. Groped for his cigarettes, lit one and pulled the smoke past the band of pain around his chest, held it until he felt the slightest easing, then exhaled on a long sigh. He sat quietly smoking, staring out at the city lights—Arlington, not Washington; his fifth-floor room was on the opposite side of the hotel, the best he'd been able to do at the last minute—and let memory carry him back to a long-ago summer afternoon...

Voices and laughter, whoops and splashes, the smell of charred meat drifting up to his bedroom window from the yard that backed up against his. A slender, dark-haired woman waving to him, calling to him: "Hi, we're your new neighbors— the Hostetlers. That's our daughter, Jennifer, there in the pool. Would you like to come over for a swim? Jenny would love some company..."

Even now the memory could make him smile, remembering the way his thirteen-year-old hormones had stirred at the sight of that dark head emerging from the water, sleek as an otter...the perfect, sunburned oval she'd turned to him, with a look of utter disdain...the way she'd pranced the length of the diving board, so proud of her budding body, to execute the most glorious cannonball he'd ever seen. Love at first sight, that's what it had been.

Time to say goodbye...

Hawk shook his head, a small, silent rejection, drew on his

cigarette one last time and stubbed it out. Emma was right, he knew that. Seven years was long enough. But try telling that to his heart. His heart seemed to have its own timetable, and about all he could do was wait for it to reach the same conclusion. He'd know the moment it happened, he was sure of that. He'd feel it.

And until then... He stood and stretched, then pulled off his shoes and lay down on top of the bedspread, flat on his back with his hands laced across his midsection. Until then, he had a job to do, and days to get through, one at a time. Tomorrow was a new day, and it was shaping up to be an interesting one, at that.

He'd pretty much accepted that his mission now had two objectives. The first—and still the most critical, of course—was to recover that painting and the vital piece of information Jarek Singh had hidden inside it. The second and probably the more difficult task was to protect Jane Carlysle.

Hawk programmed himself for sleep the way he'd learned to do as a boy of sixteen, and then perfected seven years ago, first clearing his mind, making it a blank screen on which he projected a pleasant, relaxing vision. Most often the vision he chose had something to do with the sea, a calm sea with sunlight streaming through clouds, sparkling on gently rocking swells...the cries of seagulls and the swish and murmur of waves washing on warm sands.

Tonight, though, for some reason, the image that came to fill the screen in his mind and refused to leave, no matter how hard he tried to supplant it, was...a face. A woman's face. A nice face with a kind smile and sea-gray eyes with telltale laugh lines at the corners, eyes that could light with sudden joy, the way the sea does when the sunlight hits it a certain way...or go dark and deep with sadness, anger or fear. Jane Carlysle's face.

He found it an oddly comforting vision.

Jane woke to find sunshine streaming through her uncurtained window, and beyond it a soft spring sky with only a few fat puffy clouds scurrying in pursuit of the cold front that had blown through in the night.

How different things always look in the morning, she thought, buoyed by thoughts of spring. But she was a naturally optimistic and resilient person; like bad dreams, the night's doubts and fears had vanished with the daylight, leaving her with only an edgy sense of anticipation and excitement.

The first thing she did, after the morning mists and cobwebs had cleared, was reach for the phone. A check-in call to the girls was long overdue. They were full of the anticipated questions and reproaches, the loudest of which were in response to being roused at seven-thirty on a weekend morning.

Maybe she was only under the influence of the champagne sunshine, but Jane found that she had no trouble coming up with the necessary lies and reassurances that had been beyond her capabilities last night. Since lying had never been one of her talents, she was surprised and relieved that hers were so readily accepted. She thought it probably had a lot to do with the fact that Tracy was nursing a homework hangover and Lynn's head was swimming with the details of her latest scheme to postpone her final year of college.

"Eurail Youthpasses, Mom. Kevin says that's the only way to go. You can go *anywhere,* for three months. You have to go with a companion, so that's okay, and we can extend it, if—"

"Hey, wait, who said anything about extending?"

"How was the auction, Mom?" That was Tracy, with a yawn that sounded as if it could have sucked in the whole phone. It was followed by a sleepy snicker. "Meet lots of cute guys?"

Knowing that it was safe because they'd never believe her anyway, Jane told the truth. "A couple, actually." She paused for a chorus of "Ha-ha's" and "Yeah, rights," then added her diversion. "I bought some things."

More yawns, politely smothered this time. Then a duet: "Hmm...really?" "What'd you buy?"

"Just some small stuff." They'd never understand about the Roy Rogers six-shooter. She wasn't sure she did, herself. "A painting—kind of nice, I think you'll like it. I'm going to have it appraised this morning. A gallery in Georgetown—somebody Connie knows."

"Do you think it might be valuable?" That was Lynn, the analytical one. Jane could almost see her, suddenly sitting up straighter, back against piled pillows, her interest hooked by the tantalizing thought of money. She was David's daughter, alas, but a darling in so many ways that it was easy enough to over-look one small avaricious streak.

"Oh, no, not really," she said quickly, anxious to head *that* idea off at the pass. "I didn't pay much for it. I'd just kind of like to know what it's worth."

"Good idea. Kev says you should have everything in your household appraised anyway—for the insurance. He's got all his mom and dad's stuff on their computer. You should do that, Mom. Kev could probably do it for you. There's this neat pro-gram—"

"So, when are you coming home?" Tracy, of course, trying to sound casual, though Jane could almost see her daughter's forehead creasing with anxiety, worrying about dwindling re-frigerator stores. With a few more months yet to fledge, she seemed content for now to cling to the safety of the nest, feath-ers fluffed, plaintively chirping. Which was okay with Jane; she wasn't in any great hurry to see her last baby fly away. One at a time was about all she could handle.

She made soothing, mother-bird noises into the phone. "Soon. Tomorrow, probably. I'll call you when I know ex-actly—by the way, I'll need one of you to pick me up at Ra-leigh-Durham. I just want to see a few of the sights in Wash-ington while I'm here. I told you I might."

"That's great, Mom, I think you should," Lynn said. "Wash-ington's really big with the baby boomers right now. Oh—and Kev says you *have* to be sure and see The Wall."

"The wall?"

"The Vietnam Memorial? They have all the names—"

"Oh, yes, of course. I plan to. And the Lincoln Memorial and the Washington Monument and all that good stuff. Listen, Tracy?"

"I think...she's in the bathroom."

"Oh, okay, well, remind her to keep the bird feeders filled, will you? And if you need anything, you can give Connie a call. She should be home soon—might even be there now. She left last night. Don't forget to bring in the Sunday paper tomorrow—you'll need it for the TV guide. And save the coupon—"

"Mom, we've got it covered, okay? Don't worry about us. Have a good time in Washington. But be careful, right? I've read about their crime rate."

"I'll look both ways before crossing the street, and I promise not to talk to strangers," Jane said, laughing. Inwardly cringing. "Listen, I'm getting a late start, as it is. You guys be good and I'll see you soon, okay? Call you tomorrow. Love you both. Bye."

She hung up the phone without waiting for the response, then sat for a minute or two waiting for lightning to strike her dead on the spot for telling her children such lies.

When, she wondered, did they become the parents and I the child?

In his room two floors below Jane Carlysle's and on the opposite side of the hotel, Hawk emerged from the bathroom freshly showered and dressed for comfort in khakis and a favorite old cable-knit pullover sweater. As he stowed away his wallet and weapon in their customary places, his eyes sought out the coordinates on the GPS monitor purring away in the middle of the unrumpled bed. Thank God. She hadn't moved.

He lit a cigarette and drew deeply on it, waiting for the nicotine to ease the knots of tension in his belly. He couldn't afford any errors in judgment; too many lives depended on it, not the least of which was Jane Carlysle's.

It didn't help matters that he'd slept so badly. It was almost funny, when he thought about it, the way her face had come to him—which had surprised the hell out of him, but he'd allowed it to stay because it had seemed sort of...comforting, at first. He'd liked having it there in his mind, the laughter in her eyes, that nice smile. Not a bad vision to carry him into sleep.

Except that somehow the vision had gotten away from him, and instead of her face he'd suddenly begun seeing other parts of her, particularly the part he'd enjoyed watching so much while she was walking away from him down in the lobby, the part that was responsible for the jolt he'd gotten just below his ribs when she'd leaned over to prop the painting on the pillows. The part he'd most like to...

Dammit, he couldn't keep having these lustful thoughts about the woman!

Not that he'd mind, ordinarily, or that he hadn't enjoyed his fair share of lustful thoughts during the last seven years—on the contrary, he figured he probably fell in and out of lust a couple of times a year on average. He considered lust healthy and a pretty good tension reliever. But this was different. He couldn't remember ever being in lust before with somebody he actually liked.

So you like this woman?

The question came like a whisper of a playful breeze, skirling around the corner from the very back of his mind, stirring memories still so painful he almost cried out in agony, and instead lashed back in anger. *Dammit, why shouldn't I like her? It'd be pretty near impossible not to like her!*

The whisper became a chuckle, amused and satisfied. *You do, you like her....*

Hawk snatched the phone, muttering curses under his breath as he punched in the number for Interpol's Washington bureau. He reported to Devore on the previous evening's activities and got the answer he'd expected to his request for information on Mrs. Jane Carlysle, of Cooper's Mill, North Carolina: Clean as a cookie sheet. Nothing. *Nada.* At least as far as the FBI was concerned, the woman was exactly who she claimed to be.

Which didn't mean much, of course. A well-planted agent's cover wouldn't be so easy to crack.

He turned off the GPS and restored it to his briefcase, then plucked a scuffed and well-worn bomber jacket from the foot of the bed and shrugged it on. Sunglasses and a Baltimore Orioles baseball cap completed his "disguise." High-tech toys would be useless to him today; he'd play this cat-and-mouse game the old-fashioned way.

A glance at his watch confirmed what he already knew. Time to go. Time to get himself into position so he'd be certain to pick up Carlysle the minute she left the hotel. He'd use the GPS as backup in case he lost her, but he knew he wasn't going to do that. He couldn't afford to. As long as she had that painting, one woman's life wasn't worth squat to the cold-blooded killer who'd put a bullet in Loizeau's forehead.

Jane loved subways. More than skyscrapers, more than tangled freeways, to a girl raised on a Southern California farm they'd always seemed the very essence of City, the heart and arteries pulsing away beneath the surface streets and sidewalks, carrying the endless flow of humanity that was the life's blood of any metropolis. Nowadays, even medium-size cities had their skylines, and the smallest towns their soaring freeway interchanges. But only the grandest of cities—San Francisco, New York, Boston, Paris, London, Washington—had subways.

The Washington Metro took her breath away. First the descent, down, down, down into the earth...the gleaming caverns echoing with hurrying footsteps, and then...the slightest stirring of wind, the faintest vibration, felt with the most primitive of senses, the way animals sense a distant storm. And all at once, with a rush and a rumble, it was *there.* Joining the crush of people, like catching a wave...heart pounding, wait for the right moment...*now.* The moment of panic: *Oh, God, I hope this is the right train!* The euphoria as she settled into her seat, confident in the knowledge that, yes, it was the right train, headed in the right direction, and all she had to do now was watch and listen for the right stop. *Whew!*

If she hadn't been so caught up in it all, she might have noticed him sooner. But it wasn't until the train had left the station and was rocketing beneath the Potomac River—next stop, Foggy Bottom, a name she'd always adored—that she caught a glimpse, through several layers of windows and flickering reflections, of a dark-browed, scimitar-nosed profile.

Her heart, just settling down to normal rhythms, jolted once more into high gear. It was *that man,* the one from the auction—Aaron Campbell! Yes, she was sure of it—she'd recognize that dark hair and Arab sheikh's profile anywhere.

What could he be doing on this train, if not following *her?* Oh, God, what should she do?

And now—even worse—he seemed to have disappeared. *Where was he?*

The train was slowing, the loudspeaker announcing the Foggy Bottom stop. She was supposed to get off here, according to her maps and Metro schedules. But *now* what should she do? Get off and go for help?

Ridiculous notion—what would she say? "Excuse me, Officer, but I think a man is following me... Why? Because he wants my painting... What painting? Oh, well, I have it right here...

No, it's not valuable. I bought it yesterday at an auction for seventy-eight dollars and fifty cents.''

As Tracy would say, *Yeah, right.*

The train was stopping, the doors whooshing open. She had to make a decision...*now.*

The instant the doors cracked open, Hawk squeezed through, stepped out onto the platform and headed for the escalators without looking back.

The one big advantage he had in this game was that he knew what Carlysle's next move was going to be. A gallery in Georgetown, that was what she'd told him—assuming, of course, that she hadn't thrown him a red herring. Which he was fairly confident she hadn't, since he'd spotted and made note of the address her friend had jotted down for her and left on the dresser in her hotel room.

Plus, he was rapidly coming to the conclusion that Jane Carlysle didn't have a devious bone in her body.

Unless, of course, she was the most devious person he'd ever met.

In either case, his strategy was the same one he'd been following since leaving his room at the hotel. It was easy, since he knew his way around Washington so well, to get ahead of his quarry, find himself a hidden vantage point and wait and watch to see which way she went. There—he had her spotted now, in the crowd making for the GW University exit. So she'd told the truth this time, at least; Georgetown it was.

He was feeling pleased with himself as he stepped onto the escalator, figuring Mrs. Carlysle ought to be just about reaching the top. And then he got a nasty surprise.

Damned if that wasn't her, coming back down the other side!

He was able to turn away before she spotted him, but not before he'd gotten a pretty good look at her face. And what he saw there didn't make him happy. What he saw was fear. That was unmistakable. But he also saw *purpose.* No doubt about it, the woman was taking deliberate evasive action.

Dammit, how in the hell had she spotted him?

Roused and fuming and marooned on the Up escalator, Hawk could only watch helplessly while his quarry, his supposedly guileless innocent, dodged through the crowd like a broken field runner as she sprinted toward the exit at the far end of the station.

It was while he was silently and bitterly cursing the duplicity of women and his own gullibility that he gradually became aware of a commotion somewhere above him on the moving escalator. It merely distracted him at first; someone—a man— seemed to be pushing and shoving through the standees, trying with some haste to make his way to the top and generating considerable unhappiness among the passengers in his wake. It was only after the man had done a one-handed vault onto the Down side and was hurtling toward him at great risk to life and limb that Hawk got a really good look at the "rude commuter." What he saw altered his frame of mind completely.

Campbell! So that was it. That was who Jane must have spotted. No wonder she'd taken off like a vixen with a pack of hounds on her tail.

Those weren't good moments for Hawk. Another hunter was after his quarry, and he was stuck on the damn escalator!

But it was more than that, and something as yet unacknowledged deep within him knew it. The terrifying truth was, he was beginning to care what happened to Mrs. Jane Carlysle of Cooper's Mill, North Carolina. He hadn't counted on that.

At least he hadn't lost her. Not this time. Thank God, he thought grimly as he tightened his grip on the handle of his briefcase, for high-tech toys.

Jane told herself that she was acting like a crazy person. She was jumping at shadows, behaving like a complete ninny. She'd never been paranoid before in her life. What she needed to do was stop a minute, get her bearings, get a grip on herself. Think.

Bursting out of the Metro station like a flushed pheasant, she found herself in the midst of a throng of camera-bearing tourists, all of whom seemed to be wearing Bermuda shorts, never mind that the temperature wasn't likely to hit sixty. It seemed enough that it was Saturday, the sun was shining and spring was officially four days old. In spite of her not having a camera with her, Jane seemed to fit right in with her sunglasses and oversize tote bag, so she allowed herself to be swept along with the crowd toward the Lincoln Memorial.

No one paid the slightest bit of attention to the fact that she kept turning to look behind her, to the right, to the left, and behind again. After all, they were all doing much the same thing, jostling one another and pointing out landmarks along the way.

By the time she'd reached Constitution Avenue and there was no sign whatsoever of either Aaron Campbell or Tom Hawkins, she began to relax and even enjoy the sights a little herself. Walking through the park, with the pristine white columns of the Lincoln Memorial visible through the charcoal-gray skeletons of trees, she no longer felt fearful at all—merely foolish.

This is all so silly, she scolded herself as she settled onto a sunny bench with a sigh. I surprised a burglar last night—big deal.

And Mr. Hawkins was some sort of law officer on some sort of assignment that had nothing to do with her. No one was following her, nobody was trying to take her painting away from her. That was just…silly.

She was just plain Jane Carlysle who worked at a bank in Cooper's Mill, North Carolina, divorced mom facing empty-nest syndrome, gardener, bird-watcher, closet romantic, daydreamer…to whom nothing exciting ever happened.

But all the same, she checked to make sure the paper-wrapped parcel was secure in her tote bag, and looped the handles carefully over her arm as she rose.

Well, now. Since I'm here, she thought, why shouldn't I see the Lincoln Memorial, at least? And The Wall, of course.

She could always go to Georgetown later this afternoon.

Besides, the Lincoln Memorial would be crowded with tourists; she'd be safe there.

What in the hell is she doing? Hawk wondered.

The woman had been sitting on the Lincoln Memorial steps for a good twenty minutes. Just sitting there. He couldn't figure it out. He'd even taken the risk of getting close enough to see her, to make sure she was actually there, thinking she might have found the tracking device in her purse and left it behind to throw him off her trail.

But no, there she sat, soaking up sunshine, enjoying the view, apparently waiting...for what? Or who? He couldn't decide whether she was waiting for a contact, carrying out some sinister agenda, or whether, with the instinctive cunning of a hunted animal, she was merely seeking high ground in order to sniff the wind, to see who might be on her trail.

Campbell had spooked her badly; she had to be wondering whether he was still out there somewhere. Hawk was wondering about that, too. He hadn't spotted him yet, but that didn't mean much. Unless the guy was a complete idiot, he wouldn't make the same mistake again.

One way or another, intentionally or not, Jane Carlysle was proving to be a lot better player at this game than he'd expected.

And why couldn't he make up his mind about her? After giving himself a severe talking-to this morning, he was pretty sure he had the lust thing under control, but still the picture in his mind labeled Jane Carlysle remained cloudy and out of focus. His usually keen instincts didn't seem to be functioning where she was concerned. He couldn't for the life of him figure out who she was and where she fit in all this. And that worried him. In fact, it was driving him crazy.

For a long time Hawk sat still, hands resting on the GPS monitor lying open in his lap, with The Wall there at his back and the sun soaking into the leather of the old brown bomber jacket, like a warm hand resting on his shoulder.

Finally, like someone coming out of a doze, he shook himself, checked the monitor one more time to reassure himself that Mrs. Carlysle was still keeping her enigmatic vigil, then shut it down, and closed and locked the briefcase.

A young couple was moving down the paved walk in front of The Wall, close together, hands linked. Hawk watched them, for a moment envying their closeness. He wondered if it made it any easier, having someone there. Or if it was a thing better done with only one's own ghosts for company.

Seeing as how he had no choice in the matter, he squared his shoulders, walked over to the directory, peeled back the pages and ran his finger down the endless list of names. Rapidly, at first, but then his trailing finger slowed...and paused. He felt a tremor deep in his belly.

He drew a long breath, then did an about-face and walked

quickly down the slope, into the long black gash in the earth's green skin known as The Wall.

He moved along without pausing, part of him noticing the details of his surroundings, as was his ingrained habit, taking in the tokens left here and there along the base of the black granite wall—American flags, flowers, photographs, hastily written notes—and the subdued presence of park security. He noticed that the casual visitors tended to keep a certain distance, strolling by quietly, almost reverently, on the outside of the walkway, now and then pointing, like polite strangers in church. Mostly it was those on a more personal quest who moved in close. Who seemed to feel a need to reach out and *touch.*

He found the name he was looking for at The Wall's highest point, where the names were thickest, the numbers the most overwhelming. He was glad that it was only a little above head height and easy to reach. Slowly he lifted his hand and traced the letters: Walter T. Hawkins. Then the diamond that designated KIA—killed in action. He opened his fingers and placed his palm flat against the polished granite. He hadn't expected it to feel so warm, almost like a living thing instead of polished stone.

In that moment something swelled and burst inside him, as unpreventable as an unexpected sneeze. It was a few minutes before he was able to mumble the words he'd waited so many years to say.

"Hey, Dad. I guess I should have come before. I'm sorry it's taken me so long...."

Jane lost track of how long she sat on the cold marble steps of the Lincoln Memorial, watching the tourists come and go, seeing watchers in the shadows, a terrorist behind every tree. So she wasn't sure exactly when it was that she began to get angry. When she came to realize that the intruder in her hotel room might have stolen something from her that was of greater value than any painting, even a real Renoir. When she became determined that if it was the last thing she ever did, she was going to get that something back. No art thief or petty burglar was going to run *her* life!

What was it that nice young instructor in the self-defense

class she'd taken in those first nervous, vulnerable months after
the divorce—what was his name?—Shing Lee, that was it. What
had Shing always said?

Take control, take action!

Yes, that was it. To get over this awful fear and sense of
violation, she had to take back *control.* She had to take *action.*
It was all up to her.

The first thing she made up her mind to do was what she'd
planned to do in the first place—see the sights of Washington.
Later on, if she felt like it and it was convenient, she'd take the
painting to a gallery and have someone tell her what she already
knew: that it was an undistinguished Impressionist-style painting, not especially good, but it would look quite nice hanging
over her piano.

And if, during the course of the day, anyone tried to push her
down, step on her back and render her unconscious,
well...thanks to Shing Lee, she had a trick or two up her own
sleeve.

Just let them try, she thought as she rose somewhat stiffly
and started down the steps. Riled and ready, she was almost
disappointed not to catch a glimpse of Aaron Campbell lurking
in the trees between the Lincoln and Vietnam Memorials.

But as she made her way slowly down the walkway past the
rows of makeshift tent stalls manned by disabled veterans in
their long hair and beards and tattered camouflage fatigues, selling memorabilia and souvenirs of a war they couldn't leave
behind, she found the incident in her hotel room, and all her
fears and unanswered questions slipping into the back of her
mind. As always when confronted with reminders of that war
and those times, she developed an irritating little itch of guilt.

At the height of the dying and the turbulence and dissension,
she'd had other things on her mind. In the early years of a
marriage that had been troubled even then—though she'd never
have admitted such a thing—she remembered feeling only a
mild sense of sorrow and regret when her mother had called
with the news that a boy Jane had gone to school with was
MIA—missing in action in Vietnam. In recent years, though,
she'd found herself thinking quite a bit about Jimmy Hill,
though she'd never known him well at all. He'd been two years
ahead of her, and in a different crowd altogether. But still...she

had known him. She could recall his face even now. Where would he be today if he'd survived the war? Might he be like one of these men, with their maimed bodies and nightmares, their grizzled faces and haunted eyes?

So it was partly to scratch that little itch of guilt that Jane decided to look up Jimmy Hill's name in the directory, partly to try to feel some sort of connectedness to a period of history that had inflicted such grievous injury on an entire generation, while leaving her virtually untouched. Beyond that, she had no idea what she hoped to accomplish by finding Jimmy's name on that wall of so many thousands of names. Touch it, maybe? Say a little prayer for his family? She didn't know. But it seemed important, somehow.

Her heart began to beat faster when she found the name in the book, followed by a cross that, according to the directory, meant MIA. But the awe didn't hit her until she was approaching The Wall itself...until she saw the first of the names. So many names. That was when she knew that she should not have come alone, and that she would leave something of herself behind.

What was it about the place? She vaguely remembered controversy when it first opened...probably the statues added since had assuaged any disappointment that might have lingered. But it wasn't the statues people came to see. It wasn't the statues that made strong men cry.

Like that one there, the tall, lean man in the brown leather jacket, standing with his palm pressed against the mirror-like surface of the monument, head bowed, shoulders hunched with pain.

Chapter 6

She halted as if the wall itself had suddenly shifted to block her path, while her heartbeat stumbled and then lurched on, like a drunk running downhill.

Tom Hawkins. Yes, it was—and she'd have known him at once in spite of the old, worn-looking bomber jacket, baseball cap and aviator sunglasses he was wearing, and the oddly out-of-place briefcase he was carrying, if it hadn't been for the grief that seemed to weigh him down like an invisible net.

For a few moments she stood motionless, in shock not so much at seeing him *here*—she was beginning to half expect him to turn up ''coincidentally'' wherever she happened to be—or even at the giddy *lift* she'd felt beneath her ribs at the moment of recognition. But seeing him like *this*. Hurt and suffering, and so dreadfully vulnerable. It seemed almost indecent that she should see him like this, like surprising a stranger in the shower.

And yet it was her nature to comfort and nurture, and the urge to go to him and offer what solace she could was all but overwhelming. Or...maybe after all it would be better if she just turned and walked away and left him his privacy and solitude.

How long she stood there in breathless indecision she didn't know, but in the end he looked up and saw her, and the choice wasn't hers to make.

"Well," he said in a cracked-sounding voice, "we meet again."

Jane mumbled something equally inane and was rewarded with his crooked smile, which seemed to her even more heart-breakingly poignant than usual in that context.

"Are you—" he gestured toward the scrap of paper on which she'd written down the coordinates for Jimmy's name "—looking for someone?"

"What? Oh, well, yes, sort of. Just a..." The guilt flooded her, filling her cheeks with warmth. She shook her head, erasing that self-conscious denigration, and said firmly, "A friend. He's officially MIA."

"His name'll be here," Tom said, his tone dry, the curve of his lips becoming even more ironic. "It'll just have a little cross after it."

"Yes, that's what... And then, I guess, if they're ever found, they just chip out the rest." Jane watched her finger trace the diamond after a name and was astonished that her hand could appear so steady when she felt so jangled inside.

With that same soft irony, Tom drawled, "I don't think they're gonna be doing much more of that, do you?"

Uncertain what he meant, Jane glanced at him, but was unable to see anything at all of his eyes, just her own reflection in the sunglasses. She looked away again, down at the paper in her hand, and muttered distractedly, "I think...it should be somewhere near here."

They weren't the words she'd meant to say. Where were those words, the words of motherly comfort and sympathy she'd meant to offer a wounded and grieving stranger? They seemed impossible to utter now. He didn't seem at all wounded, and she felt not the least bit maternal. What she felt most like was a girl—a very young girl, shy and awkward and out of her depth.

He took the paper from her, slipping it from between her nerveless fingers, asking permission with a quirk of his eye-brows. Silently she watched him as he moved along the walk-way, scanning the list of names. She could see him reflected in the polished granite, along with the other visitors, a small V of American flags and the Washington Monument.

"Here," he said, pointing to a spot about two feet from the base of the wall. "Is that the one?"

Jane nodded. Lowering herself to one knee, she slowly traced the letters with her fingertips. *James P. Hill.* And then the cross.

From behind her, his voice came, dry as the sands that blew day and night across the California deserts of her childhood. "Was he somebody close to you?"

She looked up, startled by the gruffness and by the unmistakable compassion in the voice, to find a face as unreadable as stone, the lenses of the sunglasses that gazed back at her as opaque as the face of the wall itself.

She shook her head, surprised to find that her throat was tight, and that for those few moments, at least, the denial she was about to utter was a lie. "No," she murmured. "Just somebody I went to school with. A long time ago."

"Yeah, but I'll bet you remember his face." Tom's smile twitched off center as he held out his hand to help her up.

He saw it come, then, that *lighting* deep in her eyes, that little flare of gladness and recognition.

"Yes—yes, I do. How did you know?"

He shrugged and felt her hand warm his as he steadied her to her feet. The sun struck reddish highlights into her dark hair and tipped her lashes with gold. For the first time he noticed the faded ghosts of freckles across the tops of her cheeks and on the bridge of her nose.

She took a deep breath as she brushed off her slacks and looked sort of sideways at him, and he knew it was coming. He braced himself, but she said it so softly, so gently, that the question didn't seem an assault at all. "And you...the name you were touching...he was someone close to you?"

He tried to take some of the pressure off his chest by releasing air in a short little laugh. It didn't help much, and neither did the deep breath that followed. "Yeah, you could say that," he said finally, focusing his gaze somewhere above her head, on the white puffy clouds racing across the blue spring sky. How had it got to be so beautiful, he wondered irrelevantly, after such a crappy day yesterday?

"A friend?" she persisted. "Or..."

"My father."

"*Oh.* Oh dear, I'm so sorry."

He could see that she was startled, that it was a possibility that hadn't occurred to her. He didn't know if it was that or the genuine compassion in her eyes that made him explain, in a drawl that tried hard to be casual. "Yeah, he was a naval aviator—a commander at the time of his death, promoted posthumously to captain, which I guess made a difference to someone—my mother, maybe. He was stationed on a carrier in the South China Sea. Flew one too many missions, I guess you could say. And..." he could feel his face cramp with his attempt at a smile as he touched the name he'd located for her, and the MIA cross that followed it "...I guess you could say we were one of the lucky ones. We got a body to bury. It's over there—" he made a gesture with his hand "—in Arlington."

He could feel her eyes on him, hear even the tiny throat-clearing sound she made before she said, "That must have been very hard for you." And then, again so gently he didn't even notice that she was chip-chipping away at his carefully constructed barricades, "How old were you when it happened?"

And again he was mildly surprised when he heard himself answer. "I was sixteen."

"A difficult age."

He shrugged. "I guess. It was for me, anyway."

They were strolling along the paved walkway now, close together but nowhere near touching. In spite of that, he was aware of everything about her, the clothes she wore—same slacks and blazer as yesterday, but a different turtleneck, teal blue this time—every movement she made, no matter how slight. Aware that once again she'd turned her head to look at him. He wondered what she saw when she gazed at him like that, so thoughtful and silent. Wondered why it made him so uneasy. And why he allowed it.

"I was pretty difficult at all ages, if you want to know the truth," he said, taking a breath. "My dad was gone a lot, and I didn't get along with my mom. Hell, nobody did—including my dad, which was probably why he was gone a lot." He glanced sideways at Jane to see if she'd smiled at his poor attempt at humor, and was inordinately pleased to see the laugh lines deepening at the corners of her mouth and eyes. He found himself relaxing, at ease with her in a way he couldn't remember being with anyone in many, many years.

"Anyway, I was already mad at my dad for going to 'Nam—he'd volunteered for the duty, he didn't have to go. And I was mad at my mother, blaming her for making him so miserable he'd rather be in that hellhole than home with his family. After he was shot down, well...I was one pretty angry, messed-up kid. Truth is, I don't know what might have happened if it hadn't been for—" He stopped, quivering with shock at what he'd almost said.

She glanced at him and, instead of pursuing it, asked, "Do you have any brothers and sisters?"

"A brother." He said it on an exhalation, relaxing again, with a chuckle that was more fond than ironic. "Jack. He's navy, too, a real chip off the old block—lives somewhere in Texas, at the moment. Has a wife and three...no, four kids." His mouth twisted in a way that was familiar to him; afraid of what his companion might read in that expression, he looked over at her and turned it into a grin. "As you've probably gathered, we don't see a lot of each other."

For a moment, those thoughtful, compassionate eyes seemed to bore right into his, though he knew they were safely hidden behind the dark lenses of his sunglasses. But she didn't say anything, and he shrugged and went on, "Jack was pretty much the only one who could get along with Mother, so of course he always took her side. He was at the academy when Dad died. Naturally he came right home—we were living here in Washington then. And needless to say, that didn't help my attitude any. Like I said, I don't know what I would have done..." he took a deep breath and this time let himself finish it "...if it hadn't been for...a friend of mine."

"A friend?" The prompt was so soft it seemed almost to come from inside his own mind.

He nodded. She's good, he thought; really good. She could dig the life story out of a stone. "Their house backed up to ours. She was...I guess you could say she was my best friend."

My best friend. How odd it was to hear the words, not like anything that might have come from him, but like the vibrations of chords played by some unseen musician and left hanging in the cool, winy air. He paused for a moment to listen, thinking that if he only listened hard enough...

"It's good that you had someone," Jane said gently. So much pain, she thought, watching his averted profile, the strange, almost expectant tilt of his head. *So much grief...but not all, I think, for his father.*

She said nothing more, but settled onto a vacant bench with a little sigh and pulled her tote bag into her lap, leaving it to him whether to tell her about the friend whose name he couldn't bring himself to utter.

But he swore suddenly and threw her a hard, fierce look, the one men use to mask extreme emotions. "Ah, hell, what am I telling you all this stuff for?" Only he didn't say "stuff," and he didn't apologize for the word he did use.

Jane just smiled; she used the word herself, on occasion. She said comfortably, "I expect because I'm a good listener."

Watching him take cigarettes from a pocket inside his jacket with jerky, impatient motions, tap one out and light it, she found herself noticing the way his throat moved, the way his lips shaped themselves around the filter, the hard, brown look of his hands. Only when he'd tucked the pack away again and was blowing a thin stream of smoke into the morning's brilliance did she realize that her mouth had gone dry.

She swallowed with an effort and asked, "Was this one of your appointments?"

"What?"

"Last night, you said—"

"Oh. Yeah, sort of." The smile flicked briefly at one corner of his mouth but never made it as far as his eyes. He made a restless gesture with the hand that held the cigarette, then sat rather abruptly on the bench beside her, tucking his briefcase carefully between his feet. Also taking care, she noticed, to hold the cigarette between his knees so the smoke wouldn't drift her way.

Her heart gave a skip when he did that. It's the little things, she thought. That's what makes it so hard to explain when somebody asks, "Why? What is it about *him?*"

"I should be asking about you," he said after a moment, turning toward her so that once again she couldn't see anything of his eyes except the dark lenses of his sunglasses. "How are you this morning?'' She shrugged and tried a smile, which he didn't return. ''Sleep okay?''

She shook her head, but of course she couldn't tell him why she hadn't been able to sleep. And as she tried to efface it by adding, ''I never do, really, in hotels,'' she looked away, reluctant to have him see the doubt that must be in her eyes.

I wish, I really do wish I could trust him, she thought. This morning, seeing him there at The Wall like that, it was hard to remember why she couldn't. Surely the grief had been genuine.

But, she reminded herself, villains have fathers, too.

''No more dizziness?''

''What?'' She jerked her head around to look at him again, heart thumping. His arm lay across the back of the bench behind her shoulders; it was the feathery touch of his fingers on her neck that had startled her so. ''Oh—no.'' Her swallow made a stickery sound. She laughed and made a dismissive gesture toward her own throat. ''No, I'm perfectly fine. It didn't even leave a mark, whatever he did. I'd have thought being almost strangled would have more of an effect, you know?''

''You weren't strangled.'' His hand dropped casually, almost negligently, to her nape; his thumb traced up and down the side of her throat.

''No?'' Jane whispered. His hand was heavy and warm; she had to resist an urge to lean her head back against it. *What is he doing? What does this mean?*

He shook his head. Without the influence of his eyes, his smile had an almost unbearable sweetness. ''It wasn't your air supply that was cut off.''

She tried desperately to look intelligent. ''It wasn't?''

Another head shake. ''See, if you press right here...'' He did so, gently, and instantly she felt that awful, remembered pressure. ''What you do is, you cut off the blood supply to the brain.''

Jane gasped and pulled away from him, heart thumping. ''But that's...'' She could hardly get the words out; she felt cold. But of course, she thought, being a policeman, he'd know about things like that. ''So I could have...he really could have killed me.''

''*Could* have. But *didn't*.''

He took his arm away from the back of the bench, leaving

her feeling unsettled, as though someone had picked her up, shaken her vigorously and then set her down again slightly askew.

Gesturing at the tote bag in her lap, he casually asked, "Had it appraised yet?"

She gave her head a quick, hard shake, more in an effort to set herself to rights than as a response to the question, and shifted the tote bag unnecessarily as she considered how she should reply.

It wasn't that she feared Tom Hawkins; she didn't, not anymore. No matter how hard she tried, she just couldn't make him out to be a villain. And not only because he'd said he was a policeman, either. Because neither did the fact that he was a policeman mean she trusted him. Cop or villain, she was quite certain he wasn't being honest with her. She could just *feel* it. He had some sort of agenda he wasn't telling her about, which struck her as being particularly unfair of him since she seemed to be involved in whatever was going on, at least indirectly.

For goodness' sake, she thought in exasperation, if he was some kind of law enforcement officer, why didn't he just show her his ID and tell her what was going on? Why all this cloak-and-dagger, cat-and-mouse stuff? It was all beginning to seem like some sort of elaborate game, and she was quite frankly fed up with being the only one who didn't know the rules!

On the other hand, someone *had* broken into her hotel room last night and attacked her. That was no game.

She took a deep breath and released it. "I was going to. But then I saw that man again—Aaron Campbell—the one from the auction? He was on the Metro, on the next car. And he got off when I did. I'm almost sure he was following me. At least..." She let her words trail off into uncertainty, exasperated with herself now. She *wasn't* sure. She wasn't sure of anything, that was the problem.

Tom took a final drag on his cigarette. "Campbell again, huh?" he said on a soft hiss of expelled smoke.

Jane shot him a look and said flatly, "You think it was him last night, don't you? In my hotel room."

He shrugged and dropped the cigarette onto the packed, moist earth at his feet. "I told you, he had on—"

"—a ski mask. I know, I *know*." Furious with the evasion, she lapsed into silence.

"Look, just to be on the safe side, would you like me to go with you? I could take you..."

Why do I have a feeling you're going to anyway, whether I say yes or not? Jane thought resentfully. She said with a slight smile, "Take me...to your friend at the Smithsonian?" and was more satisfied than surprised when he looked momentarily nonplussed. So he had been lying about that, too.

"Uh, I guess we could still do that," he hedged as he tugged back the sleeve of the brown leather jacket and frowned at his watch. "I don't know if he'd be in or not, but we could give it a try."

"I'm sure I'll be fine," Jane said gently, "but thank you for the offer." After a quick look around, she added briskly, "In any case, I seem to have ditched Mr. Campbell—if he was following me at all. Maybe it was just my imagination."

Except for the faint sigh of an exhalation, there was no reply. But her awareness of Tom's silence seemed to grow with each of her heartbeats, like the ticking of a clock in the wee hours of the morning. His presence seemed to swell, too, taking up more than his share of the bench, filling up all the space between them. She could feel his body's heat, the sleeve of the old bomber jacket like melted butter against her arm. She could feel the warmth spreading to her face and throat, and down into her chest...her breasts.

And then...

"You don't trust me, do you, Mrs. Carlysle?" It was spoken quietly for so blunt and unexpected a question, almost in a murmur.

She shook her head, not smiling at all now, nor looking at him, either, focusing instead on the knuckles of her hands where they gripped the handles of her tote bag. "You do seem to keep turning up, Mr. Hawkins. Everywhere Campbell is, everywhere I am...there you are. You must admit, it's quite a coincidence."

There was a sharp bark of laughter, and then more of that strange, pulsating silence. Jane's mouth grew dry and her chest tight before he stirred and said in that same caressing voice, "What would you say if I told you you were right—that it wasn't a coincidence, that I have an ulterior motive for...turning up, as you put it?''

Jane smiled. *I'd say you were telling me the truth for a change.* She turned to him, but the words never made it past her lips. He'd taken off his sunglasses finally, and the message in his eyes was crystal clear.

Here it comes. Hawk watched her eyes for the expected flare of awareness and surprise. He'd caught the shocked little bump in her breathing. All's fair, he reminded himself when his belly tightened with guilt and self-disgust. If seduction is what it takes...

And then, to *his* great shock, she laughed. Without malice or artifice, just a warm little ripple of pure amusement, her eyes sparkling with it, crinkling up at the corners in that way he liked so much. He hadn't thought it possible for so small and innocent a thing to have such an effect on him. It hit him in places he hadn't known he still possessed—guy-places like *ego,* and *pride,* and others even more deeply buried and longer dormant that he couldn't bear to give names to.

Detachment, his greatest defense, enfolded him in a shell of ice. It enabled him to coolly arch his eyebrows and inquire, ''Why is that funny?''

She shook her head, still chuckling, and looked down at her hands. But Hawk had noted a faint blush of color in her cheeks, the slightest tremor of her lips. Now he zeroed in on them and unleashed his imagination. It didn't take much. Good old reliable lust.

He concentrated on the shape and texture of her lips, until he could feel the heat of her mouth and taste her essence on his tongue. He thought about her hands, too...thought about those nice, strong, no-nonsense hands unbuckling his belt and peeling off his pants, encircling him, stroking him to that edge-of-explosion readiness. He called up the memory that had haunted him in the night, of that nice, firm fanny of hers pressed up against him, her breasts tumescent in his hands...

''You're a very attractive woman,'' he said, noting the sultry timbre of his own voice with detached satisfaction. ''Don't you know that?''

She lifted amused eyes to his. ''Oh, please, Mr. Hawkins, I know perfectly well what I am. And *who* I am.''

Hawk shifted uncomfortably and muttered, "What's that supposed to mean?"

He was beginning to feel just a little lost, as if he'd suddenly found himself in a foreign country, with unfamiliar language and customs; the woman's responses weren't what he'd expected and not at all what he was used to. Plus, the pounding in his belly and the intense heat in his loins was making him wonder if he should have been more careful about giving his libido free rein, considering how long it had been since he'd had a woman.

"I mean," she began, and then paused, head tilted to one side, while she thought about it. Watching her, Hawk saw the flush in her cheeks deepen, caught the flicker of a pulse beat in her throat and felt a primitive surge of triumph at the realization that she wasn't as immune to him—or his comments—as she wanted him to think she was. She drew a deep breath, and he felt his own pulse thumping against his breastbone.

"I'm hardly the *femme fatale* type," she went on finally, speaking in a low, husky voice, and this time when she looked him in the eyes, although she was still gently smiling, he had the impression it wasn't easy for her. Her vulnerability made him feel thoroughly ashamed of himself. "Certainly not the type of woman attractive and dashing strangers make passes at in the middle of a public park in broad daylight. I'm sorry—I don't mean to be rude—but those things just don't happen, except in movies and romance novels, I suppose. At least not to me." She shifted to face forward again, giving the words a note of finality, like a sentence from a merciless judge.

In the silence that followed, Hawk realized that his jaw was aching from the tension of his tightly clenched teeth. And that his hands itched with the sudden urge to grab her by the shoulders and shake her out of that damn composure of hers, shake her until her head fell back and her mouth opened and her breath came quick and shallow, and then... "You're wrong, you know," he growled.

She shook her head, implacable and yet serene. "I don't think so."

"What would I have to do to convince you?" he asked, masking his frustration with a smile he knew must look as crooked as his motives. "Kiss you?" *It would serve her right...serve her right!* "Right here and now? In broad daylight...in a public park?"

She looked at him and, with that maddening serenity, replied, "Probably." Calling his bluff—he couldn't believe it.

It would serve her right, he raged silently. *Do it. Do it now.* He thought about her lips crushing under the onslaught of his, her mouth opening...the clashing of teeth, the mating of tongues...her hands raking his back, her breath sobbing in her throat... *Do it!*

Sudden, unexpected desire curled inside him like tongues of flame, twisting his belly into knots, pounding in his temples. He felt almost sick with wanting... *Do it now.*

He almost did. He even reached out his hand to touch her, to take her chin and turn her to face him, to tilt her mouth to his pleasure. But then, for some reason, his lust-fogged gaze happened to focus on the little fan of crow's-feet at the corner of her eye. And he thought, *Nice...*

And just like that the fog cleared, and he was rational again. But not detached. Hardly. Shaken. Shaken to his core.

She turned to look at him when he put on his shades—and a damn good thing she hadn't done so before, he thought, or no telling what she'd have seen in his eyes, and he'd have lost her for good, for sure—fixing him with a look more rueful than amused. Perhaps even, he thought, with a touch of regret.

"You see," she said softly, "I was right, wasn't I?"

He gave a short laugh, a sound like sandpaper scraping over stone. Hearing it, her lips smiled without changing her eyes, and she reached up to touch his face along the hard, raspy edge of his jaw. "For some reason, I think...you're too honorable to lie about such an important thing."

With a movement like a snake striking, he caught her hand and imprisoned it in his grasp, holding it like a captured bird in the space between his face and hers. Looking across it, he caught and held her eyes, as well, knowing his were safely hidden now behind the hunter's blind of his sunglasses.

Still vibrating and reckless from the effects of his brush with disaster, he said roughly, "About kissing you? Who said I was lying? Lady, you misjudge me. I do want very much to kiss you." He was surprised to find that he meant it. Surprised, too, by that same primitive something in him that surged at the flicker of uncertainty—even alarm, and yes, desire, too!—he saw in the bottomless depths of her eyes. "Just not *here,* in broad daylight in a public park, as you put it. That's not my style. When I kiss you..." he smiled at the almost imperceptible jerk of response he felt in her hand "...*when* I kiss you, I'd want it to be private enough for what comes after. You follow me?"

He didn't wait for her nod; the small, convulsive movement of her throat, the slight parting of her lips and the shine of perspiration across the tops of her cheekbones were enough for him.

Changing the nature of his grip on her hand, and with it the mood and tenor of what was between them, so that even he wasn't sure now that the sexually charged moments had really happened, he rose and pulled her to her feet.

In a different voice, a light, teasing voice, he said, "And now that we've established that we both think the other is attractive..." He paused to smile at her gasp of protest. "You did, you know. You said attractive—*and* dashing. I have a very good memory."

He was delighted by the grace with which she accepted his words, like a shifting of gears, or the change in tempo that signals a new movement in a symphony. Turning her hand in his so that it was more like, and more than, a handshake, she said sweetly, "Well, don't let it go to your head, Mr. Hawkins. I also happen to think the bald guy in the Maytag commercials is adorable."

Hawk grinned and touched his temple with two fingers in an unspoken touché. The heat was ebbing slowly from his body, leaving his mind clear and once more focused on the game at hand. And already plotting strategy several moves ahead.

"So," he said as he bent to retrieve the briefcase from under the bench, breaking the vibrating silence that was threatening the tenuous truce between them, "you'll be heading off to Georgetown, I suppose?"

There was no answer from Jane. Straightening, he saw that she was standing just where he'd left her, gnawing thoughtfully at her lip. He smiled to himself. Was she having second thoughts about turning him down, or thinking over the promise he'd just made to her? Both, probably. And if he were to ask again right now to accompany her to Georgetown, he wondered which of her fears would win.

He didn't ask, having already decided that the trek to Georgetown on foot would give Campbell—not to mention any other players he might have missed—too many opportunities to play his hand. Hawk wanted Campbell completely out of the picture, if at all possible; dealing with this Carlysle woman was becoming complicated enough one on one. He didn't even want to think about how complicated. So he said instead, with just a hint of exasperation, "Will you at least let me put you in a cab?"

He watched her eyes flare bright with relief. "Oh, yes, I'd appreciate that very much. Thank you."

"There used to be a cab stand on Constitution, not far from here. Come on, I'll walk you over." He touched her elbow briefly and they set out together across the grass, taking a shortcut through the trees.

As they walked, briskly and in silence, not touching...with the part of his mind that wasn't busy scanning and monitoring everything around him, Hawk found himself wondering, for the first time in many years, what the woman beside him was thinking.

Chapter 7

The door of the taxicab slammed with a harsh and final *thunk.*

I'm not going to look, I *won't* look, Jane told herself as she leaned forward to speak to the driver.

Finally, as the cab groaned into gear and lurched away from the curb, she did look back, just once. But Tom Hawkins had already turned to light a cigarette, his shoulders hunched in the brown bomber jacket, hands cupped beneath the brim of the baseball cap, the incongruous black briefcase wedged between his feet. He didn't look up, or wave.

Odd, she thought, settling once more into her seat, and into a boggy little slough of depression for which she could find no reasonable cause.

He says he's going to kiss me, and with such conviction I almost believed him, but as far as I can see, this is goodbye. And he doesn't ask for my phone number, or give me any way of reaching him. Why? I wonder...

Well, okay, she could think of two logical answers to that question. One, he was just a very good actor and hadn't meant it, after all, about kissing her. Or two, he had no intention of saying goodbye, and simply had his own way of finding her.

Both scenarios seemed equally possible to her. And oddly enough, neither one made her feel happy.

Tom had told her the truth about one thing, at least; it wasn't far to Georgetown. It seemed only minutes, in fact, before the taxicab was pulling up to a curb on a bustling street filled with shops and restaurants offering every kind of cuisine imaginable, many of them housed in converted residences dating back she could only guess how many hundred years. Ordinarily, she'd have been delighted at the prospect of an afternoon of window-shopping and exploring, including the quaint and narrow side streets she could only catch glimpses of. Now, though, all she wanted was to find Connie's friend's gallery as quickly as possible and lay to rest all these wild imaginings about valuable art "finds" and mysterious strangers with sinister agendas.

She paid the driver and extricated herself from the back seat of the cab, a little awkwardly because of the bulky tote bag. She slammed the door and stood for a moment watching the cab pull away from the curb, absently smoothing the front of her slacks and tugging her jacket into proper order. Somewhere nearby, a car door opened and quickly closed again.

She glanced once more at the piece of paper in her hand and then at the number etched in the semicircle of glass over the door of the nearest shop. Ah-hah, she thought. *Left.*

But she'd taken only one step in that direction when something—someone—a man—suddenly brushed against her, filling up all the space on her right.

Aaron Campbell! Even with one panic-stricken glance out of the corner of her eye, she'd recognized that angry black glower and hawk-faced profile. But before she had time to react, even to draw breath for a scream, a hand closed around her elbow and a voice just loud enough to override her soft gasp of surprise, said, "Mrs. Carlysle, I'm going to have to ask you to come with me, please."

How polite he seemed. But she saw him reach inside his jacket with the hand not holding her elbow, the *right* hand. And it was reaching into the *left* side of his jacket, the side next to her, where she was absolutely certain she could feel something hard, like a... Oh, God—the man was wearing a shoulder holster with a gun in it, and he was reaching for it *now*. What should she do? *What should she do?"*

Take control! Take action! Shing Lee's commands shrieked inside her head like an alarm klaxon.

With adrenaline already tingling her nerves to readiness and her heart racing in high gear, she searched for, and found, the quiet place in her mind, the place where all things moved in slow motion, the place in which *she* had absolute control. From that place of peace and tranquillity, she willed her breaths to come slow and even, gathering her strength as she wrapped her left hand over her right fist.

A split second before the strike, she uttered a loud, "Eee-*yuh!*" which had the effect of startling Aaron Campbell so that he eased his hold on her elbow just long enough for her to drive it, with all the combined force in her upper body, into the softness of his belly, just below the apex of his ribs.

Jane found the sounds he made as he dropped to his knees on the sidewalk somewhat disturbing; Shing's demonstrations had somehow neglected to include that ugly little detail.

Fortunately, she was pumped up enough by her success to carry her through the next step, which was to drop the tote bag to the sidewalk and bring her clasped fists down as hard as she could, with all her weight behind them, onto the back of her opponent's neck.

She was considering whether to follow that up with a good solid knee to the underside of the chin, or perhaps a swift kick to the, uh, groin, when something struck her arm—not hard—and a voice hissed urgently, "Carlysle—quick! This way—*come on!*"

She whirled, still riled and combative, arms raised in the defensive position. Tom Hawkins, poised like a relay runner about to accept the baton, relaxed momentarily and looked pained. "For God's sake, put that away. I'm on *your* side, dammit! Come on, give me that bag and let's go."

"Over my dead body," Jane shouted.

She only meant that in response to the first half of Tom's command, of course; the second part seemed only good sense. Though she thought it probable that only seconds had elapsed since she'd stepped out of the taxi and into Aaron Campbell's clutches, a few curious spectators had already begun to drift in her direction, drawn by the always-mesmerizing specter of violence. It would only be a matter of time before it occurred to one of them to summon someone in authority. Which Jane, being a law-abiding citizen, would definitely have welcomed if it hadn't become apparent that her fallen foe was only temporarily vanquished. He was already on his feet, in fact, and shaking his head like a dazed prizefighter. And there was still the matter of that gun.

No time to think about alternatives—she just snatched her tote bag and ran.

No time to wonder how it was possible Tom Hawkins could be here, when just moments ago he'd said goodbye to her in the shadow of the Lincoln Memorial—it was toward him she ran, and reached for his outstretched hand.

No time to question the surge of joy she felt inside at seeing his face, hearing his voice, feeling his fingers close around hers. Because at that point, her arm was nearly wrenched out of its socket.

"Slow down," she gasped. "I can't...run that fast."

"Sure you can. You're doing it, aren't you?" Tom retorted, pulling her down a side street. "Here—this way."

At first she thought she'd surely fall flat on her face, but when she didn't, she began to feel exhilarated instead. It was as Tom had said—she *could* run that fast. Imagine—at her age!

"Why don't you let me carry that damn bag?" Tom asked in a bumpy voice as he ran, matching his stride now with hers. He no longer had the briefcase, she noticed. He'd also ditched the baseball cap and sunglasses.

"No way, you can run faster than I can."

He grunted, glanced her way and then ran for several paces in silence before growling, "You think I'd take the damn painting and leave you to Campbell, is that it? What the hell kind of guy do you think I am?"

"I don't know," Jane managed to say. "That's pretty much...the problem." She ran a few more steps. "I think...you owe me...an explanation."

"Yeah, well, this is hardly the time or place for it. Look who's got his legs back."

One brief, wild glance over her shoulder confirmed it: Campbell had just turned into the narrow residential street behind them, running hard. "Oh, God," she moaned. Her chest was on fire and she was developing a side ache. "He's gaining on us, isn't he?"

Her companion didn't answer that but instead veered suddenly, yanking her after him as he dodged between two parked cars. She gave a horrified squeak as they narrowly missed a collision with a bicyclist, skittered on across the street with her heart in her throat and almost tripped over Tom's heels when he ducked into an even narrower cross street. She was following blindly now.

Hawk had had a reason for choosing this particular street. He'd spotted a moving van parked about halfway down the block, facing out, taking up most of the pavement. He could see that the doors on the side facing the sidewalk were open, and that the interior of the van was all but filled with boxes and indeterminate shapes shrouded in packing blankets. And also that no one was in sight.

A quick look over his shoulder told him Campbell hadn't made the turn into this street yet, although he couldn't be far from it, and had surely seen them do so. And Jane was tiring; she couldn't keep this up much longer. It wasn't a hard decision to make.

"In here." Jerking Jane up beside him, he pushed her ahead of him into the van.

There wasn't much room; the van seemed to be fully loaded, though whether going or coming he had no way of knowing. After wasting precious seconds in search of a nook or cranny big enough to hide them both, he shoved Jane down into a space between a washer and dryer and what appeared to be an upright piano wrapped in blankets. He then squeezed in after her as best he could, pulling a blanket over the part of him that didn't quite fit.

And not a moment too soon. In the sudden breathy stillness, he could hear the sound of footsteps slapping on the pavement outside the van.

"Not a sound," he hissed. And then there was silence, so heavy it seemed to thunder with the beat of his heart.

It was stifling under the blanket. The footsteps grew louder, scraping past, finally, only inches from their hiding place. They receded, but only a short distance, then stopped...hesitated...

scuffled around first one way, then another. And then came back.

Hawk uttered a very nasty word under his breath. Feeling Jane's body jerk slightly—whether because of the language he'd used or the gravity of their situation, he couldn't be sure—he reached out a hand to touch her, to steady and caution her, while with the other he found the comforting shape of the gun nestled in the small of his back. Braced and ready, he waited.

The footsteps drew nearer...and nearer. Slowly this time. In his mind's eye, Hawk could see his adversary, see the suspicion in his face, feel the tension in his body as, so cautiously, so carefully, he advanced, knowing his prey was cornered, but suspicious, too, of traps and ambushes. He could see him in the doorway, now, every nerve, every muscle vibrating, his own breath suspended... One foot, now, on the floor of the van—he could feel it give a little with the weight...then—

Suddenly, just like that, he was gone. In the distance, Hawk heard voices, low and casual, bantering voices. The movers were returning.

He let his gun hand relax and with the other, the one still touching Jane, gave her a couple of reassuring strokes and encouraging pats.

But relief was short-lived. He barely had time to register it in his consciousness before a new series of sounds elevated the short hairs on the back of his neck and sent a fresh shot of adrenaline into his system. First, a loud and prolonged squeak, metal on metal...then a reverberating clang...and another...and then a sliding *thunk*. And finally...dead silence.

"Uh-oh," said Hawk, and muttered that word again.

"They've shut us in," said Jane, her voice small and airstarved.

Hawk drew his head out from under the blanket and into total darkness.."Yep," he grunted. "Looks that way."

"Sh—shouldn't we do something? Yell, or bang on the door?"

"Yeah, and then what? They let us out, listen to our explanation—you've got one, I suppose?—and assuming they buy it, drive off and leave us here? Campbell's still out there, you know. He won't have gone far. He knows we have to be here somewhere."

Just then, there was a belly-deep roar, like a growl from the throat of some gigantic beast, and then a low, continuous rumbling. Under their hands and knees the floor of the van had begun to vibrate.

"Oh dear," said Jane. There was a pause, and then a surprisingly meek and tremulous, "So, what do we do now?"

"Hope and pray it's not a long-distance move, I guess."

There was another pause during which the van lurched from one side to the other, but in an almost stately manner that reminded Hawk of a very large and tipsy lady.

And then in an altogether different voice, one he couldn't quite interpret, he heard Jane say, "Tom? Would you stop stroking my bottom, please?"

He snatched his hand away from her as if she'd bitten him, and muttered, "Sorry," under his breath.

"Under the circumstances, I forgive you." And now there was no mistaking her amusement. That teetering-on-the-brink-of-laughter quiver in her voice was contagious, too; he could feel the almost-forgotten sensation building inside him like an oncoming sneeze. Well, hell, he supposed it was one way to react to a crisis.

"Let's get the hell out of this hole," he said in a monotone, fighting hard against the influence of that insidious itch.

Squirming backward until he'd managed to free his shoulders, he stood up gingerly, feeling the blackness above his head for obstacles. "Damn," he said gruffly. "Wish we had some light."

Jane's voice drifted up from somewhere near his feet. "I have...a flashlight, if I can just—"

"You're kidding! You do? Where?"

"I always carry one. I grew up in California—earthquakes, you know. It's in my bag. Just let me...okay, I'm out. Now, where did I...oh, here it is."

She came crawling out backward on her hands and knees, kneeling on his feet, brushing against his legs. He tried to give her more room, but there just wasn't any; his back was smack up against a wall of boxes. When he leaned over to help her up, he got a mouthful of her hair.

"Mmpf. Ptoo," he muttered, spitting it out.

Breathless and obviously still quivery with laughter, she whispered, "Oops, sorry," and rose to her feet, clinging to his arms and unfolding her body along the front of his.

"Tight quarters," he said stiffly.

"Yes, isn't it."

Her hair was on a level with his face again. This time, he kept his mouth closed, and discovered that he could appreciate the tickly softness of it on his lips and chin. And the smell of it...nothing he could place, just a part of that indefinable "nice-woman" smell he'd noticed before.

His stomach growled suddenly. For Hawk, that had always meant one or the other of two different kinds of hunger, and he couldn't have sworn, at that moment, which one this was. It had been a long time since breakfast, but even longer since he'd had the sweet scent of a woman in his nostrils and her breasts brushing up against his chest like this, and her legs shifting to make room for his...

"I know—I'm starving, too," Jane said with a sympathetic chuckle, certain *she* at least knew which hunger his juices were giving voice to.

"Don't suppose you have any food in that bag of yours along with the flashlight?" He could feel his pulse in his loins.

"As a matter of fact, I do. Here—hold this." She thrust something large and flat against his chest.

Clutching the painting, hearing the crackle of the paper it was wrapped in, Hawk's blood pressure and temperature began a slow descent back to normal. *This is it, Hawk, the game ends here, and you've won.* He took a deep breath and let it out slowly.

"Here it is—got it!" There was a little cackle of triumph as a thin beam of light stabbed through the blackness. It danced giddily for a moment, like a sprite set free, flashed briefly in his eyes and then stabilized at chest level between them, illuminating her features—and his, too, he imagined—with ghoulish shadows.

Maybe something in those shadows gave her the inspiration, who knows; he'd stopped trying to figure this woman out. She waggled the flashlight playfully, and her face seemed to grow longer and her voice got higher, and she quipped, "Well, Ollie, here's another fine mess you've got us into!"

Hawk snorted to keep from laughing—damned if he was going to let this woman make him laugh. "Carlysle," he growled, "damned if I don't think you're starting to enjoy this. Give me that." Laying the painting carefully on top of the washer—or the dryer, he wasn't sure which—he took the flashlight from her and pointed it downward. "We're gonna want to conserve the batteries. You say you have food in that thing?"

She had her head down, already digging in the tote bag. Her voice came muffled. "Well, not *food* exactly. But I still have the peanuts they gave me on the plane—Connie's, too. And these." She held it out to him—a package of fat-free cookies.

He sighed. "Nothing to drink, I suppose?"

She slowly shook her head, her eyes glistening, over-large in the oblique illumination of the flashlight. Her voice was calm, but with no traces of laughter in it, when she asked, "How long do you think we might be stuck in here?"

Hawk shrugged. "No telling. If this is a coast-to-coast move, it could be days before they get where they're going. On the other hand..." Her face looked so stricken he couldn't bear to look at it, so he thumbed the flashlight off and went on in the darkness. "On the other hand, these guys have to stop sometime—to use the john, to eat..."

"There's no place to go to the bathroom in here." That was pointed out in a small, horror-stricken voice.

"You noticed that, did you?" said Hawk dryly. Taking pity on her, he added, "Look, the first time they stop, we'll bang like hell on the door and hope somebody hears us. That's all we can do."

"This van isn't...airtight, is it?"

"Airtight? Hardly. Other good news is, this is a diesel, so we don't have to worry about carbon monoxide poisoning. The bad news is, it's probably gonna get colder'n hell in here pretty soon."

"Well, at least we seem to have plenty of blankets." She sounded calmer, even brisk and purposeful, as though she was quite ready to deal with the situation now that she knew what, exactly, the situation was.

Hawk was just glad she seemed to be okay again. He refused to let himself admire her spirit; he was already getting to like her too much as it was. "I think there's room for both of us right here in this space by the door—gonna be a little snug..."

With faultless timing, the truck chose that moment to turn a corner. Jane swayed slowly and inexorably against him, weighted by centrifugal force and utterly helpless to stop herself. Her head eased in under his chin like a boat going into its slip. It would have been a pretty nice fit, Hawk thought, if it hadn't been for her arms being full of stuff and all doubled up between them.

From the darkness came a doleful, ''I knew I shouldn't have let myself gain those five extra pounds.''

A snort burst from him, like a pressure valve letting go. He couldn't think of anything else he dared add to that, but he was thinking that if she *was* carrying around five extra pounds, they felt perfectly all right to him.

It seemed an hour or two before the truck slowly righted itself. Hawk took Jane by the elbows and gently pushed her back to vertical, muttering something like, ''There y'go...''

Her contribution was a breathless whisper. ''Thanks...sorry about that.''

''Don't mention it.''

''How 'bout this,'' she said brightly, after a brief, mysterious silence. And then he could feel her stirring at his feet, spreading blankets. ''We sit facing each other—you know, legs alongside? Come on—you sit right there, like that, and I'll sit—'' and once more he heard her huffing and scuffling around as she got herself settled ''...like this.''

He thought about turning on the flashlight again but didn't. It was bad enough imagining the close quarters; at least he didn't have to see the legs that lay warm and firm along the outside of his, the feminine hip nudging his ankle, the slender foot—

''Hey,'' he said, ''you took your shoes off.''

''Take yours off, too, if you like,'' she said generously. ''I don't mind if they smell.''

Hawk gave a single whoop of laughter; he couldn't help it.

But it was a struggle, trying to push off one laced-up athletic-type shoe with the toe of the other. And he didn't dare lean over too far, because he knew if he got the taste of her in his mouth again, the smell of her... Then he felt her hands, strong, no-nonsense hands. A moment later, first one foot, then the other experienced the chill of suddenly exposed, sweat-damp socks. ''Thanks,'' he said gruffly.

"Don't mention it." Her voice was as cool as his socks. "Want a blanket?"

"Yeah, please." He felt the weight of the packing blanket fall across his knees, felt her pull and tug it until she had it wrapped snugly around his ankles and feet. "Hand me a blanket," he heard himself say, "and I'll do you."

There was a curious pain in his chest, like something stuck way down deep in his esophagus, something he couldn't get rid of. And hard as he tried to stop the memory, it came anyway...

He and Jen, sitting on opposite ends of the old sofa in the den at her parents' house...a fire roaring in the fireplace and half-drunk mugs of cocoa on the floor. He'd been home from college on Thanksgiving break, her parents were out for the evening at some party or other, and they'd just been roughhousing in the unexpected snow, the first fall of the season. He could hear Jen's voice, with that bossy self-confidence he'd loved so much, saying, "Here—you do me and I'll do you." His icy-cold feet in her lap, hers in his...he couldn't remember who'd started the tickling, but inevitably they'd wound up in a tangle on the rug, kissing breathlessly and with escalating passion. It had been the first time they'd made love....

"There you go," he said as he shoved Jane's swaddled feet back down beside him, wishing he could do something about the roughness in his hands and voice, hoping she wouldn't read into that things about him he wasn't ready for her to know. "Hey, how about some of that food, now, huh?"

"Okay, let's see, which do you prefer, peanuts or cookies?"

"Oh, hell, I don't care—you choose."

"Well, maybe we should each have some of both—protein and carbohydrates—what do you think?"

God, she sounded like his mother. Well, okay, not *his* mother, but somebody's. Like June Cleaver. "Fine. Need the light?"

"No, that's okay. Give me your hand."

"Come on, Tom, you get on, too! Quick, give me your hand, give me your hand!"

"Wait—I want to take one more picture...wave next time you come around, okay? Jase, wave at Daddy, now..."

He put his hand into the darkness and felt her cool fingers close around his. He could feel his heart beating.

"Ooh...I hate the way they make these darn packages of peanuts so hard to open, don't you? I just hope I don't lose them all in the dark…''

He took a breath. It was like dragging shards of glass through his chest. ''Want some help?''

''No, that's okay, I've got it now… Mmm, boy, those taste good.''

For a while, Hawk sat with his mind in neutral and listened to the sounds of her genteel munching, giving his emotions time to drift back into quiet waters. When he felt pretty sure he was back on course again, he opened his own stubborn little foil pack and downed the peanuts in a couple of greedy handfuls, figuring they'd make more of an impact on his stomach that way. The cookies he nibbled; he wasn't much of a sweets person. Jen had been the one—

''For once I'm not sorry I have a bit of a sweet tooth,'' said Jane with a sigh. The cookie wrapper crinkled softly in the darkness.

Suddenly feeling as if he had rocks under his butt, Hawk shifted and growled like a bad-tempered dog, ''All right, let's cut the crap. Out with it. Get it over with.''

He felt her legs twitch as she gasped, ''I beg your pardon?'' But she said it on a little ripple of laughter, and he had a feeling she wasn't really all that surprised.

''You're wondering what the hell this is all about,'' he went on, his voice still guttural and harsh with diverted emotions. ''You said I owe you an explanation. So go on. This is your chance. Ask your questions.''

There was a pregnant little silence, and then a solemn, ''You'll tell me the truth?''

He gave a short, hard laugh. ''Well, I'll try.''

Questions. Jane took a bite of cookie and chewed thoughtfully. Funny, up until the moment she'd stepped out of that taxicab in Georgetown, all she'd been able to think about was questions. And boy, had she wanted answers! She'd been feeling angry, victimized, threatened and just plain scared.

But ever since that tussle with Aaron Campbell, well, how on earth to describe it? She'd felt…exhilarated. And at the same time, calm. Right now she felt strong. Confident. And yes, Tom was right, in a strange way, she *was* sort of enjoying this. She was alive, uninjured, and it didn't really matter what the explanation was for whatever it was she'd stumbled into; never again would Jane Carlysle be able to say that nothing ever happened to her!

"I'm not sure I know where to begin," she said finally. She frowned, trying her best to inject a degree of sternness into her voice and thinking that what it reminded her of was when the girls were little, and she'd been forced to discipline them when actually she was secretly entertained by the mischief they'd done.

It wasn't that she didn't still want—*need*—answers and explanations; goodness no. But somehow the urgency was gone. She felt strangely at ease with Tom Hawkins now—this mystifying stranger she hadn't even met before yesterday, and whose bundled bare feet were now snuggled cozily under her elbow. She wasn't sure she could have explained why, it was just a feeling she had. The feeling she was going to have all the time in the world to learn about this man, including the answers to questions she hadn't even thought of yet.

"I guess," she said at last, dabbing cookie crumbs from her lips with the tip of a forefinger, "you could begin by telling me who you are."

Chapter 8

"*Interpol?*" For one wild instant she thought he must be joking. But for some reason, she didn't follow up on her initial impulse to laugh.

The flashlight's beam slashed across her blanket-covered legs. When it steadied, and she saw that Tom was reaching for something inside his jacket, she jerked slightly and frowned; that gesture reminded her of something, but she couldn't think what. Then he pulled out a wallet—no, an ID case—and without a word handed it to her and trained the light on it. She studied it carefully and then gave it back, heart thumping.

"My goodness," she said faintly.

Her thoughts were racing. So he'd told her the truth, about being a policeman, at least. And this was what he meant by "not in this jurisdiction." But who'd have thought...*Interpol?* It seemed so exotic to her, like something out of a movie, or a spy novel—James Bond stuff.

Her head was spinning, and she couldn't think which question should logically come next. She also felt a little testy. She wished he'd just explain, dammit. But she could tell by his silence that she was going to have to drag this, whatever it was, out of him, piece by piece. She had an idea that the habit of secrecy was deeply ingrained in this man.

But it hasn't always been so. Oh, yes, somehow she knew that. Once he'd had a friend, a best friend, with whom he'd shared his innermost thoughts, his secrets, his anger and pain. A friend for whom he still grieved.

"But why..." Her throat was suddenly filled with gravel. She cleared it and tried again. "Why are you *here?* What do you want with *me?*"

Then her breath caught, and she blurted it out in a rush, even though she was sure she already knew the answer. "It's the painting, isn't it? I was afraid of that. It's valuable, after all, isn't it? And of course it's stolen. I knew I liked that painting too much. Damn."

She felt Tom's knees move restively beside hers. "It's not stolen," he said gruffly. "And as far as I know, it's not valuable."

"Well, it certainly is to someone," Jane snapped, impatient with the stingy way he was doling out information. "Aaron Campbell, for starters. Not to mention the person who was in my hotel room last night. Which reminds me..." She was relieved to feel the anger, finally, which was much more comfortable and a lot less complicated than what she'd recently been feeling toward the man whose legs lay so firm and warm against hers. So relieved that she fired her suspicions and questions at him recklessly, and without her usual diplomacy. "*You* being there, that wasn't any accident, was it? So, who were you following, *Agent* Hawkins? Was it Campbell, or me?"

"You, of course." His voice, in response to her anger, was hard and without expression, though it took on a note of dark irony when he added, "I'd rather hoped we'd left Mr. Campbell behind."

"Okay, so who *is* he?"

She heard the soft hiss of an exhalation. "I wish to God I knew."

"But you *do* think it was him in my room last night?"

"Let's just say I hope it was."

"You...hope? *Why?*"

There was another sigh, a whispery sound like wind-driven sand. He said almost gently, "Think, Carlysle. Would you rather have one other player out there somewhere, dogging our trail, or two?"

"Player?" The word exploded on a puff of air, as if something had squeezed her chest. She wondered what had become of her former serenity and confidence; all of a sudden, her mouth was dry and her heart was hammering against the wall of her chest. "What is this," she demanded, "some kind of *game?* You know, dammit, for somebody who's supposed to be enlightening me, you're making me awfully confused!"

"I'm trying," he muttered, shifting again. "To enlighten you, I mean. It's just...not easy to explain."

She wished he'd stop moving. It made it hard for her to hang on to the anger. She muttered unsteadily, "You're making this sound very complicated."

"Trust me, it is. And there's a lot I can't tell you."

There was a long pause. Jane listened to the monotonous drone of eighteen tires on asphalt, fighting for the calm that had deserted her, searching for an anchor of normalcy in a world that had suddenly become unreal. As if, she thought, she'd somehow stepped into a movie—a Hollywood thriller, something starring Sylvester Stallone, or Arnold whatever-his-name-was.

But the painting. That was certainly real. And dammit, it was hers.

She cleared her throat and said with a great deal more firmness, both in her voice and her resolve, "Okay, then, tell me about the painting. If it's not stolen, and it's not valuable—"

"It's not the painting." There was another, shorter pause, during which she heard a familiar crackle, which she identified as the wrapper on a pack of cigarettes. Then the crackling ceased and his arm relaxed, coming to rest on the mound of her swaddled feet. She heard him sigh; evidently he'd decided that under the circumstances he was going to have to get through this without the aid of nicotine. She could almost feel him girding himself, and the words came as if each one represented a victory in a small, private tug-of-war. "I—we have...there's reason to believe that a piece of information was, uh, hidden somewhere on or in that painting. A piece of information that would make it very valuable indeed to...certain people." He subsided, seemingly exhausted by that effort.

But if he thought he was finished, Jane had news for him. "Information? Hidden? In my painting?" She fired the volley at him without drawing breath. "What sort of information?"

"I'm afraid I can't tell you that." He sounded every inch an officer of the law. Jane had to resist an urge to kick him.

"That's ridiculous," she said in exasperation. "If there was something you wanted in my painting, why didn't you just *say* so? If you'd only told me who you were and what you wanted, don't you think I'd have been more than happy to cooperate?"

He was silent for just a little too long. Illumination came as he was finally drawing breath for an explanation, and she got there first, overriding it with a startled gasp, then a squeak of incredulous laughter. "You thought *I* was after the...whatever it is in the painting? That I was one of the, uh... That's it—you did, didn't you? Oh, for heaven's sake." And borrowing one of her daughters' favorite expressions, she added, "Get *real.*"

"You did bid on the painting," Tom said in his stuffiest and most inflexible policeman's monotone. "You and Campbell were the only ones hanging in there. And then..." he paused a chilling instant "...there was just you."

"Yes, because Mr. Campbell fainted..." The word trailed off as she suddenly found herself running short of air. "Oh, but— oh, God, you don't mean you think somebody *did* something to him, do you? That he didn't just...faint?"

It must have been then that full comprehension finally hit her. It was like a blast of cold, dank air from a freshly opened tomb, a vault filled with dreadful, frightening, unthinkable things from a world that was totally alien to her. A world of violence and evil. Chilled and clammy, she whispered, "Oh, you *can't* think I would do anything like that."

"It seemed a possibility at the time," said Tom in a neutral voice.

"That's why you followed us," Jane went on as if he hadn't spoken. Her voice was low and still tinged with the horror that had overtaken her when she added curiously, "How did you manage to do that, by the way? When Connie and I left the auction, you were standing on the loading platform smoking a cigarette. I saw you. You couldn't have gotten to your car in time to see which way we'd gone. It's impossible."

"Nothing's impossible." She didn't need light to see the

twisted, ironic little smile. "But as a matter of fact, I used a GPS tracker."

"GPS? What on earth's that?"

"Global Positioning System—tracking by satellite. I put a signaling device in your friend's van when I was helping you stow your stuff." She felt him jerk slightly, and thought perhaps he'd shrugged. And then he offered an ambiguous, "Sorry."

"And that's how you found me today," she said flatly, choosing not to hear the apology, if indeed that's what it had been. "Isn't it? You didn't just 'happen' to be there, either, at The Wall."

"Yes..." there was a long exhalation "...and no."

Her throat was tight suddenly, her eyes itchy. Why did she feel such a sense of disappointment and betrayal? Remembering the way her heart had gone out to him in his vulnerability and pain, she thought, *God, Jane, how stupid you are.*

She was silent for a long time, waiting for that constriction in her throat to relax, all the while running his explanations over and over in her mind. Several things bothered her. "But," she said finally, "you said the device was in Connie's van. So how come—"

"There's also one in your bag." His voice was soft, almost diffident. "I put it there last night."

"I see." Last night, in her room. And she'd been so grateful for his nearness and comfort. God, she felt awful. Hollow...queasy. She took a deep breath, trying to fill the emptiness inside her, if only momentarily.

"Tell me," she said, and was both startled and pleased that her voice sounded so steady. "Was any of what you told me true? About your father, I mean. And...your friend." She wondered why his answer mattered so much.

Or why she felt such an odd little twinge—relief that was almost like pain—when he answered, with the gravel of sincerity in his voice, "Oh, yeah, that was true. All of it."

"And when..." *Carefully, carefully, Jane.* She began again, now with forced lightness. "When did you, uh, change your mind about me being involved in all this? Or maybe I should ask—"

"Oh, that was last night." He still sounded hoarse but with a note of anger himself, now. "To be precise, when I saw you standing there in that doorway with the light behind you and that damn toy pistol in your hands. Right then and there I said to myself, *nobody's* that stupid. She *must* be innocent.''

"Thanks," said Jane tartly, "I think." Then she cocked her head to one side, listening, trying to catch a replay of the exchange. There was something he'd just said...

But he wouldn't let her concentrate, plunging on in that newly charged, guttural voice. "Lady, you've no idea what you're mixed up in. There are people who'd kill for what's hidden in that painting. People who *have* killed. Do you understand me?''

Her hands, she discovered, were knotted tightly together in her lap. In spite of that, and the fact that all her muscles were quivering with tension, her voice once again emerged with gratifying calm. "*Have* killed... Do you mean Campbell?''

"I can't be sure. All I know is, three days ago somebody killed a shopkeeper in Marseilles—"

"Marseilles? *France?*''

"—by the name of Loizeau. And I have very good reason to believe that whoever did it was at that auction yesterday.''

Jane said nothing, just listened to the words he'd spoken in a tone of such flat certainty, playing them over and over in her head to the accompaniment of the steady thumping of her heart. Funny, she mused, how unbelievable things become quite believable when they are actually happening to you.

Presently she took a breath and said, "Well. Since you're fairly sure now that it wasn't me, and since we have the painting right here, don't you think perhaps we should examine it?''

She felt minute air currents, stirred by his almost silent amusement. "We?''

"It is," she stiffly reminded him, "still my painting. You're welcome to remove this...whatever it is that's supposed to be inside, but I intend to make sure it doesn't get damaged in the process.''

He snorted and muttered, "Damaged..." Then, grudgingly, "Well, okay, here—hold the light.''

He switched on the flashlight and gave it to her, sending shadows leaping over the mounds of shrouded household belongings and across the ceiling of the van. Jane trained the doughnut of yellow light on Tom's chest and held it steady while he lifted his arms and swiveled his upper body in order to reach the package he'd placed on top of the appliances behind him. As he did so, the brown leather jacket he was wearing pulled up and bunched across his shoulders, leaving a gap between its bottom edge and the top of his trousers. She made an involuntary hiccuping noise. The beam of light wobbled.

"You have a gun," she said.

"You bet," Hawk responded with a muffled grunt. He said nothing more while he lifted down the package containing the painting and placed it flat across his knees. Then he looked for her across the thin stream of light, and his lips quirked sideways in a smile. "What did you expect?"

He could barely make out her features in the reflected glow of the beam she'd pinned to his chest. In the deep shadows, her eyes seemed as unfathomable and mysterious as the sea by moonlight. So when she spoke, it was odd to hear her voice sound so normal, as everyday-normal as a housewife discussing roses with the gardener.

"I'm kind of glad, actually. I mean, if there are killers around... What kind is it?"

He had to hand it to her; she was nothing if not resilient. "A Walther 9-millimeter," he said as he took it from its nest, double-checked the safety and placed it on top of the brown-paper parcel across his knees. She skewered it with the light beam but made no move to touch it.

"I'm afraid I don't know very much about guns," she said after a moment. "Real ones, anyway. This one certainly looks, uh, effective. Mine, by the way—" and from the sound of her voice, she had to be saying this with an absolutely straight face "—happens to be a genuine Roy Rogers six-shooter revolver. It fires real caps."

"Don't tell me," said Hawk in a strangled voice, "you brought it with you?"

"You bet. What did you expect? It's right there in my tote bag."

Laughter bumped around inside his chest, wanting out. He clamped down on it, made an exasperated hissing noise instead and returned his pistol to its resting place at the small of his back. "Just do us both a favor and leave it there, okay?" he muttered, adding a few choice words and "get us both killed," under his breath.

There was no response from Jane, no sound or movement at all. He paused with his fingers under the taped edges of the painting's paper wrappings to glance over at her, wondering about her sudden stillness, and saw that her head appeared to be tilted slightly, as if she heard voices.

"What?" he asked, oddly unnerved. Her shadowed eyes seemed to be staring right through him.

Her voice came from a distance, with an odd lilt to it. "How did you know?"

"Know what?"

"How did you know I was standing there, in the light, with the gun? I remember you said you saw the other guy running out of my room with the painting. But that was after he'd knocked me down. So, how could you know?"

Hawk silently indulged in his favorite cussword and added every other vile phrase he could think of, for good measure. Aloud he had to content nimself with, "Hell, I don't know, put two and two together, I guess. Wasn't exactly hard—the damn gun was on the floor and so were you."

The lie made him squirm, like having an itchy spot he couldn't reach. He wished he knew why he so hated the idea of her ever finding out that he was the one who'd put her on the floor. It had seemed like the best strategy at the time, and a whole lot more reliable and a lot less painful than slugging her in the jaw. Now, though, remembering the feel of her body struggling, pinned under his knee, and her pulse surging against his fingers...it made him feel sick to think about it.

So, Hawkins, you'd rather have been kneeling in her blood, the way you did Loizeau's, and feeling for a pulse that wasn't there?

Angry with himself for allowing those doubts, and annoyed with her for raising them in the first place, he snarled, "You want to watch this, or not? Put the damn light where my hands are!"

"I do," she replied evenly, "and I am." Something in the way she said it made him feel pretty certain she hadn't bought his explanation for what had taken place last night in her room. Not for a minute. That was the trouble with nice women who were also people's mothers, he thought gloomily. They were too damn hard to lie to.

The masking tape was loose—the painting had already been unwrapped once—so the brown-paper wrappings came apart easily. Hawk quickly folded and laid them aside. He barely glanced at the painting itself, having seen it the night before, but once more turned it facedown across his thighs. It was as he remembered, heavy pinkish-brown paper covering the entire back of the painting, apparently glued to the frame. He hitched himself up and dug in his pants pocket for his knife. He heard her make a small ambiguous sound as he slid the tip of the pocketknife under the edge of the brown-paper backing. When he had it loosened on three sides, he folded the knife and slipped it back in his pocket. He could feel his heart beating. Hell, he could *hear* it. He wondered if she could, too.

Oh so carefully, he lifted the paper and folded it back. Under it was a pale rectangle of canvas.

"Lemme see that light," he said gruffly, snatching it from Jane's outstretched hand.

Then all he could hear was the harsh sound of his own breathing as he bent over the painting and examined every inch of brown paper, every square millimeter of canvas, every sliver and grain of wooden frame. Nothing. He'd expected—hoped—to find a computer disk; unable to accept the truth, he searched now for...something—anything—a slip of paper, a code word, a number. He felt with his fingertips for the slightest irregularity, took out his pocketknife again and probed the wooden frame for hollow places. He peeled off the framer's label and searched it for some kind of clue, a microdot. *Anything.*

Finally, ice-cold and light-headed, he raised his eyes and the flashlight beam to Jane's face and croaked, "Where is it?"

Her eyes blinked at him, silvery and unfocused in the light. One hand fluttered into the path of the beam like a large pale moth, trying to shield her eyes from the glare. He grabbed it, imprisoning her wrist.

"Dammit, where is it?" His teeth were clenched so tightly he thought his skull would split. "When did you find it? Last night? You...took it out...you must have put it somewhere. *Tell me, damn you!*"

He couldn't hear anything but the roaring in his ears, but he could see her shaking her head, see her lips forming the word, "No, no, no..."

It was the terror in her eyes that got to him, finally. He let go of her hand, throwing it away from him, almost, that small act of violence the only ember he allowed to escape the firestorm raging inside him. Utterly defeated, he leaned his head back against the washing machine and switched off the flashlight.

And now, in the darkness, he could hear her whispering, "I didn't take anything, I swear. If you'll just think a minute..."

He shook his head, not wanting to hear anything she had to say, primarily because he knew she was right. She hadn't taken anything out of the painting. How could she have? The backing had been glued on, and it obviously hadn't been tampered with. He'd had to remove it with a knife. But he didn't want to hear her, because then he'd have to face the alternative. He'd have to think about the unthinkable. Accept the unacceptable.

"I'm sorry," he said, his voice dull and flat. "I was out of line."

There was no answer, no sound at all from Jane. He could feel her hurt withdrawal, like a dog he'd just kicked.

He closed his eyes and tried to force his brain to grapple with this new turn of events, but he suddenly felt overwhelmed, exhausted. He'd been following this trail for days now, with little or no sleep, a trail he'd first picked up in Jarek Singh's ransacked apartment on the outskirts of Cairo. Noticing that slight discoloration on Singh's wall—that had been his first break. After that, tracking the missing painting to the antiques dealer in Marseilles had been easy. Finding Loizeau dead had been a setback, but then he'd managed to lift the information about the auction from the blotter. Rathskeller's Lot #187—March 22. He knew he wasn't mistaken about that. Yesterday—that was the twenty-second, Rathskeller's auction in Arlington, Virginia.

And *this painting*—his hands curled, gripping the wooden frame with sudden fury—dammit, *this* painting was Lot #187. He'd made no mistake about that, either. So where had he gone wrong? He'd lost the trail somewhere, but he couldn't for the life of him think where. *Where, dammit?*

A small sound broke his tenuous concentration, collapsing his careful progression of thoughts like a pebble tossed into a house of cards. Jane, clearing her throat. Though her voice was still rusty with uncertainty when she said, "Hmm...Tom? Can I ask...can you tell me what it is, exactly, that you're looking for?''

He shifted irritably, resenting the hell out of her at that moment, just wanting to be left to his own misery. But he owed her something for the way he'd treated her, grabbing her like that, scaring her to death. He really did regret that—more than he liked to think about—but it was too late to take it back now.

So he tried to soften his tone, and managed a grudging gruffness when he replied, ''I'm not exactly sure. Computer disk, probably. Maybe just an access code. I don't know. Just that it was supposed to be in this painting, Lot #187... What? Did you say something?''

He switched on the flashlight. Her face seemed to float in the light, disembodied and pale as the moon, the tips of her fingers barely touching her lips.

''I just thought of something,'' she said, still hesitant at first, but gaining confidence as she went on. ''I don't know if it's important, or if it makes any sense, but, well, I'm not exactly sure that painting was supposed to be number 187.''

''What do you mean?'' He felt a stillness, as though even his heart and all his body functions had paused to listen to her answer.

''When I first saw it, when I marked it down in my catalog, you know, so I'd know which one to bid on... I don't remember now what the number was, but I'm absolutely certain it wasn't 187.'' She hesitated, waiting for him to comment. But he didn't trust himself to speak, and she went on in a nervous rush, sensing the tension in him, perhaps, the words tumbling from her like pebbles before an avalanche.

''I think there must have been some kind of mix-up—my friend Connie said it happens sometimes—anyway, I wasn't expecting it to come up in the bidding until later, and I was just about to go to the snack bar to get something to drink. If Connie hadn't spotted it just in time, and told me about it, I'd have missed bidding for it.''

''Whoa,'' he croaked. ''Back up a minute. Some kind of mix-up? Like what, exactly? You mean, a *switch?*'' His heart had resumed beating, hard and fast. Alarm bells were clanging inside his head. *A switch.* Jeez Louise, one of the oldest tricks in the book.

"Well," Jane said, "it seemed like it would be easy to do. In the catalog, all the paintings were listed the same—just, Oil Painting, Framed, or something like that—and then the lot number. So I guess if—"

"And the lot number—how was it attached to the painting? Some kind of tag, sticker, what?"

"A sticker—on the bottom edge of the frame. It was pretty small. I remember I had to—"

"I don't remember any sticker. Here. Take this." He thrust the light into her hands and began to turn the painting over, turning it upside down and around, even though he'd already been over the damn thing with a fine-tooth comb and knew perfectly well there'd been no sticker on it, large or small.

"It was there last night." Her voice was breathless, as if his agitation was contagious. "I'm sure of it. Maybe it fell off. Check the wrappings." The light beam danced, alighting like a butterfly on the brown paper he'd folded and set to one side.

And a moment later came a satisfied, "*There* it is." Her hand darted into the light to pluck from the sea of brown a white rectangle of paper half the size of a postage stamp. "See? I knew it had to be here." She handed it to him, saying, "No wonder it fell off. It's not sticky at all. That's probably what happened, don't you think? Maybe it happened to more than one item, and the auction employees just stuck them back on as best they could, figuring no one would notice."

Hawk grunted. "Yeah, right." He was squinting at the sticker, holding it between the nails of his thumb and forefinger. "Hey, let me see that pistol you bought—you did mean it when you said you have it with you?"

"Right here."

He could hear her scuffling around in the dark. A moment later, the silver Colt revolver poked into the puddle of light. He gave her a look as he took it from her, wondering if she knew she'd handed it to him butt-first and carefully, as if it was a real gun, and loaded. Strange woman.

The lot-number sticker was still on the butt end of the pistol, right where he remembered seeing it when he'd picked it up from the floor in her hotel room last night. It was stuck on good, so good he had to scratch with his fingernail to peel up one corner. So good there was no way in hell one could have come unstuck by accident.

Wishing to God he had a pair of tweezers, he tore off a piece of the brown wrapping paper and dropped the numbered sticker onto the middle of it, then folded it into a credit card–size packet and tucked it carefully away in his wallet. If he ever got out of this damn truck, he'd see that the boys at Quantico got a look at it. Who knows, maybe they'd get lucky, turn up a print, although in reality the chances of that were pretty slim.

No, his best bet was going to be to backtrack to that auction house, try to pick up the buyer of the other painting. The *original* number 187. Unless the guy had pulled a multiple switch, in which case he'd have to track down every one of those damn paintings. He was going to have to call in help, of course, but even so, the odds were, by the time they got to it, the key to Jarek Singh's computer files would be long gone on its way to the highest bidder, in another sort of auction altogether. The thought of that happening chilled him to his very bones.

"Any chance of you remembering that other number?" he asked without much hope. He felt very tired.

Jane made a small sound, either a sigh or a stifled yawn. "Probably not. I have a terrible memory for numbers. But I could look it up in my catalog for you, if you like."

Hawk, whose last remaining hopes had collapsed with her first sentence, didn't know whether to strangle or kiss her. Well, to be truthful, he did know. And it was surprising the hell out of him, the way that notion kept popping into his mind.

"That would be nice," he said with polite irony. Then he added, as she instantly began digging in her tote bag again, "I didn't mean *now*. No point in it. Why don't you wait until we've got some light?"

"Oh—okay." She paused, her hands and the flashlight draped over her tote bag, to say thoughtfully, "So, I guess whoever bought the other painting, the one with my number on it…must have this disk, or whatever. Is that what you think?"

"Looks like it."

Jane was silent, chewing her lip, her shadowed, unreadable gaze directed away from him, staring at nothing. But something about her seemed to radiate tension; Hawk's own heightened senses picked it up, like the subtle vibrations of electricity near power lines. A tiny chill of warning crept across his skin, the way it always did when he knew someone was lying to him. But he thought, No, not Jane. And ignored the sensation, putting it down to nerves, frustration, his own general antsyness.

"If we could just get out of this damn truck!" The vehemence in her voice as she spoke his own desire out loud surprised him; she'd seemed so unflappable up till now.

"Yeah, well, nothing we can do until they stop," he reminded her. "Meanwhile, why don't you turn that thing off, save the batteries? Try and get some sleep."

She made a funny, high sound, like a laugh—as in, "Are you *kidding?*" But she didn't say a word about being hungry, or thirsty, or wanting to use a bathroom, or any number of other things she must have been in need of. He knew he sure was—all of the above.

The light went out. A few moments of silence ticked by, filled with the rhythmic thrumming of the truck's tires on pavement. And then she began to sing softly, huskily, "'Hello, darkness, my old friend...'"

It had been one of Jen's favorite songs. She'd loved Simon and Garfunkel.

What the hell's going on? Hawk's heart was pounding. Who the hell *was* this Carlysle woman, anyway? And why was it every time she opened her mouth, one way or another she seemed to say something that made him feel as if he'd been punched in the gut?

I sure didn't count on this, he thought as he stared into the blackness above his head.

And then he wasn't certain what he meant by that. Because he hadn't counted on a lot of things. He hadn't counted on Jane Carlysle, for one, and the way he kept seeing her face in his mind, and thinking about how good it would feel to touch her. To make love to her, yes, but also, and much more incomprehensibly, just to hold her, and go to sleep with her wrapped in his arms.

He also hadn't counted on running into memories of Jen every time he turned around. It couldn't help but occur to him to wonder if the two were somehow connected.

For almost seven years he'd kept those memories locked away in the deepest, darkest dungeons of his soul, ruthlessly squelching every attempt they'd made to break free. Now, suddenly, ever since the moment this woman had entered his life, somehow or another things kept reminding him of Jen.

He didn't know why, either; she didn't look at all like Jenny...well, except maybe in a superficial way. Both had dark hair worn short and curly, and were on the tall side of medium height. But Jen's eyes had been golden brown, warm and intriguing, the color of brandy, not the sea. And where Jane had a certain quietness about her that seemed to invite confidences, Jenny had been feisty, with that arrogance he'd fallen for the very first time he'd laid eyes on her.

He found himself smiling even now, in the darkness, thinking of the way she'd pranced out on that diving board....

Smiling? How was it that a memory of Jenny could make him smile? But hurt, too, way down deep inside. What was happening to him?

Whatever it was, he wasn't ready for it. The timing couldn't be worse.

"Carlysle?" There was no answer. But even though he thought she was probably asleep, he went ahead, in a voice he didn't know. "Just wanted to say thanks."

There was more he'd meant to say, more he should have said, but hell, she wasn't going to hear it anyway. Just as well. Evidently she'd been tired enough to override all her discomforts, after all. Let her sleep, he thought. He'd take the first watch—he didn't want to risk being asleep when the damn truck finally did stop.

Chapter 9

Jane was very tired but too keyed up to sleep. It had been a long time since she'd experienced so many emotions, a roller coaster of emotions, in such a short span of time. Right now she didn't know *what* to feel. She didn't know what to think.

And she didn't *want* to think. The notion that had come to her was so...unthinkable. And so persistent. It kept tapping her on the shoulder, trying to get her attention, and she kept pushing it away, telling herself, No...it can't be. It's ridiculous. I won't believe it.

But how else to explain everything? It all *fit*.

She supposed that what she felt more than anything, besides hungry, of course, was frightened. She actually had knots in her stomach—though that could have been hunger. But she didn't think so. And she kept shivering, with a deep-down-inside cold that had nothing to do with the temperature of the van.

"Carlysle?" Again Tom Hawkins probed the blackness with what he probably imagined was a whisper. "Hey—you cold? You're shivering."

She didn't want to answer, afraid that if she did she might have to give voice to her thoughts. *Terrible thoughts. Impossible thoughts.* She fought to control the trembling, tried to make her breathing slow and deep and even.

She heard rustlings, felt Tom moving around next to her, felt the faintest brush of air against her cheeks. And then something warm came across her arms and chest, settled around her shoulders, enveloped her like a warm bath, seeped through her insides like a cup of cocoa on a cold morning. It smelled strongly of tobacco, and old leather and man. It was Tom's jacket. He'd taken off his own jacket and put it over her.

A curious warmth crept over her, and again it had nothing to do with temperature. It was more like a sunrise, the warmth that comes from light, touched with wonder, a revelation of sorts. When had anyone ever done such a thing for her before? She tried hard to remember. Certainly David never had.

It's the little things, she thought for the second time that day.

And then she wondered if she'd been wrong about that, and whether maybe those things, the thoughtful little gestures, like holding a cigarette so the smoke doesn't blow in someone's face, the caring touch of a jacket selflessly shared...maybe those were the biggest things of all.

She'd never been able to explain, to her own or anyone else's satisfaction, just what it was that had driven her to tell David, on the eve of their twenty-first wedding anniversary, that she wanted a divorce. She remembered that David had asked her, still in shock and disbelief, "Why? What have I done? Have I ever abused you, been unfaithful to you? *What?*" So many of her friends, and even her mother, had suggested she was only suffering the normal discontent of middle age. How she'd come to loathe the term "midlife crisis."

Oddly enough, it had been the two people closest to, and most affected by, the breakup who'd been the most supportive of her decision. As much as they loved their dad, Lynn and Tracy had always seemed to understand. Never once had they contributed to Jane's already overwhelming burden of guilt. She'd always wondered if it was perhaps because they'd been old enough to witness and judge from a woman's perspective rather than a child's. Because, already experimenting with relationships of their own, they'd sensed on an almost instinctive level the soul-crushing loneliness she'd suffered in hers.

Married, Jane had been the most "alone" person she knew,

a single in a world of couples. She'd never even known what it *felt* like to be a couple. Other married people she knew always seemed to refer to themselves as "us," or "we." Jane had never thought of herself and David that way. How could she, when every decision, all the work and worry and responsibility involving the children and household had been hers and hers alone? David's world and only concern had been his work, his business, and it had been a world he'd kept separate and secret from his wife, guarded as jealously as a miser hoards his riches.

After so many years, she'd stopped questioning the way things were between them, even made little jokes about it: "Oh, yes, David and I get along great, as long as we don't do anything together!" And she'd known all along that *something,* something important, was missing.

But this is what I wanted, she thought as she lay awake in the swaying moving van, steeped in the warmth and wonder of Tom Hawkins's old leather jacket. This is what I meant when I told David I wanted a chance before it was too late. A chance...to feel loved. A chance to feel cherished. Valued. *This.*

The "little" things? But that's what makes it all work. Things like this. Now I know.

And she thought how ironic it was, and how *damned* unfair that she should have to learn this from a stranger, a man just passing through her life, this man from Interpol with eyes like broken promises and a face that looked as if it had been caught between a rock and a hard place.

The van had stopped again. It had done so before, briefly, but not under circumstances where it would have been advisable, or even possible, to attract someone's attention by pounding on the doors. Twice they'd gone over scales, and once over what Hawk was almost certain was a very long bridge, or perhaps a causeway. Since then their progress had been slow, stop-and-go, which made him fairly sure they were no longer on the interstate, and therefore, logic told him, most likely nearing their destination.

And then the truck's tires had rumbled across something hollow-sounding—another bridge perhaps? But no, too short to be a bridge. And now at last the van sat almost motionless, the floor vibrating with the idling purr of the tractor's powerful diesel engine. Far off and very faintly, he heard a door slam.

"Carlysle," he said hoarsely, nudging the part of her closest to him, which he suspected was, once again, her bottom. Thumbing on the flashlight, he confirmed that yes, she had scooted herself down and was sleeping curled on her side with her head pillowed on her tote bag, and that it was indeed her fanny tucked in cozily against his thighs.

He leaned across the swell of her hip and pulled the collar of his jacket away from her face. She stirred, and he said again, "Carlysle—hey, wake up. Rise and shine."

And then, for some reason, he left the light there and watched her come awake, watched her features warm and liven and become magically, uniquely Jane, while thoughts and emotions flitted through his head like bats in the twilight. Thoughts that came and went too quickly to identify, emotions he wouldn't have wanted to hold on to even if he could have managed to capture them. *I want...I wish... No! I don't. I don't.*

He realized that she was squinting, blinking in protest at the light, and moved it to one side. "Hate to wake you," he said gruffly, "but it looks like we may be getting out of here soon. Thought you might want to, uh, make yourself presentable."

"Mmm, thanks." She hitched herself around and sat up, coming out of his jacket like a kitten out of its nest, first one arm, then the other. He watched each hand in turn perform the little touching, patting gestures women use to put themselves to rights as she murmured, "I really didn't expect to sleep. Have we really stopped? What time is it, do you know?"

"About five, last time I looked."

"Five—in the evening? My goodness, I must have slept several hours, at least. Did you sleep at all? You really should have woke me."

He shook his head and said, "That's okay, I probably wouldn't have slept anyway." He watched her fidget, locating her tote bag, tugging at her clothes. Watched her identify and recognize his jacket, pull it slowly down and across her lap, her hands straightening and shaping it, her fingers lingering in the buttery softness of it, almost caressing.

"It was very nice of you to give me this," she said, and the husky burr of her voice rubbed against his nerves like fur. "Thank you. I hope you weren't cold because of it."

He coughed and said, "Nah...keep it if you want to. I'm warm enough."

"Thanks, but...I really am fine now." She was holding it out to him. "It's a very nice jacket. Nice and warm."

He took it from her, grunting a little as he shrugged it on. "It was my father's," he heard himself say. And surprised himself even more by continuing, "I'd always wanted one like it when I was a kid. I just sort of...confiscated it after he died. Sometimes I think I can almost still smell him."

And now it was warm from *her* body, and if he closed his eyes he could catch just the barest hint of her elusive scent....

His stomach rumbled loudly.

"I'm hungry, too," she instantly responded in that comfortable, unflappable way she had as she was rummaging around in her tote bag. Producing a brush, or anyway one of those things with plastic spikes instead of bristles that women seem to use nowadays, she began to rake it briskly through her hair. "And I could sure use a potty. Do you think anyone would hear us if we banged on the door?"

"Don't know," said Hawk. "I thought I heard the truck's doors slam, but haven't heard anything since."

She'd finished with the brush and was poking it back into the depths of her bag, although as near as he could see in that light it hadn't done much to change the way those curls of hers wanted to lie along her neck and around her ears and temples. He decided not to tell her about the endearing little flip that stubbornly persisted on the side she'd slept on, and which for some reason made his fingers itch with the urge to touch it.

"Well, I'm ready if you are," she said, puffing slightly as she struggled to unwrap her feet and disentangle her legs from the mounds of packing blankets. That accomplished, she heaved herself upright, holding on to the piano for support. He heard her say with a laugh and a groan, "Mercy, I'm stiff!"

Hurriedly freeing himself from his own swaddlings, he joined her, still in his stocking feet. He was stiff, too, though his ego didn't let him say so, and he tried to get in a few limbering-up stretches as best he could in that cramped space. The flashlight's batteries were noticeably weakening; he turned it off and jammed it into his jacket pocket. "Okay, here goes," he muttered.

An instant later he froze, his upraised fist suspended in darkness.

"What's *that?*" gasped Jane.

The long, drawn-out, deep-throated bellow was a familiar sound to Hawk. As it died, he clutched her arm and hissed, "Shush!" although she hadn't said another word. Because now he could hear what he'd missed before—beneath the gravelly growl of the truck's diesel was another, deeper, rhythmic throbbing. A second and even more powerful engine.

"Hear that?" He said it with a note of triumph. Now he knew, or was fairly certain he knew, where they were and where they were going. "You know where we are? We're on a ferryboat. That's what this is—a damned ferryboat!"

"A...ferryboat?" Her voice sounded faint and worried.

"Yeah." He chuckled exultantly, his hand traveling up her arm and along her shoulder to the back of her neck, to give her what he thought he meant to be a friendly and reassuring little squeeze. "Can you believe that? Now, the bad news is, everybody's probably gone topside, so there's not going to be anybody to hear us if we holler. The *good* news is, we've got to be pretty close to where we're going."

"How do you know?" It burst from her with a lot of breath, as if she'd been holding it.

It occurred to him just then, if he were to ease his hand across, say, to her opposite shoulder, and turn her a little bit, he'd have her neatly in his arms. It seemed so right, so easy, almost as if it was meant to happen just that way.

"Think about it," he snapped, self-discipline making him testy. "Where do ferries go?"

"On water," said Jane in a dismal voice.

"Across water," he smugly corrected. "To islands, mostly. And the only reason this eighteen-wheeler is going to be sitting on a ferry is if that's the only way to get there, right?" If memory served him, there was only one set of islands served by ferry that was about six hours or so driving time from Washington, D.C. "Mrs. Carlysle, I'll bet you a fresh seafood dinner as soon as we get out of this box that we're in North Carolina. The Outer Banks, to be exact."

Jane's response was utter silence. Then a tiny gulp—an audible swallow, and a whispered, "Oh."

"So," he expounded, feeling pleased with his powers of deduction, "way I figure it, we've got maybe forty-five minutes or so for the crossing, then no more than fifteen, twenty minutes, tops, to get wherever we're going. These islands aren't very big, and it's the off-season, so there's not going to be much traffic. We should be out of here in—"

And then she did turn, of her own accord. And she was in his arms, but not quite in the way he'd imagined. Trembling, but not the way he would have liked, which was in response to, or hunger for, his touch. Her arms were doubled up again, making a barrier between them, in fact, and her hands must have been pressed against her mouth, because her voice came small and muffled.

"I get seasick."

Though they weren't exactly words he wanted to hear, he found his arms going around her, and felt an indulgent, unfamiliar tenderness. Soothingly, he said, "The crossing shouldn't be rough this time of—"

"I get seasick tied to the dock."

All Hawk could think of to say was, "Uh...well..."

"It usually helps if I can watch the horizon, but in here..."

"Don't panic." That was for his benefit. To her, he said calmly, "The best thing to do is, don't dwell on it. Think of something else."

She was gripping his arms, shaking her head; he could feel the tickle of her hair across his lips. Her voice was hushed and breathy. "I'm sorry. I'm just not good with boats. I grew up in the Mojave Desert. I saw the beach for the first time when I was twelve. I've only been—"

"It's okay..." Soothing words, comforting chuckles. But he found that his chest felt as bumpy inside as her voice sounded, as if something vital that held everything else together had broken loose. His hands were just lightly stroking her arms, her shoulders. But he wanted...needed...he *knew* that if he could only hold her close, hold her tightly, that the hollow, shaken feeling inside him would ease. His jaw ached with the effort it cost him to keep her that small, essential distance away.

"I guess you don't, huh? Get seasick?"

Her arms had relaxed a little; he could feel her hands on his chest, her fingers playing with the textures of his cable-knit sweater. He snorted softly and said, "I live on a boat."

And realized that with those five words he'd revealed more about his living arrangements than he ever did, even to casual friends and the people he worked with, much less to total strangers.

Although...he wasn't sure Jane Carlysle would still fit that latter category, after the way they'd spent the past few hours. He was surprised to discover he didn't want her to. He just didn't know quite how to make that metamorphosis from stranger to...something else. It had been too long since he'd even tried.

Her response to his revelation was, "You're kidding!" It was spoken not in the tone of flat dismay he might have expected, but with the interested *quickening* in her voice that went with that sudden brightening he knew would also be there, now, in her eyes. He cursed the darkness for making him miss it. He realized he'd come to watch for it the same way he watched for dolphins leaping in the sunlit sea.

Maybe that was why, when she asked him where his boat was, he told her. In fact, he told her about many of the places he'd tied up, never for too long at a time. And he told her, with a touch of undeniable pride, about his '46 Grand Banks classic with the teakwood trim, two staterooms and galley down, twin CAT 3208TA's, and all the options, including a big generator and full electronics.

"What's her name?" she asked.

"No name," he told her. He'd never found one that suited.

"Like Cat," she murmured, and he could feel her nodding. "In *Breakfast at Tiffany's*."

He wondered if she knew they were under way. If she didn't, he sure wasn't going to be the one to tell her.

"How wonderful it must be, to live on a boat," she said. "So...adventurous." It may have been the darkness, or he may have imagined it, but he thought she sounded wistful.

Well, it did have its moments. He wanted to tell her about the dolphins, and about seeing double rainbows after a summer squall, and about a little cove he knew of on an island off the coast of Maine where the pines came right down to the water's edge and the smell of the woods and the sea on an autumn morning was like the finest champagne. But he didn't.

He cleared his throat and said, "Well, to tell you the truth, I'm not at home all that much."

"So," she said, "I guess you must not be married."

"No."

"But you were." She said it softly, and with such certainty.

He didn't ask her how she knew, just replied, "Yes."

It was then he discovered that his left hand had not stayed in its safe, friendly berth on her shoulder, that while he'd been busy navigating perilous conversational shoals it had gone wandering off on an even more hazardous quest of its own. That his palm now curved around the side of her neck, his fingertips flirted with the curls on her nape and his thumb was beginning an exploration of the ridge of her jaw and the velvety curve of her cheek. From out of nowhere a pulse began to pound in his belly, like an impromptu solo from a surprised but eager drummer.

He couldn't for the life of him figure which would be more dangerous, the turn the conversation had taken, or the direction his wandering hand was leading him. He did know that if she asked one more question, the next obvious question, he was going to find himself churning through some emotional rapids he wasn't at all sure he was ready to handle yet. On the other hand, he'd kissed plenty of women before, and never had a problem handling the consequences.

Then again, he'd never kissed Jane Carlysle.

He would have liked to think that he'd reasoned it all out like that ahead of time, and that what happened next was a carefully planned tactical maneuver on his part, a diversion and nothing more. He certainly tried his best to justify it that way afterward. But, there was that delighted little drummer in his belly, the pounding of it a thunder in his ears that completely drowned all thought. And there was her lip, full and vibrant against the sensitive pad of his thumb. So in the end, when he felt her lips part and the moist warmth of her breath bathe his skin, he put his mouth there simply because, like taking his next breath, it seemed impossible not to.

A second or two later, Hawk knew he was in big trouble. If he'd thought that by substituting physical intimacy he could avoid the emotional, he'd miscalculated—badly. And if he'd thought that just because it was dark he could forget that crinkly fan of lines at the corners of her eyes, or the compassion, or the warmth of her smile, well, that was another mistake.

There was the "nice" smell of her, the earthy, womanly feel of her body against him, so familiar and yet so long denied it seemed utterly and completely new. He knew then that kissing this woman could never be just a physical thing. That with her, the physical and emotional were inextricably tangled, and that, far from steering himself a safe course around the maelstrom, he'd suddenly found himself capsized, in up to his neck and swimming for his life.

Odd, though, that with so much going on inside him, the kiss was such a gentle thing.

It seemed almost as if she'd expected it. There was no gasp of surprise, no initial resistance, but no overwhelming response, either. Neither advancing nor retreating, she simply accepted, with a faint, almost inaudible sigh, asking of him no more than he wanted to give her. Her lips were warm and compliant, denying him nothing, and yet he sensed she held most of her *self,* her passions and feelings, in reserve. He drew away from her, finally, feeling vaguely frustrated and emotionally battered.

She whispered, "Did you do that to distract me?"

His first reaction was to mutter epithets under his breath, and he remembered how she'd laughed at him the last time he'd tried to put a move on her. He also remembered the elbow to the solar plexis that had dropped that Campbell guy in his tracks, and he thought that she sure did have a way of catching a man off guard and with his defenses down.

Then he realized, belatedly, that she'd thrown him a lifeline.

He reached for it with a grateful laugh and asked, "Is it working?"

She considered in silence for a moment. "Hmm. Apparently. I'm not upchucking all down your front, anyway."

"Don't know when I've had a more enthusiastic testimonial," said Hawk cheerfully. And after a pause, "Want to do it again?"

She gave the smallest of shrugs and said, "Sure."

So it was on that basis that he was able to put aside the emotional baggage, finally, and just enjoy her on a purely physical level. By deluding himself, and her, too, into believing, for the moment, at least, that it was only an exercise in psychology, a recreational diversion. The thing he was best at—a game.

As games went, it was engrossing, to say the least. One hell of a diversion, recreational or otherwise. Having given himself permission to indulge in lust he made the most of it, and was gratified to discover that she was no slouch at this particular game herself. In fact, when he finally did come up for air, he figured he'd pretty much have to call it a draw.

"How're we doin'?" he inquired in a thick mumble, leaning his forehead against hers and stroking her shoulders in a solicitous sort of way. For his part, the answer to that would be, not great; his tongue was something fat and furry, and his heart was beating way too fast.

"Still okay, I think." But her voice wasn't steady.

She tilted her face up and he ducked his head to meet her mouth once more, this time like a thirsty man going for his cup. She gave a little sigh and her arms came around him. His slipped into place around her, and her body eased in against him like a perfect, sweet meshing of well-oiled gears.

He felt a tremor run through her...the *right* kind of tremor. And before he could do a thing to stop it or control it, a violent shudder caught him and rocked him to his toes. He felt a rolling shock wave of heat and pressure, heard the thunder of his own blood in his ears. Nothing to do then but go with it...

A low growl vibrated through his chest as he shifted his arms and caught her hard against him, making her feel all the heat and strength and power in his body, making her know, on the most primitive of levels, his maleness and her own femininity.

She gave a strange little cry; her head fell back and her mouth opened still more under his, both a surrender and an invitation. He took advantage of it with a single, fierce thrust, found the deepest and most perfect melding, the mating of mouths that is unmistakably symbolic of, and almost always a prelude to, the joining of bodies.

Of course, that kind of kiss has only two possible conclusions: complete satisfaction, or total frustration. Hawk knew that going in. He also knew, given the circumstances, that there wasn't much doubt which way this one was going to wind up. So all he could do, finally, was peel himself away from her, feeling tense and creaky as an overwound watch, mentally kicking himself and swearing under his breath.

He listened to the sounds of their breathing, like storm surf lashing against rock, and waited for her to say something. He could have bet money it wouldn't be anything expected. And it wasn't.

"Well," she said after a careful clearing of her throat, "I suppose this is private enough. But I don't imagine it's quite what you had in mind, is it?"

He was still so jangled he wasn't sure he'd heard her right. He even laughed a little before he realized he didn't have any idea what she was talking about. Still chuckling uncertainly, he said, "I beg your pardon?"

"This morning. You said, *when* you kissed me, you wanted it to be private enough...I think you said, for what comes after. But I don't think this is what you meant."

He had no idea how to answer her.

"Of course," she went on, her voice shaken and raspy, but gentle in the darkness, a reminder to him both of the kind of woman she was and of the shameful way he'd just used her, "I know you didn't mean it, then—about kissing me. I know you were just trying to find a way to stay close to me—or to the painting, rather. Funny, isn't it, how things work out sometimes?"

His stomach was roiling and coiling—the watch spring coming unwound. He snapped, "For God's sake, Jen." And stopped, shock freezing his insides.

He couldn't have done that. Couldn't have said what he thought he'd said. Could he? Even with the echoes reverberating through his entire being, he didn't believe it. Had she noticed? What would she think? He waited, paralyzed by a wholly uncharacteristic panic, for her to say something. Anything. It seemed like forever.

In fact, it was only a second or two. And it had just entered his head that he'd never mentioned Jen's name to her at all, and that she'd probably only think, at worst, that he'd gotten hers wrong, when there was a loud, echoing *clang* outside the truck, only a foot or two from where they were standing. Hawk's favorite all-purpose epithet was drowned out by an ear-shredding screech, and then the door of the van was rolled violently back, letting in the cold fresh smell of the sea and the rosy pink light of sunset.

And a voice belonging to a large man wearing dark green coveralls and carrying a crowbar, a cracking, high-pitched Southern voice, tense with fear, suspicion and surprise: "Hey! What the hell's goin' on here?"

Chapter 10

"What nice guys," Jane said as she paused to wave at the moving van lumbering off in the direction of the harbor.

Tom, who was holding the door for her, merely grunted. She cast him one quick glance as she slipped past him into the warmth and bustle of the restaurant, but he was avoiding her eyes.

She sighed inwardly and wondered, as she often did, why things always had to be so difficult between men and women, and why, in her case, at least, she always had to be the one to smooth things out, make things work. I'm just as tired and hungry as he is, she thought resentfully. And I didn't exactly ask to be mixed up in all this.

She thought it was reasonable enough that Tom had been moody and preoccupied since they'd left the ferry terminal. Jane had emerged from the ladies' rest room to find him hunched over the pay phone, his face looking like a thundercloud. She'd figured he was probably checking in with his superiors, or headquarters, or whoever it was he answered to, filling them in on the latest developments in the case of the missing...whatever it was. Which couldn't have been very pleasant for him. In any case, she'd given him a wide berth.

And when he'd finally joined her, she'd tried hard to be cheerful and positive, making light of their situation, laughing about the moments following their discovery in the back of the moving van, barefoot and blinking, breathing hard and clinging to each other like orphaned babes in the woods. And it *had* been funny, watching the poor man—whose name, they learned, was Isaac—as Tom offered his Interpol ID and an explanation of sorts, watching his expression transform from hostile suspicion to disbelief, then to a sort of good-natured uneasiness. "As if," she'd said to Tom, "any minute he expected Allen Funt to pop out from behind all those boxes and shout, 'Smile—you're on "Candid Camera"'!"

As for what had happened between them in those minutes just before Isaac had rolled back the door of the van...well, Jane wasn't any more eager to talk about that than Tom was. At least not then. Not now. She was still too shaken; she knew she'd experienced some sort of trauma—to her body and soul, her emotions, her heart—but it was too soon to tell what the consequences were going to be. For now, she just wanted to guard and protect the wounded parts of herself as best she could.

Meanwhile, she was good, had always been good, at pretending things were normal when they were anything but, at smiling and making friendly conversation and going on as if nothing had happened.

But it had happened. Oh, it had. And she was becoming weary of carrying on the charade all alone.

The restaurant they'd chosen, of the many that lined the only highway on the island, was called Teach's Pub, a reference, Tom told her, to the notorious pirate Blackbeard, who'd supposedly been killed somewhere near here. A casual, friendly and well-lit place, it was busy on a Saturday night even in the off-season, with people calling out to each other and a basketball game going on a big-screen TV. The smells of good things cooking made Jane feel a little faint.

"Okay?" Tom asked her as they were settled at a table, with menus spread in front of them and a promise of coffee to come.

Already hungrily poring over the menu, Jane wasn't sure whether he was asking after her own well-being, or for her approval of the table. She looked up, smiling vaguely, and nodded—and found that he was meeting her eyes for the first time since they'd left the back of the moving van. Her heart shuddered and began to pound.

Okay? No, she wanted to say, of course I'm not okay. You idiot. You jerk. You dropped a hand grenade into my life, and I will never be the same.

"I wonder if they have she-crab soup here," she murmured, diving back into the menu.

They didn't, of course, so she ordered clam chowder instead.

"Is that all?" Tom asked her while the waitress hovered. "I promised you a seafood dinner."

"You *bet* me a seafood dinner," Jane said with a small smile. "And I was smart enough not to take you up on it. If I had, I guess I'd owe you one, wouldn't I? Anyway," she added, with a wider smile for the waitress as she handed back the menu, "I only have room for so much, no matter how empty I am to start with."

Tom ordered a medium-rare steak and French fries. "I'm not big on seafood," he explained in response to Jane's raised eyebrows. "Never have been."

"Funny," she said thoughtfully as she watched the waitress walk away with the menus tucked under her arm, "that you live on a boat."

"I wasn't after the fishing." She looked at him, drawn by the growl in his voice, and found that he was staring fiercely out the window now, at the jumble of umbrella tables on the deserted deck. "I was looking for a particular life-style, is all. Simple. Uncomplicated. Uncluttered."

"Solitary," murmured Jane.

His eyes flicked at her. He shifted uncomfortably as he reached for his cigarettes, looking around for No Smoking signs. Jane slid the table's ashtray over to his side, saying nothing. After he'd lit his cigarette and smoked in silence for a few minutes, he transferred that passionate glare to her and said in a cracking voice that might have been blamed on the smoke, "My wife had died."

Having already guessed as much, she only nodded and said softly, "You wanted to get away from the memories."

He didn't reply. The waitress bustled by, dropping a basket of rolls on their table in passing. Jane took one and buttered it, bit into it with a sigh. Tom smoked on in silence. Intensely aware of him, Jane chewed and swallowed, discovering only then that her throat already had a lump in it. Damn him, she thought, furious. Damn him.

She looked away, her eyes pricking with the tears she couldn't allow herself to shed. She wondered if he'd done it deliberately, picking a time and place for such revelations when emotions could not be allowed to run rampant.

Almost as if he'd heard her thoughts, he broke that charged silence with a cough and said, "About what happened—" Jane made a reflexive motion of protest, which he overrode by increasing the intensity, not the volume, of his voice "—between us, back there..."

"It's okay," said Jane faintly. "I understand." Is it better, she bleakly wondered, or worse, talking about it like this, in a crowded, well-lit place? If we were somewhere in private, would I fall apart? Make a fool of myself? Again?

Blessedly, the waitress arrived with coffee just then. Jane doctored hers with artificial sweetener and creamer and made a neat pile of the trash, conscious all the while of Tom's brooding presence across the table, and of his expression, black as the brew steaming unheeded before him. She wondered how she would swallow past the lump that was still wedged in her throat, and whether her hand would shake when she lifted her mug.

"I don't—" he said, just as she began, "I know—" And it was she who paused and said politely, "Go ahead."

He looked at her for a moment, and she thought she'd never seen eyes so intense. Then he smiled unexpectedly, his mouth slipping awry in that poignant and so familiar way of his, and he shrugged and said, "That's just it—I don't know what to say."

Jane laughed. Unevenly. I don't dare pick up my coffee, she thought. My hands will shake and I will spill it for sure. Lightly, she said, "It's okay, really. I know what you were trying to do. And congratulations—it worked very well. I didn't get seasick."

He shifted in his chair. "Well, I think there was more to it than that."

She couldn't for the life of her think what to reply. It would have been easier, she thought, if he'd just shrugged off what had happened between them in the van, made nothing of it.

Pretended it hadn't mattered. And then, perhaps, she could have done the same.

Heat engulfed her, setting her cheeks on fire. Don't do this, she pleaded silently. *Don't do this to me.*

"I think I got a little carried away," he said, lopsidedly smiling.

"I think we both did." Jane lifted her mug and, supporting it with both hands, lowered her mouth to the rim. She closed her eyes as fragrant steam misted her hot cheeks and sweet warmth filled her insides, and thought that from now on, as long as she lived, she would always remember this particular cup of coffee. Just as she remembered the piece of cherry pie that had been sitting before her when she'd uttered the words, "David, I don't want to be married to you anymore."

She lowered her cup and smiled brilliantly at the man across the table. "No big deal. Completely understandable, under the circumstances. I consider my honor unsullied, and I promise not to cringe and blush every time I look at you." *At least, I hope I won't. Oh, God, I hope.*

"I sure wouldn't want that." And studying her, he added with unexpected and devastating softness, "I'd really miss your smile."

"Here you go," the waitress trilled, blowing in like a nor'easter, dispersing the sultry, weighted atmosphere that had settled over them with gusts of good cheer and wonderful fragrances. And as she briskly deposited plates and bowls in their proper places and left them with instructions to "Enjoy your meal!," Jane thought what a relief it was, for a time, to have to deal only with a hunger so uncomplicated, and so easily assuaged.

After the waitress left, for a while they did just that, other needs put aside while they attended with silent concentration to one perhaps even more fundamental. Perhaps. Because, with an empty bowl and a full stomach, Jane found her thoughts returning to—if indeed they'd ever really left—that other hunger, the one so rudely, so voraciously awakened by the gentle press of this stranger's mouth on hers. By the weight and warmth of his body, the electrifying caress of his fingers. The hunger that, once awakened, stubbornly refused to creep back into hibernation.

Tom Hawkins... Always a fast eater, having disposed of her bowl of chowder while her companion was barely beginning his assault on his steak, she watched him narrowly through the steam from her refilled coffee cup and thought how strange it was that features so forbidding and irregular should have become, in so short a time, so pleasing to her eyes.

Man From Interpol... How alien that sounded, without reality, like the title of a book, or a movie. And how impossible now to think of him that way. Now he was just...a man, a flesh-and-blood man, in need of a shave, a shower and a good night's sleep, a man who had covered her with his jacket and watched over her while she slept, a man whose hands had touched her in intimate places, a man whose tongue she'd tasted.

A man who played games in which the stakes were human lives.

How could this have happened? she thought. *To me.*

"I think," said Hawk, pushing aside his plate and reaching for his coffee, "we'd better talk about what we're going to do." He felt much better for having a decent meal under his belt, much less off balance, much more in control. A good night's sleep, he thought with dogged optimism, and I'll be back on track again.

Jane was nodding, regarding him steadily, as she had been for a while now, across the rim of her coffee mug. She'd been hiding behind that damn mug, it seemed to him, ever since they'd sat down. Which was probably just as well. Her eyes were bad enough, dark and disturbing as the sea just before a storm, but vulnerable, too, and smudged with shadows. He wasn't sure that in his own exhausted state he would have been able to look at her mouth and have the willpower and concentration to block out the way it had felt...tasted... Or to stop himself from thinking about how much he wanted to taste her again.

He lit a cigarette, then said, "I still don't think there's much use trying to get back to the mainland tonight. It would take us till morning to get anything accomplished anyway. Better we check into a motel here, get some rest. I've, uh, arranged for a flight out in the morning."

She'd been nodding, going along with him, but when he said that, she pulled up, looking surprised. "A flight? You mean, an *airplane?*"

"Yeah, there's an airstrip here."

"Air...strip. You mean, a small plane."

He quirked a smile at her. "Little one."

She murmured, "Oh," and her eyes flicked sideways in a way that made him uneasy.

"Don't tell me—you get airsick."

Her eyes were wide, the smudges under them making her seem very young and apprehensive, like a child contemplating a Ferris wheel. "I don't know. I've never been in a little plane before."

He felt a sudden and unsettling tenderness toward her, which probably accounted for the brusqueness with which he said, "Hey—don't worry. You're gonna love it."

The funny thing was, he realized as he stubbed out his cigarette, reached for the check and shoved back his chair, that he knew it was true. Once she got used to the idea, she *would* love flying, the adventure of it, the breathtaking thrill, the excitement. And it wouldn't make any difference to her if she did get airsick, she'd enjoy it anyway, just because the experience was new. And how was it he knew so much about her, when he actually knew her barely at all?

"My kids are never going to believe this," he heard her mutter as she followed him to the cash register.

He turned to scowl at her, one hand in his pocket, groping for change. "You got kids?" Of course she had kids. The woman practically had a sign around her neck that said MOM. Just another thing he'd managed to forget while he was doing the tongue tango with her back there in the truck. One more reason why he had to forget about it, put it out of his mind.

Sure. The way he could forget the taste of a ripe peach, or a fine, sweet Tuscany wine.

"Two daughters," she said, hitching her tote bag onto her shoulder. "Lynn's in college and Tracy's a senior in high school. What about you?"

He didn't reply, pretending his business with the cashier was occupying so much of his attention that he hadn't heard the question. Because another thing he'd come to understand about her in the brief time he'd known her was that she was too polite—or maybe too sensitive—to ask again.

He turned from the register with a frown to inquire as he

tucked away his wallet, "You need to call? Let somebody know where you are?" Like your husband, he thought, and put the leaden feeling in his chest down to tiredness.

The question had been meant to distract, and it did, even though he had a feeling she knew perfectly well what he'd done. She made a wry little grimace. "I tried, from the terminal." Then, with a smile and a shrug, "It *is* Saturday night. I got the answering machine. I left a message—just told them I'd call tomorrow. Even if they had tried to reach me at the hotel, I don't think they'd worry. They'd just assume I was out seeing the sights in Washington, or maybe having dinner, or something."

As he held the door for her, he played back what she'd said, frustrated to realize he still didn't know whether or not she had a husband, angry with himself for wanting to know. And damned if he was going to ask her.

"We'll call the hotel," he said, "as soon as we get settled in here. Take care of checking out. You're probably going to want to have your things sent." He reached for her tote bag, shrugged it onto his own shoulder. He did it unthinkingly, an automatic response to something he'd all but forgotten, like hearing a song he hadn't thought of for years and discovering he still knew the words. "I can have somebody from headquarters take care of it for you, if you like."

Again he felt her eyes flick at him, quickly and then away. "Thank you. I'll try the hotel first. If there's any problem..." She let her words trail off into nothing.

They were walking unhurried in the cold March night, the breeze damp and sea-smelly, the sandy pavement gritty underfoot. Jane suddenly shook herself and wrapped her arms across her body as if she was cold, but when she spoke it was in a soft, ecstatic voice, full of wonder and a fierce kind of joy. "How quiet it is here, have you noticed? No man-made sounds at all, only nature. And look how bright the stars are. It reminds me of when I was a child, the mountains...the desert... I wish—"

She would have left it there, but for some reason, not knowing why he did, he prompted her, "You wish...?"

She shrugged and laughed her low, self-deprecating signature laugh. "Oh, just that I guess I wish I'd known then how lovely

it was—the desert, I mean. I hated it—really. I wanted to
go...somewhere else. *Anywhere* else. And everywhere else. I
wanted to see the whole world...backpack all over Europe, see
London, Paris, Rome, Madrid. And I was so afraid I was never
going to get to see any of it, except for that damn desert.''

"Well, there you go," said Hawk gruffly. "See how wrong
you were?"

"Yes..." But he thought she sounded sad. After a moment,
in a different, lighter tone, she said, "This was one of the places
I dreamed of going, do you know that? The outer islands...I'd
read about the wild ponies, you see. And the Atlantic
Ocean...wow, it seemed as far away as Mars."

Restless and reaching for his cigarettes, he said dryly, "It's
okay now, I guess. Not so nice in the summertime. Sure as hell
not quiet."

He could feel her eyes touch him with that brightening look
of hers. "Oh—have you been here before? Really?"

Kicking himself, he drew hard on his cigarette and exhaled
with the answer. "Yeah, I've been here."

He was here with his wife. As soon as the thought touched
her mind, she knew it was true, just as she knew his wife must
also be the childhood friend whose name he refused to speak.
The friend and wife whose death had cast him into a lonely
exile of grief from which he couldn't seem to find his way back.
How did she know? She just did. *She knew.*

Compassion filled her, spreading like Novocain through her
heart so that she no longer felt her own pain. Softly, knowing
what a risky thing it was, she asked, "Was it your honeymoon?"

He threw her a startled look, drew one last time on his cigarette and tossed it to the ground, extinguishing it with the toe
of his shoe before walking on. She was surprised when he answered, and thought he was, too. "Not my honeymoon." He
laughed, a sound like the creaking of an old structure swaying
in the wind. "We weren't married, just...together."

She held her breath, held back the questions she wanted to
ask. It was a long time before he went on, almost as if she
wasn't there at all, and he was talking only to himself.

"This is where we decided to do it, finally. Decided to get
married. We'd been together forever—since we were kids. We'd

talked about it before, but...I guess we were both afraid of ruining a good thing.''

"What changed your mind?" Jane dared to ask, as softly as she knew how.

They were walking on a quiet street lined with picket fences, beneath the branches of enormous live oaks. She thought it was like being in some ancient, ruined cathedral, except that there was light now from some of the houses they passed, distant music, canned laughter from someone's TV.

"Children," said Tom, after she'd given up hope of an answer. "We decided, since we both wanted kids, we should get married first."

"You have children?"

Unable to trust his voice, Hawk only nodded, knowing she'd misunderstand.

It had been a long time since he'd hurt this bad, not since those first terrible weeks and months, after the shock had worn off and before he'd learned other ways to numb the pain. Part of him wanted to hate the woman beside him, this woman whose gentle insistence was like a dentist's probe on an exposed nerve. But he couldn't. He knew he could have put an end to her probing, could have cut her down as he'd cut down so many before her, coldly, cleanly, bloodlessly as a surgeon's scalpel. But he didn't.

And when she fell silent for a time, he was bewildered to find that there was a part of him that was sorry.

They'd come back to the highway, the lights of the motel he'd telephoned from the ferry terminal visible up ahead of them, before she spoke again. It was late and cold; few people were still out and about. She was hugging herself, and he imagined she must be shivering. So he was surprised by the softness, the easiness of her voice when she said, "You must have lovely memories of this place."

Memories? Memories weren't lovely, they were his enemies. But...yes, he remembered the little house they'd rented, he and Jen. They'd spent the weekend walking hand in hand on the beach, looking for shells, strolling the unpaved street under the great old oaks, looking at gravestones in the family cemeteries. They'd been like children playing house. They'd fought some and laughed some and made love in the quiet afternoons.

He reached for his cigarettes instead of answering.

"You should treasure them," she went on, her voice sighing gently across his auditory nerves. "I always think that good memories are like beloved keepsakes. You put them away and keep them safe—but not buried so deeply you can't get at them when you need them. They don't cause you pain, they bring you pleasure. Sometimes a little sadness, too, when you bring them out and look at them. But you'd never want to lose them, and you wouldn't trade them for gold or diamonds."

He could only nod, his jaw clenched so tightly it hurt. Unable to look at the woman beside him, he plunged ahead of her, across the street and into the brightly lit motel lobby.

Jane insisted on registering separately, paying with her own credit card, though he'd offered to put it on his expense voucher. They had adjoining rooms on the second floor, his smoking, hers non. They smiled through the formalities, chatting with the desk clerk but not with each other.

They climbed the stairs together in silence, Hawk once again carrying the tote bag. He waited while she unlocked her door and turned on a light, then stuck his head in for a cursory check of the room before he handed over her bag.

She thanked him in a polite, expressionless murmur, then cleared her throat and said, "Um, what time do I need to be ready in the morning?"

"Plane should be ready to go at eight." His voice was like a cement mixer full of rocks. "I'll knock on your door at seven—we can go get a bite first, if you want to. Need a wake-up call?"

She shook her head and held up her bag. "I have my little travel alarm."

Absolutely devoid of makeup, her mouth looked vulnerable as a child's. Looking at her, Hawk felt something inside him begin to loosen, to ease and soften, like a balloon that had been filled to the danger point slowly deflating. He had a sudden urge to touch her. And then he did, even though he knew it wasn't wise.

When he touched the side of her cheek with his fingertips, he felt her tremble. "Get some sleep," he said softly, and letting his hand drop to his side, stepped back out of her doorway. "Good night."

"Good night," she whispered as he turned away. But she hadn't closed her door yet when he suddenly turned back, his heart beating hard and fast.

"Her name was Jennifer," he said. "My wife. She and our son, Jason, died when a terrorist's bomb went off on a merry-go-round in Marseilles. In April. Seven years ago next month."

Chapter 11

For the second day in a row, Jane found herself bone-tired and unable to sleep. After delivering his terrible revelation, Tom had gone into his room and shut the door, leaving her standing in her own doorway, appalled and trembling, icy with shock. Inside her room now, she paced, thoroughly rattled and furious, too. And frustrated. Furious with him for doing such a cruel thing to her, and frustrated because how, after all, could she be angry with someone who'd suffered so devastating a loss?

The cold inside her would not go away. A nice hot soak in the tub seemed the most sensible remedy, but first she had to compose herself enough to try calling the girls again. She sat on the edge of the bed and counted seconds up to sixty, then picked up the phone and dialed. The machine answered on the third ring. She was almost glad, and left the same message she'd left earlier: "Hi, this is Mom, I'll try again in the morning, Love you, Bye."

She did not leave the number where she could be reached, because she couldn't think how to explain what she was doing on an island in North Carolina's Outer Banks, when she was supposed to be in Washington, D.C. She wasn't accustomed to lying to her children, but how could she tell them about any of this?

Perhaps, she thought, there were just some things about their parents children were better off not knowing. And vice versa.

While the tub was filling, she emptied the contents of her tote bag onto the bed. The painting and Roy Rogers six-shooter she set aside in their jumbled brown paper, to be rewrapped later. She checked the batteries in the flashlight, made a mental note to put in new ones as soon as she got home, and threw the cookie and peanut wrappers in the trash. Everything else went back into the bag except for her hairbrush, toothpaste and tooth-brush, and the little zippered pouch in which she carried tiny sample bottles of deodorant and hand lotion, and the packets of shampoo and conditioner she'd taken from the hotel in Arling-ton. Had it only been this morning? It seemed a lifetime ago.

She undressed and hung her clothes neatly on the motel hang-ers, except for her knee-high nylons and bra and panties, which she was determined to wash, even if it meant she had to put them on wet tomorrow. She brushed her teeth, unable to avoid her reflection in the mirror and vaguely disheartened by it, hav-ing reached an age where it was sometimes a shock to see her-self, especially like this, tired and without makeup. She'd al-ready made the discovery everyone makes, sooner or later, which was that the human heart is ageless; on the inside she still felt exactly the same as she'd felt when she was eighteen. So how is it, she wondered as she contemplated her tired-looking eyes and the parentheses of lines at the corners of her mouth, that I have this middle-aged face?

She lowered herself into the tub slowly, her body shuddering and cringing with delight at the heat, and as she closed her eyes and lay back in the warm water's embrace, something inside her gave in and let go, and tears began to seep between her lashes.

She knew it was silly, even shameful that she should feel so bad about such a thing, but that knowledge didn't change the fact that she did, not one bit. The truth was, Tom Hawkins had touched her, and it had felt wonderful. And every nerve and cell in her body waited, ached, begged and screamed for him to do it again.

How did this happen? she wondered. How could I have gotten so desperately hungry, and not have known it?

Sex had been one of the few things about her marriage that had seemed to work, until the last few years, anyway. David had prided himself on being a vigorous and imaginative lover; it was part of his self-image. Satisfying his wife in bed had been important to him, and over the years he'd learned just which of her buttons to push in order to elicit the physical response he desired. Emotional response wasn't something he required, or understood, and if Jane had often found their lovemaking lacking in tenderness, or joy, and if she'd ever tried to tell him so, he wouldn't have known what on earth she was talking about.

Oh, but how was it that those few kisses of Tom's in the back of a moving truck, and now just the touch of his hand on her *cheek,* for God's sake, could have elicited from her more emotion, more tenderness, more joy, more anguish, than twenty-one years of regular and abundant sex with David ever had?

Having admitted to herself that she wanted Tom Hawkins, she tortured herself further by allowing herself to think about him that way, to imagine his body, for instance, to wonder what it would look like without clothes. He was tall and lean, that much she knew, and she rather imagined his build would be wiry, his proportions naturally pleasing, not artificially pumped up and filled out from lifting weights, or some such narcissistic pursuit. He didn't have the stiff, straight, almost militaristic posture she associated with most of the law enforcement people she knew, seeming much more casual in his bearing, with a slight stoop to his shoulders, as if he'd spent a lifetime listening carefully to people who were shorter than he was. And he moved, even with the smallest of motions, like opening a menu, or holding a door, or lifting her tote bag onto his shoulder, with the completely unselfconscious grace of a cat.

She realized suddenly that her tears had stopped, and that she was smiling, her body relaxed and languid, steeped in sensual pleasure. Thinking about Tom, envisioning him naked, was a joy, it seemed, not a torment. The torture, the terrible drumming of her pulse, the pressure, the ache and the fire, only began when she recalled the way he'd touched *her* body. When she felt again his body's heat against hers, the brush of his fingers across her skin. When she remembered how she'd tasted his mouth, breathed his breath, and finally surrendered to the mastery of his tongue.

And then...when she saw in her memory's eye that same mouth tilt sideways in that poignant remnant of a smile, and, glimpsed almost by accident, the unimaginable pain in his eyes, the ache inside her became like a knife twisting in her heart.

Oh, God, help me, she thought, gasping with the pain. *What am I going to do?*

Hawk put through a call to Interpol headquarters, and while he waited for someone to locate Devore at such an hour on a Saturday night, opened the fresh pack of cigarettes he'd bought at the ferry terminal, tapped one out and lit it. After the first puff, he looked at the lighted end with disgust and thought he really ought to do something about the damn things.

He'd actually given up smoking once, before Jason was born, mainly because it made Jen sick. He'd taken it up again after they'd died, and until this moment hadn't given even the smallest thought to quitting. He wondered why he should think of it now.

Devore came on the line, sounding far away and annoyed. "About time you called. Why the devil did it take you so long to get settled in? I thought that was a very small island."

"It is, and there are no superhighways on it, either," Hawk said in a surly growl. "And we stopped for dinner. Anyway, I'm here now, and I'm tired as hell. What have you got for me?"

"I've got someone tracking down the auction company's records. We should have the names and addresses of the buyers of the other paintings by tomorrow morning. Oh—and Fritz will be there for you at eight—be ready. How soon can you get here?"

"One stop," said Hawk, squinting through smoke. "Probably Greenville. Got to drop Mrs. Carlysle where she can catch a shuttle or something to Raleigh-Durham. Then I'll be on my way." Something he'd detected in the bureau chief's tone made him ask with quickening pulse, "Why, what's up? You got something?"

"We've heard from Lyons—just about an hour ago, right

after you called, as a matter of fact. It seems Loizeau's body has yielded some interesting bits, in spite of your mucking about. Quite a number of fibers. Most of them appear to be from those little blankets airlines provide.''

"Which only tells us our shooter might have recently taken a flight, probably of long duration,'' Hawk observed. "Which doesn't narrow it down much.''

"True. But a few of the others might be a bit more significant, I think. Merino wool, which I believe is a component of better-quality outer garments.''

"Sweaters,'' muttered Hawk. "Topcoat, maybe?''

"I doubt it,'' said Devore dryly. "These happen to be pink.''

"*Pink?*''

"That is what I said.''

"Pink.''

"Yes. Pink.''

"Are you telling me,'' said Hawk slowly, while his belly tied itself in knots, "that we could be looking at a *woman?*''

"It is a possibility that must be considered,'' said Devore, with enough diffidence in his voice to make Hawk very uneasy.

"There's something else,'' he growled. "Let's have it.''

There was a moment's hesitation, and then, "Yes, there is something else. Hawk, I must ask you to get for me a set of Mrs. Carlysle's fingerprints.''

"Why?'' He exhaled sharply and reached to stub out his cigarette, breaking it in half.

"I know you have told me you believe she is not involved, but we must be certain. You know that. We must at least eliminate—''

"Eliminate? From what? Are you telling me you have a *print?*''

"We do have a print, yes. Several, actually. Most are smudged, but there is one very good one—a thumbprint.''

"My God. Where was it?''

"On some papers in one of Loizeau's pockets. He had some small things—a grocery list from his wife among them. The pocket was buttoned. Possibly the shooter had difficulty opening the button with gloves on, took them off, rifled through the papers, then was in a rush, perhaps—you said you arrived only

moments after he—or she—had left. And made a mistake."
There was a pause. "A fatal one, let us hope."

"Don't tell me," said Hawk on an exhalation of disbelief.
Rarely in his experience were forensics scientists, particularly
fingerprints experts, blessed with such luck. "You have a
match?"

"We do." Another pause, longer this time. "You will not
like this, Hawk."

Impatient, he said through clenched teeth, "Tell me."

Devore made a sound that was almost a sigh. "The print lifted
from the shopping list in Loizeau's pocket matches perfectly
one found on bomb fragments recovered from the wreckage of
Flight 310—the plane that went down off Sicily five years ago.
If you recall—"

"I remember," said Hawk in a tone as leaden as his heart.
He remembered it as he remembered his own name, his own
signature, because the bomb that had brought Flight 310 to a
premature end, along with the lives of all hundred eighty-three
people on board, had born the same signature as the one left on
a merry-go-round in Marseilles.

"So," Devore was saying, "you will do this—get us something with Mrs. Carlysle's prints on it? Just to be sure."

"Yeah," said Hawk. "Sure." His thoughts were spinning
crazily. He was trying to imagine Jane wearing pink. Problem
was, he thought she'd look terrific in it.

The knock on her door came as Jane was raking off the
skimpy motel shower cap, shaking her head and combing
through her hair with her fingers. Her heart skidded and began
to pound.

"Oh, God," she whimpered to herself as her naked body
froze in a posture of panic and indecision. Her clothes were
hanging within reach, but her underwear was dripping on the
towel bar in the bathroom. The motel towels were typically
skimpy. Impossibly skimpy.

"Who is it?" her voice quavered. Stupid, she thought, who
would it be?

The answer came muffled. "It's Tom. Sorry to bother you..."

"Just a minute..." Breathing like a cornered fugitive, she

quickly wrapped the extra towel around her waist and rolled the top edge down to secure it, then grabbed the damp one from the floor and covered her top half in the same fashion. Finally, hoping her pounding heart wouldn't shake the towels loose, she gave her sweat-damp hair a futile pat and opened the door a crack.

"Hi," she gasped through the gap. "Sorry—I was just..."

Tom was standing there with his hands in his pockets. "Maybe I'd better come back," he said. "When you're, uh..." His forehead creased in a scowl of Godzillian proportions. But he looked as if he wanted to say something and was making no move to go.

She shrugged her bare shoulders, keeping a death grip on the top of the towel that covered her breasts as she stuttered, "It's okay—if there's—did you want...can I help you?"

She opened the door wider and he slipped into the room, moving stiffly, without his usual grace. "I, uh, just wanted to say I'm sorry." He was looking around her stock motel room as if he'd never seen one like it before. Looking anywhere but at her.

"Sorry?" As she closed the door, a trickle of sweat emerged from her hair and began a journey across her forehead toward one eyebrow. She mopped it self-consciously with the back of her hand as she turned back to him. "What for?"

He waved a hand in a vaguely self-disgusted sort of way. "For saying what I did—earlier. I shouldn't have thrown it at you like that. I'd been trying to think how to tell you."

"It's okay," Jane murmured. "Really. I'm just...so terribly sorry."

He nodded, finally looking at her. Cloaked in terry cloth from her armpits to her knees, she'd never felt so utterly naked. "It's not something I normally tell people," he said.

Another sweat trickle traced its way between her eyebrows, and his glance flicked at it, his eyes alert while his body remained still, like a lazy cat following the dartings of a fly.

She lost track of time and space; it might have been an hour or a second before he said, in a voice like a rock slide, "I was wondering...you don't happen to have any toothpaste, do you? That tote bag of yours..." His smile tilted. Her heart did, too.

"Oh, sure. As a matter of fact, I do." A laugh jerked her

body like a hiccup. "I'll just..." Amazed that her legs still functioned, she padded to the bathroom on bare feet, her knees all but creaking with self-awareness. "It's...in here. You're welcome to it. I'm, uh, finished..." Returning, she thrust the tube of toothpaste at him. "So you might as well keep it. Sorry I don't have a spare toothbrush." Her smile and shrug were nervous and apologetic.

"That's okay—I'll make do." He grinned as he held up a finger and made brushing motions across his teeth with it. The smile slipped back into its customary place as he added, "This'll help a lot—thanks, I 'preciate it."

Smiling brilliantly, Jane murmured, "Oh, no problem. Glad I could help. Any time." I hate this, she thought. *Hate it.* Why did this have to happen?

Again he nodded, saying nothing. And then his eyes dropped unexpectedly to her chest, to the spot where her fingers were knotted in the join of her towel. Her pulse throbbed so loudly in her ears that when he spoke she heard the words as if she were underwater.

"Were you able to get hold of your family?"

"There's just the girls. They were still out. I left another message."

"Ah. Well, at least they won't worry."

Her smile was as lopsided as his. "I just hope somebody remembers they have to pick me up at the airport."

"You'll probably be able to get them in the morning."

He was moving toward her, moving toward the door. She stepped aside to let him pass, every muscle, nerve and sinew groaning in protest. Close to her he paused...intolerably close, close enough to touch, close enough that she could hear him breathing, breathing as if he'd just been running hard. Her eyes found and clung to his mouth, and though she fought it desperately, of course the memories had to come, too. Tormenting memories of how it had felt on hers, the way it had tasted.

"Well, thanks again for the toothpaste. See you in the morning. Seven o'clock, right?"

"Right."

"'Night."

"Good night." It was almost a gasp, as if she'd been in desperate need of air.

And then he was gone, and she slid the security chain into place and leaned against the door, limp and exhausted, trembling, wishing to God she could cry.

Twenty-one years of a bad marriage, five years divorced...I thought I knew what loneliness was. Dear God, I thought I knew.

But lying in bed that still, dark night, with seabirds calling in the marshes and Tom lying near enough to touch but for a few cruel inches of wall, she understood that she'd only begun to know real loneliness. Only begun.

They left the island in a single-engine Cessna, lifting into a lovely pink and lavender haze that reminded Jane of cotton candy. She did not get airsick; in fact, she enjoyed the flight so much she thought she might even decide to take flying lessons. After this, she was definitely going to need something exciting and new in her life. Something big enough to fill a void created by a man she hadn't even known existed until two days ago. Except she was very much afraid there wasn't anything in the world big enough to fill that particular void.

Tom had very little to say to her that morning, brooding in silence on the flight to Greenville while Jane chatted with Fritz, the pilot, a serious young man with a blond crewcut and a military manner who somehow seemed too American to be with Interpol. She wondered, but didn't ask, if he might be FBI. In any event, by the end of the flight he'd warmed up and softened enough that he gave her the names of two people he knew of in North Carolina who might be willing to teach her to fly. He'd have taught her himself, he said, except he was a little too far away for her convenience.

"Wasn't he nice!" Jane said to Tom as he walked her to the terminal, Fritz having stayed with the plane, which was idling on the tarmac.

His only reply was an ambiguous grunt, which she didn't try to interpret. She was determined to keep herself cheerful, the tone of their leave-taking casual and light. Which had proved to be easier than she'd expected, because after the trauma of the previous evening she felt quite numb. She felt that she'd learned a valuable lesson, and that never again would she allow herself to be so vulnerable. So needy. *Never again.*

"Did you manage to get hold of your kids this morning?" Tom's voice was like a truckload of gravel—about normal, for him.

"Oh, no," she said politely. "But that's all right. I didn't want to disturb them on a Sunday morning until I knew what flight I'd be coming in on. I'll buy my ticket first, then call. By that time, they might even be up." She said it with a smile, inviting him to join her, but his face remained somber.

"So," he said, "you sure you'll be okay? Anything you need?"

"Quite sure. Thanks for everything." She stuck out her hand, and though he looked momentarily startled, he took it. Steeling herself against the warmth of his grasp, she said brightly, "Listen, good luck. I hope you find...the whatever-it-is you're looking for."

"Yeah," said Tom, "me, too."

"Well, so long." She managed not to add, "It's been fun."

"See ya."

No, thought Jane. We both know that you won't.

She watched him walk away, and the numbness held. She turned and began to make her way toward the USAir ticket counter, and it occurred to her suddenly that Tom still had her toothpaste. Well, of course, it was Connie's toothpaste, actually.

That was when her legs got wobbly, and she had to go and sit down for a while and wait until the trembling stopped.

Hawk had never liked FBI headquarters much. Something about the long, polished corridors and closed doors, and so many improbably fit and unsmiling people gliding silently and efficiently about their business made him think of some futuristic society where all the people had become machines. He wasn't sure why that was so; most of the FBI agents he was personally acquainted with were okay people.

Devore met him at the security station. "I thought it would be simplest to meet here," he said by way of a greeting as Hawk pinned an ID tag to the front of his shirt. "We will have the results of the fingerprint analysis directly from IAFIS the moment they are available," he said, referring to the FBI's extensive fingerprint data bank.

"Fritz delivered the sample okay, then, I assume," Hawk drawled. It hadn't made him happy, letting that tube of toothpaste out of his sight.

"Approximately one hour ago." Devore looked at his watch. "Meanwhile, they are expecting us upstairs—come." His wheelchair hummed softly as he led the way across the foyer to the bank of elevators.

Andreas Devore was Belgian, a large-boned, gaunt man with shaggy hair, an aristocratic nose and a long, rather cruel mouth women found attractive. Before the helicopter crash that had broken his back and mottled his skin with burn scars, he'd been one of Interpol's best field agents. Now he headed ATDI—the Antiterrorism Division's Washington bureau—and acted as chief liaison between ATDI and DECCA—the FBI's Development of Espionage, Counterintelligence and Counterterrorism Awareness. But Hawk had no doubt that Andreas Devore still knew more about how to play the game than any man alive. He'd learned a lot from him. Especially patience.

The DECCA coordinator was waiting for them in the doorway to his office. He ushered them across the hall into a carpeted meeting room furnished with a large polished table and a dozen or so comfortable chairs. On the other side of the room, windows looked down on the old Ford's Theater, but Hawk wasn't interested in the view. One of the four chairs drawn up to the table was already occupied by a young man wearing a medium-gray suit and starched white shirt, and a maroon tie with silver stripes. His eyes were black as bullet holes, and he had the nose and bearing of an Arab prince.

"Our field agent on the case," the DECCA coordinator said, beginning the introductions.

"We've met." Hawk managed to keep his face impassive as he leaned across the table to shake Aaron Campbell's hand.

"Well," said the coordinator briskly as he took the chair at the head of the table, "let's not waste any more time. Just to recap, so we know we've all got the same information up to this point." He picked up the file in front of him, set it down again and laced his fingers together on top of it as he gave everyone at the table his eyes in turn.

"On March fifteenth, our agents in Kuwait received a, uh, communication purporting to be from Jarek Singh, who, as you know, was an Indian computer expert reported missing and presumed kidnapped from his home in Cairo at the end of the Gulf War.''

Devore said, ''Ours came to our bureau in Ankara.''

''They were apparently identical. We know Scotland Yard, the CIA and the Israelis each got one, too. We don't know how many others. In the, uh, communication—'' which Hawk knew had come via computer, in the mysterious and incomprehensible manner fully understood only by hackers and wizards ''—Mr. Singh claims to have been kidnapped by agents of Saddam Hussein and forced to design and program the security system for an elaborate secret facility built as a hideaway for Hussein's stockpile of chemical and biological weapons. Most of which, as you know, did not turn up during our inspections after the war. We know they existed. Where are they now? Mr. Singh claims to know exactly where, as well as how to circumvent the facility's security system, and has offered this information to the highest bidder. Unfortunately—'' he paused as Devore coughed and shifted in his seat ''—we have reason to believe this offer was also made to some very undesirable and dangerous bidders.''

''Khadafy, for one,'' said Devore.

The coordinator nodded. ''For one. North Korea and China, almost certainly. Others we can only guess at.'' He looked unspeakably glum.

''In all fairness to Singh,'' Campbell remarked, speaking for the first time, ''he must have known he was a marked man. It would have taken a lot of money to put himself and his family out of Saddam's reach.''

''He expected Saddam to pay him off,'' said Devore, ''with the promise that, if he didn't, or if anything happened to him in the meantime, the information would go elsewhere.''

''Something like that. We can't know precisely what Singh had in mind. We know he delivered only enough with his offer to demonstrate the probable accuracy and authenticity of what he had. The rest is inaccessible except with a key, which is what he was offering for sale. It was a clever enough plan.''

''Except,'' muttered Hawk, ''Singh wound up dead anyway.''

Once again the coordinator nodded. ''His body turned up in an alley not far from his home in Cairo on March seventeenth.

Estimates are he'd been dead at least three days. So apparently, Saddam's agents caught up with Singh before his communication reached Baghdad.''

"And so," Devore said dryly, "begins the treasure hunt."

"Some treasure," said Hawk,

"A treasure map, certainly. The map to enough chemical and biological agents to wipe out the entire population of the globe several times over. And unlike conventional weapons, almost impossible to detect by existing security systems. A vial the size of a cigarette, a few drops of a deadly virus in the water supply of a major city..."

The coordinator took a breath and went on, "It's absolutely imperative that Jarek Singh's key doesn't fall into the wrong hands. We searched Singh's house immediately, of course; it had been ransacked before we got there." His eyes flicked to Devore and settled appraisingly on Hawk.

Hawk said nothing. Devore sat forward in his wheelchair, leaning one forearm on the table as he quietly said, "We also found it so. However, our agent—" he indicated Hawk with a nod "—observed a faint marking on one wall, which suggested a painting had hung there—a mark that did not fit any painting in the house. It seemed reasonable to assume that whoever had broken into the place had taken it, but when asked about it, Mrs. Singh said her husband had suddenly shown up the day before the communications from him began arriving—"

"That would be the day we assume he was killed," said Campbell.

"Right. According to Singh's wife, he was very excited about something, and in a great hurry. She thought he seemed frightened, as well. Anyway, he packed up this particular painting and told her to mail it, then pack her things and go stay with her mother in Giza until she heard from him. He gave her the address of an antiques dealer in Marseilles—"

"Loizeau," the coordinator offered, although everyone there knew the name.

Devore nodded. "Then Mr. Singh left again and that was the last his wife saw of him. She did as he'd told her and went off to her mother's, stayed there until she learned of her husband's death, when she returned to find her house a shambles." He raised his eyebrows at Hawk. "Would you like to take it from here?"

Hawk didn't say anything for a moment. He'd rather not have been there at all, if the truth were told. He hated meetings like this, always had. In his opinion, they were a waste of time. He knew where he needed to be, which was out there tracking down those other paintings. Most of which, it appeared, according to the records of the auction house, were in a town called Cooper's Mill, North Carolina.

Sprawled in his chair, idly spinning a pencil on the polished tabletop, he looked across at Campbell and said casually, "You know, something else Mrs. Singh couldn't seem to find was the shipping receipt from when she mailed that painting. She said she came straight back home to pack, and left it on top of the dresser in the bedroom. You guys take it?"

Campbell and the coordinator looked at each other. Campbell said quietly, "We found out about Loizeau's having the painting the same way you did. Mrs. Singh told us."

"So," said Hawk, sitting up straight, "that means whoever trashed Singh's place probably found it, went straight to Loizeau's, got the information about the auction from him and then killed him. I'd be curious to know," he added, looking across at Campbell, "how you guys found out about that auction."

There was another uncomfortable silence; rival law enforcement agencies never enjoyed revealing their sources and methods. This time it was the coordinator who said, without expression, "We had immediately placed Loizeau's shop under electronic surveillance."

"Ah," said Hawk, smiling slightly. Phone tap, of course.

"I'd like to ask you that same question," said Campbell, his eyes glittering. "Loizeau was dead when you got there?"

"That's right," said Hawk evenly, showing his teeth.

"So, it would appear," said the DECCA coordinator, unnecessarily shuffling through the file in front of him, "that only three people were able to follow the trail as far as Rathskeller's. The two of us—" his nod took in Hawk as well as Devore "—and whoever ransacked Singh's house and killed Loizeau. Are we in agreement that those two are most likely one and the same?"

Three nods answered. "All right, then—"

But whatever the DECCA coordinator had been about to say would have to wait, because right then someone's beeper went off. The coordinator reached for his, checked the number and handed it to Campbell. "It's IAFIS."

Alarm ran through Hawk like an electrical charge. It couldn't be his sample, the prints lifted from Jane's tube of toothpaste. It was too soon. A futile search through the millions of prints in the FBI's data banks should take hours, even days.

Campbell went to a phone on the wall near the door and punched in a number. He spoke quietly, then listened, eyes on the floor. After a moment or two, those same eyes, glittering bright, found Hawk across the room. And then, carelessly covering the mouthpiece with his hand, he said, "That fingerprint sample you delivered this afternoon? It seems IAFIS has a match."

Chapter 12

"Impossible," Hawk muttered. He stood by the windows, tensely smoking. *Not Jane. No way. I don't believe it. Impossible.*

"I'm afraid," the coordinator said mildly, "it's not only possible, it's a fact." He glanced at Campbell, who nodded.

"Atkinson says he's never seen IAFIS get a hit so fast, or so positively. The thumbprint lifted from that toothpaste tube you sent them is a perfect match with the one you guys found on the shopping list in Loizeau's pocket. And—" it was his turn to flick a confirming glance at Devore "—the one from the Flight 310 bomb fragment."

"I'm not saying it isn't," growled Hawk, "I'm just saying it can't be Jane's. My God, if you'd ever met the woman—"

"I have met her," Campbell said under his breath. There was a rueful twist to his mouth, and he was absently rubbing a spot on his midsection, just below his ribs.

Hawk snorted, and muttered for the FBI agent's ears only, "Why in the hell didn't you just ID yourself?"

"I was about to when she decked me. I don't know how—"

"Lucky shot. Don't feel bad. Believe me, she was at least as surprised as you were."

Then aloud he said as he strode angrily across the room to stub out his cigarette in the ashtray the coordinator had politely produced, ''Dammit, I'm just saying this woman is no terrorist. There has to be some explanation.''

''I can think of one,'' Campbell unexpectedly said. Three pairs of eyes focused on him. It was Hawk's he chose to meet, his own eyes glittering dangerously. ''Carlysle wasn't alone at that auction. She shared a ride, and she shared a hotel room. Maybe that's not all she shared.''

No one spoke. Hawk felt his heart lurch and his pulse quicken, not sure whether or not to be glad that someone else had finally given voice to the suspicion that had been nibbling at him for a while now.

Devore coughed and said, ''You are suggesting Carlysle had an accomplice? The woman she was with...''

The coordinator glanced down at his file and supplied, ''Connie Vincent.''

''I'm saying, when I went down—'' and Campbell flushed brick red under his olive skin ''—Carlysle was in her seat, bidding. Vincent wasn't. I felt something—a prick, like an insect bite—on my thigh. I remember thinking I must have an ant in my pants, and what the hell was I going to do about it, because I couldn't leave the bidding right then, and the next thing I know I'm looking up at all these worried faces.'' He shook his head and made a sound replete with self-disgust. ''All I know is, there's no way Carlysle could have been responsible.''

Again there was silence, until Devore diffidently cleared his throat and said, ''Agent Hawkins?''

''Vincent bought the other paintings,'' Hawk said with a carefully noncommittal shrug. ''She could have pulled the switch.''

And Jane knows it, he thought. He was remembering their conversation in the truck, Jane's sudden silence and subsequent evasiveness.

He paced again to the windows, reaching for his cigarettes with jerky, angry motions. He was furious with her for not telling him her suspicions, with himself for not figuring it out sooner. Most of all, though, he was furious with himself for dismissing someone as a suspect solely because she was a woman. Well, perhaps not solely—he'd suspected Jane, after all.

But for God's sake, he thought in disgust, Vincent looks like somebody's *mother*. All right, so Ma Barker was somebody's mother, too. But...she wore those damn glasses on the end of a chain, like a librarian, or his second-grade music teacher. And button-up-the-front sweaters.

He stared out the window and drew deeply on his cigarette while a chill scattered goose bumps down his spine. *Pink* sweaters. That's what he was thinking of. Pink sweaters made of Merino wool.

She knows.

Yes, there was no doubt in his mind that Jane had figured it out. The question was, what was she thinking of doing about it? He thought again of Loizeau, and the possibilities terrified him.

Behind him, Devore coughed and said, "If Vincent does have Jarek Singh's painting..."

"I think it's safe to assume it's for sale," said the DECCA coordinator.

"And," said Campbell, "we're fairly sure she hasn't moved it yet."

"How do you know she hasn't?" Hawk asked, turning.

"We've had agents in Cooper's Mill since early yesterday," the coordinator said blandly, while Campbell again flushed dark underneath his tan. "Since we, uh, lost track of Mrs. Carlysle in Georgetown. They've been concentrating on Carlysle, of course, but it's a small town. They haven't reported any unusual activity, any strangers in town. My guess is, it'll take some time to broker a deal and arrange for pickup or delivery—"

"But not too much," murmured Devore. "She must know we would be onto her sooner or later."

The coordinator nodded, looking grim. "It's possible Mrs. Carlysle has been a red herring—designed to give Vincent just enough time to complete her deal. Once Singh's key is out of her hands, we'd have a devil of a time proving it was ever there."

Hawk made a growling sound deep in his throat. The DECCA coordinator glanced at him as he placed both hands on the table and abruptly stood. "All right then—Agent Campbell, you will leave immediately for Cooper's Mill. You will coordinate the surveillance efforts down there, concentrating now, of course, on Mrs. Vincent. And we'll have a Hostage Rescue Team in place and ready to move in if anything does break.

"I imagine you—" he nodded to Hawk with a thin smile "—will want to clarify as soon as possible exactly which of the prints on that tube of toothpaste belong to Mrs. Carlysle and which do not." Hawk nodded a grim confirmation. The coordinator also nodded, making it a dismissal. "A helicopter is standing by. Agent Hawkins, you're welcome to hitch a ride."

Hawk glanced at Devore for a confirming nod, then muttered, "Thanks," and headed for the door. Behind him, Aaron Campbell pushed back his chair and rose to his feet. Hawk could feel the FBI man's glittering black eyes resting appraisingly on him as he followed him out of the room.

It was late afternoon by the time Jane got home, tired, depressed and still frustrated and fuming over the fact that she'd been forced to fly all the way to *Charlotte,* for heaven's sake, and then wait for another connection back to Raleigh-Durham, because, as it turned out, there was no such thing as a direct flight from Greenville to Raleigh.

Then she'd had to explain to Lynn, who'd been anxiously waiting for her at the gate, why she'd arrived on a flight from Charlotte instead of Washington. But that was easy. She'd simply told her daughter the truth, that she'd been unable to get a direct flight. These days, who could?

And it had been equally easy explaining her lack of luggage. "It got lost—they're sending it on later," she'd said in an irritable tone, and instantly won her well-traveled daughter's sympathy.

"Did you file a claim?" was the first thing Lynn had thought of. "You know—in case it doesn't turn up. The things you bought at the auction—"

"Those I have," Jane had said, holding up her tote bag. "And I took care of everything in Charlotte. By the way, where's Tracy?"

"She's at Dad's. And could you please drop me by there, on your way home? That's why we haven't been home all day. Good thing we thought about checking the messages, huh? We've been trying to reach you at the hotel all weekend. Dad wants us to go skiing with him. We're driving up tonight. He's got the resort booked for the whole week, isn't that cool? He got this great deal at the resort, because it's the end of the season, you know? That's always the best time to go—either that or really early. He said I could bring Kevin, and Tracy could bring anybody she wanted, but it was such short notice Kevin couldn't get off work, and Tracy couldn't find anybody that could go either, so it's just us. And Dad and Pamela, of course.''

"Who's Pamela?"

"Dad's new girlfriend. She's pretty cool. She's only a couple years older than me, I think.''

"Than *I*," Jane had murmured automatically, feeling unspeakably tired.

Much too tired to fight David on this ski-trip notion of his, not that she would probably have done so anyway. It wasn't that she never stood up to her ex-husband; she'd just learned to pick her battles carefully.

And so, it was without further argument that Jane made the detour into Raleigh to drop off Lynn and her baggage at her father's tree-shaded two-story brick house on its elegant, old-money street. Though maybe there was a little bit of selfishness in her lack of resistance, as well. It wouldn't be such a bad thing, she thought, to have a week by herself to decompress. Recover her equilibrium. Reestablish contact with reality.

And there was that other matter, too. The one she'd been trying so hard not to think about. *Tomorrow,* she thought. Tomorrow I'll find out. Tomorrow I'll know.

She pulled into her own graveled driveway just in time to watch the sun drop into a lake of molten gold.

No dogs came running to greet her as she drove her station wagon into the carport; no cat came to wind, complaining, around her ankles when she unlocked her door. Since dogs and cats did not tend to mix well with the local indigent wildlife, it had long ago been put to a family vote whether to opt for pets or for bird and squirrel feeders, and salt licks for the deer that came at twilight and dawn, and cracked corn for the mallard ducklings that hatched in the sheltered coves in the spring, and the Canadian geese that grazed and made messes on the sweep of grass that ran from the rear deck down to the water's edge. The vote had been unanimous, although there had been times when the girls, particularly Tracy, had been sorely tempted by the frequent kitten-and-puppy giveaways in front of the Winn Dixie.

The house seemed unnaturally quiet, its rooms filled with an aura of expectancy, as if they waited in hushed suspense for the return of laughter and running footsteps and the blare of MTV. This is what it will be like soon, thought Jane. From now on.

From the kitchen windows she watched cardinals and chickadees and goldfinches peck at the overflowing feeders, pleased to see that Tracy had remembered to fill them before she left, as she'd been told to do.

Carrying her tote bag into the living room, she placed it on the couch and withdrew the painting. Eagerly, she tore off the wrappings. She carried the painting over to the nice little spinet piano she'd bought with part of her divorce-settlement money, and moving aside the metronome and her parents' framed wedding portrait, placed the picture on top of the piano, leaning it against the wall. Then she took a step back.

She sighed. "Perfect." As she'd known it would be.

The living room was part of the original cinderblock summer cottage, the walls paneled in a highly varnished and outdated knotty pine. She'd always intended to remodel someday, and modernize with sheetrock and wallpaper, but now she wasn't so sure. For some reason, the painting's vivid colors brought out the warmth in the old wood walls, so that they seemed to be lit by candle- and firelight.

Which, far from cheering, only made the house seem more empty.

Unable to bear it another minute, Jane pressed a disk of Strauss waltzes into the CD player and turned the volume up high. Throwing wide the French doors, she went out onto the deck and down the stairs, leaving the doors open even though the evening chill was settling in. Across the sparse winter lawn she went, running a little on the downhill slope, clattering along the board pier and onto the landing. There she stopped, hugging herself against the cold and her quickened breathing, to watch the salmon sunset fade to bronze, and then to softest mauve.

The helicopter deposited Hawk, along with FBI Agent Aaron Campbell, in a small field sandwiched between the high school and a textile plant. They were met by a sheriff's deputy driving a white unmarked Ford with dashboard- and rear-window lights and siren. Beside him was a composed-looking black man wearing a navy blue windbreaker and Atlanta Braves baseball cap, who got out of the car and stood waiting as they ducked their heads and plowed toward him through the dust and chaff stirred up by the chopper's rotors.

"We've got you rooms at the Best Western," the man said, after identifying himself as Agent Monroe and the driver as Deputy Schaefer. "It's pretty much the only game in town, if you don't count a couple bed-and-breakfasts on Main Street. We've got a command post set up at the fire station—by the way, you guys are representatives of rural volunteer fire departments, in town to learn about firefighting techniques and equipment." He shot Campbell a look. "So lose the suit."

"I'm gonna need a car," said Hawk, muttering around the cigarette he was lighting. He hadn't been able to smoke on the flight down and was pretty sure he wasn't going to be able to in that deputy's car, either. Funny how it was getting so he could tell a nonsmoker just by looking at him. "Preferably something without red lights and a siren."

"Radio?" Monroe inquired, politely deadpan.

Hawk thought about it, then shook his head. "Just a cellular phone'll do."

He dropped his half-smoked cigarette to the ground and stepped on it, and they all got into the white Ford. Monroe sat in front but turned around to fill Hawk and Campbell in while Deputy Schaefer drove and mumbled unintelligibly into his radio mike.

"We've got surveillance in place on Vincent, both her home and the shop. She's got a place just outside of town—we were able to get in this morning while she was at the shop unloading the stuff she bought at Arlington. It's secluded, and there's a field nearby big enough to land a chopper in. We're watching that, too."

A thought occurred to Hawk, and he said, "What about Mrs. Carlysle? You have 'surveillance'—" a term he knew very well was just a big word for "bugs" "—on her too?"

Agent Monroe just looked at him and didn't answer. Damned

electronic toys, thought Hawk, inexplicably disturbed by the thought of Jane's every move being scrutinized by unseen strangers. He definitely had mixed feelings about listening devices.

"According to our local sources," Monroe continued, and was interrupted by Aaron Campbell.

"Which are?"

Monroe grinned. "Name's Loretta. She's a waitress at the coffee shop next door to Vincent's place. She says Vincent didn't open the shop at all yesterday, and as far as she knows, never came near the place. We had a chance to go through Vincent's home pretty thoroughly this morning and didn't find anything, so we think we're reasonably safe in assuming Singh's key is still with the stuff she brought back from the auction, and is there in the shop now."

"What makes you think she didn't unload it somewhere on her way home from Virginia?" Campbell asked.

"I guess we don't, for sure," Monroe replied. "But I don't think she did. For one thing, she couldn't have known for sure she'd be successful in getting the merchandise, so I don't see how she could have held her own auction and put together a deal in advance. It makes a lot more sense for her to put the word out she's in possession, then go home and wait for the offers to come in. As long as we're all hot on the trail of her red herring, she knows she's got time. That's assuming," Monroe added, with a glance at Hawk, "she and Mrs. Carlysle aren't in this together."

Ignoring that, Hawk said, "What happens when Vincent finds out we're onto her and not the herring?"

Agents Monroe and Campbell looked at each other and didn't say anything. Hawk felt his jaw clench.

He was heading across the Best Western parking lot, thinking he'd have time to stow his bag and maybe wash up and at least put on a clean shirt before heading out to Jane's place, when a sporty red Nissan pulled up behind him and the driver tapped the horn. Recognizing the young sheriff's deputy, Schaefer, he went around to the driver's-side window.

Schaefer ran the window down and grinned up at him. "How'll this do? B'longs to Sheriff Taylor's wife, but he says you're welcome to borry it, since she's off visitin' her mother till Wednesday. Got you your cell phone, too, right here. Sheriff says to just let him know in case there's anythin' else you need.''

"Thanks," said Hawk as he waited with one hand on the door for the deputy to extricate himself from the low-slung driver's seat, "this'll do fine. And be sure and tell Sheriff Taylor I appreciate it.''

"No problem." Half in and half out of the car, Schaefer paused suddenly to pull a folded piece of paper out of his uniform shirt pocket. "Agent Monroe said to give you this—said you'll need it. Get's confusin' out there around the lake.''

Hawk unfolded enough of the paper to see that it was a hand-drawn map to Jane Carlysle's house. He muttered, "Thanks," to himself, since Deputy Schaefer was already loping off across the highway, where two regular police cruisers were pulled up in the Waffle House parking lot.

He was glad to have Monroe's map, because there was no doubt he'd need one, and it saved him the time and trouble of stopping to ask for directions. But it bothered him, too. Bothered him to have the map spread there on the seat beside him, tangible evidence that FBI agents had already been to Jane's house, had almost assuredly been inside it, invading her personal space and privacy. It bothered him even though he'd been doing just that himself, not so long ago.

But that was *then,* he thought. Things have changed.

He wasn't even exactly sure when they'd changed, but he was only beginning to understand how much.

Even with the map he managed to make a couple of wrong turns, and the sunset's glow was fading fast by the time he finally turned into the graveled driveway he was sure at last was Jane's. When he turned off the Nissan's engine, he could hear a stereo thumping. The daughters, he thought. Naturally they'd be home on a Sunday evening. It gave him a peculiar feeling to think of Jane in a warm, cozy kitchen, surrounded by boisterous teenagers. And yet, wasn't that how he'd always pictured her? *Supermom.*

No, something inside him corrected, that's how your conscience told you you *should* think of her. *You* thought of her in a different context entirely.

He got out of the car, and then he could actually hear the music. A *waltz?* Strange choice for teenagers, he thought.

He went up to the front door and knocked, but the music was so loud he knew no one inside would ever hear him, so he went through the carport and stepped out onto a covered deck that ran the entire length of the back of the house. He saw planters filled with pansies and the green spears of budding daffodils, and hummingbird feeders hanging from the rafters. He saw wind chimes gently swaying, though he couldn't hear their music. Just off the deck and reachable from it, he saw a bird feeder hanging from the branch of an oak tree, still rocking slightly from the customers scared away by his sudden appearance. He saw that a set of French doors leading into the living room was standing wide open, though the air temperature was dropping rapidly with the coming dusk. Alarmed, realizing now that the house was empty, he began to look around in earnest, his eyes lifting to scan beyond his immediate surroundings. And now at last he saw her.

She was standing on a broad platform—a boat dock, it looked like—far out on the water at the end of a long pier. She had her back to the house and was watching the sunset fade, her arms wrapped around herself for warmth. She couldn't have been home long, he realized. Even from that distance he could see that she still had on the blazer and slacks she'd been wearing since yesterday.

He walked rapidly down the steps and across the lawn, slowing as he went, realizing he didn't know how to approach her. He didn't want to startle her, and with the music on she couldn't possibly hear him. With her back to him, she wouldn't even know he was here. As he stepped onto the pier, he could feel his heart beating.

He'd only taken a few steps before she turned and saw him. She'd felt him, he imagined, felt the vibrations of his footsteps on the wooden pier. He lifted his hand in greeting, knowing what light there was would be on his face, and that she should be able to identify him well enough. *Her* face was in purple shadow, and unreadable. She didn't move a muscle, didn't raise her hand in response to his wave, but simply stood with her arms crisscrossing her body, and waited for him to approach. Something in the way she held herself, in her very stillness, told him she wasn't smiling.

What do I say to her? Hawk thought as he walked toward that silent, waiting figure, his heart thumping now in rhythm with his footsteps on the planks of the pier, to the music soaring out of the stereo into the cold, winy dusk. *What am I doing? What's my reason for being here?* He realized that for once in his life he hadn't prepared a cover story in advance.

At the join of the pier and the dock he paused, one hand resting on the railing. A few feet still separated him from Jane. He could see her face now but still couldn't read it. She had the slightly dazed look of someone who couldn't quite believe what she was seeing.

"Hi," he said, making a feeble attempt to smile.

"Hi," she responded, and he saw her shoulders hunch suddenly, as if a chill had just shaken her.

Now what? She didn't say anything more, refusing to ask the expected question, "What are you doing here?," to which he was certain inspiration would have provided him with a clever and believable reply. Instead, the music abruptly ceased and the evening filled with silence, a timeless void marked only by the faint creaking of the dock and the hollow thudding of his heart. *My God,* he thought, *what's happening here?* Another minute and he'd be shaking like an adolescent standing on his first date's doorstep.

The silence ended as abruptly as it had begun, on the opening chords of "The Blue Danube Waltz." And Hawk, hearing the familiar melody of the introduction, felt something happening inside him. Something seemed to stretch and reach...to struggle, then suddenly lift, like a bird making its first leap toward the sky. For the first time in many years he felt...*happy.*

He kept his face straight as he made a small, stiff bow from the waist, but laughed as he held out his hand, making a joke of it when he said, "Ma'am, may I have this dance?"

Chapter 13

He seemed to her to come from nowhere, as if conjured from the purple shadows by a cruel and heartless genie. In spite of that, she never doubted for a moment that he was real; in fact, she wondered if, in some locked-away part of herself, she had even been expecting him.

Oh, God. Of course. He's figured it out. He knows.

In the next moment, bewildered, she thought, but if that's so, then why is he *here?* Unless...he still thinks it's me.

"Hi," he said. And she responded, somehow, though her heart was pounding so hard it hurt.

And then she saw the unmistakable, unbelievable leap of gladness in his face, in his eyes, and felt the very same within her entire being. *Glad to be here? Glad to see...me?* Her body shivered and tingled with shock, and her legs weakened. She wanted to run into his arms, touch his face, feel his hands on her body, and know once again those kisses that had seemed to reach into her very soul.

Instead, she stood still, and silent, and so did he.

She saw his hand extend toward her, and she stared at it uncomprehending. What does this mean? she thought. *What does this mean?*

Then, unbelievably, he laughed and said, "Would you like to dance?"

To see joy and laughter in his face was what she'd wanted, longed for. In response, she should have felt joy, too. But she didn't. Instead, it was anger that began to rise like steam from the churning soup of her emotions.

Why is he doing this? she wondered. What does he want from me, when he has nothing to give me back? I won't let him do this to me—I won't. *I can't.* I promised myself, she inwardly whimpered, wanting, childlike, to slap at his hand and shout, *Go away! Leave me alone!* Hadn't she just vowed, after last night, never again to let herself need anyone so much? *Never again.*

A sharp, breathy sound escaped her; it might have been mistaken for a laugh, but it was pain. Pure anguish. But the music filled her ears and invaded her mind like a drug, and she saw her hand reach out as if it were guided by someone else's will. She saw herself like the young girl in the painting, in a graceful and low-cut gown and high-piled coiffure, as Tom, elegant in embroidered waistcoat and silk cravat, took her hand in his and raised it briefly to his lips. For a moment she was sure that on the cold March breeze she had caught the scent of lilacs.

She took a step backward and Tom followed her onto the landing, as if they were the choreographed first steps of the dance. He guided her gently into position. Then for a few beats they stood still, listening to the rhythm, adjusting to it with their bodies while they gazed at one another. And he was smiling, but she was not.

Their eyes never left each other's faces as they began to move and sway to the tempo of the waltz, small, tentative steps at first, but gradually gaining in confidence and gusto, until they were whirling around on the gently rocking platform as if it were a ballroom floor. The last of the light faded, and the sky filled up with stars. Yard lights came on and swam in the dark water like reflected moons.

The platform dipped suddenly, riding the wake of a distant and long-departed boat. Jane gasped and lurched toward Tom, off balance. He caught her close while he steadied them both, then murmured, "Feels just like old times."

"We're both going to wind up in the water," she said, her

voice bumpy with frightened laughter. She tried to pull away, but he wouldn't let her.

The song ended, the last one on the CD, and silence came to stay. And still he wouldn't release her from the warm and heart-wrenchingly wonderful prison of his arms. She drew her hands from his neck and shoulder and brought her folded arms between them, and tried to lighten the moment by saying mockingly, "You *are* surprising."

She heard the familiar irony in his voice as he responded in the same mode, "You, too, Miss Jane."

"I've always loved to dance," she said, and the irony faded from her voice as she added, "I guess that's why I liked the painting so much."

He didn't speak. His arms shifted, one hand coming to cover hers and press them against his chest. She could feel his heart beating beneath her fingers as his head slowly descended.

As well as she knew he was going to kiss her, as much as she wanted him to, she knew that she would be truly and forever lost if he did. So she turned her face away before he could, saying on a ripple of laughter as false as it was light, "Tom, what in the world are you *doing* here?"

She could feel his breath sigh soundlessly through his body as he let her go. "I came to see you, what else?" And she *knew* he was smiling his familiar crooked smile.

"I thought you were going back to Arlington, to try and find out who bought the other paintings." She was moving away from him, onto the pier, heading back toward the shore, moving quickly to hide the fact that she was trembling.

"I was, and I did." Tom's voice and footsteps followed her up the pier. "Seems all but one of 'em are right here in Cooper's Mill."

"Really?" said Jane faintly. "Imagine..." What is he saying? she wondered, trying desperately to read the thoughts behind that dry and casual voice. *What does he suspect? Or does he know?*

"Yeah, one that I guess didn't sell was still there at the auction company's warehouse. Didn't take us long to check it out. The rest, it seems, your friend Connie Vincent bought."

"Really!" said Jane, her voice high with feigned surprise.

"Yeah, looks like I'm gonna have to wait until tomorrow to

see about those, though. Apparently, they're locked up tight in her shop.''

But you're lying, Jane thought. Because as important as whatever it is you're looking for seems to be to you, I know you'd go in after it right this minute, locks or no locks. If you're waiting for morning, there's a reason for it. What is it? What are you up to, Agent Hawkins? Why are you lying to me?

''I'm just amazed you got here so fast.'' Words tumbled over themselves in their rush to leave her, the way they did at parties, or other occasions when she felt ill at ease. ''Actually, I just got home myself, a little while ago. I haven't even had time to change my clothes, or—''

''Yeah, how come? Greenville's...what? A hundred miles from here?'' And she could hear the tenor of his voice change with his frown.

''It's a long story,'' she said, tossing it off with light, rueful laughter. I know he still suspects me, she thought, shivering as the evening chill found its way inside her jacket and penetrated instantly to her bones. *And I'm making it worse.*

But she couldn't tell him. Not yet. Not until she'd had a chance to find out for sure. Because...what if it wasn't true? There still might be an innocent explanation for everything. Oh, God, she prayed, please let there be an explanation. She couldn't bear the thought that she might have been so wrong, so stupid.

As soon as he could, when they'd left the narrow pier behind and begun to trudge uphill across the broad expanse of lawn, Hawk moved up to walk beside Jane. ''Where are your daughters this evening?'' he asked, making it sound like an effort at polite and casual conversation, though it was something he really did need to know.

She paused at the bottom of the stairs that led up to the deck, smiling gamely, as if trying hard to remember her manners. He was surprised to find that he had to fight with every ounce of will he possessed to keep from reaching for her and pulling her back into his arms. Surprised by how much he wanted to stroke her and hold her and murmur soothing things into her hair, until she trusted him enough to tell him what she was trying so hard not to. *Dammit, Jane, don't lie—you're not good enough at it.*

''The girls are with their father,'' she said in a gracious-hostess voice as she started up the stairs, once more preceding him. "Skiing. They'll be gone all week. Where are you staying, the Best Western?"

"Uh-huh," said Hawk absently. What he was wondering as he topped the last step and moved across the deck, was whether he could expect the bureau's "surveillance" to extend this far outside the house. He was amazed how much it unsettled him to think of someone listening to *his* private conversations, for a change.

"I understand the rooms there are quite nice. Please come in." She pulled the French doors shut after them and bustled through the living room and into the kitchen, turning on lights, setting thermostats and firing questions over her shoulder at him as she went. "Can I get you something to drink? Have you eaten?"

Her kitchen was like her, he thought. Nice. Ordinary. The kind of kitchen you felt comfortable in right away. White curtains at the windows of a breakfast alcove, blue checks on the walls, touches of yellow in sunflowers and daisies...

"Would you like coffee?"

Still thinking of bugs, he shook his head and coughed over his muttered reply.

Her smile was brilliant and painful. "Well. All right, then. Please make yourself comfortable. We're a very casual household—really. Just help yourself from the fridge if you're hungry."

"Thanks, but I think I'll just step outside for a smoke, if that's all right."

"Oh—of course. But you don't have to go outside. I can get you an ashtray—"

"No, that's okay, I'd rather—really."

"Oh, well, then." A valiant smile flickered across her face. "I won't be long..."

He waited until he heard a door close somewhere down a hallway before he let himself out the kitchen's side door. In the carport he paused to light up, and managed a couple of deep drags on the way out to where he'd parked the red Nissan. With the cigarette stuck between his lips and smoke curling into one eye, he unlocked the trunk and opened his travel bag, removing from it a small black object which he put in the pocket of his jacket. He then closed and relocked the trunk, took one last pull on the cigarette, dropped it onto the gravel at his feet and went back into the house.

He could hear the water running as he tiptoed down the hallway and into what had to be Jane's bedroom. Please, God, he thought, curling his fingers around the electronic receiver in his pocket, let her take long, long showers.

It took him all of fifteen seconds to zero in on the frequency and then locate the first bug, behind the headboard of her bed. That made him mad. Just what in the hell, he wondered, were they hoping to hear from that one? He quickly found another one behind the mirror above her dresser, then spent a suspensefilled and futile five minutes going over the rest of the room before he was willing to call it clean.

Ignoring the girls' bedrooms, he moved on to the kitchen next, one ear always tuned to the sounds coming from the other end of the hall. He was just finishing up in there when he heard the water shut off. Hurrying now, he skipped the phones and went straight to the living room. So far, two per room seemed to be the limit; he could only hope he'd found them all.

Back in Jane's bedroom, a door opened. Another closed. Jeez, thought Hawk, grinding his teeth, take your time, dammit! For a woman, she sure was fast. Probably what came from having two daughters and apparently only one bathroom in the house.

He was standing in the middle of the living room, shaking and jingling a handful of small metal objects—about the size of watch batteries—when he heard her bedroom door open.

Damn! he thought. What in the hell was he going to do with the blasted things? He couldn't very well carry them around in his pocket.

There was pretty much only one thing he could do. Casting one quick look over his shoulder, he opened the French doors, stepped onto the deck and hurled the handful of expensive, stateof-the-art listening devices as far as he could into the woods that bordered the lawn. He broke into a smile when he saw one hit a branch of the oak tree nearest the deck and fall into the bird feeder. Let them try to figure that one out, he thought, envisioning with a great deal of enjoyment the faces of the FBI techs monitoring the mikes when they heard nothing but twitterings and chirpings and random pecking sounds.

"I told you, you don't have to do that outside," Jane said from behind him.

He turned to find her standing in the softly lit living room, one hand on the frame of the open door, and almost groaned aloud. She was wearing cream-colored leggings and a long-sleeved knit tunic in a dusty rose shade of pink. And he'd been right about the way she looked in it.

"I actually have ashtrays for my guests, believe it or not." The shower seemed to have restored her natural serenity. She was smiling slightly, her head tilted a little to one side, and her hair was brushed back from her face and damp from the shower. He didn't think she'd washed it; she sure as hell hadn't had time to blow it dry. Her face had the scrubbed-fresh, no-makeup look that always seemed to make her appear so vulnerable, as if she lacked a certain critical layer of protection. The elusive and indefinable scent he associated with her drifted to him on the cold night air.

Nice, he thought, and felt his heart quiver inside him.

"Come inside," she said gently. "It's getting cold out."

Once more he followed her into the house. "I'm going to warm up some soup," she said as he was closing the door behind him. "Want some?"

"Sure," he said after a moment's hesitation, following her into the kitchen. "What've you got?"

She'd opened a cupboard and was scanning its contents. "Uh, looks like clam chowder, minestrone and chicken noodle. Oh, and here's a can of lentil." Her nose wrinkled; obviously she wasn't fond of lentil.

"Minestrone's fine," he told her. "Unless you'd rather—"

"No, no, minestrone's good. I'm not a gourmet cook," she warned him as she deftly opened cans. "As you can tell."

"Oh. Well, then, forget it," he said, straight-faced. And got a quick, startled look before she laughed.

He watched her while she worked, only half listening to the tale of her day's travels, the promised "long story" about why it had taken her so long to get home from Greenville. He was thinking about how he was going to do what he'd come to do. What he had to do. Wondering just how he was going to manage to get his hands on something he could be absolutely certain had her fingerprints on it and no one else's.

It was when she opened the dishwasher and began taking cups and bowls out in preparation for setting the table that he knew he had his answer.

"Here, let me do that," he said, stepping quickly forward as she turned with her hands full of dishes, catching her by surprise.

"Oh—no," she automatically began. "You don't..." But she had no stock protest ready, and could only juggle the dishes clumsily as he took them from her.

She uttered a soft gasp when he let one—a soup bowl—slip through his fingers.

He spat out his standard, all-purpose cussword under his breath as it shattered, then mumbled, "Ah, jeez—I'm sorry..." He deposited the rest of the dishes haphazardly on the table and dropped to one knee beside the scattered shards, his handkerchief in his hands.

But she was already there before him, on her knees and pushing his hands away, saying in a breathless, almost panicky voice, "Oh, don't—please. Here, let me—I don't want you to cut yourself..."

"Can't believe I did that. Here—put 'em in here." He held his handkerchief like a basket and watched her while she carefully deposited the larger shards in it.

"It's okay—really. I told you, we're a casual household."

"I'll replace it. Just tell me—"

"Don't be ridiculous. I don't think I have a complete set of dishes in the entire house. There, I guess that's most of it."

He rose to his feet, cradling the broken china in his hands. "Trash?"

"Under the sink. Here, let me—"

"'S'okay, I got it." He kept his back to her as he dumped the shards into the trash, so she couldn't see him fold two of the largest pieces into his handkerchief and tuck them away in his pocket.

He was smiling lopsidedly as he turned back to her, saying, "Listen, I sure am sorry..." It was only when he saw her swiping blindly at the floor with a paper towel that he realized she was crying.

Like most people in law enforcement, Hawk had long ago become inured to women's tears. Not only was it a matter of self-preservation; it was also his experience with both sexes that tears usually tended to flow in amounts directly proportional to the degree of guilt of the weeper.

But *this* woman? *Crying?*

He couldn't believe it. This was Jane, the woman who'd confronted an intruder in her hotel room with a Roy Rogers cap pistol and brought an experienced FBI agent to his knees. She'd been knocked out, chased through the streets of the nation's capital and endured six hours locked in a moving truck without food, water or toilet facilities, had even braved seasickness, all without so much as a sniffle. This he couldn't understand at all. This he couldn't tolerate.

"Hey, Carlysle, what is it? What's wrong?" he growled, awed and fearful, thinking maybe, possibly, even hoping she'd cut herself. Hoping it was something so simple. He squatted in front of her, balancing on the balls of his feet, and gently touched her beneath the chin, trying to get her to look at him. But she turned her face away from him so abruptly he felt the cool splash of her tears on the back of his hand.

She rose, eluding him, and threw the balled-up paper towel into the sink with an angry, jerky motion.

"Why are you here?" she asked suddenly, in a voice like the cry of some small, hurt animal. "What do you *want* with me?" She'd asked him the very same things once before, he remembered, but with different inflections. It was amazing what a difference those inflections made. This time he felt her words like arrows in his heart.

He hesitated, thinking of the pieces of broken china in his pocket, wondering if there was some way she could have seen him put them there, some way she could know. "What do you mean?" he asked warily as he stood, moving slowly and with great caution, the way he would in the presence of a cornered and unpredictable suspect.

She kept her face averted and didn't answer. He studied her, the curve of her ear, the side of her neck and the damp hair curling there. He remembered how soft her skin was, and the way she smelled. And he told her the simple truth: "I came because I needed to see you again."

She laughed. Not a comfortable, gently mocking chuckle, like the last time she'd skewered him so deftly with that particular weapon. This was a high, sharp bark of sheer disbelief, and he thought about the irony of being rejected for telling the God's-honest truth, when he was accustomed to having his glibbest lies taken as gospel.

"Why is that so hard to believe?" he asked, approaching her cautiously. He put his hands on her shoulders, and his jaw clenched involuntarily when she flinched. He turned her toward him, his hands firm but gentle when she resisted. Still she kept her face lowered, hidden from him, and he understood finally that she was distressed and humiliated by her tears.

Since he couldn't very well offer her his handkerchief, he reached for the roll of paper towels she'd left on the counter, tore one sheet off and then, instead of handing it to her, began oh so gently to mop her cheeks with it. He was probably clumsy—tenderness didn't exactly come naturally to him—but in any case, she gave a funny little sniffle, sort of a half laugh, and finally looked up. Her eyes were open, and gazing straight into his.

And once again he thought of the sea, and of dolphins, and of rain, and sunshine breaking through clouds, and rainbows over gray water. But now, for some reason, there was a poignancy in her gaze that touched him deep inside. The towel he was holding brushed the tear-filled creases at the corner of her eye and then was still. And he lowered his head and kissed her.

At first he thought it was going to be all right. He felt her breath sigh through her body, and her lips begin to soften as he touched them. It felt to him as though he were kissing her for the very first time. So sweet, so sweet, he thought, although it was salt he tasted, and he wondered why he suddenly ached so much inside.

Until he realized he was remembering the first time he'd ever kissed Jenny...

He thought it must have been autumn, following the spring he'd turned sixteen. Grief-stricken and rebellious, he'd fled his house, heading straight and true across the backyard to Jen's house, as usual. Meeting at the boundary between their two properties, they'd gone for a walk in the woods nearby. He'd been hurrying, furious. He remembered the swish and crunch of leaves underfoot, and the squirrels that fled, scolding, before them. *Don't cry,* Jen had said, reaching for his hand. And she'd leaned over—he'd had several more years of growing to do, and she'd been as tall as he was then—and she'd kissed him. He'd stopped and faced her, daring her to run away. But she'd just looked solemnly back at him, never blinking, never wavering. He'd never kissed anyone before. He'd thought his heart might punch a hole in his chest. He'd tasted salt then, too, he remembered. Only then, the tears had been his....

He felt her lips—Jane's lips—quiver, and almost groaned aloud when she turned her face aside. He held himself still, except for his jackhammer heart, and whispered, "What's the matter?"

He could feel her trembling. She said in a cracked and testy voice, "Please don't do this."

He felt as if he were balanced precariously on the edge of a chasm, afraid even to breathe. "Why not?" She shook her head desperately. He gave a short huff of puzzled laughter. "We've done it before."

"Yes."

"I thought it was..." *Phenomenal* was the word that came immediately to mind, but he settled instead for "good."

She gave a little gulp that was more like a whimper than a laugh. "Oh, yes."

"Well, then..."

She drew away enough so that she could look at him, and he was left tensely stroking her shoulders, simply to keep himself from pulling her against him. She whispered, "But it's different now."

"Yeah, it is." God, he wished his heart wouldn't beat so hard. His lips quirked wryly. "We're not in a truck anymore. Looks to me like we've got all the time, space and privacy we need for what comes—" He stopped suddenly, thinking he understood. That unaccustomed tenderness assailed him.

Thoroughly ashamed of himself, he rubbed his hands up and down her arms, drawing her cold hands into his and cradling them both against his chest. "Hey," he said gruffly, "is that what's bothering you? The 'what comes after'? Look, we don't have to do anything you don't want to do. Far as I'm concerned, 'what comes after' is always a mutual decision. Hell, I'm no Neanderthal."

Her eyes stabbed at him like darts when he said that, and she muttered almost angrily, "Don't be ridiculous—I know that." Then her lashes dropped like curtains, and she gave a small, helpless sigh. "It isn't that."

"Then..."

She shook her head, drew breath for another sigh, and he could see her struggling with it, working toward a decision of some sort. Part of him—the heated and lusty, eternally adolescent part—waited, panting and confident, for the moment when he could pull her back into his embrace, knowing that it would be only one endless kiss from there to her bedroom. The other, the wounded and wary adult part of him, knew that nothing would ever be so simple for him again.

"It's different," she said, so carefully he wondered what it must have cost her to keep her voice steady. "Because I care about you."

A chuckle rattled around inside his chest. "I care about you, too." But it was the kind of thing he'd said many times before. It was too glib and came too easily, and he could tell by the bottomless look she gave him as she pulled her hands from his that she knew it.

She shook her head and turned away, rubbing her arms as if she was cold. "Hey, what's wrong?" he said, reaching for her again, still half laughing, "That's supposed to make things better, not worse."

He was completely unprepared when she rounded on him, flinching angrily from his outstretched hand. "I care about you...too much," she said as her eyes leaked liquid fire. "*Too much*. Do you understand?" He waited, dumbstruck and scarcely breathing, for her to finish. "And you're still grieving for your *wife!*"

Chapter 14

It was the last thing she'd ever wanted to say to him. She regretted the words the minute they were out of her mouth, but of course there was nothing she could do about it then. She knew all too well that words once spoken can never be taken back.

With a furious, choked-off sob, she turned her back on Tom's stricken face and tried her best to erase from her heart and soul the memory of the pain she'd glimpsed in his eyes. And she waited, breath held and trembling, the way one waits after the lightning flash for the thunder.

What she heard instead in that tense and breathless silence was the faint rustle and crackle of paper. The click of a cigarette lighter. The softest of exhalations. And then at last she heard his footsteps scuff the vinyl-tile floor, moving away from her, toward the breakfast nook. Away, not closer. As of course she wanted him to do. Had all but asked him to do.

And still she felt a vast sense of loneliness and loss.

"Yeah, I still grieve for my wife and my son." His voice was harsh in her friendly kitchen, so warm and fragrant with the homey smell of steaming soup. "I probably always will. I loved Jenny for twenty-two years, dammit—that's almost half my life. Jason was my child—my *only* child. You don't stop loving somebody just because they happen to *die.*''

"Of course not," Jane whispered. She opened a drawer, took out an ashtray and stood for a moment holding it, keeping her back to him as she drew a courage-building breath. Why not? she thought. *Why not? I have nothing else to lose.* "But," she said, her voice shaking, "does it mean you can't love anyone else, ever again?"

He didn't answer, and when she turned with the ashtray in her hands, she saw that he'd moved around the table so that it stood between them, like a barrier.

"I don't know," he said, and for a moment his eyes blazed at her with the brightness of pain. Then he shook his head and looked away, reaching blindly for the ashtray she'd placed on the table. "I know I loved my wife. I don't know if I'll ever love anyone else that way again. I know, well, hell, I haven't exactly been a monk in the seven years since she died, but there hasn't been anyone that even came close." He pulled his gaze back to her then, as if it was a hard thing to do, and there was no escaping the anguish in his face, and the confusion, the longing, and...fear.

He's afraid, she thought, suddenly understanding. *Afraid of letting go.*

"And where," she softly asked, "does that leave me?"

She saw his jaw clench, and he punched the words through them. "Damned if I know!" He brought his fist down gently on the tabletop, but his knuckles were white and his voice rose, rocky with anger. "I don't know what's going on with me right now, if you want to know the truth. I know I like you, dammit. I like your company. I know I want you, and not just to have sex with, either, though God knows—and I think you do, too—that I do want that. I mean I want you *around*—to talk to, *be* with—and that's not something I've said to anyone in seven years, let me tell you!" He glared at her as if both blaming and daring her to dispute him.

She stared back at him, eyes burning, her whole face aching with the need to relieve the tension with tears. But I can't cry, she thought. It will make it so much worse. *I won't cry.* She said nothing, and watched the anger and frustration in his face turn to bewilderment.

"But the thing is, ever since I met you, it seems like I keep being reminded of Jenny. Not...*you*, exactly—I mean, it's not that *you* remind me of Jen. You're nothing like her. Just...things. Little things. It's like...you've brought her back to me, or something." His red-rimmed eyes stabbed her accusingly. "Now every time I turn around, seems like I bump into a memory of Jen."

"And is that such a bad thing?" Jane asked, her tongue thick with unshed tears.

"It's *hell*." Again he ground the words out through tightly clenched teeth. "Do you know how hard I've tried to *forget*? For *seven years?*"

"Maybe," she ventured, hugging herself now, hoping he wouldn't see or notice that she was shaking, "you aren't supposed to forget. Maybe it's time to remember...and then—" she caught a quick breath and whispered it "—say goodbye."

There were moments of suspenseful silence. Then he uttered a surprised-sounding "Huh!" and unexpectedly smiled. It was the same little lopsided smile that had always struck her as being so poignant; now, at least, she thought she understood why.

"Funny," he muttered as he stubbed out his cigarette in the ashtray, "someone else just said the same thing to me a couple of days ago...."

When he looked back at her, his eyes had softened and the smile was slipping. "Look, all I know is, I wanted to see you again. *Needed* to see you, actually. So—" he gave an offhand shrug she knew was only meant to hide his terrible vulnerability "—I guess that's the answer to your question, why I'm here."

But not the second question, thought Jane. *What do you want with me?*

Because we both know exactly what you can't ever bring yourself to admit. Simply put: *You need me.*

She didn't know which she wanted to do more—laugh or cry. If she'd thought David a master when it came to knowing how to push her buttons, then Tom Hawkins must be in a class by himself. He'd known her only a few days, and already he knew the one way to short-circuit her resolve, the one button she could never resist. *He needs me.*

But, her heart protested, what about me? I need too. I want. I *deserve*. Someone who loves...*me*.

Before she knew she was going to, she heard herself speaking softly, almost musingly. Leaning against the countertop with her arms folded across, and pressed hard against, the quivering ball of nerves that had taken the place of her stomach, she began to tell him about herself. And about David.

"I met my husband when I was just seventeen, Tom. I was in high school, a straight-A student, and I had so many dreams. David was very jealous, possessive and controlling, which I, of course, thought meant that he loved me. Because I was young, and didn't know then that loving someone doesn't mean putting them in a cage. It means giving them room to *fly*."

Her voice cracked on the last word, and she had to look away quickly and wait until she was sure she had both her voice and her face under control again before she dared go on. All the while, Tom said nothing, but simply watched her, quietly smoking. He seemed to be waiting for her to continue, and after a while, in a low, husky murmur, she did.

"When I was nineteen, I found that I was pregnant. I'd just started college, but I dropped out, and we got married—familiar story, right? Especially in those days." She smiled wryly, not quite meeting his eyes. "I must tell you that I didn't look forward to my wedding day and future life with joy and optimism. It was more like...resignation. I knew life with David would never be easy, but I believed I was doing the right thing.

"Anyway. Two weeks after the wedding, I had a miscarriage." Tom exhaled audibly. "It was early in the pregnancy. The child wasn't real to me," she said gently. "I didn't grieve for it. What I grieved for were my dreams, my...possibilities." She took a deep breath. "But only for a little while. I told myself David was a good man, a hard worker, that he would love and provide for me, and I told myself that I loved him and it was up to me to make him a good wife and a happy home.

"And I did, dammit." There was anger now, and she didn't even try to hide it, to keep her voice from grating or one hand from curling into a fist. "For so many years I followed him dutifully from place to place, pouring all my energy into trying to be the perfect wife, the perfect mom, spending all my creativity to make our home lovely and serene. And David, well, to give him credit, he was indeed a good man, a hard worker, a good provider, and after Lynn and Tracy were born, a very good dad. What he never learned how to be was a partner, a friend, a mate...a husband.''

She paused, knowing she was getting more carried away than she'd planned, meaning to apologize to Tom for boring him with her life story when he was so obviously more in need of a listener than a lecture. But he'd pulled out a chair and seated himself at the table, and was gazing at her intently, listening to her, it seemed, with every cell in his body. So she gave him the apology in a shrug and a smile and continued.

''As the years went by, I realized that David not only didn't love me, that in fact he probably isn't capable of loving anyone. He only possesses people. He loves the girls, because to him they are extensions of himself. Me he cared about only in terms of what I provided for him—his home, his children, his meals. Sex. I was expected to do my job, like any good employee, while his function, like that of any good boss, was to delegate as much work and responsibility to me as possible, and in return provide me with a living wage. Period.''

''God,'' said Tom under his breath, almost involuntarily.

Jane glanced at him and found that this time it was impossible to look away again. She said softly, ''Little by little, I came to understand that I was very much alone. And that I was lonely. I decided that I had to do something, because if I didn't, I was going to die of loneliness. I believe it, you know—that you *can* die of loneliness. You die inside, the part of you that really matters, a little at a time.''

''And so,'' he murmured, not disagreeing, ''you got a divorce.''

''No,'' she said. ''I took up dancing.'' And she had to laugh at the look on his face. ''It's true. I signed up for dancing lessons. I meant it as a way for David and I to share something, to actually do something together for once. But he thought it was silly, said he was too busy and refused to go, and because I'd already spent the money, I went ahead anyway. It was pretty awful, at first. I hated the group lessons—as one of several unattached women, I always seemed to wind up dancing the man's position—but the instructor was very good. So I signed up for private lessons.

''I know what you're thinking,'' she said when Tom restlessly stirred, frowned and reached for his cigarettes. ''It's what David thought, too—that I was having an affair with my dance teacher. How trite, huh? And actually, I did adore Hans—''

''Hans?''

''He was Dutch, I think—maybe German. Probably gay, but so what? He was young and lithe and graceful and charming, but more to the point, he made *me* feel all those things. When I was on that dance floor with Hans, I felt…as if I could fly. As if I were a bird, just released from a cage, and I was soaring…and that there was no limit to the sky.''

She stopped on a high note that was too dangerously close to being a sob, and after a few restorative moments, gave a low chuckle and murmured, ''Oh, boy, David was furious. He demanded that I quit. But…'' She paused then, remembering, reliving the terrible sense of panic and futility she'd felt as she'd tried to make David understand. She felt it again now as she wondered how she could ever expect Tom, a man, to know what it felt like to be a woman and trapped by other people's expectations.

Passion filled her chest with pain; once more she doubled her fingers into a fist and used it to press against the ache. ''He might just as well have asked me to give up *light*. I mean, I felt as if I'd been living in the dark for so long, you know? And now someone had come along and turned on the light. And here was this man who supposedly loved me, and he was asking—telling—me I had to go back to the dark! *I couldn't.* I just couldn't. He didn't understand. He kept saying, 'How could you put a *dance* class above your marriage, for God's sake?' He didn't know it wasn't a dance class he was asking me to give up, it was *life.*''

''And so,'' said Tom in a rough, quiet voice, exhaling smoke, ''you got a divorce. Hell, I don't blame you.''

''Not even then,'' Jane said, relaxing slightly, but not quite believing he really understood. ''Believe it or not. It never entered my head. All I wanted then was to do some of the things I'd always dreamed of doing, in spite of his disapproval. I enrolled in some college classes, for instance.'' She gave a soft, derisive snort, and said the rest with a little smile on her face, knowing it would sound too angry, too bitter if she let all her pain and frustration show. ''Well, when David found out he couldn't control me any longer, he just withdrew from me completely. Punishing me, I suppose. Sex was the last thing to go, probably because that meant a certain amount of inconvenience for him, as well. Eventually, all I was getting from him was hostility and disapproval.''

"That's no way to live," Tom said in a voice so gravelly it almost hurt to hear it.

"No," Jane agreed softly, "it isn't. And I knew that. But it still took a couple more years of pain and fear and the most awful guilt before I was finally able to tell David I wanted out. It was on the eve of our twenty-first wedding anniversary. I think it was partly that—'' she smiled a little ''—partly the fact that I'd just turned forty. Maybe a little that Lynn was a senior in high school, and I knew she was going to be leaving home soon. Then in a few more years, Tracy...and I'd be truly alone.

"Anyway—'' she drew a deep, shuddering breath ''—I did it, and it was a hell I wouldn't wish on my worst enemy, and I vowed that I would never, ever go through something like that again. I also vowed,'' and finally she had to whisper, ''that I wouldn't let myself settle, ever again, for anything less than someone who would love me, cherish me...and give me the freedom to fly. It's been five years, dammit, and I haven't.'' She paused to snatch an agonized breath before blurting out, ''Do you think it's too much to ask?''

Tom shook his head. There was a long silence while he scowled at the floor.

"And now,'' she said gently, and his eyes came back to her, warily, still frowning, as if he knew what she was going to say, ''you are asking me to give you...all these feelings I have for you.'' As hard as it was, she gazed at him without wavering, letting him see everything that was in her heart at that moment, knowing how it must hurt him to acknowledge it. ''You want me to give all that I have to give—because that's the only way I know how, Tom. When I feel something, I give it *all*. And believe me, that's a *lot*. And in return, you can give me...nothing?''

There was another long silence before he finally coughed and said in that voice that was as raw as tearing cloth, ''Right now, yeah. That's about the size of it.''

He stubbed out his cigarette clumsily, like a blind man, and got to his feet. His smile was as skewed and painful as she'd ever seen it when he looked at her and muttered, "I always have been pretty much of a sonuvabitch."

He paused, then shook his head and added on a note of wonder, "That's what made Jen such a miracle, I guess. A man can't expect to get two such miracles in one lifetime."

And she knew that he was leaving.

It was what she wanted, of course. It was what had to happen. It was the way things had to be—for *her* sake. For *her* well-being and happiness, for all that she'd promised herself, all that she'd dreamed. Tom, of the gentle hands, the thrilling kisses, the unthinkingly caring little gestures...Tom had nothing left of his heart to give her. He'd invested it all in a woman and a child and buried it with them when they died. And she was sorry for him. She ached for his loneliness and need. But she couldn't sacrifice her need for his. *She couldn't.*

Oh, God, she thought, please don't let me do this.

He knew he had to leave. It wasn't what he wanted. *God knows...* Hawk actually thought it might have been easier to leave behind one of his appendages—at least for that they gave you some kind of anesthesia.

This was almost as bad as losing Jen and Jason all over again. In a way, he felt as if he was reliving it, those terrible days after the bombing...the hospital...leaving Marseilles, returning to their house in Florence...walking away from it that last time. Feeling as if his whole body had been tied down with lead weights, as if he were swimming against a powerful undertow, and every move he made, even the smallest move, required a tremendous effort, all the strength in his body, all the power of his will.

How many times he'd railed against his own strength and will, wishing he could just give in, give up and let the undertow take him down. But he hadn't. Something inside him had made him keep making that next stroke, taking that next step, waking up to face one more day. Doing what had to be done. Simply because it was the way things had to be.

That was what it felt like to him now. Like his whole body was lead, and it took all his strength just to move his arms, to pick up his jacket, put one foot in front of the other. But he did it because it was what had to be done. He had to leave Jane standing there looking at him with her rain-drenched eyes. Walk

out of her house, get in his borrowed red Nissan and drive away
and never, ever come back. Never see her again.

It wasn't what he wanted. It was the way things had to be.
For her sake, because what he wanted from her was something
he couldn't give her in return. And for his sake, because he
knew she'd give it to him if he asked her, and he wouldn't be
able to live with himself if he did.

He didn't say goodbye. He didn't trust himself to speak. He
went outside into the March night, carrying his jacket in one
hand, not even feeling the cold, feeling only numbness and a
terrible sense of urgency. Because he knew that if he didn't get
to the car, get it started and get the hell away from Jane's house
as fast as he possibly could, he might still do the unforgivable.
He could still walk back into her warm happy kitchen and take
her in his arms and pull her warm, giving body against him and
kiss her until she begged him to stay. He could do it.

Please, God, don't let me do it.

He had the car started, the lights on and his seat belt fastened,
and was just putting the car in gear when suddenly she was
there at his window. Adrenaline hit him, and it was like running
full tilt into a wall. She lifted a hand and knocked on the glass,
but he could only stare at her, shocked and jangling like a mal-
functioning fire alarm, all his impulses and responses hopelessly
scrambled. *Don't do this. For the love of God, just drive away....*

But she was opening the door, bending down to him, and he
knew it was too late for that now.

"Jane," he growled just as she was whispering, "Please,
Tom. Come back inside."

"For God's sake, what are you doing?" Angrily, he threw
the gear lever into Park. The heater came on and blew gusty,
humid air against the windshield, fogging it.

"I'd like you to stay."

He could only look at her, everything inside him vibrating
like a badly timed engine. Her face was a pale blur in the artificial moonlight given off by the mercury vapor yard lamps. He
saw that she was hugging herself in the loose, soft tunic, and
from the sound of her voice, he knew that she was shivering.

He stared at her and didn't know what to say or how to feel.
A moment ago he'd been engaged in a tug-of-war with his own
impulses, requiring every ounce of willpower he possessed to

keep from doing what she was now asking—begging—him to do. And perversely, now that she was asking, it was both easier and harder to resist.

Finally, of all the emotions rattling around inside him at that moment, anger seemed safest, the one least likely to produce a boomerang effect. Because it was impossible, under any circumstances, to imagine Jane angry.

"You want me to *stay?*" he said harshly. "And all that stuff you just told me in there—what was that, a bunch of garbage?"

"I meant every word of it," she said in her soft, serene way. "And I still want you to stay."

"Why?"

Why? Because, Tom Hawkins, in looking back over the last few days, I've realized that the happiest I've ever been in my life was when I was with you. And that the most miserable I've ever been in my life, since I met you, was when I wasn't with you. Bottom line? Under any circumstances, it seems I'm happier with you than without you. Go figure, huh?

"Because," she said, bumpy with shivers of cold and fear, "I want you."

He almost laughed, and was fully aware of how ironic it would be if he did. After all, she'd done the same thing to him—twice. He didn't laugh, not out of any particular sense of chivalry or nobility, but because, even in the bad light, he could see the fear and vulnerability in her face. It had about the same effect on his anger that the Nissan's defroster was having on the fogged-up windshield.

"You want me?" he said roughly. A pulse began to scrabble behind his belt buckle. "Hell, I want you, too—I told you that. That's not what this is about, is it?"

She didn't answer; her face appeared frozen, her eyes fathomless pools. He realized that he'd never wanted anything so much as to have her close to him at that moment, wrapped up in his arms, naked, legs entangled, breaths comingled, and to drive the chill from her body with the raging heat in his. It was like nothing he'd ever felt before, a wave of desire so intense it was like a sickness; his head swam with dizziness. Struggling with it was like fighting to remain conscious.

With thickened tongue, he said, "You were right, you know—what you said in there—you do deserve a whole lot more than I can give you. For right now, for sure. Maybe not ever. I don't know. That's the problem—I just don't know. I can't give you any promises.''

"I'm not asking for any.''

He drew a breath that sounded like a sigh and said under his breath, "What do you think I am? I'd have to be a real sonuvabitch, you know that? To stay...''

And it occurred to Jane for the first time that maybe *she* was the one who was being unfair, that maybe she was asking too much of *him*. She thought about stepping away from the car door, letting him go. But her body wouldn't obey her.

"I should drive away right now," he muttered, his scowl fierce and furious. "I should—''

I should let him go. Panic zapped through her like a current of electricity, weakening her knees. *If I do, I'll never see him again.* Desperately, she clung to the door, wondering how she'd ever manage to stand if he drove away and left her there. Wondering how she'd survive if he did. And how would I stop him, she thought, if he's determined to go? Shoot out his tires with my Roy Rogers cap pistol? *I won't beg—I won't!*

"Ah, dammit.'' He lanced her with an accusing stare and growled, "You're gonna freeze to death—either get in here or go back in the damn house!''

Instantly, as if he'd said a magic word, she let go of the door. He pulled it shut while she darted around the front of the Nissan, flitting like a moth through the headlights. A moment later the passenger-side door opened, letting in a rush of cold air and her sweet, familiar scent. She settled into the seat and the door slammed with a quiet *thunk,* and together they sat listening to the rush and growl of the heater, and their own uneven breathing.

"This is ridiculous," Hawk muttered after a moment. "You know that, don't you?''

"Yes," she agreed, breathless, "it's much warmer in the house.''

He shook his head, laughing soundlessly, and looked sideways at her. Her presence, her being...her smell, her warmth, all that she was...swamped his senses. His stomach growled audibly.

"And, there's soup," she added pointedly.

"Carlysle," he growled, "what in the hell am I gonna do with you?"

Neither of them spoke. There was no sound in the car; even the heater's gale seemed to Hawk to have become part of the rush and surge of his own life forces; he could hear them echoing inside his head. And the answer to his question lay teetering between them like a live grenade....

Later, he wondered if it was something she'd done—the faintest of sounds, the most infinitesimal movement, perhaps—that triggered it. He couldn't think how else to account for what happened—the sudden *shift* inside him, the almost audible click as if someone had thrown a switch, and a whole complex set of gears had settled smoothly into place. He had a vague awareness of changed rhythms and altered perspectives, a half-fearful sense that the changes might be both profound and permanent, and then he was reaching for her, his hand going like a homing missile to the back of her neck, and his fingers were pushing roughly through her hair as he pulled her to him.

This time there was no kidding himself that the kiss would be some kind of diversion, something fun to pass the time, a game. Before his lips had even touched hers he knew that this was going to compare with the frolic in the moving van about the way his Walther 9-millimeter compared to Jane's Roy Rogers cap pistol. This was the real thing. Dangerous. Devastating. He knew that going in. What he wasn't prepared for was the jolt. It was like getting hit in the chest with a sledgehammer. Like taking a slug in a bullet-proof vest, right over the heart.

I'd forgotten, Jane thought. Forgotten how good this feels. *Forgotten?* No...she wondered now if indeed she'd *ever* known.

She was sure she hadn't known about the ache. About pleasure so intense, so exquisite, so poignant it *hurt*. Never, not even as a naive girl imagining herself wildly, heedlessly in love, had she known such sweet, unbearable joy. Her heart scrambled into her throat, squeezing from it a gasp that was instantly swallowed up in his mouth. She whimpered his name, and he took that, too, hungrily, greedily, as if he was famished, and could never, ever be filled.

Oh, but he was gentle, too...giving, but not forcing; taking, never demanding...almost, she thought, as if he were guiding her in the steps of a dance. The most beautiful, breathtakingly wonderful dance. A dance through heaven…and beyond. So this is what it feels like, she thought. *Flying…*

Her mouth tasted like a drug, a magic potion, pure sin…something with the power to make him forget completely how wrong it was, or that he'd ever tried to resist its spell. Now he could only think about how good it was, and how long it had been since he'd felt like this, and how could he manage to get even closer to her, preferably inside her, and how soon. His heart was pounding, trying to punch a way out of his chest; he had a fire raging in his belly and a volcano in his loins, and a thirst he couldn't seem to quench. Whatever it was she had— potion, drug or sin—he thought he could have drowned in it and died happy.

It had to end, of course, because there simply wasn't room for it to go anywhere. Though for a time, Hawk tried his best to ignore that fact. He filled his hands with her—her hair, her shoulders, her neck—even let them find their way under the loose tunic she wore to the smooth, soft skin and the unexpected fullness of breasts beneath, urging her closer…closer.

And she tried…oh, she tried. Her back arched, her rib cage lifted and her belly pulled taut with yearning. But it was no use. The force was irresistible, but there were too many immovable objects—a console and a cellular-phone box, for starters—between them.

Finally, with a gasp of pure frustration, Hawk pulled his mouth away from hers and skimmed it instead down the side of her throat to the hollow at its base. There he rested, while her pulse jerked against his lips and her fingers tangled in his hair, and tried to restore some kind of order to his thoughts.

Order? There was only one thought in his head. *Where?*

Okay, maybe two. The second being, *How soon?*

Working his way back up the cords of her neck, he found her mouth again, found it soft, pliant, unreasonably sensual. Discovering that he was now in extreme, and rather adolescent, discomfort, he was even considering the back seat, God help him, when she said, moving her lips tantalizingly over his, "What is it…about cars, anyway?"

Hawk had to either groan or laugh. He did both, and into her mouth murmured, "I think I'm too old for this."

Her laughter was shaken and bumpy. "Well, I *know* I am."

But her mouth was there, open and inviting beneath his. He sank into it one more time...and once more...and yet again.

"Tom." It was high and frightened, almost a whimper.

But he was too far gone with passion now for tenderness. He kissed her again, ruthlessly, until her neck muscles let go and her head fell back against the seat, and he heard her give a helpless little moan of surrender. He pushed his hand under the tunic, found a nipple already hard and sensitized and rolled it between his thumb and fingertips until her breath shuddered and her body trembled.

He found her responses to him—her trembling, her whimpers, her helpless surrender—exciting beyond belief. A primitive thing, he knew—a dark and, to the best of his knowledge, heretofore unexplored part of himself, but irresistible as the call of a wild wolf to its mate.

Her chest rose and fell like a bellows. His wandering fingers brushed her soft belly and he exulted when it quivered and tightened beneath his touch. Deft as a surgeon, sure now of his goal and his purpose, he slipped his hand beneath the elastic of the leggings she wore, burrowed his fingers through the springy cushion of hair and took possession of the most intimate and closely guarded part of her. And with that claiming, knew that there would be no going back.

Without his urging, she shifted, and he drove his fingers deeper, parting her, searching for her body's most sensitive places. With his own body he felt the jolt of desire that rocked her when he found it. He took her desperate cries into his own mouth, and forgetting where he was for the moment, tried again to turn, struggling to bring their bodies into still more intimate alignment.

The steering wheel punched him in the vicinity of a kidney. A groan, more of frustration than pain, rumbled through his chest and into his throat. As far as he could figure, there was only one way to avoid that damn steering wheel, and if he did that he didn't even want to *think* about where the gearshift was going to hit him.

Defeated, he let his hand relax so that it cradled her gently and he could feel her pulse throb against his fingers. He withdrew from her mouth with a long sigh and diminishing kisses touched with reluctance and apology to her lips, her cheeks, her throat, her eyelids. Pulling away at last, he looked down into her dazed and fathomless eyes and said thickly, "This is a ploy, isn't it—to get me back into the house."

She made a small, almost comically polite, throat-clearing sound and murmured, "Not at all. There's always the back seat."

Hawk snorted. "I thought we agreed we're too old for that sort of nonsense."

Her voice was hushed and shaken. "It's been a long time, but I think I can still remember how..."

"Yeah?" Something dark and primitive jolted through him; he didn't like to be reminded that any man besides himself had ever touched her. Ridiculous, he told himself. She was married for twenty-one years—almost half her life, for God's sake. She's divorced, has two children. And you have no claim on her whatsoever. Absurd.

She'd been young, she'd told him, when she'd met her husband. Still in her teens. He wondered if she'd lost her virginity in the back seat of a car. His own, he remembered...

That was when it hit him. That from the moment Jane had materialized outside his car window, he hadn't once thought of Jenny.

"Seems to me," Jane was saying, "it's doable, if you don't mind a complete loss of dignity."

Shocked and frightened laughter shuddered through him. "Since when," he croaked, "is sex ever dignified?"

"Well, since you put it that way..."

And there was her mouth again, calling to him like Temptation itself, and her feminine pulse beating against his fingers like a captive bird's wings, and it was easy to close down his mind and his memory again, and hard...so hard to remember why it was he had to stop this, even for the few moments it would take to find them a better place. Hard to remember he'd ever been a separate being, capable of existing on his own. Parting from her at that moment seemed like an amputation.

"One of us has to be sensible," he said at last under his breath, not knowing even as he was doing it where he'd found the strength to lift his mouth from hers, or pull his hand from between her legs. "For God's sake, let's go in the house."

Chapter 15

"**Y**ou okay?" Hawk asked as he waited for her to come around the car. She was moving slowly, he noticed, and wondered if she felt as shaky as he did, or if, perhaps, now that he'd given her breathing room, she was having second thoughts.

She shook her head and gave him a look that implied he'd said something incredibly stupid, but smiled a little, too, as if she'd already forgiven him for it.

Okay? Are you crazy? She wasn't even sure her legs would carry her as far as the house.

She thought it would have been so much easier if they could have just stayed where they were. Or if, at least, he would sweep her up in his arms and charge boldly into the bedroom, like Rhett Butler carrying Scarlett up those stairs. The good old caveman fantasy—let him take the responsibility, and the decision out of her hands!

"Can you walk?"

She met his familiar black scowl with gently arched eyebrows and murmured, "I think so. Can you?"

He chuckled and reached for her hand, lifting it to his lips in an impulse that seemed both out of character, and at the same time oddly familiar. For some reason, maybe because of that,

Jane felt as if her heart had jumped into her throat; she actually felt it would stop her breath.

It's what I want, she thought, fighting panic. *I've made my choice. I won't regret it.*

But still...it would have been so much easier if they could have stayed in the car like teenagers and let passion govern, and not have to think about it at all.

The kitchen was warm and light, and smelled of soup and, faintly, of cigarettes. Jane closed the door and made straight for the stove, picking up a spoon from the countertop with one hand and at the same time reaching efficiently for the burner knob with the other.

Hawk stood with his jacket draped over one shoulder, hooked on a finger, and watched her.

"What are you doing?" he asked after a moment.

Breathlessly, not looking at him, she said, "It just needs warming a little...it'll only take a minute..."

Unnamed emotions, treacherous as rapids, tumbled inside him. "Jane, for God's sake, turn off the stove."

"I thought you were hungry."

"Yeah, I am," he growled, "but sure as hell not for soup."

She had her back to him, her hands resting on the edge of the counter. He had a feeling if she lifted them from that support, they would tremble. He took a step closer to her and said softly, "Jane, look at me." She lifted her head and gave him her profile, but didn't turn. He raised a hand and almost—not quite—touched her. "Come on...please."

And then she did finally face him, leaning against the counter with her arms folded across her middle. He noticed that she was still gripping the soup ladle, as if it were a weapon she might brandish in her defense, if necessary.

His voice was gruff when he said, "You can still call this off, you know. Now you've had a chance to think about it, if you've had second thoughts..."

"No," she said softly. "It's what I want." But her eyes looked scared.

"You're sure?"

"Yes."

"After what—"

"Tom." And now something—could it have been anger?—

crossed her face like daytime lightning, barely discernible except as a flicker in the corner of an eye. But instead of thunder, her voice was a sultry rumble, humid and tense as a hot summer afternoon.

"Everything I told you was true. Including the part about it having been five years—more than five—since I've been with a man. If I'd never met you, if you hadn't kissed me, if you hadn't come here tonight, I'd have gone right on doing without one, and—" her voice rose slightly, a little lift of belligerence that touched him "—very nicely, too, believe me." She paused, then said quietly, "But...I did, and you did, and here we are...and, I'd like you to stay."

Again something darkened briefly in her eyes, but this time he had no trouble identifying it as uncertainty, and she added belatedly, over a choked little swallow, "If you want to."

He frowned and muttered, "You know I do." He felt wired and itchy, as if heat lightning crawled just beneath his skin.

Her eyes met and held his across the well-lit distance between them, and it seemed as though the lightning that was in both of them arced the chasm, as well, met and joined in a charge of electricity that was almost visible.

"Then," she said, "I'd ask of you no more than that. And as for your...scruples—" her mouth tugged sideways in a smile as wry as his own "—you told me you'd been with other women since your wife died. Women you didn't love. What's one more? It's just sex, Tom."

He couldn't account for the spasm of pain that sliced through him, and something he could have sworn was disappointment. But he growled, "Dammit, Jane, this is different."

"Is it?" she said gently. "How?"

He couldn't for the life of him think how to answer her. He only knew it *was* different. It was the reasons why, the possibilities, that terrified him. And the fear kept him silent.

After a moment, she went on in that same gentle tone, "We're both adults, Tom. And we've been adults long enough to have collected quite a bit of emotional baggage. Things are a lot more complicated now than they were when we were kids." Her smile flickered and went out. "It's occurred to me that maybe *I'm* the one who's asking too much, to think there could even be such a thing as love—I mean, you know, falling *in* love—for people our age.''

"Dammit, Carlysle—'' He stopped midsentence. He wasn't sure why it had occurred to him to refute what she'd said; a week ago, if you'd asked him, he'd probably have agreed with her. Hell, he supposed he still did. Sure he did. One to a customer, and he'd already had his.

Frustrated and off balance, he tossed his jacket in the general direction of a chair. It slid to the floor, landing with a faint *clunk*.

Guilt jolted him. But Jane didn't seem to have noticed, and he had more pressing things to think about just then. It wasn't that he'd forgotten why he was there in the first place, or the importance of the game he was in, or what was at stake. But it wasn't *his* game anymore, it was the FBI's, and·they had all bases covered. In a matter of hours, Jarek Singh's key and Loizeau's killer would both be in custody, and all that would be left for Hawk to do was paperwork.

Even what had become his own personal stake—getting Jane cleared of any suspicion of complicity in the whole affair—had lost its sense of urgency. Being as certain of her innocence as he was that the sun would rise tomorrow, and just as certain that the shards in his jacket pocket would prove that beyond any doubt, he didn't see that there was any particular rush to get the evidence back to the FBI labs. Tomorrow would do fine. Tonight was for...

What? Suddenly he wasn't sure exactly what he was really doing there, or what was going to happen. He just had a vague, jumpy idea it might be something important.

He knew what he wanted to do more than anything at that moment, which was haul Jane into his arms, touch her the way he'd been touching her out there in the car and kiss her until neither of them could stand. Sensing it wasn't the best moment to do so, he took out his cigarettes instead.

He frowned as he lit one, thinking about what she'd just said about love, afraid that with the electricity still so intense and dangerous between them, if he touched her the way he wanted to right now he might appear to be saying things he didn't mean, things he wasn't ready to say. He told himself he had to be careful with this woman. He couldn't risk misunderstandings. He told himself he'd been honest with her up to now—about his feelings, anyway—and he didn't intend to start lying at this stage of the game.

It occurred to him that he wished she'd be as honest with him.

Suddenly frustrated beyond bearing, he stuck a cigarette between his lips and muttered furiously around it, "Sometimes I can't figure you out, you know that?"

She gave a small, surprised laugh and leaned to snag the ashtray and move it closer to him, an automatic gesture of consideration and courtesy, and so completely typical of her. "I know women who'd take that as a compliment," she said lightly, then frowned. "I don't know why. I've always wanted more than anything to be understood."

He snatched the ashtray from her and stubbed out his barely touched cigarette, then pushed it away, took her by the shoulders and pulled her closer, but not yet into his arms. Caught by surprise, she put her hands on his chest, the fingers of one still curled around the handle of the soup spoon. He could see her mouth pop open as she stared at it, and he felt her body vibrate with deep-down-inside tremors.

He removed the spoon from her fingers and tossed it into the sink, wincing at the clatter. Then, cupping her jaw and chin with one hand, he tilted her face upward. "Look at me," he commanded. She did, trustingly, lifting those sea-gray eyes to his. And he felt as if the ocean were rising up to meet him.

"I always know what you're feeling," he said, wondering why his tongue felt thick. He felt woozy...dizzy, as if riding a heavy swell—and he'd never been one to get seasick. "Your eyes tell me. They show everything. Did you know that?"

He watched a little pleat of lines appear between her eyebrows, and felt her pulse hammer against his palm. *His* pulse was in his throat.

"I don't know—sometimes you seem so damn frank and open it scares me. Hell, I never know what's going to come out of your mouth. And then sometimes, I look in your eyes and what I'm seeing doesn't match what I'm hearing." He paused, staring down at her as if he might see inside her soul if he only looked hard enough. It was like trying to see the bottom of the ocean. "I can't tell what you're *thinking,* dammit!"

Dear God, thought Jane as a new and heretofore unknown

kind of fear shivered and sparkled like crystal dust just beneath her skin. *This man has known me for a matter of days, and already he knows what David never could figure out in more than twenty-one years.*

Was this what it would be like? Intimacy? To be one of a couple, wholly and completely *with* someone...did that mean she'd have to learn to share her innermost thoughts? Oh, surely not *all* her thoughts. But at least, not to lie about her feelings? Her *true* feelings...

Oh, what a terrifying thing! Imagine having the courage to let someone know when you felt angry, or hurt, or disappointed, or just plain out-of-sorts. Imagine trusting someone enough to let yourself be cranky and disagreeable and moody in his presence, trusting that he would still love you in spite of it. Imagine not having to be *nice* all the time. Imagine being allowed to have flaws. Imagine not having to be perfect in order to be loved. *Imagine...*

A tear appalled her by slipping from the corner of one eye and rolling down to puddle in the crack between her cheek and Tom's fingers.

"Don't!" he cried sharply, and smeared the moisture across her hot cheek with his fingers as if trying to make it disappear.

"Sorry," she murmured, dropping her lashes across the other tears that wanted to follow the first. "It's just, you know, emotions..."

The growl he gave had more frustration in it than lust, but his lips, when they touched hers, were unexpectedly gentle. Incredibly sweet. Unbelievably wonderful. A sigh shivered through her as for a moment—just a moment—she seemed to hang suspended in a fragile, crystalline bubble of happiness, happiness so pure and rare it felt like shimmers inside her, and ran along her skin like the cold-hot prickle of a sparkler's shower on the Fourth of July.

If this is all there is to be, she thought—and for that moment believed—then I will settle for this. And be happy.

Her hands crept around his neck and her head relaxed into the cradle of his hand, and she sighed as though she'd found something for which she'd been searching a very long time. As she had.

"You must know what I'm thinking now," she whispered

when his lips left hers to travel upward across her cheek, tasting the dampness her tear had left there.

"I know what you're *feeling*," he corrected, murmuring the words across her eyelid like the tiniest of caresses. "That's all."

Drunkenly she mumbled. "Right now it's the same thing anyway...I can't think." And she wished—oh, how she wished—that it were true.

She never knew how they got from the kitchen to her bedroom; certainly Tom didn't sweep her into his arms, Rhett Butler–like, and carry her—she'd have been mortified if he had—but she had no recollection of walking down a darkened hallway, no awareness of sidestepping the living-room furniture or squeezing entwined through doorways. It was only when Tom turned on the light in her bedroom that the deep, enveloping fog of desire lifted long enough for her to make an inarticulate sound of protest. He instantly turned it off again.

On wobbly legs she moved through the semidarkness to the bed, tossed pillows onto the floor and folded back the comforter. Separated from him, she felt cold, isolated, off balance, as if she'd stepped onto the deck of a ship in a storm. When she felt his hands on her waist and the warm and solid bulkhead of his body there behind her, her relief was so profound she almost whimpered.

"Easy," Hawk murmured as he turned her, wondering why she was shivering when it wasn't cold in the room.

He was glad of that; he wanted very much to see her while he made love to her, and was glad not to have to resort to huddling under the covers like Puritans. To that end, he kissed her until he felt her relax and her shivers subside and her knees begin to buckle, then leaned over to turn on the lamp beside the bed.

And as before when he did that, she uttered a little yelp of protest. Only this time, he ignored it, left the light on and went back to doing what he'd been doing so pleasurably before.

"Have a heart," she whispered, clutching his shoulders and laughing weakly as he reached under her tunic to stroke the sides of her waist.

"Come on," he teased, pulling her torso against his and at the same time bending her backward a little, nibbling the side of her neck, delighting at the way her body moved in his hands, the way her muscles flexed and tightened, supple as a green willow. "You don't mean to tell me you're embarrassed..." Her shaky little half laugh confirmed it. Still not believing she was serious, he pulled back and looked at her, smiling himself, expecting to see a teasing light in her eyes. "Carlysle?"

But she wouldn't let him see her eyes, and he wondered if it was because of what he'd told her, that he could read her feelings in them.

"Well, of course I am," she murmured, sounding a little testy, licking her lips as if she could taste him still. "I told you, it's been more than five years...and before that there was only..." She paused, drew a breath and blurted out, "You're only the second man who's ever seen this body, not counting obstetricians, and, well..."

That tenderness that surprised him every now and then, and that unnerved him so whenever it appeared, was lurking about again, playing a little goblin-game with his emotions. He fought it, keeping his frown in place as he said solemnly, in the best John Wayne imitation he could muster, "Well, ma'am, from what I've been able to see of it, it looks like a damn fine body to me."

She made a disparaging sound, half snort, half whimper. "It's forty-five years old, and looks every year of it."

God help me, he thought, suddenly remembering what she'd said to him about people collecting baggage, and about nothing being as simple now as it was when they were young. Nothing about this woman was simple, that was for sure, and neither was the way he felt about her. Where in the hell was good ol' lust when he needed it?

You've been with other women, she'd said—what's one more? But he'd never felt like this, not under these circumstances, anyway. He felt protective, strong, but a little bit awed and humble, too, as if he was taking part in something...special. Out-of-the-ordinary. And there was that word again: *Important.*

Even the first time with Jenny hadn't felt like this—but he'd been a virgin then, himself, and Jen, well, Jen had always been so sure of herself, so sure of him. In some strange way, he thought, Jane seemed younger now than Jenny had then.

He felt her shudder when he began, slowly, to lift her tunic, but she didn't stop him, and he pulled it over her head and let it drop to the floor. Her hands fluttered nervously to the center clasp of her bra, but he gently pushed them aside and put his there instead. And then, instead of unhooking it immediately, he leaned down and kissed her a long, slow time, until her breathing grew uneven and she had to reach for him to keep from falling.

And still he didn't free her breasts from that last bastion of modesty and protection, but began to rub the nipples through the lacy fabric that covered them, until he could feel them grow hard and tender, and chafe against that restriction. Until her breaths became tiny pants and whimpers that he took from her lips like sips of warm brandy.

He knew she would have torn off the rest of her clothes then herself, if he'd let her. But now, perversely, he denied her, holding her captive with his mouth and hands, and when she finally tore her mouth free and clung to him, incoherently gasping, instead of undressing, he began to talk to her. Blowing the words past the sensitive channels of her ear so that every nerve ending shivered to attention, he began to tell her about how he'd spent most of his adult life in Europe, where people have different attitudes toward women and age.

"Someone told me once..." *Someone...* He didn't tell her just then about Ava, the mistress of a notorious drug kingpin with whom he'd had a brief but mutually profitable liaison, and who, last he'd heard, was enjoying a comfortable retirement in Morocco while the kingpin was serving a life sentence in a Gibraltar prison. But he knew he would...someday. *Someday.* And that, in itself, was a revelation.

For now, though, he told her what Ava had said to him once, on a warm summer day in Tuscany. "A woman's body is a receptacle, *caro mio*...in which she collects life's pleasures and experiences. And the more she collects, the more of life she experiences, the more she is able to give and receive pleasure..."

"In other words," Jane gasped, "I'm not getting older, I'm getting better?"

"You got it." He heard her breath catch as he finally released the catch on her bra. Slowly, he drew the halves apart, pushed the straps over her shoulders and down, until the thing fell of its own accord. Then he didn't say a word, just looked at her, watching her face until he saw her lips soften in a smile...sleepy, seductive and wholly female.

"What are you waiting for?" she said huskily, licking her lips. "This receptacle has got some catching up to do."

He laughed then, and he'd never known laughter to feel so good.

She'd wanted to make him smile, she remembered, the first time she'd ever set eyes on him. But she hadn't known it would feel like this to look at him, full to bursting with wonder, joy and fear. Stunned, she lifted a hand to touch his lips with just the tips of her fingers, awed by the firm satiny warmth of them, hardly able to believe those same lips still bore the glaze of moisture from her own mouth, and that she could still taste him on her own tongue.

It was with a sense of shock that she realized she'd felt this same confusing mix of happiness and terror twice before, when she'd first gazed upon the faces of her newborn daughters, first tremulously touched the velvety fuzz on their heads with an awestruck finger. *Love.* No gentle emotion, this. No hearts-and-flowers and giddy birds tying ribbons into lovers' knots. This was something fierce and frightening, powerful and ungovernable. Not a choice at all, but a force of nature.

"Tom," she cried, "I—" But she stopped herself in time, and didn't say it out loud.

Instead, she gulped and said, "Hey, when do I get to see *your*—" And stopped again.

"—*My* forty-five-year-old body?" he finished for her with such gallantry her heart, if it hadn't already, melted completely. Grinning, he held out his arms. "Feel free..."

Feel free. Oh, she wanted to, more than anything. She wanted to *feel,* to experience, to relish and enjoy, to lose herself in almost forgotten sensations, languish in unimagined pleasure. But it was all so new, and *that* she hadn't expected. Her mind was so busy discovering, sorting, comparing, questioning, wondering... She didn't want to think at all, and instead she was overwhelmed with thoughts.

Have I ever done this before? she wondered as she lifted Tom's sweater and helped him push it up and over his head, clumsily, so that he emerged tousled and grinning, like a mischievous boy. She couldn't remember, and it didn't seem likely she would have. Unwilling to relinquish even that much control, David had always preferred to undress himself. Should she tell Tom that? And would he believe her if she did?

He is beautiful, she thought as she tugged his soft white T-shirt free of his trousers and skimmed it upward, running her hands over the almost geometric symmetry of his abdominal muscles, brushing the tickly thicket of chest hair with her arms and biting her lips to keep from following her impulse to bury her face in it. *Beautiful...just as I imagined he'd be.* Should she tell him so? Would she sound like a silly, besotted girl if she did?

And all the while, he was cradling the weight of her breasts in his hands, teasing and tormenting the nipples with his fingers until they hardened to the point of hurting—a good hurt, a delicious hurt, a tugging she could feel deep down inside—and all she wanted to do was close her eyes and sink into that glorious sensation and forget everything in the world but his hands...his mouth...his body.

This is worse than being a virgin, she thought, swaying drunkenly into his hands, trying not to moan at his touch. I should be better at this...I have no excuses for being so scared.

"Hey, look at me," Tom said in his familiar gravelly murmur, his breath pouring like liquid sunlight over her eyelids. She tried, but her eyes wouldn't focus, and she saw him only in a shimmering blur. From inside it his voice came, softer than she'd ever heard it, soft as the voices of bees on lazy summer afternoons. "You *are* beautiful, but that's not the reason I wanted the light on. The part of you I really want to see is your eyes..."

She felt his hands moving, fanning down her rib cage to the sensitive sides of her waist. She sucked in air when his fingers feathered across her belly, dipped under the elastic waistband of her leggings and eased them gently over her hips. With his hands firmly cupping her bottom, he paused and murmured, "Your turn..."

She struggled with his belt buckle, her fingers nerveless and stiff as wire. It parted more of its own accord, she thought, or some kind of miracle, perhaps, than from anything she'd done. But when she slipped her hands inside his waistband, his skin felt warm and smooth, like silk. She wanted desperately to kiss him there. Do I dare? she thought. Would it be too bold?

"Look at me," he said more insistently now. "You look scared. Tell me what you're thinking."

It took a moment; her tongue felt wrapped in cotton wool. When she did try, her words kept getting caught in her breathing and bumping into her wildly pounding heartbeat, so they came out in broken gasps. "I keep...thinking I feel...like I've never...done this before." She tried to laugh and failed miserably. "Silly..."

"But you haven't," he said. *And neither have I.* He kept trying to believe otherwise, that it was as she'd said, that she was no different than any of the other women—lovely women, each and every one—he'd been in lust with during the past seven years. He was trying his best to make it all about sex, but it kept getting away from him and turning into...something else. What, exactly, he didn't know. What he *did* know was that all the women he'd made love to in his lifetime hadn't prepared him for making love to *this* woman. Nothing had prepared him for Jane.

Prepared. The thought hit him like a bucket of cold water.

How, he wondered, silently cursing himself with all the virtuosity of half a lifetime's international experience, could he have been so stupid? He felt as clumsy and ill-equipped as an adolescent boy.

"What?" The word was a warm, frightened puff against the base of his throat, and he realized that he'd gone stiff and still as a post, with his hands neatly cupping the part of her that had contributed most to his lustful fantasies, not to mention a couple of recent sleepless nights.

"Carlysle," he groaned, "please tell me you're on the Pill."

"I'm not." She pulled back a little, frowning. "I mean, there wasn't..." He sighed, and slowly eased his hands away from her bottom. "Wait," she gasped. "Don't go 'way." And before he could stop her, she'd slipped out of his arms and was darting across the bedroom, forgetting to be self-conscious about the fact that she was wearing only a pair of formfitting leggings.

A diaphragm? he thought, bemused. Would such a thing still be functional after five years? But no, she was making, not for the bathroom across the way, but down the hall to one of the bedrooms he'd assumed belonged to her daughters. He heard a door open, then drawers scraping in and out.

A moment later she was back, looking embarrassed but triumphant as she came to him, all too aware now of her nakedness, but determined not to cower. He wondered if he could ever make her understand how sexy she looked to him. She was right, hers was a forty-five-year-old's body, not a young girl's, and all the more beautiful because of it...lush and ripe as the fruits of summer, or a velvety, full-blown rose.

"How's this?" she said breathlessly as she dropped a foil packet onto the nightstand. She flushed and nervously pushed her hair back from her face, and didn't look at him as she explained, "I got them...a while back. For Lynn. She's on the Pill now, so I don't think she'll mind."

"You bought condoms...for your *daughter?*" Hawk didn't know why he felt so shocked; some sort of residual fatherhood instinct, he supposed.

Jane leveled a look at him and said in her quiet way, "She's twenty-two and has a steady boyfriend. What would you have me do?"

He didn't answer. But he was thinking again as he gently pulled her against him and felt her breasts nestle in his chest hair, about what she'd said about nothing being as simple as when they were young. He was wondering what his life might have been like if Jason had lived, and what kind of father he'd have been. Wondering how it was that he could think of Jason now and feel only a twinge of pain, and the bittersweet ache of regret.

Wondering if it might have something to do with the woman he held so closely in his arms that right now he could feel her heartbeat as his own.

They finished undressing each other quickly after that, and lay together side by side...almost, for that moment, at least, like old lovers. As if, Hawk thought, they'd both accepted that this time, the first time, there was just too much tension for languid explorations, too many nerves and inhibitions for prolonged and inventive foreplay.

And yet, when he reached for the foil packet, she leaned across him and placed her hand over his and whispered,

"No...don't. Not yet. I want to touch you first. You feel...so
good."

He didn't say a word, just drew her down onto his chest and
cradled her head in his hands, and gently wove his fingers
through her warm, damp hair while she explored his body with
her hands and her mouth and all the speechless wonder and
curiosity of a child with a newfound treasure. He wondered later
where he got the self-control to keep his hands so gentle and
his body so still, when he felt as tight and tense as an overwound
spring, and full to the point of pain. Her mouth, her tongue, her
sweet, warm breath felt cool as rain on his fevered skin...

This feels so good...he feels so good, Jane thought. *I'd forgotten. No—did I ever know?* It was so different, not like anything she'd ever experienced before. Not like David with another name, but something completely new, completely
wonderful. The way he gave himself up to her so completely,
encouraging her so gently, never urging, never forcing,
just...enjoying. Enjoying *her.*

And when he finally growled, "Enough..." and took back
control from her, it didn't seem like a taking at all, but more as
if they were two pianists making music on the same keyboard,
first one taking the melody, then the other, in beautifully syn-
chronized rhythm. Or like a dance. *Yes,* she thought again as
she had before, in the car. That was what it was like. The most
glorious...incredible...beautiful dance.

He became her partner in the fullest sense of that word. He
seemed tuned to her body's rhythms, seemed to understand better than she did how she felt, what she needed, when to go
slowly and when to pick up the tempo. And like the very best
of partners, he telegraphed his every move, so that she never
felt clumsy, or awkward, or shy. She felt graceful, beautiful and
incredibly sexy. She felt earthy, and daring, and...free.

Chapter 16

It was so easy. So incredibly easy.

Somnolent as a cat, she watched him put on the condom and felt no apprehension at all, not one smidgen of tension, urgency or doubt. She felt glazed and dewy as an overripe plum, warm and weighted, and at the same time pulsing with anticipation and excitement. And joy...oh, yes, that most of all. What she was most conscious of as he gently, so gently, so perfectly filled her, was...happiness.

He chuckled when she sighed, and leaned over to kiss her, languidly, deeply, a long sweet kiss, intoxicating as champagne. And then she laughed, too, partly with relief because it was so easy, but mostly with sheer joy.

Braced on his forearms, he held her face between his hands and kissed her nose, her eyelids and then her mouth again, and all the while he was moving inside her, moving to the rhythms of her own body, fitting himself to her so perfectly, it seemed as if he'd become part of her.

And as he came into her body and became part of it, it seemed as if he'd also entered her mind and her heart and her soul and become part of those, too, so that she knew nothing, thought nothing, felt nothing, except him. At last there was no such thing as thought. Only feeling.

Only him...and her...and such incredible, overwhelming emotions...feelings...sensations. She could feel them gathering strength and power within her, like a tsunami, building and building until they took her over completely, until finally all she could do was close her eyes, cling helplessly to Tom and hold on for dear life while the wave broke upon her. While it battered and tossed and pummeled her and finally flung her, dazed and sobbing, into the quiet eddy of his arms.

"Oh," she whimpered, awed and shaking. "Oh, dear...oh...my."

"Stay with me," he gasped, his voice raw and grating. "Stay with me, love...."

And she did, and felt the wave take him, too. She held him safe as he had held her, and afterward they clung to each other like castaways, like shipwrecked and battered survivors flung up on the same shore.

Inevitably, thought must return. Her first was *What now?* This was the scary time. Now, when she was at her most vulnerable, what would he say? What would he do? Trembling, she waited, knowing he could spoil it all, shatter her joy and crush her spirit with the wrong word.

But what he said was the most beautiful, most perfect thing she had ever heard, lovelier than a sonnet, more stirring than an anthem. Breathed like a benediction across her sweat-damp temple, one single word: "Wow."

Emotion tumbled through her and emerged in the form of laughter; words were limiting, and risky besides. Words were hard to organize and easily misunderstood. Silence was better, a sweet, lazy silence filled with the thump of heartbeats, the whisper of breathing, the settling-down rustles, twitches and sighs of their cooling bodies.

I wish I could stay like this forever, Jane thought, and was awed by the fact that Tom seemed to feel that way, too. Even when he finally, and with obvious reluctance, separated from her and shifted his weight to one side, he pulled her with him and wrapped her warmly in his arms, tangling his legs with hers in the damp tumble of sheets, as if he meant to stay there for a good long time. No jumping up and dashing off to the bathroom to wash, the way David always did, as if her body had somehow soiled him.

Hating the fact that she should think of David at a time like this, she stirred restlessly, spreading her fingers wide across the hills and valleys of Tom's chest, turning her face against the wet-silk roughness of his hair. Instantly he responded, stroking her back, her hair. She felt the warm press of his mouth on the top of her head, heard the sleepy rumble of his voice in her ear.

"Well, Carlysle, what have you got to say for yourself now?"

She thought about it, laughed a little and ventured, "I don't know...I feel a little bit dumb, I guess. To think I was so worried..."

"Hmm, I could have told you, it's not something you forget how to do."

"I guess not... Hey," she said when his stomach growled suddenly, stroking her hand downward into the shallow, hard-muscled valley below his ribs, "you must be starving. How 'bout that soup now?"

"Mmm, what's this preoccupation you have with soup?" He took her hand and pushed it farther down, across his belly and into the damp, springy thicket of hair below. Her breath caught, and he laughed softly. "Worried about keeping my strength up?"

"How can you?" she said weakly. "So...soon?" But she was already exploring the hardening shape of him, and delighted when he groaned with pleasure.

She was unreasonably delighted, too, when he said, "It's been a long time for me, too...guess I've been saving up." For a while, then, he let her hand have its way, before he stopped her with a little chuckle of regret. "But you're right, I can't live on...sex alone. And neither can you. Maybe we should both have some of that soup."

"It'll just take a minute. I'll go turn it on..." Eager to please him, she was already scrambling out of bed, bending to pick up the tunic that lay abandoned on the floor.

"Hey, you don't have to wait on me."

She turned, the tunic still clutched to her chest, to find him propped on one elbow, watching her with a peculiar half smile, half frown on his face.

"I just thought..." she faltered. "Would you like to take a shower while it's heating?"

The frown disappeared as the smile pushed it aside. "Why, do I stink?"

"No!" she cried, mortified. "I didn't mean..." But there was something about his smile, a glint in his eyes that made it devilish rather than poignant. And something in that which banished her embarrassment like a mist in a hot desert wind.

With one knee on the mattress, she leaned across to kiss him, and said in a throaty murmur, "You smell...delicious. Very sexy. Earthy. I just thought you might like to wash some of that off before you..."

"I'd love to..." his mouth opened under hers, and she sank into it gladly "...if you'll come...do my back. Soup can wait..."

Soup...life...the world...reality. They could all wait. Sooner or later, she knew, daybreak would come and she would have to wake up to the reality that Tom's place in her life was fleeting at best; an Interpol agent who called a boat home, who lived and traveled mostly in distant, exotic places, he was like a wild mountain lion taking a daytime stroll through the quiet, sunlit garden of her life. By sheer chance, because of a case he happened to be working on, his world had brushed briefly against hers. But the truth was, he had no place in her life, nor she in his.

Tomorrow...tomorrow she would find out the truth. And when she did, and told him what he needed to know, he would have no more reason to stay. No reason at all.

So, there was only tonight. For now, *this* was the only reality. She would think about everything else...tomorrow.

For now, she would be happy to once again shut down her mind, and just...feel. Feel the gentle sluice of warm water over her skin, the slippery caress of soapy fingers. Feel the teasing tug of his teeth on her nipples, the drumming of her pulse against his hand...his mouth...his tongue.

How could she think at all, when his fingers were pushing...probing...filling her, when his tongue was following the water's course into valleys and deeps...into her body's secret and most sensitive places...the hollow of her throat...her navel...the soft, swollen petals between her thighs?

How could she think...breathe...stand, when her whole body

was being rocked by such exquisite torture, such unimagined sensations, when she was being torn apart, shattering into a million quivering pieces?

What could she do but feel? And cling, sobbing, to Tom's broad, slippery shoulders while he held her, oh so tightly, and stroked her back, buttocks and thighs, and whispered words of love against her belly that he didn't mean.

"Easy...easy, love..."

They were words, just words. Of course he didn't mean them, she told herself afterward as she stood in the kitchen stirring soup, her wet hair dripping onto the shoulders of her tunic, her knees still weak from the residual effects of her body's most recent cataclysm. She could hear Tom whistling as he toweled himself dry in her bathroom. Probably, she thought, he didn't even know he'd said that—it was doubtful he'd be so cheerful if he had known.

She sniffed a little as she wiped away shower drips with the back of her hand, set aside the ladle and turned off the burner under the steaming minestrone. Turning to survey the table, she murmured, "Oops," and bent to scoop up Tom's jacket, which she'd just noticed lying on the floor behind one of the chairs. For a moment she stood and held it, stroking the old, butter-soft leather with her hands, bringing it to her face, inhaling deeply of the musky, already-familiar smell. *Tom's smell.*

Was that when it happened? she wondered. Did I fall in love with him there in that moving van, when he put his jacket over me, thinking I was asleep? Almost certainly that was when she'd known she *could* fall in love with him.

There was something in one of the pockets. Something hard, and...

A peculiar vibration began in her spine, right between her shoulder blades. I won't look, she thought. *I won't look...I mustn't look. It's not what it seems.*

She could just see the corner of a handkerchief sticking out of the pocket. The vibration spread from her spine and into her chest as, in a kind of hypnotic and unwilling fascination, like someone passing by the scene of a traffic accident, she watched her own fingers touch the handkerchief, then slowly, slowly pull it forth. Pull it until the folds of clean white cotton parted, and she could see the pale blue gleam of china. China that perfectly matched the soup bowls sitting on the table a few feet away.

The shaking was all through her now. She shook as if with a terrible sickness, unable to do anything but stare down at the broken pieces of the bowl she held in her hands, nestled in Tom's handkerchief. *What does this mean? What does this mean?*

Moving slowly and stiffly, like a mechanical toy forgotten too long in the garden, she turned her head toward the doorway, trying to listen through the roaring in her ears. She couldn't hear Tom whistling now. Any minute he might walk in. *Any minute.* Jerkily, she shoved the handkerchief back into the pocket from whence it had come and dropped the jacket onto a chair.

What does it mean?

It wasn't an oversight, a forgetful accident. She remembered very clearly. He'd deliberately hidden the pieces from her, wrapped them in his handkerchief and tucked them carefully away in his pocket. *Why?*

Oh, but she knew why. There just wasn't any other reason she could think of that Tom Hawkins would have pieces of her broken china in his pocket. China only she had handled. She just couldn't bear to admit it. *So…that's why. That's what he really came for.*

Of course, she thought, aching and sick inside. I should have known.

Interpol. The word conjured up such exotic, romantic images, it was easy to forget that it was just another police department. And that Tom was, first and foremost, a cop. He was working a case, a case in which she, obviously, was still a suspect. Of course, she thought, drawing in deep breaths and trying desperately to calm her trembling before she had to face him again. Why hadn't she realized she'd still be a suspect?

But he didn't know what she knew—all right, *suspected*—so why wouldn't she be?

Maybe I should have told him, she thought. Then he wouldn't have had to go to all this trouble.

But she'd been so shocked and devastated to think she could have been so badly fooled, so stupidly naive, such a lousy judge of character…all right, and just plain hurt, too, to think she'd been used by someone she'd considered a friend, someone she'd trusted. She'd wanted to find out for herself if it was true. She'd wanted to be sure.

And if I'd told him, I wouldn't have had this. I wouldn't have had tonight.

Calmer now, she leaned against the edge of the sink and gazed at her image in the night-darkened window. Her forty-five-year-old reflection stared back at her, with eyes full of inexpressible sadness. "Dummy," she whispered, and her image did, too, mocking her.

Feeling lost and adrift in a sea of unfathomable sorrow, she took a deep breath, affixed a smile on her face and went to see what was keeping Tom.

Just inside her bedroom doorway she halted, then continued, the smile gone, now that there was no longer a need for it. A tear began a lonely journey to the place where her smile had been.

"Oh, Tom," she whispered as she stood gazing down at the face of the man now sound asleep in her bed. He was lying on his side facing toward her, his head pillowed on his hand, mouth half-open...vulnerable, unguarded, in need of a shave. She reached out a hand to touch the hair that had fallen across his forehead, then pulled it back. After a moment she raised her arms and drew her tunic over her head and let it fall to the floor. Then she carefully lifted the edge of the comforter and slipped between the sheets.

Tom stirred in his sleep, and his arms came around her, pulling her close as he nestled her bottom against his belly. "Cold?" he murmured when a shiver she couldn't control coursed through her.

"No," she whispered gently. "I'm fine."

His only reply was an unintelligible mutter, followed by a faint snore. Lying very still so as not to disturb him, Jane settled down to wait for morning.

Hawk knew even before he opened his eyes that something was wrong. *Something* had awakened him—some sound—but whatever it was, it was quiet now.

And that was it. The thing that was wrong. It was *too* damn quiet. He couldn't hear Jane anywhere, not in the bathroom, or

the kitchen, or anywhere in or around the house, as far as he
could tell. The place sounded—*felt*—empty.

He threw back the covers, swung his feet around and stood
up, found his pants on the floor where he'd dropped them, briefs
still neatly in place inside his khakis, and pulled them both on
in one swift, smooth motion. Zipping and buckling as he went,
he crossed the room, bypassed the empty bathroom and stalked
in his bare feet down the hallway to the kitchen. *Empty.*

Through the kitchen window he could see the red Nissan in
the driveway. For some reason it looked lonely. A quick check
of the carport confirmed his suspicion: Jane's car was gone. He
figured it must have been her starting it up and driving off that
had waked him. He didn't know why that realization filled him
with such unease, but it did. Something was wrong. He knew it
was. Why had she left without waking him? Why hadn't she
said goodbye?

Swearing under his breath, he closed the door and was about
to bolt back into the bedroom after his shirt and shoes when he
saw the note printed in Magic Marker on the magnetic message
board stuck to the refrigerator door:

TOM! HAVE TO GO TO WORK. THERE'S COFFEE
AND ENGLISH MUFFINS. PLEASE (underlined) EAT
SOMETHING!

She'd signed it simply, *Jane.* Her signature looked smudged,
as if she'd written something else, wiped it out and written her
name over it instead.

Well, sure, thought Hawk, momentarily relieved. It's Monday. She had to go to work. That explains it.

But the cold, uneasy feeling came creeping back, twice as
bad as before. Because hadn't somebody told him—Campbell,
probably, or Devore, or maybe she'd told him herself—that she
worked in a bank? What the hell kind of bank opened at this
hour?

"Carlysle," he groaned aloud, "what are you up to?"

His stomach was burning and churning, and only partly from
lack of food. He was so keyed up already he didn't think coffee
was a good idea, and he didn't have time to wait for muffins to

toast. He noticed that the kettle full of untouched soup was still there on the back burner of the stove; he poured some into the coffee mug she'd set out for him and drank it down cold, swallowing the lumps of meat and vegetables whole. He knew it was going to hit his stomach like a hand grenade, but he couldn't help that; he needed the food, and the idea of eating nauseated him.

He had a bad feeling about this. He couldn't remember ever having had such a bad feeling.

As if someone had been watching him, the cellular phone began to ring as he was settling behind the wheel of the red Nissan. He let the seat belt snap back into its well, snatched up the phone and barked, "Yeah!"

"Hawkins—where the hell've you been?" It was Agent Campbell, sounding more excited than vexed. "I've been trying to get you all night. You weren't in your—"

"No," said Hawk as the ignition fired, "I wasn't. Listen—"

"Things are about to pop over here. If you want to be in on it, better get your butt in gear now. It's turning into a regular circus, you want to know the truth—CIA arrived last night, that's one thing I wanted to tell you—and a bunch of guys from Mossad just called in to say they're on their way, and not to do anything until they get here. Seems they think they oughta have first crack at her, I guess, because of that Israeli jet that went down two years—"

"Jeez," Hawk broke in, "who the hell've we got here, anyway? Khadafy's wife?"

"That's the other thing I wanted to pass along. We've got a tentative ID on the lady with all the paintings. Took a while—still sorting things out over there at the Kremlin, it seems. Finally came through about four this morning." Campbell paused. Hawk ground his teeth and spun gravel as he turned the Nissan onto the paved road. "Ever hear of Galina Moskova?" Hawk frowned and grunted a negative. "Alias Emma Butterfield Parker?"

Something began to nibble at his memory. Something ugly.

"Code name...The Duchess?"

"Holy..." Hawk went on to further embellish his favorite word, and when he ran out of possibilities, muttered, "We thought she had to be dead. Jeez. You're sure?"

"Sure as we can be. It was that fingerprint your people turned up that did it. There's never been a decent photo, and any descriptions would be, what, ten years out of date? And it's likely she's altered her appearance anyway. But the prints don't lie. It's her, all right."

Hawk didn't say anything for a few moments. He was on the highway now, pushing it as hard as he dared on the narrow country road, made more treacherous with patches of ground fog that had collected in unexpected places. He felt as though some of that fog had settled inside him. *Jeez...Galina Moskova. The Duchess. Emma Butterfield Parker.*

He remembered it all now. No wonder the hit on Loizeau had seemed so clean and professional. Back in their glory days, Galina Moskova had been one of the KGB's most ruthless and successful assassins. As sought-after interior designer Emma Butterfield Parker, she'd moved almost unnoticed through Britain's upper crust, pulling off an unbroken string of high-profile hits, many of them so discreetly done, it wasn't until the fall of the Soviet Union that it had been known for certain they *were* hits, and not unfortunate accidents or death from natural causes. Discretion and restraint—those had been Emma's trademarks. She'd had a reputation for never using an ounce more muscle than it took to get the job done.

Like at the auction, Hawk thought. Using just enough poison on Aaron Campbell to knock him out, but not enough to kill him. That was Galina, all right.

And Loizeau? But he'd seen her, spoken to her, face-to-face. So of course he'd had to die. Neatly, cleanly, hadn't even seen it coming. That was Galina, too.

Dear God...Jane. It came to him suddenly, like a hard left to the midsection. If anyone in the world could identify the woman, Jane could. They'd been friends. Shared meals, confidences, a hotel room...a tube of toothpaste. Would that make a difference to Galina Moskova?

Hawk knew the answer to that. His heart felt like a lump of ice.

"Ten years or so ago," Campbell was saying, "apparently our Emma saw glasnost coming, saw the handwriting on the wall, and went AWOL."

"We assumed her own people had shut her down," Hawk said in a leaden voice. "Permanently."

"Yes, well, I'm sure Emma saw that in her cards and that's why she split. Anyway, seems she went underground for a while, then quietly opened up for business, near as we can tell, about seven, eight years ago—private business. Now she works for the highest bidder."

"Hired gun on an international scale." Hawk swore softly.

"Yeah, but apparently not limited to that. She's been a busy lady. We've turned up connections to the Libyans—"

"God. Not—"

"Yeah, and as I said, the Israelis want her for their crash also—"

And we've connected her to Sicily. And that means...

"—And we've got suspicions about half a dozen other terrorist bombings in Europe over the past eight years...."

Marseilles...April 1990. A beautiful spring day, warm sunshine and a mistral blowing, making the masts in the small-boat harbor clank with their own kind of rhythm, like a band of children making music with spoons and pots and garbage-can lids. Two days left of spring break from Tom's job teaching history at the American School in Milan...They'd spent the morning on the beach, watching the windsurfers dip and dart though the waves like butterflies. That afternoon they'd planned to explore La Canebière and look at the model ships in La Musée de la Marine. Jason had been promised ice cream, but it was sieste time, and everything was closed. They'd walked past café after café, teasing Jason and telling him stories to distract him, when they'd come upon the street...he couldn't remember the name of it now...a street with no traffic, paved with stones and lined will all sorts of little shops and cafés. And in the middle, the merry-go-round, playing a tune...what was the name of it? It was from a movie with Leslie Caron, he remembered, and for years he'd heard it in his dreams. Hi Lili, Hi Lo, *he thought it was called.*

"Hawkins? Are you still there?"

"Yeah." It came out so garbled, he cleared his throat and repeated, "Yeah, I'm here."

"You know this changes things."

No kidding.

"If this is Galina Moskova we're dealing with, then she's got to be working for somebody with big bucks. I mean, government-big. She wouldn't come cheap." Campbell paused. "I'm thinking Libya."

"Well, whoever it is," Hawk said through the truckload of rock in his throat, "I don't think she's gonna be sitting here in Cooper's Mill, North Carolina, waiting for her customer. She's gonna be going to see the boss. So if you're figuring on waiting for the rendezvous and getting both birds with one stone..."

"Right. So we move on her as soon as we know she's got the disk. Uh, by the way, Hawkins?"

"Yeah."

"What can you tell us about Mrs. Carlysle? We, uh, seem to have lost our... Ahem. The, uh, surveillance equipment we had on her seems to be down for some reason. You wouldn't know anything about that, I don't suppose." Campbell's voice was carefully neutral. "Or where she might be at the moment?"

"No, I don't." Hawk rubbed a hand over his eyes and then across his unshaven jaw. He felt like nine miles of bad road. "But I've got an idea she may be headed your way."

"Say again?" He could hear the FBI agent's voice crack.

"You heard me. I don't know where she is. But I think she might be on her way to a meeting with our suspect."

Campbell borrowed Hawk's word and made it his own. "You don't think she means to *warn* her?"

"Warn her of *what*, for God's sake! Use your head. She doesn't know anything. Look—I don't know what she's up to, but I'll tell you this—she hasn't got a clue who she's dealing with."

There was a pause, during which Agent Campbell held a mumbled conversation with someone on his end, and Hawk made the discovery that none of the cow pastures he was driving past now bore any resemblance to the ones he'd driven past last night.

"Hawkins?"

"Yeah."

"You figure Mrs. Carlysle to be heading for the suspect's house or her store?"

Hawk thought about it while he was peering through the windows and checking all his mirrors, hoping to find something that looked the slightest bit familiar. "My guess would be the house," he muttered. "Too early—the store wouldn't be open, would it?" Damn. It seemed to him one cow looked pretty much like every other cow. And the same went for daffodils.

"Yeah, you're probably right. In that case, we should be okay."

"How's that?"

"I just got word—suspect's on the move. She just left her house in a blue van, and is heading into town. We are in position. What's your ETA?"

"Damned if I know," Hawk snarled, and disgustedly hit the wheel of the red Nissan with the palm of his hand. "I think I'm lost!"

"My goodness, such a lot of cars for this early in the morning," Jane said to herself as she glided through the green signal light and onto the brick-paved square. She wondered if it was jury-selection day over at the courthouse, or if maybe the Rotary Club was having a breakfast meeting at the Cooper's Corner Café.

Connie's Antiques looked dark and empty, but that didn't mean anything. Connie was almost always in her shop early on Monday mornings, especially if she'd been on a buying trip over the weekend. Often Jane would leave for work half an hour early on Mondays, just so she'd have time to drop in at the shop and see what treasures her friend had brought home this time. Connie would have the teakettle on, and a tin of those English biscuits she liked, and she'd tell Jane all about her trip, and Jane would admire—and sometimes wistfully drool over—her latest purchases.

Right now, Jane thought, she'd most likely be in the back of the shop somewhere, just as usual, busy unpacking, cataloging, pricing and marking the things she'd bought at the auction in Arlington. *Just as usual...*

Oh, God, she thought, please don't let it be true. This is *Connie.* Connie...my friend.

But her heart was pounding so hard it hurt, and she kept taking deep breaths that didn't do any good. Her hands were like ice, and her legs felt weak and shaky.

Okay, she was terrified.

But she had to know. *She had to.*

Connie's van wasn't in its usual place in the tiny unpaved parking lot behind her store. Jane pulled into a spot far enough away from the back door so there would be plenty of room for the blue van and settled down to wait.

Alone in the quiet car, Tom came to her. She could smell him…feel his warmth soaking through his sweater and into her skin…feel the tender roughness of his whiskers against her softest places. If she closed her eyes, she could almost imagine he was there with her now…hear his emotion-scratchy voice saying, "Well, Carlysle, what have you got to say for yourself?"

No regrets. Even now. How could she regret something so wonderful, so lovely and rare, just because it was for only one night? She might as well regret lilacs, because they only bloomed once every spring…or bluebirds, or shooting stars, or dolphins. *Once in a lifetime.*

Her lips even curved in a smile as she remembered the gift he'd given her, that she would carry with her for the rest of her life, like a secret keepsake, hidden close to her heart. The gift of a single word. *"Wow…"*

She was debating whether to turn off the engine or leave it on so she could run the heater, when she heard the van bump down the potholed alley and roar into the parking lot behind her. Her hand shook as she turned off the ignition.

Shivering, she stood beside her car and waited while Connie backed the van into its place and climbed out, jingling keys. Giving Jane a little wave, she bent to unlock the back door of the shop, then straightened, calling out cheerily, "Hullo, dear—back from Washington so soon?"

Sidling closer, Jane thrust her hands into the pockets of her coat and gave a nervous laugh and a little shrug of vexation. "Oh—wouldn't you know, the girls have gone off skiing with their father? Very spur-of-the-moment—typically David. Of course, I'd have had to come back to work today, anyway. Unless I took a sick day, I suppose. I could have, but if I'd stayed longer, I wouldn't have had anyone to pick me up at the airport, would I? So I guess it's just as well…" She was babbling. She never babbled.

Take a deep breath, Jane.

"There, dear, you're shivering." Connie was standing beside the back door of her shop, holding it open for her, smiling in her usual friendly way. "Do come in—I'll just put the kettle on."

Chapter 17

Hawk was climbing back into the driver's seat, having just received directions to the main highway from a farmer in a pickup truck with a bale of hay the size of Delaware in the back, when the cellular phone rang.

"Jeez," he muttered to himself as he grabbed at it, "they got a camera in this thing, or what?"

Campbell sounded out of breath. "Hawkins? Not good news here. Mrs. Carlysle just showed up at the suspect's shop."

Hawk threw the Nissan into Drive and swore with a vehemence unprecedented even for him. "Get her out of there," he snarled. "Now."

"No can do. The suspect's en route, due to arrive any minute. Can't risk being spotted."

"So, what now?" The Nissan's tires spun briefly on wet grass before they made contact with pavement. Hawk set his jaw and pressed down on the accelerator pedal. "You can't go in. Not if there's a chance—"

"Look, Hawkins," Campbell said with the arrogance that made the FBI such a pain in the butt to work with sometimes, "you're just gonna have to trust us, okay? We're not any more anxious than you are for some innocent civilian to get caught in the crossfire, but we both know what's at stake here. We've taken every precaution, and we have every reason to believe we can pull this off without anybody getting hurt.''

Every reason to *believe?* thought Hawk. Great. Just great.

"We've got the whole place wired," Campbell went on in a smug Bureau purr that made Hawk grind his teeth. "Both picture and sound. We'll be monitoring the situation from the word go. We've got both front and rear exits covered, plus the alley, the parking lot and the whole damn square, and a Hostage Rescue Team ready to roll just in case."

In case? In case what? Hawk wanted to shout. In case Emma/ Galina puts a gun to Jane's head, the way she did to Loizeau's? If she does that, you moron, there won't be anything for the Hostage Rescue Team to do except carry in the body bag!

A vision came to him then, a vision of Jane's face, her eyes lifting to his with that sudden, miraculous leap of light and joy that always made him think of dolphins. Then he saw her eyes go dull and flat, the light in them forever quenched, and with it all the joy and light there was in the world. *His world.*

Carlysle...you idiot...why couldn't you have trusted me? After last night...after everything...was that too much to ask?

"O...kay...suspect has arrived." Agent Campbell was trying without success to bury his excitement in a monotone drawl. "She's pulling into the parking lot at the rear of the shop. Mrs. Carlysle has exited her vehicle. So has the suspect...she's waving at Mrs. Carlysle...suspect now appears to be unlocking the door of the shop. Okay, both Carlysle and the suspect are inside...we have them on the monitors. Hawk?"

"Yeah?" Becoming aware that his chest was hurting, he grabbed for a breath.

"What's your ETA now?"

"I dunno." Hawk glanced down at the speedometer needle, which was hovering around seventy-five. How far could it be to the damn town, anyway? "Five minutes?"

"Take your time. Doesn't look like Mrs. Carlysle's in any immediate danger."

"How the hell you figure that?" Hawk growled.

Campbell exhaled audibly. "They're having tea."

* * *

"There you are...honey...and lemon."

Jane watched while Connie, who preferred milk in her tea, poured herself a generous dollop and returned the carton to the camp-size refrigerator that shared the limited space in her cluttered workroom with a working, 1930s-vintage gas stove. An equally old-fashioned teakettle sat on one of the stove's burners beneath its tea cozy, comfortably steeping.

"Would you like a biscuit, dear?"

"Oh, no...thanks." Jane stirred and sipped her tea, tasting nothing. Her mind, from the moment she'd entered Connie's shop, had seemed capable of only one coherent thought: *It can't be true. It can't be. This is Connie...my friend.*

Thank goodness Connie had done most of the talking, as usual, telling her in great detail, as the kettle was coming to a boil, all about her newest customer, something about a fantastically wealthy businessman who apparently wanted her to decorate his villa in Miami Beach.

"He's Iranian, I believe—seems to have pots of money and no taste whatsoever." Connie's eyes sparkled with avarice as she bit daintily into a cookie. "I do believe I may have already found a home for some of those dreadful paintings I bought at Arlington. Oh—and that reminds me, dear—" her eyes came to rest on Jane, causing her heart to give a painful bump "—what did you find out about that nice little one you bought? Was my friend in Georgetown able to have a look at it? What did he say?"

Jane took a sip of tea, which did nothing to dispel the feeling that she'd somehow gotten Connie's cookie crumbs stuck in her throat. Finally, she coughed and said, "I never got around to it, actually. I told you—I had to cut the whole trip short, and anyway, by the next day getting it appraised began to seem, well, just sort of silly. I'm sure it's not valuable, and I like it anyway, so why bother? It does look very nice over the piano, though, just like I thought it would." She set down her teacup carefully, praying Connie wouldn't notice the slight clatter as it met the saucer.

"Actually, that's one of the reasons I'm here. I was, um, wondering, I still need something for that space between the windows in the breakfast nook, and now that I have the one painting in the living room, the wall above the TV looks awfully bare, so I was thinking I might like to take another look at those paintings—the ones you bought. I know you said you were thinking of taking them to Miami, but...maybe I could have first crack?''

"Uh-oh.''

"What?'' Hawk barked, as the ominous syllables came through the open cellular phone connection in Campbell's deep-throated cop's mutter.

His anxiety level shot off the scale when the FBI agent next produced a vehement rendition of his own favorite swearword, followed by an outraged, "What the hell is she *doing?*''

"You mind letting *me* in on whatever the hell it is she's doing?'' Hawk almost bellowed, ignoring a blast from a trucker's horn as he ran the stop sign and made a hard right at the junction with the main road into Cooper's Mill.

The FBI agent's reply was lost in the squeal of tires.

"Say again?''

"I said, she's asking about the paintings. How much did you tell her, Hawkins? Does she know what she's doing? Is she out of her *mind?*''

"No, she's just got one of her own,'' he said grimly, slowing reluctantly for the traffic light opposite a Burger King. "Where are you? I'm coming into town now.''

"Uh, white van, city engineer's markings, on the square across from the courthouse. There's a loading zone next to it, you can park there. And Hawkins—for God's sake, keep a low profile. The last thing we want to do—''

But the light had just turned green, and Hawk was already hanging up on him.

"I don't know...I just can't make up my mind.'' Jane propped the two paintings—one a rather dark landscape of horses grazing in a meadow, the other a vase full of overblown roses, complete with fallen petals—side by side against Connie's big leather-topped desk and stood back to study them. They weren't noticeably improved by distance. "The floral would do for the living room—it could do with some brightening, I think—but for the kitchen nook...you know, what I was really looking for was..." *What? What am I looking for, exactly? And will I know it when I see it?* "Something..."

And then she saw it, half-hidden behind the desk, the painting of a sailing ship foundering in a sickly green sea. And it was as if someone had flicked a switch in her mind, illuminating a video screen. A memory. "Something with boats," she cried, swooping upon the painting, snatching it up and whirling away with it in triumph. "Yes—like this one."

Connie, who had been leaning against a dining-room table set with an enormous set of Franciscan dinnerware, idly clicking her little jeweled pen and watching Jane's search over the tops of her half glasses, straightened suddenly. "That ugly thing? In a kitchen? No, Jane, really—that's not for you, dear."

"Not for you, dear." Connie had been holding this painting, Jane remembered, when she'd said those words at the auction. But—funny, she hadn't thought anything about it at the time—she'd been holding it so that Jane could see it, facing out, as if it had been the back of the painting she'd been looking at. Staring at it, studying it intently, with her glasses perched on the end of her nose.

"Oh, but...don't you see?" Jane said with almost desperate brightness. "Those windows in the breakfast nook look right out over the lake. Something with boats...water..." She was babbling again, but she couldn't seem to stop. "This really isn't that bad, you know that? The colors would go, kind of...I mean, my kitchen is blue and yellow, and blue and yellow do make green. And with all the plants..."

The words ceased as if she'd suddenly run out of air. She'd never seen Connie look like that before—eyes cold and hard as stone. She felt cold herself, just from their touch, as if something evil had brushed against her.

This is it, she thought. And then, *Oh, God...it's true.*

Outside on the square, in a panel truck with city engineer's markings, Hawk stared at the bluish gray images on the video monitor screen and felt himself go cold.

"My God," he whispered, "that's *it.*"

Campbell turned from the monitor long enough to throw him a glance over his shoulder. "That's what?"

"That's the one—Jarek Singh's painting." He broke off,

swearing softly. "If only I hadn't been late to that damn auction...if I'd seen it, I'd have known."

"What the hell are you talking about? How could you? None of us had ever seen the damn thing."

"Seascapes—damn." He turned angrily, looking for pacing room in the confined space and finding none. "I should have known that's what it would be. They were all over Singh's place in Cairo. You live in the middle of a desert, you put pictures of water on your walls, right?" He jerked back to the monitor. "What's she doing now?"

Campbell handed him a set of headphones. "Here—listen for yourself."

Hawk grabbed them and pressed one side against his ear, never taking his eyes from the tiny, blue-gray figures on the screen...

"I'm so sorry, dear, I'm afraid I already have a buyer for that one." Connie's voice was as polite and impersonal as a shop clerk's.

"A b-buyer?" Jane's mind seemed to have short-circuited; she couldn't think what to do next, could only stand there with the painting clutched in her hands, foolishly stammering.

The air in the antiques shop seemed to have thickened, become a tangible substance that clogged her breathing and wrapped itself around her like spider's silk. It seemed to shimmer as she watched Connie move through it, slowly, like someone wading through waist-deep water...to the front of the shop...watched her take a leisurely look through the front window.

"My, what a lot of people there are in town this morning," Connie commented as she swam slowly back toward Jane. "Have you noticed, dear? Court must be in session."

Dazedly, she shook her head, then nodded. She couldn't seem to hear properly; there was a ringing in her ears, like the keen of a high-tension power line.

Hawk wondered why the tension wasn't blowing the top of his head off. "Why the hell didn't your people take her?" he yelled. "Someone must have had a clear shot."

Campbell turned on him like a desert dervish. "We can't take her out until we know what she's done with the disk, dammit! What if she's already gotten rid of it? What if she's stashed it?

We kill her, and we're never gonna find out where it is, or who's got it. It's like a freakin' time bomb, is that what you want?''

For a long moment Hawk stared at the FBI agent, while helpless fury darkened his vision and the pounding of his blood drowned sound and thought. "She's going to kill her," he heard himself say, as if from a great distance. "You know that, don't you?"

And it could happen at any minute...any second. Right before his eyes. He would see it playing out like a television show on the monitor screen...see the gun in the woman's hand, see the neat black hole appear in Jane's forehead...the third eye, robbing the others of all light and joy and life...and there would be nothing he could do to stop it. *Nothing...*

As he'd watched that lovely April afternoon, watched through the eye of his camera lens...watched his wife and son whirl past on the merry-go-round, laughing and waving...watched it all disappear in an instant, a single instant of fire and thunder and blood that would live in his memory forever...

"I don't see any sign of a gun," Campbell said. He was back at the monitor, staring intently at the screen. "Don't think she's got one on her. In the desk, maybe?"

"Maybe..." Hawk leaned over the agent's shoulder so he could see better. "What's that she's got in her hand? She keeps playing with it."

"That?" The FBI man pointed. "Looks like a pen."

"A pen?" Hawk frowned. Campbell turned around to look at him. He was absently rubbing his thigh...

"Now then, Jane," Connie said almost gaily, "give us the painting...there's a good girl." She advanced, hands outstretched.

Jane took an involuntary step backward. And instantly saw something flare, something smoky and dark, like a guttering candle flame, behind Connie's eyes.

"She's not helpless," Campbell muttered, watching the monitor as if hypnotized. "She could probably take her. Jeez, you saw what she did to me."

Hawk growled, "That was different. She was prepared for you." He could feel the FBI man turn to look at him, but didn't take his eyes from the monitor screen as he grimly added, "She's never met evil before..."

Like a bird mesmerized by a cobra, Jane watched Connie's hand reach toward her, moving slowly through that strangely viscous, thrumming space. And all the while, screened from the other woman's view by the painting she held in her left hand, clutched against her chest, her right hand was moving too, reaching behind her, under her jacket, to grasp something hard that nestled there, tucked in the waistband of her slacks, snug against the small of her back...

With a final lunge, Connie grabbed the painting and wrested it from her grasp. But not before Jane had managed to slip her fingers under the loosened edge of the brown-paper backing. It tore away with barely a sound. Connie glanced down at it, then back at Jane, her lips curving in a regretful little smile.

"Dear Jane," she said with a sigh, "I really do wish you hadn't done that."

"There," Hawk said, straightening on an explosive breath. "What'd I tell you? There's the damn disk. What are you waiting for? Get in there—*now.*"

Campbell's breath gusted angrily as he straightened, staring down at the screen. "We go in there now, we put Carlysle at risk. She won't hesitate to use her as a hostage—you know that as well as I do." Campbell was rubbing unconsciously at the back of his neck. Hawk could see his own tension in the rigid set of the FBI man's shoulders, his own frustration reflected in the angry black eyes.

"What about your snipers? Hasn't *anybody* got a clear shot?" He watched the screen as if he were drowning and it held his only hope of survival. Through the headphone pressed against his ear he could hear Connie—Galina, Emma—telling Jane in that cultured, upper-crust British voice of hers how sorry she was....

Campbell, meanwhile, was holding a low-voiced conversation with one of the other agents monitoring field communications. The agent spoke into a radio mike, listened, spoke again, then looked at Campbell and shook his head. Campbell swore under his breath.

"Can't get a clear shot—they're too far back. The damn place is so full of stuff..." Like Hawk, he didn't say "stuff." He exhaled bleakly. "I'm afraid that, for the moment, at least, Mrs. Carlysle is on her own."

"Like hell she is," Hawk snapped. Before anyone could stop him, he threw down the earphones, dived out of the van and hit the brick pavement running.

"I don't understand," Jane mumbled. Her lips felt numb. So did all the rest of her.

"It won't do, you know," Connie cocked her head, reminding Jane of nothing so much as a little gray hen as she turned the doomed ship in its garish green sea toward the floor and peered at the torn paper backing, and at the flat square of black plastic that was taped to the canvas beneath it. "I had hoped you'd just gotten a rather peculiar bee in your bonnet, and were being silly and stubborn about it. But I can see that wasn't it at all, was it? You do know what this is all about, don't you? Well..." Her sigh overrode Jane's futile denial.

"One of the others got to you, I suppose. Who was it, that Middle Eastern–looking fellow from the auction? No doubt it was a mistake not to kill him, but you know, there would have been such a fuss...."

"Or was it someone else—the FBI, perhaps? Now that I think about it, that circus outside does seem to have their stamp on it. They have an unfortunate tendency toward overkill. The CIA would have been much more discreet."

Connie's eyes were bright with that combative gleam Jane had seen before. *She's enjoying this,* she thought. And for some reason, she suddenly felt very calm. Not angry, not even frightened, just a strange sort of quietness inside.

"Are you going to kill me?" she asked.

Connie's eyebrows arched in surprise. "Oh my—well, I shouldn't like to, you know. You are a dear girl, and you've been quite a good friend, haven't you? We shall have to see."

As she talked, she was ripping the disk from the back of the painting, setting the painting aside, tucking the disk into a manila envelope and then into a large handbag that had been lying on the desktop. That completed, she looked once more at Jane. Jane wondered why she'd never noticed before that Connie's eyes were as hard and flat as polished stones.

"I have an idea you are going to be of some use to me yet, dear. For example, right now you are going to tell me who it is you've brought with you, exactly where they are out there and how many." She picked up her little jewel-encrusted pen and studied it thoughtfully. "Then we shall see how helpful you can be in getting us out of here."

Jane gave her head a confused shake. "What are you talking about? *Who* is out *where?*"

And suddenly she thought of Tom, and what he'd said about waiting until Connie's shop opened so he could look at the paintings she'd bought. She remembered, too, that she'd thought he must be lying. And that he must be up to something.

All those cars parked in the square... Was Connie right? Were the police, or the FBI, or—good heavens, the CIA—out there even now? Was help so near, just outside these old brick walls, visible, even through the dusty front window? And yet, so far away...

Tom. Her heart gave a great leap of hope. Might he be out there, too, she wondered, right this minute? She'd left him sleeping, but then, she knew how good he was at pretending.

Oh, Tom. She'd been wrong to lie to him. That note she'd left him—he thought she'd gone to work. He wouldn't even know she was in here until it was too late. She'd probably messed up everything for him. Oh, God, what if she, with her foolhardiness, was the one who made it possible for Connie to get away, and with that all-important disk besides? Tom would never forgive her. Never.

I'm sorry, Tom...I should have trusted you.

She'd been wrong to try to do this alone. But wasn't that what she'd always done, what she'd always had to do? She had a whole lifetime's habit of handling things on her own, fending for herself, dealing with every task and crisis without help from anyone. She'd never worked with a partner before. She didn't even know how.

Out of a deep, inexpressible sadness, she said before she thought, "I came alone, Connie. No one else even knows I'm here."

The moment the words were out of her mouth, she knew how stupid she'd been.

Connie's eyes flared briefly. She gave a short, hard laugh. "You know, dear Jane, I actually believe you. Your eyes, you know. They simply don't know how to lie. So, perhaps court *is* in session, after all. Well, now..." She studied her little jeweled pen, thoughtfully clicking it, while Jane's heart began a slow, heavy thumping. "This does change things, doesn't it? It would be much more tidy, much less cumbersome, I think, if I killed you now. I'm so sorry, Jane...it's not personal, you know. And I do promise, you won't feel any pain at all..."

Like a snake striking, Connie's hand shot out and clamped with a grip of iron around Jane's wrist. The jeweled pen flashed as it caught the light. Jane gasped when she felt the needle prick her skin.

Shock rocketed through her, turning her blood to ice water. But it didn't stop her from whipping her Roy Rogers cap pistol from its hiding place and bringing it down with all her might across Connie's forearm.

It made a most satisfying sound.

There were other sounds, then, too. Connie's shriek of rage, a clatter as the jeweled pen hit the floor and went skittering away under the desk. Some loud thumps and bangs, and Tom's voice shouting, "Stay where you are—don't move!"

She tried to turn toward him, but the room tilted alarmingly. There was another, louder bang, followed by a crashing and tinkling, as if a crystal rain were falling. And then a strange male voice bellowing, "Get down on the floor! Get down on the floor!"

And the next thing she knew, that's where she was. Tom's face was looking down at her, wearing a truly magnificent scowl. She wanted to reach up and touch his face, smooth away the frown, but her arms wouldn't obey her. She heard a strange, garbled voice say, "How is she?" And then a second face joined Tom's, the two hovering above her like pale twin moons.

Her last thought was *Aaron Campbell? But that makes no sense at all!*

"I can't believe I hit a federal agent," Jane said with a groan.

It was the third or fourth time she'd said it, but she sounded a lot stronger and a lot less groggy now, and the nasty little fear-pulse that had been throbbing in Hawk's belly was finally beginning to subside.

She was lying on a gurney, much against her will, in the parking lot behind Connie's Antiques. Hawk was sitting beside her on a yellow plastic chest that belonged to the fire department's paramedics, most of whom were busy at the moment tending to Aaron Campbell. The FBI man lay a short distance away on a stretcher with his arms encased in inflated pressure bandages meant to control the bleeding from several deep lacerations he'd sustained breaking through the shop's front window. Connie had been whisked away to God knows where.

There was a measure of privacy there, "privacy" being a relative term, considering there was a small army of men wearing navy blue windbreakers with "FBI" in block letters on the back swarming over every inch of the store and the blue van, and another handful armed with high-tech rifles standing around in baseball caps and flak jackets, not to mention the four guys wearing berets who were engaged in polite conversation with two others dressed in conservative gray suits. But at least the alley had been roped off with crime-scene tape, and Sheriff Taylor's people were doing a good job of keeping both the news media and the merely curious confined to the town square.

"I think he'll probably forgive you," Hawk said gruffly.

He didn't seem to know what to do with his hands. They felt too big, clumsy and useless for what he wanted to do, which was touch her face in awe and thanksgiving, stroke her hair, gather her oh so gently against his heart. He also wanted to grab her by the shoulders and shake her until her teeth rattled.

He didn't know what to do with his eyes, either. What he was doing was looking everywhere, *anywhere* but at Jane, because she was the only thing in this world he wanted to see. He couldn't look at her, even though he feared she'd disappear in a puff of smoke if he didn't, because he feared what she might see in his face even more.

So he kept his hands clasped tightly between his knees and followed the comings and goings of the army of law enforcement personnel with burning eyes, while every nerve in his body hummed and vibrated to the same frequency as hers.

"Is he going to be all right?" Jane asked.

Aaron may forgive me, Tom, but will you?

"Yeah," Tom muttered, clearing his throat. "Just needs some stitches. They'd have taken him before now, but he won't let 'em. Not until they've got things wrapped up here."

He looks so angry, she thought. As if he can't stand the sight of me. I don't blame him.

She wanted to touch him so badly. She wanted to reach out and put her hand on his face, and smooth away the frown and make him smile again, that sweet, crooked smile that made her ache inside. But he looked so grim and isolated, so unreachable. And as if she were still feeling the effects of Connie's poison, her arms wouldn't obey her wishes.

She wanted his arms around her, holding her close, keeping her safe, keeping her warm. Even if she didn't deserve it. Her body trembled with wanting. How will I survive, she wondered, if he never holds me again?

A white-haired man dressed in a suit and tie and wearing latex gloves came stumping up to them. He had a small plastic bag in each hand, one containing Connie's little jeweled pen, the other a vial containing a small amount of murky-looking liquid. He gave Jane a nod, then spoke briskly to Tom, who'd gotten to his feet at his approach.

"Tests'll confirm it, but I'm sure it's...oh, well, forget the scientific name—let's just say it's a tranquilizer, enough to bring down a bull elephant. You were lucky, young lady." His bristly white eyebrows twitched in Jane's direction. "Looks like she barely nicked ya. Otherwise, you'da been dead for sure."

And with that he took himself off, continuing on his way across the parking lot and around the corner with the stoop-shouldered, slightly sideways gait of the still-vigorous elderly. Jane drew a shaken breath and said, "Who was that?"

Hawk didn't answer. He couldn't look at her. He couldn't, not without remembering the way he'd felt when she'd hit the floor right in front of him. He never wanted to feel like that again in his life. He didn't think he'd be able to survive it.

"Gotta...talk to Aaron," he mumbled, and lurched off to where the FBI agent was about to be loaded into a waiting EMS wagon.

"Hey, Hawkins," Campbell greeted him, sounding weak but grinning anyway.

"Hey, yourself," Hawk said gruffly. "I'd shake your hand, but..."

"Yeah, looks like I'm kinda tied up at the moment."

"Yeah, well..." Hawk stuck his hands in his jacket pockets and shifted uneasily; moments like this were never easy for him.

He coughed and muttered, "Just wanted to say thanks, before they, uh, haul you in for repairs."

"Hey, you too."

"Oh—well." Hawk made a dismissive gesture and looked off into the distance. Campbell followed his gaze.

"That's one helluva lady," he said softly. "But I expect you know that, don't you?"

Hawk didn't answer. Two paramedics hoisted the FBI agent's gurney onto its wheels and began rolling it toward the waiting van. Campbell lifted his head. "Hey, Hawk?"

"Yeah?" He took a few steps, keeping pace with the gurney.

"Take good care of her, you hear?"

He halted. "Hey, wait. It's not like that."

"The hell it's not." The gurney slid into the van, but Campbell's eyes still followed him, glowing like coals in his pale face. "Look man, just because it's never happened to me, doesn't mean I don't know it when I see it. You let that lady go, you're crazy, you hear me? Crazy."

The van's door began to close. The last thing Hawk heard Aaron Campbell say before they did was, "Hey—ask her if she's got a daughter!"

Jane watched the two men in immaculate gray suits walk away across the dusty parking lot and disappear around a corner.

"What'd they want?" Tom growled, startling her. She was still a little bemused, and hadn't heard him come back.

"Oh," she said, smiling up at him from the gurney's hard pillow, "they were just being nice." Under the edge of the rough EMS blanket, she was fingering a plain white business card.

Tom was glowering—there was no other word for it. "They're CIA."

"Yes," Jane murmured, "I know." *And they asked me to give them a call—me! Jane Carlysle.* She wouldn't, of course; the very idea was, well, preposterous. But still...*the CIA.*

Jane Carlysle...spy.

Oh my.

"They're gonna want to take you over to the hospital...check everything out," Tom said, still scowling at her, hands stuffed in his jacket pockets. "Just to be on the safe side."

"Yes, I guess." She took a deep breath. Her heart began to hurt. She pressed her fist into her stomach and felt her pulse bang against her knuckles. "And what about you? What's next for you, Tom?"

He shifted restlessly and looked off into the distance. "I'll be going back to Washington."

"Oh," she said. "Of course." *Please, God, don't let me fall apart.*

"I've got some things to do there. There's...someone I need to see."

"I see," she whispered, though she didn't, not at all. *I won't ask if he's coming back...I won't. Please, God, don't let me ask.*

"There's someone...I have to say goodbye to." His voice sounded strange...thick and husky.

Jane's breath seemed to catch in her throat. She could only stare at him, suspended in a strange, shimmering state, like a newly emerging chrysalis. *Do I dare? If he would only look at me...*

She never knew where she got the strength to say the words, calmly, quietly. "When are you leaving?"

"I dunno...depends." And now at last he was looking at her, rocking a little onto the balls of his feet, then back again, as if he felt ill at ease. His frown seemed less severe than usual. Almost wary. "I've got a few things to wrap up around here first. Then, I guess it pretty much depends on when they let you go."

"I don't understand." But she did. Oh, she did. And she felt as if her heart would fly right out of her chest. Surely he would see it. Surely he must know.

"I want...I'd like you to come with me."

Somehow she knew that was all he would say. All he *could* say. And it was enough.

She reached for his hand. He took hold of hers like a drowning man thrown a rope, and after a moment, raised it, closed his eyes and pressed his lips against her palm. She felt a shudder pass through him, and then a sigh.

Epilogue

"This isn't quite what I expected," Jane said, laughing nervously.

The woman walking beside her chuckled. It was a warm sound, to match her warm brown eyes, which glowed like fine old brandy when she smiled. "No, I suppose not." She shook her head and sighed. "Tom always did lack a certain degree of…"

"Tact?" suggested Jane.

Emma Hostetler smiled. "Grace. When it comes to matters of the heart, Tom is, well, rather like a newborn foal trying out its legs for the first time. He had so little experience with love, you know, when he was growing up."

"No," said Jane, "I didn't know." She knew so little about the man she loved. Learning about him was still a new and exciting voyage of discovery, and every detail a small source of awe.

Emma sighed. "Oh, yes…his father was seldom there, of course, and his mother…" She paused and made a gesture, as if brushing away a fly. "Well. That's for Tom to tell you. Let's just say, I don't know what might have happened to him if…"

"He hadn't met your daughter…Jenny."

Why doesn't this hurt more? she wondered, lifting her face to the April sun, drawing in a deep breath filled with the smells of new grass, flowers...lilacs. This was his wife's home, these were her parents. She'd felt so scared about coming here. But from the moment she'd met Emma Hostetler and her gaunt, twinkly-eyed, pipe-smoking, college-professor husband, Frank, she'd felt warm. Embraced. Accepted.

"He told me he loved her very much. I wonder if he'll ever—" She stopped, and sighed.

Emma looked at her in surprise. "Of course he will. He loves *you*. Anyone can see that. Don't tell me you didn't know."

Jane laughed a little and said, "Oh...well, I don't know about that. He says..."

"If you're waiting for Tom to tell you," Emma said dryly, stooping to clip a daffodil stem, "don't hold your breath." She dropped the flower into the basket on Jane's arm and paused, turning to look up at the gracious Georgian house they'd left behind. Her face was gentle, and a little sad. "He never told Jenny, either, you know. I think maybe that's why it's been so hard for him to let her go."

Jen...

Hawk stood in the upstairs corner bedroom that had been hers, looking down on the sweep of lawn and the gardens beyond. The casement windows were open to let in the soft April breezes, and the voices of the two women walking there drifted up to him like the lazy murmur of bees. As he watched, a low ripple of laughter seemed to stir across his auditory nerves like a playful sprite playing peekaboo with his memory.

You love her, Tom?

He took a deep breath, trying to ease the ache inside him.

Then why don't you say it?

His jaw tightened and his eyes burned. He'd loved Jen...so much.

The laughter skirled like a breeze around the corners of his mind. He thought it sounded a trifle smug. *Of course you did.*

The air seemed full of pollen suddenly. He felt something building like a sneeze at the back of his throat, behind his eyelids. Because he'd never told her.

But I knew. I always knew.

"I'm always going to love you, Jen," he whispered. "Always."

I know that, too. And now you have someone else to love, as well.

But can I? he wondered. He'd loved Jen, and then Jason. He didn't know how to love someone else.

Of course you do, you dummy. I taught you, didn't I?

To his surprise, Hawk found that he was smiling. He drew another long breath, and on its exhalation, heard the laughter go tumbling away like a butterfly dancing on a sunbeam, sending back a whisper.

It wouldn't hurt to tell her, you know.

The breeze came through the window and touched his face like a blown kiss. And for a moment he thought he smelled lilacs....

"Oh, I love lilacs," Jane said with a sigh. "I think they're my favorite."

Emma snipped a fat cluster and held it to her own nose for a moment before she handed it to her. "They were Jennifer's favorite, too," she said. And then, seeing the shadow that crossed Jane's face, "What is it, dear?"

Ashamed, she shook her head and tried to laugh it off. But there was something about Emma... She took a deep breath and blurted out, "I'm not anything like her, you know. Tom says I'm not, even though..."

Emma laughed. "No, you and Jennifer are quite different. For one thing, she was an only child, and undoubtedly spoiled. But supremely self-confident. You..." She paused to give her a thoughtful look. "Life has treated you a bit more harshly, I think. You're probably a little slower to trust."

Trust. There was an ache in Jane's throat. She rubbed it absently and murmured, "But he says I remind him of her. What if..."

"You're wondering whether he only loves you because you remind him of Jenny."

"Yes," said Jane miserably.

Emma said nothing for a moment, while she added one more

sprig of lilac to the overflowing flower basket. Then she stripped off her gloves and gently took Jane's hand.

"Let me tell you how you're like Tom's wife," she said as they walked together, back toward the house. "Let's see…you're independent, giving, passionate, *com*passionate. Warm. Very loving. All those things." She took a deep breath and lifted her face, for a moment, to the morning sun, as if she somehow found it a comfort. "But where you're most like her, I think, is that you have an enormous capacity for joy. Jenny had such enthusiasm for *life*. She brightened your spirits just by walking into a room. And so do you, dear, in your own way." She gave Jane's hand a squeeze and then released it. "Tom needs that. He needs *you*." She laughed, that low, throaty chuckle that made her seem so much younger than she was. "Even though he may never tell you."

"But…he *does* tell me," Jane said, suddenly understanding. "In his own way…every single day. In little things he does. The way his face lights up when he sees me, as if he's glad I'm there. Anyone can *say* it—I should know, my ex-husband used to say it all the time. But Tom makes me *feel* it. He makes me feel…*loved*."

Yes…

Jane glanced at Emma. Had she spoken? It didn't seem so, and yet the word seemed to hang in the air like the shimmer of sunshine, or the whisper of a breeze.

Up ahead, she could see Tom coming out of the house, with Frank Hostetler behind him. Even from this distance she could see that he was smiling his familiar lopsided smile. Her heart gave a great surge of gladness.

And Hawk's heart answered, *Yes!* It was all he needed, all he'd been waiting for…searching for. That *look*. That sudden *brightening*…the flash of light in her sea-gray eyes that always made him think of the joyous leap of dolphins toward the sun.

* * * * *

COMING NEXT MONTH FROM

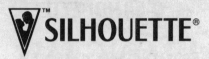 **SILHOUETTE**®

Intrigue
Danger, deception and desire

HIS SECRET SIDE Pamela Burford
THIS LITTLE BABY Joyce Sullivan
KRYSTAL'S BODYGUARD Molly Rice
THE REDEMPTION OF DEKE SUMMERS Gayle Wilson

Special Edition
Satisfying romances packed with emotion

THE SECRET WIFE Susan Mallery
PALE RIDER Myrna Temte
WANTED: HUSBAND, WILL TRAIN Marie Ferrarella
MRS RIGHT Carole Halston
BEAUTY AND THE GROOM Lorraine Carroll
LONE STAR LOVER Gail Link

Desire
Provocative, sensual love stories for the woman of today

THE PATIENT NURSE Diana Palmer
THE ENGAGEMENT PARTY Barbara Boswell
WIFE BY CONTRACT Raye Morgan
THE MIDNIGHT RIDER TAKES A BRIDE
Christine Rimmer
ANYBODY'S DAD Amy Fetzer
THE HONEYMOON HOUSE Patty Salier

On sale from 24th April 1998

Five unforgettable
couples say 'I Do'...
with a little help
from their friends!

The Engagement Party by Barbara Boswell
Silhouette Desire®, May 1998

The Bridal Shower by Elizabeth August
Silhouette Desire, June 1998

The Bachelor Party by Paula Detmer Riggs
Silhouette Sensation®, July 1998

The Abandoned Bride by Jane Toombs
Silhouette Intrigue®, August 1998

Finally a Bride by Sherryl Woods
Silhouette Special Edition®, September 1998

Always a Bridesmaid!
is coming to every Silhouette® series
so don't miss any of these
five wonderful weddings!

LINDA
HOWARD

WHITE LIES

Escorted by the FBI to her ex-husband's bedside, Jay
Granger is unprepared for her reaction. *He* doesn't
remember a thing, but his effect on her is immediate
and undeniable. Is this the man she married...or a
total stranger?

"Howard's writing is compelling"
—Publishers Weekly

MIRA®

1-55166-274-4
AVAILABLE FROM APRIL 1998

NORA ROBERTS

Hot Ice

She had the cash and the connections. He knew the whereabouts of a fabulous hidden fortune. It was a business proposition, pure and simple. Now all they needed to do was stay one step ahead of their murderous rivals.

"...her stories have fuelled the dreams of 25 million readers"—Entertainment Weekly

MIRA®

1-55166-395-3
AVAILABLE FROM APRIL 1998

4 FREE
books and a surprise gift!

We would like to take this opportunity to thank you for reading this Silhouette® book by offering you the chance to take FOUR more specially selected titles from the Sensation™ series absolutely FREE! We're also making this offer to introduce you to the benefits of the Reader Service™—

- ★ FREE home delivery
- ★ FREE gifts and competitions
- ★ FREE monthly newsletter
- ★ Books available before they're in the shops
- ★ Exclusive Reader Service discounts

Accepting these FREE books and gift places you under no obligation to buy; you may cancel at any time, even after receiving your free shipment. Simply complete your details below and return the entire page to the address below. *You don't even need a stamp!*

YES! Please send me 4 free Sensation books and a surprise gift. I understand that unless you hear from me, I will receive 4 superb new titles every month for just £2.50 each, postage and packing free. I am under no obligation to purchase any books and may cancel my subscription at any time. The free books and gift will be mine to keep in any case.

S8XE

Ms/Mrs/Miss/Mr...................................Initials ....
BLOCK CAPITALS PLEASE

Surname ....

Address ....

....

....Postcode..................................

Send this whole page to:
THE READER SERVICE, FREEPOST, CROYDON, CR9 3WZ
(Eire readers please send coupon to: P.O. BOX 4546, DUBLIN 24.)

MARY LYNN BAXTER

Raw Heat

Successful broadcast journalist Juliana Reed is caught
in a web of corruption, blackmail and murder. Texas
Ranger, Gates O'Brien—her ex-husband—is the only
person she can turn to. Both know that getting out
alive is just the beginning...

*"Baxter's writing...strikes every chord within
the female spirit."*
—Bestselling author Sandra Brown

1-55166-394-5
AVAILABLE FROM APRIL 1998